The Furnace

Book One of the Juniata Iron Trilogy

By

Judith Redline Coopey

The Furnace

Copyright 2014, Judith Redline Coopey
All rights reserved
Print ISBN: 978–0-9838918–8-8
All e-book editions, ISBN: 978–0-9838918–9-5
First Print Edition
Library of Congress Number: 2014912637

Author's Declaration

Published by Fox Hollow Press and the author, Judith Redline Coopey
Interior design by OPA Author Services, Scottsdale, Arizona
Cover Design by John M. Coopey, Mesa, Arizona
Cover Illustration: a detail from a painting, The Windmiller's Guest, circa 1898, by Edmund Blair Leighton (1853–1922), English historical genre painter.

Attention Corporations, Universities, Colleges and Professional Organizations: Quantity discounts are available on bulk purchases of this book for educational and gift purposes, or as premiums for increasing magazine subscriptions or renewals. Special books or book excerpts can also be created to fit specific needs. Contact Fox Hollow Press.

FOX HOLLOW
PRESS
Digitally Printed in the United States of America

Dedication

For Erin,

who has made motherhood

a rollicking adventure.

Acknowledgments

An undertaking of the scope of this trilogy requires the help of many contributors. Each time I returned to Pennsylvania I found more willing helpers to share their memories, knowledge and expertise with me. I know in naming them, I may leave someone out, but that is only attributable to my waning memory skills, not to the value of their contribution. In Altoona, Jeanine Treese of the Blair County Historical Society was a great help in climbing the attic stairs of Baker Mansion to haul down the dusty account books of the Etna Furnace Company and in providing stacks of bound newspapers that gave me the flavor of the times I was writing about. In Bellefonte, Pat Park and her brother, Tom Vaughn, escorted me on a tour of the Eagle Furnace and Curtin Village before introducing me to several books and memoirs about growing up there. Former residents of Mt. Etna opened their homes, pictures and memories to me: Eleanor Wolfhope, Dorothy Koontz, Cheryl Hughes, Helen Roller, Butterball Ross and Rebecca Ross. Thanks also to John Roller, who went out of his way to provide me with old maps of the Etna Furnace lands.

I am deeply indebted to Gary Discavage, owner of the former Mt. Etna store, who graciously opened his guest house to me and allowed me to wander and roam at will over the Etna Furnace property, and to Dan Detwiler, owner of the Etna Mansion, who shared his restoration project and priceless pictures of the area with me. My hat is off to those who value and preserve local history. If not for them, the memories would fade and the stories would be lost.

As always, I look with wonder on the people who so generously give of their time and thoughts in reading for me. The version they read is usually pretty far from the final manuscript, but it is their thoughts, ideas, questions and suggestions that blend it into the book it is to become.

Thanks to Mary Agliardo, Steve Brigman, Erin Coopey, Lou Coopey, Kathleen Andrews Davis, Carolyn Kennedy, Pamela Leipold, and Pat Park for reading for me—again, in many cases!

The older I get, the more I value the old friends of my youth. They knew me when, and they still put up with me now, none more than Genie Robine, who has generously offered me a home away from home where I can rest during my tours and from which I can launch my research forays. She has accompanied me through the pathless brambles of Blair Four, along the Lower Trail, up the mountain conquered by the Portage Railroad, and through the Staple Bend Tunnel, all in support of whatever the next book will address. Friends like that come along only once in a lifetime, and I am fortunate that she did—at just the right time.

A special thanks to John Coopey, who has always been ready and able to print posters and bookmarks, and who demonstrated his expertise as a cover designer for this book. Who knew he was an artist, too?

Part One

1816–1830

Chapter 1

1816–1820
Ellie

I, Elinor Abigail Bratton MacPhail, do solemnly swear that the account I shall give is the truth, the whole truth and nothing but the truth, so help me God. It won't be easy. My whole life laid out for others to observe, scrutinize and judge. But I must now make sense of it, unravel, inspect, compare what might have been to what was. Accept responsibility for how things turned out—or some of it, at least. I was so young then. I know it sounds like making excuses, but I was, indeed, very young.

My brother Alex and I were inseparable in those days. Since he was older than I by two years, Alex was the leader and I the follower in all things. Like the time we decided on a whim to go swimming in Tulpehocken Creek, which bordered our Berks County farm. We'd been out chasing butterflies for Alex's collection when the heat became too much for him and he ran to the creek bank and stripped off all of his clothes. "Come on, Ellie," he called. "The water's fine."

No need to ask me twice. I sat down on the creek bank and began to undress.

"Elinor Abigail Bratton! What *can* you be thinking?" Our mother, having seen us out the dining room window, came running across the lawn, waving her arms and yelling.

"What?" I asked, continuing to disrobe.

"You can't behave this way, Ellie. You're a young lady. Young ladies do not take their clothes off and swim in the creek with their brothers."

"Oh."

I can't say I was angered by this revelation. Just puzzled. Why did boys get to do whatever they pleased and girls get in trouble for wanting to do the same things?

"Come, dear. Pick up your things and come into the house. Alex, you come, too. I don't want you swimming alone."

There was nothing new or unusual about this regulation of my young life. I only remember it because of its association with Alex's death by drowning in the same swimming hole two summers later, when he was twelve and I was ten.

He'd gone fishing with Robert Clifton, Squire Clifton's son and our next door neighbor. Alex and Robert had grown up together, with me tagging along. There weren't any other little girls for me to play with; not that I was particularly interested in girlish things. I hadn't been invited on the fishing trip, so I was sitting on the back porch of our house nursing my indignation and working my cross stitch sampler when Robert came tearing up through the field, waving his arms and screaming.

"Mrs. Bratton! Mrs. Bratton! Come quick! Alex has drowned! He jumped into the creek and didn't come up. Must have hit his head. I pulled him out, but I can't wake him."

The ensuing excitement is indelibly stamped on my memory. My mother running to the creek, followed by Robert and me. Alex lying on the ground, still and lifeless, his face gray. Mother holding his head in her lap, crying, entreating him to breathe. I stood aside— watching, praying, crying. Alex, my only brother, my friend, teacher and protector, gone.

My parents were devastated, and I was alone. The survivor. Unless this has happened to you, it is almost impossible to understand the feeling of responsibility survival places on you. The grief of losing my brother was deepened by the need to make up for it somehow, even though it wasn't my fault. I set about to do all I could to relieve my parents' suffering. I would do everything Alex would have done, be all Alex would have been. I would replace my brother in their hearts and minds and ease their pain.

At ten, the idea of death is, for most children, so foreign, so incomprehensible that the reality of it takes days, even weeks, to sink in. A ten-year-old sees the world in black and white. If I had been a better sister, maybe Alex would not have died. If I was the perfect daughter, I could replace my brother and heal their hearts. If I carried all of the burden, I could lighten theirs.

Ours had been a happy family—the perfect balance of male and female, with a proper sense of decorum, duty and honor. We all knew our own places in the family and our family's place in the world. The future was laid out in fine detail. Alex would study law in Philadelphia, marry into a prestigious family, and become rich and famous. Our parents would bask in the glory of a son well reared and prepared for a bright future. I would marry well—perhaps young Robert Clifton or the scion of some other well-placed family—and together we would make the Bratton name respected and esteemed. When our parents died, Alex would inherit the estate and I would receive a token remembrance. All laid out in fine detail

Alex's death brought an end to all that. No son to carry on the family name. No law degree and lucrative practice. No one to brag about, take pride in, make a fuss over. That left me, adrift in a changed role I could not comprehend. Alex had been my guiding light, my exemplar, the standard by which I would judge all men.

As for Robert Clifton, he stayed away for some time, locked in whatever regret he felt, grieving, too, I assumed, for the loss of his childhood friend. We saw less of him in the ensuing years, until, as a matter of social obligation, I received an invitation to his sixteenth birthday party.

Robert, next door neighbor, son of Squire Clifton, the richest man in Berks County, stood now on the precipice of that bright future my family had conjured for Alex. Not that we begrudged him. No one blamed Robert for Alex's death. Indeed, my parents were at great pains to assure the Cliftons of that, and to ease any sense of guilt Robert might feel. My parents held the Cliftons in high esteem—

admired them, copied them, willingly subjugated themselves in order to be counted among the Cliftons' friends.

In the meantime, in my naïve desire to sooth my parents' grief, I did everything I could to make them proud. I attended church regularly, studied the scriptures diligently, said my prayers with sincerity, gave myself over to the pursuit of arts deemed suitable for a proper lady. I sewed, embroidered, knitted, played the pianoforte, sang, wrote poetry, and read. Alas that last would be my downfall.

Papa had an extensive library—not for his own consumption, for he was a trader in pelts, a merchant, not an intellectual. The library was for my brother's future and as a way of impressing our neighbors and all others who might count that sort of thing important. Having learned to read as a hanger-on when Alex was tutored, I'd been infected with an insatiable appetite for the printed word, which, once whetted, was never to be quenched.

It got me into trouble often while I was growing up so that I was expressly forbidden to enter the library unless accompanied by one of our parents—to prevent me from reading "beyond my ability to comprehend." Both of our parents were literate, but only Mother actually read anything, and that was an occasional novel of which my father heartily disapproved. She liked Gothic novels, especially Ann Radcliffe's. I often picked up books she'd lain aside and read them with delight. Once, when I was nine, I mentioned at table a story I'd read about a witch with snakes for hair. Mother caught father's eye, and the pantomime of a key turning in a lock was not lost on me. To counter their attempts to discourage my literary pursuits, I became an accomplished sneak, carrying books into a closet under the stairs and reading by candlelight, or climbing a tree in the orchard, a book tucked under my apron, to spend an afternoon in stolen delight.

Alex's death only made the problem worse, for with nothing to distract me I became even more enthralled with books and the worlds they opened up. When I announced to my parents that I intended to study law in Philadelphia, my father sputtered and said, "Why my dear, you are but a girl. Women haven't the capacity to study law. You'd bring shame upon yourself."

"Elinor, child, it's unseemly for a woman to speak so. Where would you ever find a husband?" That was my mother, ever the upholder of convention.

The prohibition didn't deter me, it merely increased my appetite for more reading. I wanted to know about the world, how things worked and why, and the stories, the endless stories about people. I continued to sneak into the library at every opportunity, careful not to disturb my parents' comfortable world, until, when I was fourteen, that invitation to Robert Clifton's sixteenth birthday party came and I was swept up in all that.

Chapter 2

1820–23
Ellie

Every one I knew was invited—everyone in *our* circle, anyway—and I saw the look in his mother's eye as she laid the invitation in my mother's hand. She liked me, and if his mother liked me, she'd see that other opportunities came my way: more invitations, parties, dinners, dances, walks in the countryside, sleigh rides in winter, picnics in summer. It seemed our mothers were engaged in a conspiracy: a spring wedding a few years hence in the blossom-laden orchard between our two holdings.

This relationship with Robert wasn't new, of course. We'd lived next farm to each since birth, Robert, an only child, having grown up with Alex like a brother. I was the not-always-welcome tag-along. Once, when I was six and Robert eight, he growled that he hated girls and pushed me off the garden wall, much to Alex's approval. My dress was soiled, and Mother made a nasty face when she saw me, but didn't let on to Mrs. Clifton. Mother would have given her best frock to be as rich and stylish as Mrs. Clifton, so nothing Robert did slowed her admiration for the Cliftons or her desire to be just like them.

Papa was every bit as bad—worse in some ways. He'd bought our farm outside Reading so he could be friend and associate to Squire Clifton. Every year at Christmas we were invited to the Clifton's party, and every year Papa selected a bottle of his finest brandy to take to the Squire as a present. When the squire came up in conversation, it was 'Clifton says this', and 'Clifton says that' or 'Clifton wouldn't' or 'Clifton bought a new horse, think I'll buy one, too.'

No wonder I grew up in the hope—planted and nurtured by both my parents, I now realize—that I would be Robert Clifton's wife, mistress of Brighton, the star around which Berks County society revolved. If Alex couldn't raise the family name to exalted heights, maybe I could.

No matter that Robert Clifton barely noticed me, left me standing alone as soon as anyone more animated, more exciting, more worldly came on the scene. No matter that he was so spoiled and conceited, he would barely deign speak to me unless prodded by his mother. No matter that he was more interested in fast horses and racing and betting than in anything I had to offer. Until...

His sixteenth birthday party was the beginning. I went, shy even though keeping company with Robert certainly wasn't new. My timidity was reserved for the unfamiliar—strangers and social gatherings in a wider circle. Alone with Robert I could be, and often was, quite sassy.

At fourteen, I lived in awe of boys—a privileged class, uncalled upon to do much of anything that resembled work, fawned over and praised for the very act of breathing. Even then it didn't seem fair, but it was my reality. I joined the other girls in shameless admiration of Robert Clifton, hanging on his every word, laughing prettily at his efforts at humor, and hoping breathlessly for a look, a smile, a nod that would set me apart from the crowd.

There was music at the party; several girls took turns playing the pianoforte in the Cliftons' parlor while everyone gathered round to sing. Games of Blind Man's Bluff and Ring Toss on the lawn occupied us for some time before a sumptuous lunch was served—dainty little sandwiches, three of which Robert, always acting the fool, stuffed into his mouth at one time, glaring around with puffed cheeks, to the delight of all the young ladies present. The other boys set about to imitate him, not a one of them as handsome nor as self-assured as our young host, so no applause for them.

When the party broke up and the guests were departing, my mother and I stayed to make sure Mrs. Clifton had all the help she needed. Why would she not? There was a full complement of servants, cooks, livery men—even a snooty and pretentious butler, but my mother never missed a chance to gain Mrs. Clifton's attention for herself and for me. She pushed me forward to cut the birthday cake into portions the guests could carry home. She offered my services as secretary to record which gift came from which guest. By the time all that was accomplished, everyone had gone except Robert, me and our mothers.

"I know, Robert, why don't you walk Ellie home through the orchard?" That was his mother, smiling and prodding him from behind while my mother reflected her smile in benign approval—the mothers in perfect accord as to the pairing of their offspring.

"Yes, you children go along. I'll be there before you if the groom ever brings my gig around." That was *my* mother, smiling over my head and giving me a gentle push in Robert's direction.

Nodding, I must say without much enthusiasm, Robert did an elaborate bow and held out his hand. I placed mine in his and we meandered down the path to the orchard. It could have been one huge orchard but for the fence that divided the Clifton from the Bratton lands, easily traversed by a stile—three steps up and three steps down. We'd played there as children, the three of us darting among the trees, climbing and swinging from low hanging branches. Both of our mothers would have cringed at our antics—mine because it wasn't ladylike to climb trees and swing from branches. His because she was such a doting mother, she lived in fear that Dear Robert might scrape a knee or, at the very least, soil his expensive clothes.

We ambled down the path, chatting about the party, Robert throwing rocks at the tree trunks and going on about the new horse he'd gotten for his birthday. Robert was all wound up about that horse. He loved to race and, in spite of his youth, was accepted in competition in whatever contest was gotten up by the young men of the neighborhood. Robert was known as a competitor, even then.

"Have you ridden him yet?" I asked, referring to the new horse, a bay stallion with huge haunches and fire in his eyes.

"Oh, yeah. He's a beast. He can outrun Charles Worthington's Master."

"Really?" Charles Worthington's Master was the fastest horse in Berks and probably two or three surrounding counties. I knew this because Robert followed every contest, had every horse and rider ranked, and talked about it incessantly.

"Really. I'm putting Achilles up against Master this Saturday. Wanna come?"

I would have loved to go, but that was another area where my mother had put her foot down: young ladies did not attend horse races. End of it.

"You know my mother won't allow it."

"Oh, yeah. Well, I'll let you know how much I win by." Robert's confidence in his prowess as a rider knew no bounds. "The purse ought to be as much as a hundred."

We walked along in silence until we reached the stile, where Robert, always the gentleman, offered me his hand to steady me climbing over. Once I'd climbed down on my side, he waved and turned to go back home.

"Aren't you going to walk me all the way?" I asked.

He stood watching me, head tilted back, arms crossed. "I might, if I get paid."

"Paid? What can you be talking about? I've no money."

"So pay me with a kiss."

I giggled. It was the first time such a proposition had come my way, and I found it amusing, exciting, titillating. Stepping back from the stile, I took a running start. "You'll have to catch me first!" I shouted over my shoulder.

Of course, I was no match for him. As fast as I could run, hampered by skirts and petticoats and pantaloons, the catching was easy. He bounded over the stile, tore after me, and in about five steps overtook and pulled me down into the grassy space between two apple trees. He rolled me over, pinned me down and kissed me. Just a short peck on the cheek at first, but then, seizing the advantage, a longer, harder kiss on the lips. I struggled to free myself, laughing at my predicament, but he held me down and kissed me again. This time it wasn't hard, but long and lingering. Suddenly my body relaxed beneath his and we rolled on our sides, looking at each other as though we hadn't known each other all our lives, as though we hadn't played together in this same orchard, as though we were strangers meeting for the first time.

I sat up, unsure of myself, feeling shy and puzzled. What had just happened? I was sure I shouldn't have let it happen, but I wasn't sure why I didn't feel wrong about it. Robert lay on the grass, turned to face me and picked up a fallen apple from the ground, grinning.

"Whew! You're a wild one, you are!" He threw the apple against a nearby tree trunk.

"Wild one? Me? Whose idea was it, Robert?"

"Mine, I guess. But you were into it. I could tell."

I felt my face redden. "Well, maybe. Just a little."

Robert rose and turned to offer me his hand. I pulled myself up and stood beside him, brushing the grass from my skirt. The look in Robert's eyes was different. He saw me, as I saw him, as some one new,—interesting, exciting, transformed. He held onto my hand.

"I'll have to walk you home through the orchard more often."

I walked beside him the rest of the way to the edge of our lawn, thinking, wondering, delighted and afraid. Robert liked me. After all, you didn't go about kissing girls you didn't like, did you? That must mean I was Robert's girl, his choice, his pick. It probably meant I would someday be his bride. Mistress of Brighton. My parents' dreams come true. And mine? I didn't think about that. All I knew was this was how it was supposed to be. Two marionettes, dancing and bowing as others pulled the strings.

In the weeks and months that followed, Robert Clifton took advantage of every opportunity to be alone with me. There weren't many, to be sure, but Robert never missed one. He would take my hand and lead me around a corner, down a hall, into another room, to steal a kiss, touch my cheek, hold me close. I was a willing accomplice, choosing not to notice that when in public, Robert paid me no attention whatever. I attributed that to shyness, or to not wanting the world to know about us, accepted it as part of Robert's charm.

By the time I was sixteen and he was eighteen, we had come out into the light of public acceptance as a couple. Sure that I was on the path that led to Brighton and a life of romance and ease as the wife of the young squire, I was compliant, anxious to please and uncritical, a simple child, the product of a fine upbringing and proper training, ready to love, honor and obey. I smile as I look back on it now.

Before drawing conclusions from such compliant behavior, one should have asked my mother. She would have told you that I was a headstrong, willful, disobedient child, constantly stepping out of bounds, testing the rules, and generally making life difficult for her. My father, on the other hand, would have said I was a first-rate horsewoman, afraid of nothing, and obedient only when I chose to be. He'd lost his boy, you see, but what he had left was a daughter with a mind of her own, except for that brief period when I came under the sway of Robert Clifton. Papa was as delighted as could be with me, except that before the world I was still just a girl.

But I was more than ready to cast aside my true character in order to be all that Robert Clifton wanted me to be. I liked whatever Robert liked. I believed whatever Robert said to be true. I lived by whatever rules Robert put forth. Looking back on it all now, I wonder how I could have been so naïve and so willing.

But those times with Robert were exciting, thrilling, so full of life that I couldn't imagine it any other way. I didn't know who I was or what I wanted, but that didn't matter as long as I could have Robert Clifton for my own.

Chapter 3

October 1823
Adam

I strode along the riverbank trail, studying the terrain all the way from Water Street, rock outcroppings, hollows, the river on my left and rugged tree covered hills on my right. The river, too shallow to float much of anything except in spring high water, glistened in the sharp October afternoon. I'd studied the maps, so I knew where I was going, crossing what I judged to be the mouth of Fox Run and angling along the base of the hill, close to my destination. My eyes scanned the hillsides for limestone—plenty everywhere I looked. Plenty of timber, too. My study of the geological maps told me the ore was here, but I needed to see it, feel it, find it for myself.

When I heard Roaring Run tumbling into the Frankstown Branch of the Juniata River maybe a quarter mile away, I felt a kind of joy—anticipation, hope—at the wonderfully powerful stream living up to its name, a three-story stone grist mill standing tall at its mouth. Long strides carried me up the steep hillside above the mill, where I could see the valley laid out below—the furnace, sitting cold and barren beside the mill race, the ore bank on top of the next ridge. This was it. Etna Furnace. I'd heard about it, read about it, studied it in my sleep and waking hours for the past three months. Now I took it all in, savoring the dream.

A broadside for a sheriff's sale described in matter-of-fact terms the assets to be sold at auction: furnace, quarry, woodlands, ore bank, two-story stone house, flour mill, blacksmith shop, tenant houses. I didn't remember where or how I'd come across the sale notice, but I'd carried it folded up in my pocket ever since, read it again and again, dreamed on it.

I was nobody, former iron worker, former apprentice to the Birdsboro Works in Berks County, penniless, full of dreams and ambition and not to be denied. My first plan was to attend the sale, introduce myself to the buyer, and make myself indispensible. My dearest hope was that said buyer would not be interested in running the operation himself, happy to turn those duties over to me.

I eased myself down the steep slope, holding onto saplings for brakes and balance, brushed myself off and loped around to the door of the mill, its overshot wheel turning slowly in the afternoon chill. As I entered, the roaring of the water, the creaking of the mill wheel, the grinding of stone on stone prohibited conversation, but, nodding, the miller handed a half-filled sack of flour to a boy and stepped toward me.

"Is the owner around?" I asked when we'd stepped outside for conversation.

"What owner?"

"The owner of the furnace—the whole operation. Is he around?"

The miller grinned, wiped his hands on his apron and extended one to me. "Jefferson Baker. I lease the mill, but the furnace is another story. Ain't seen the owner—that's George Crissman—in a month a Sundays. Word is, he's gone belly up. Didn't even show up to collect his lease money this fall. Wouldn't wonder, what with the pains he had trying to get his pigs to market. Cost more to ship 'em than to make 'em. Hear tell the whole operation's going up at a sheriff's sale in a couple of weeks."

Grasping the proffered hand, I managed a halting introduction. "Adam MacPhail, of Berks County. Yes. I know about the troubles." I opened my jacket to fish the wrinkled broadside out of an inside pocket. "That's why I came."

"You up for buying it?" Jefferson Baker shielded his eyes against the bright reflection off the river.

I shook my head, looked away, scanned the rugged terrain. Steep ridges converged on the river, blocking visibility beyond a few hundred yards. It was wild and beautiful, tree-covered and rocky, and to my iron-making eye the most beautiful land imaginable. It was all here. Wood for charcoal, limestone in abundance, ore banks waiting to be dug—a new and promising land where a man could make his mark, build a life doing what he loved.

"Would that I could. No. I'm hoping to meet the new buyer—maybe sign on as a foreman. I know the business." It was a lie. I didn't really want to sign on as anything but ironmaster. I'd spent the last fifteen years, ever since I was a lad of twelve, apprenticed out by my widowed mother, learning and following the iron-making trade. I was good at it, that I knew. Good enough to run my own furnace, but without even the minimum funds needed to buy, open or operate it.

"How'd they transport the bars? Horses?" I asked, bringing my mind back to the miller's remark about getting pigs to market. The operation produced pig iron, so called because the shapeless iron blobs that came out of the bottom of the furnace resembled a nursing sow lying on her side. The pig iron was so heavy, transporting it was the major impediment to profitability.

"Yep. Forged them pigs into bars and bent them to a U-shape so they'd lay over a horse's back, but the horses wore out with crossing the mountains. About one trip to Pittsburgh was all they was good for. Took too long. Cost too much."

I looked around at the rugged terrain once more, almost—but not quite—daunted by the prospect of transporting the precious product over and around these ridges.

"How's the furnace?" I knew it couldn't be good, being out of blast for more than two years.

"Pretty poorly. Needs re-lining, and the bellows is cracked. I wouldn't want the job."

"Know where I can find this George Crissman?"

"Water Street'd be my guess. Hangs around the inn down there, looking for somebody to stand him to a drink."

"I'll try to find him there, then. Do you know of any interest in this sale?"

The miller shrugged. "Pretty remote, this place. Some other furnaces around, but profits is hard to come by. Guess it'll sell, but it won't bring much of a price."

I thanked the man, tipped my hat, and turned back the way I'd come in long loping strides, giving no thought to the wasted time and effort. My mind was on the derelict furnace and its owner. Even as I walked, I planned. This was, indeed, a pretty place for producing iron. Everything came together to make the circumstances almost perfect, and Juniata Iron was the finest iron in the world. I wanted to be—nay—had to be a part of it.

I arrived back at Water Street around four o'clock in the afternoon and went directly to the public house where I'd spent the previous night sleeping in the barn, unbeknownst to the proprietor. I'd breakfasted at the inn that morning, so the innkeeper nodded in recognition as I entered and found a seat at an empty table.

"Thought you had business at Etna."

"I did, but I learned that the man I sought was here all the time. George Crissman?"

The barkeep finished wiping the glass he was holding and nodded to a table in a dark corner, populated by one, head on arms on table, snoring loud enough to compete with the broiling spring outside. I rose and approached him, calling up my courage to speak as though I really were a prospective buyer.

"Sir, I wish to do business with you."

The snoring man dropped one arm from the edge of the table and raised his head with a bleary-eyed glare. "What you want of me? I told them all I hadn't the money. No money at all. Take your business someplace else."

"Are you the owner of Etna Furnace?"

"Told you to go on, now. I'm finished with all that. There it sits. Take it if you will. Sheriff's sale in three weeks. If you're a creditor, you'll be paid."

I pulled a chair up to the table and called for hot tea, intent upon learning as much about the history and means of the operation as I could.

"No tea! More grog!" my companion growled.

15

"No more grog. I want you sensible."

We sat at the corner table through the afternoon and into the evening as Crissman sobered up and I waited patiently for the return of sensibility. By nine o'clock, Mr. Crissman was clear-eyed and forthcoming about Etna Furnace, its brief struggle for survival, and the reasons for its early demise.

"Can't get the pigs to market. Costs more to move them than to make them. Pittsburgh's the place, but the mountains stand between. Good market there. They need everything we can produce, but I'm damned if I know how to do it and make any money."

The problem seemed insurmountable to Mr. Crissman, but I'd heard talk that brought me all the way from Berks County to this western outpost where the future loomed bright in my mind.

"What about this canal they're talking of?"

"Maybe for the next owner, not for me. Can't get it built soon enough. I'm done already. Anyway, you know how slow things proceed. The legislature only just approved the plan. Take maybe ten years to get it out this far and beyond. Besides, ain't no canal going to get iron bars up over the Alleghenies. Maybe send 'em downstream to Philadelphia, but they's too much competition down that way. Three, four furnaces in every county, keep the price too low."

I nodded. Pittsburgh was the market.

"How you know so much about iron?" Crissman's head was getting clearer now, his curiosity awakened.

"I was apprenticed to the Birdsboro Works in Berks County for ten years, then worked as a journeyman for five. I learned my trade."

"How come you don't stay down there, then? What're you doing out here in this wilderness, out of God's knowledge?"

"There the problem's charcoal. The woods are all gone. Bringing in fuel raises the cost. Besides, I wanted to make my own way. I've little money, but I know working iron. I could be a benefit to anyone who buys the Etna works if they'll listen. We could get that furnace back in blast by spring and be shipping iron all summer."

Crissman wiped his mouth on his coat sleeve. "Well, whatever happens, it won't be my problem anymore. Now, if you'll excuse me, I need to get on home."

"Would you go up there with me tomorrow and show me around? Show me the operation?"

"Young man, I've told you, I'm done with it. It can rot in hell as far as I'm concerned. I put my all into it and failed. I don't ever want to see the place again."

George Crissman rose and called for his horse. Outside, in the cold October night, he mounted for the short ride to Alexandria while I turned and ambled toward the stable, sneaked in, crept up the ladder to the loft, and slept in the hay above the horses.

Chapter 4

October 1823
Adam

The next morning, shivering, I awakened to frost, breath coming out in foggy clouds, and made my way to the public house before the fire was up, waiting for Crissman. I'd no money for breakfast, my hopes resting on Crissman's generosity, but my would-be benefactor didn't wander in until after ten o'clock, and he was not in a mood to eat.

"One up!" he yelled at the innkeeper as he settled himself in his accustomed chair in the corner away from the fire.

I stepped up to the table, taking hold of the back of a heavy oak chair. "Mr. Crissman, sir, I was hoping you'd change your mind about riding up to Etna to look at the furnace today."

Crissman gazed at me through watery eyes. "Don't give up easy now, do you young man? All right. We will. Just give me a few minutes to warm up my innards," he replied, taking a long draught of his grog.

"But, sir, I can't have you drinking when there's business to discuss."

Crissman peered over his tankard. "Business, you say? Whose business?"

"Yours, sir. And mine, I hope."

"Tell you what, young man—what'd you say your name was?"

"MacPhail, Adam MacPhail."

"MacPhail, yes. MacPhail. Good old Scotch-Irish name. Well, young man, I'm not of a mind to go all the way up to Mt. Etna on a fool's errand with some young pup who thinks he knows iron. I'd as soon sit here and watch the ducks and drink me grog. Man's got to know when he's licked. I'm licked."

Crissman turned his chair to look out the window at a pond fed by the waters of a small run flowing into the Frankstown Branch nearby. A pair of Mallards swan around in a circle, in the company of three sturdy Canvasbacks. Studying the pond over his shoulder I said nothing, nor did I move. If Crissman's intent was to ignore and discourage me, it wasn't going to work. I stood staring at his back and waited, studying my threadbare trousers, worn out shoes and ill-fitting jacket. I knew I didn't present as much of a prospect, but I was undaunted, full of hope and plans, and I could wait.

After more than a quarter hour, Crissman turned in his chair and grunted. "You still here?"

My message was clear: hope and determination—hard-headed, stubborn determination that George Crissman couldn't help but be moved by. He sat silent for some time, staring into his grog. Then he picked up his hat, plopped it on his head and rose, motioning for the barkeep to write the tab, and headed for the door with me in his wake.

In the dooryard, Crissman turned to address me. "Where's your mount?"

I shook my head. "Don't have one."

"How'd you get all the way up here from Berks without even a mule to ride?"

"Took a stage when I could, begged rides on farm wagons. Got here, anyway."

Crissman snorted and kneed his horse into a walk. "Hope you can keep up."

My stride was almost as fast as the horse's, and I kept up a respectable pace as we made our way along the river back the same way I'd gone the day before. With Crissman astride his horse a few paces ahead, conversation was sparse, but my head was full of plans and ideas, innovations I wanted to try. Crissman's lack of talk and pointed lack of hospitality made little impression on me, focused as I was on the future.

We arrived at Etna Furnace around noon and set about inspecting the works, or I did, while Crissman sat astride his horse, saying little and looking bored. It was clear he set very little store by the dreams and machinations of this nobody from Berks County—clear he wanted nothing more than to be back at Water Street having a grog and a smoke by the window, watching the ducks.

But I was not to be denied. I climbed the steep hillside to the charging house, built against the slope, supported by huge stone buttresses, and stood on the bridge staring down into the mouth of the furnace. Below I studied the deteriorating roofs of the Tuyere room and the casting house, both sagging in disrepair. To anyone with a head for business, the whole operation was a wreck, but to my naïve eyes it was a beautiful sight. Seated on a boulder at the base of the furnace I looked up at Crissman, still astride his horse, and pelted him with questions as to the whys and why-nots of the operation.

Crissman, who took a perverse pride in being hard-hearted, must have wondered what had persuaded him to even ride up here, not to mention what made him listen to naïve, empty-headed, pie-in-the-sky ideas. Considering what little I had to offer, I couldn't help but wonder why Mr. Crissman didn't just turn his horse around and ride back to his hiding place at the inn. But as the afternoon wore on Crissman warmed to the subject, his conversation more animated and intense. He sat a little taller in the saddle, studying the drawings I made in the dirt, even nodding now and then.

"These ideas of yours—how can you make all this happen when no one will lend you a farthing? You may know iron, but I doubt you know money, man. Money is what drives it."

"How much would it take to get the furnace back in production?" I asked, shivering at the thought of estimating the costs.

"Plenty. We'd have to set a crew out cutting wood for charcoal right away and through the winter so we'd have enough to keep the furnace in blast once we got her blown in. There's a good store of charcoal in the coal bank now, maybe enough to get you 'round to next fall when your new supply'd be ready." Crissman spoke with authority now, sitting forward in his saddle, even leaning down to point out flaws in my scratchings in the dirt.

"There's plenty of ore up on that hill." He pointed to the ridge above the furnace stack. "That's no problem, except my creditors own it now. Own the whole place. Somebody with money'll have to come along and save it. It won't be no wet-behind-the-ears iron-making apprentice from Birdsboro. That's for sure."

"What if I could find someone—knew someone who might be interested in buying? What then?"

Crissman peered at me through a wispy cloud of pipe smoke. "Know someone? You'd have to prove yourself, even so. Make some iron. Can't expect investors to back a man on talk alone, but if you should happen to find the means before the sale, it could be called off."

I stood up and brushed the leaves from the seat of my pants, reminded again of their worn condition. "I'll go back to Berks. Ask around. See who might be interested."

It was all a pipe dream. I had no money, no rich friends, no acquaintance with possible investors. Still, I couldn't get the idea of running Etna Furnace out of my head. I could go back to Birdsboro and get a steady job, work iron for the rest of my life, but this gnawing need wouldn't be denied. I wanted to run the place. Nothing less. I wanted to make it work.

Crissman pulled on a pair of warm leather gloves and turned his horse's head downstream. "Well, I'll wait and see if you ever show up around here again." He kneed his horse, waved the back of his hand and rode off down the river trail.

The afternoon shadows were growing long, and the cold along the river had a bite to it. I watched Crissman ride off, uninterested in trying to keep up, pulled my coat closer, shivered, and turned toward the mill in hope of the possibility of a night's shelter. Jefferson Baker was just closing the door, locking up.

"Sir! Mr. Baker! Might I prevail upon you for a place to sleep the night? I'm too tired to walk back to Water Street."

Baker turned and gave me a quizzical look. "Did that old bastard ride off and leave you to walk back? Sure. Sure. You can sleep here, and welcome." He stepped back to the door and opened the lock. "Won't be very warm, but it's better than outside. You can sleep on them sacks over there and use the empty ones for blankets."

I followed him inside, grateful to be out of the elements—and for a sheltered place to sleep. "I don't have any money, Mr. Baker, but I'll see you're paid someday."

Baker waved a dismissive hand. "Don't suppose you've had any supper."

"No, sir." Head down. Poverty taking its toll.

"I'll send my boy over with something to eat. Make yourself to home. It ain't fancy, but I 'spect you're not very used to fancy."

Then Baker was gone, and I set about making a bed out of the sacks, then sat down on a pile of full sacks of unground wheat, elbows on my knees, contemplating my predicament. Here I was, alone, penniless, with no prospects. Why had I even implied that I could get investors? I didn't know a soul with more than a few coppers under the bed, and yet, when I looked at that furnace, sitting forlorn and abandoned, I couldn't deny the drive to do something—anything—to get it working again.

The door opened and Baker's boy Joel, a lad of ten or so, carried in a basket with a cloth over it. Inside, a meat pie, still steaming, two apples, a small cloth bag of dried corn, and a flagon of ale. I thanked the boy, promising to repay the kindness, and started in to eating the first meal I'd had in two days.

Once the food and drink warmed me I fell to planning again—drew diagrams of the furnace in the dust on the mill floor and estimated the cost of rebuilding. I'd need sandstone for relining the fire chamber, wood for rebuilding the charging house and sheds. Hands. Lots of hands to do the repairs, burn the charcoal, mine the ore and quarry the limestone. Hands meant wages. Months of wages before a single pig was poured, before a single bar was forged. I racked my brain for anybody I knew who could afford to back such a project. No one. Not a single soul came to mind.

Chapter 5

Fall 1823
Ellie

Well, I'd done it now. Got myself into a pretty pickle, thanks to Robert Clifton. Here I sat, writing in my diary all the secrets of my young life, while the honorable (?) Mr. Clifton rode off to Philadelphia to study at the university. We'd probably never meet again. My father and his would see to that. Not that Robert would object. I hadn't seen or heard from him—not a whisper, mind you—since I gave him the news of my impending motherhood—not face-to-face—in a note. It should have been edged in black, it caused such a tumult.

I thought Papa would die of apoplexy when he learned of my condition. Never had I seen him so discomposed. That was later—by two months—after it was clear that Robert Clifton had no intention of marrying me. Papa was so affronted, I don't know what upset him most—my pregnancy, Robert's abdication, or Squire Clifton's obstinate refusal to make Robert stand up to his responsibility. It was all an insult to Papa's dignity. I honestly thought he might pop a blood vessel or whatever older men do when all their plans and schemes come to a bad end. Mama, too, but she was less volatile than Papa. She just told me, "You've made your bed, Elinor. Now you must lie in it."

Papa, used to getting his way in all things save one, the death of my brother, decided first to visit Squire Clifton with a plan to get him to be reasonable and pressure Robert into marrying me. I protested aloud and doubled my hands into fists at the idea, so adamant was I that Robert not be forced. But Papa wouldn't hear it. He rode right over to Brighton, unannounced, and called on the squire. I guess it came to shouting because Papa returned more awash in consternation than ever. Swore about the Cliftons. Damned them to hell—for three days running.

After about a week of pacing and raging, Papa went off to Reading—on business, he said—and came home a few days later much becalmed—went about like there was nothing amiss. Even smiled at me once and pecked Mama on the cheek—a sure sign that things were better. That was in early November. I was preoccupied with my own condition—a slow but sure expansion of my waistline and a frustrating effort to pinpoint the date of my impending confinement. As near as I could tell, it would be winter—February maybe, or March. Autumn was upon us in waning splendor, so I was either four or five months into my condition. I wondered, of course, what I was going to do, having been used to comfort and respectability all my life. This child would be a life-long reminder of last summer's indiscretions in the Cliftons' orchard.

I was in love with Robert Clifton, had been blindly so since he pushed me off the garden wall when I was six and he was eight. My feelings for him were magnified by my pity for his role in Alex's death. Poor Robert must have been devastated by the experience. So when he asked me to go riding with him, and took me for long walks in the woods, when I was sixteen and he was eighteen, of course I was taken with him, sure of my mission to salve his wounds and help him forget. Mama accompanied us at first—at a respectful distance—but after a few months she began complaining about her rheumatism and stayed close to home, allowing us more privacy than might have been considered proper. Mama and Papa, pleased with the match, were open to relaxing the rules just a little.

Then, one day just after Christmas, Robert and I went on a sleigh ride by ourselves—unchaperoned. It was on that sleigh ride that I should have set some boundaries, but I was too busy picturing myself wedded to the handsomest bachelor in three counties, and by far the richest. Maybe a Christmas wedding at Brighton Hall or a spring wedding in the orchard under the apple blossoms. Mama and Mrs. Clifton would have such a grand time planning it.

So when Robert pulled up the horse in a dark patch of woods, grasped me to him and kissed me with a passion, I can't say I resisted. Not even when he tucked his hand inside my cloak—said he was cold—and fondled me through my clothes. He ardently proclaimed his love, said he wanted me to be his bride, and my weakening resistance melted like honey on a hot day. He kissed me again and again as he reached inside my jumper and fondled my breasts. I jumped in surprise, pulled away, but in the end I couldn't find the resolve to put an end to his explorations.

After a short while I admonished him gently, reminding him that I was but a girl and he shouldn't take such advantage of me. Propriety prevailed and he reluctantly withdrew his hand, clucked to the horse and we glided silently back onto the track, driving home through a lovely snowfall. My heart beat a tattoo so loud I was sure my mother could hear it as the maid set out cookies and hot chocolate for us. Robert ate heartily while I simply nibbled. He glanced in my direction, caught my eye and licked his lips in a way that sent a chill down my spine and a patter of delight in my heart.

After that there was unspoken acceptance by my parents and me that Robert and I were destined for marriage. I expected some token for my seventeenth birthday in April, but instead I got a soft wool scarf. Expensive, yes, but hardly personal enough to be considered a token, and obviously chosen by his mother. I resisted the urge to wind it up and throw it back at him, taxing my will power. And sometimes I felt a leaden feeling in the pit of my stomach where Robert was concerned, a vague, uneasiness that maybe I'd been too free with my favors, or that Robert was only toying with me. Still I hoped, planned and schemed.

Robert was in no way to be persuaded to limit his exploration of my body. He continued to arrange meetings where we could be alone and spent the whole time urging, pleading, demanding and cajoling me for more, more, more. And I must admit that I was a willing participant, hoping to whet his appetite for the wedding night.

Alas, one 'specially warm afternoon in May, he finally had his way with me in my father's orchard abutting the Brighton lands. Robert and I daily left our respective houses and wandered off in the direction of the orchard as though by accident, meeting alone and unobserved. We loved in the fullest sense, breaching every rule, every prohibition in my young experience. Once it was done, it became easier, and though we went to elaborate lengths to keep our meetings secret, it was clear that stopping was beyond us.

So fled the summer, but by mid-August I was aware something was amiss. I had no menses, and in the mornings I couldn't bear the thought of rising, lest my stomach turn on me. A few discreet discussions with friends made the situation all too apparent. I was with child.

Chapter 6

November 1823
Ellie

The truth was perplexing but not daunting. In my naïveté, I judged that we would just have to move our wedding day up to, say, October. It was not a problem. It happened all the time and no one cared, as long as...

But as the fall ensued, Robert's visits became less frequent, and with the cooler weather it was not so easy to find privacy to continue our trysts. He had other obligations—had to go on business into Reading City quite often, two or three times a week. Sometimes he stayed in town and I didn't see him for days. His ardor was just as strong when he came to me, but it felt spurious somehow, and when I tried to press him without revealing my condition, dropping hints like, "Wouldn't it be fine if we had children right away?" Robert shrank from any mention of children, or even of the wedding, which up until then was my own singular dream and only tentative, anyway. As his visits tapered off, the leaden feeling in my stomach deepened. What if he...? No, surely not. Not after all his professions of love.

But as summer inevitably gave way to fall he visited less and less often, to the point that both of my parents asked why we saw so little of him these days. Then came word by way of the Brighton farm hands to our farm hands that Robert was preparing to go to Philadelphia to the university. It was then I wrote the note, in haste and despair, wretched with fear that he had already abandoned me. I waited. No reply. No visits. No notes. When I heard he had departed for Philadelphia, I cried. That did no good at all.

By the end of October I had to tell my parents, for it was obvious that Robert had gone his merry way. My papa went wild. He roared, held his head in both hands, gave voice to the unspoken urge to blame Robert for Alex's death, strode around the house almost bumping into things, and even hauled back as if to strike me.

"How could you be so foolish, Elinor? How could you let this happen?" He looked helplessly at my mother and stalked out the door, slamming it in his wake.

I turned to my mother but found no sympathy there, only grave disappointment at not having our family joined to the Cliftons by marriage.

By mid-November the storm had passed, but the aftermath left us with damaged hearts (me), hopes (Mama) and egos (Papa). My father, Stephen Bratton, was a self-made man—had amassed a fortune as a young dealer in beaver pelts for the hat industry. He'd married Mama, the third daughter of a seemingly wealthy and prominent Philadelphia family, the Rightenours—the poor branch of that renowned family—only to learn after the wedding that the money was gone and the social standing with it. He brought Mama to Berks County, where land was cheaper and no family history prevailed, and proceeded to set himself up as a country squire.

It was no accident that he bought a farm adjoining Brighton and that he cultivated a friendship with Squire Clifton. Papa strove to promote the friendship between Alex and Robert Clifton—and thereby his own association with Robert's father—in every possible way. Mama wanted to be Martha Clifton's lady-in-waiting, if there was such a thing. It's clear to me now that they were preparing me to marry Robert from the time I was born, with no resistance from me, a naïve but willing participant, my brother's death notwithstanding.

Now the Bratton world burst wide open. While everyone county-wide knew Robert and I were promised, his enrolling at the university didn't raise an eyebrow. People would have expected us to wait until he was through to marry, but the small detail of my expanding waistline made that scenario null and void. Papa barely spoke to me in the days leading up to his trip to Reading City, but upon his return he was a different man—relaxed, friendly, even jovial. I wasn't long in discerning that Papa had a plan, and he wasn't long in carrying it out.

The first time I saw Adam MacPhail I thought he was a business associate of my father's come for dinner, nothing more. Lumpy. That's what he looked like. All angles and bumps showing through his ill-fitting clothes. Bony wrists protruding from his sleeves, knees almost bulging through his threadbare trousers. There was nothing about Adam MacPhail's appearance to make you want to know him more—except his eyes. Blue. Enshrouded under heavy brows. Deep. Intense. Determined. One look at those eyes and you'd stand back and let him pass.

Handsome would have been a long way down my list of descriptors, as would charming. His face was thin, his hair thick. His Adam's apple bobbed when he spoke. That was barely a problem because he spoke little—only when spoken to—and then only in brief, quiet replies.

He was intensely interested in the iron industry in the western part of the state and little else. Papa said he'd come back to Berks County, where he'd been raised, to find investors for an iron furnace and forge he wanted to revive in Huntingdon County. I was polite to Mr. MacPhail but let my mind wander to more stimulating topics until it dawned on me that Papa seemed more than interested in my making Mr. MacPhail's acquaintance. Indeed, he was falling all over himself with conviviality, fairly bubbling with praise for this poor, boring, homely man. I looked across the table at Mama for an ally and realized that she, too, seemed to find Mr. MacPhail acceptable company. I felt the noose slowly tighten around my neck.

"How could you even consider this?" I demanded of my father that evening after Mr. MacPhail had taken his leave.

"Consider what, my dear?" Papa's play on innocence angered me even more.

"You know what. You're setting me up to marry that oaf. Offering to pay him off to make an honest woman of me."

"Oaf? Really now, Elinor, a young lady in your circumstances can't afford to go about with her nose in the air."

"I can't believe you'd entertain such a notion without even consulting me. What if I refuse?"

My father looked at me over his spectacles. "I don't think you will. Nor will he. In a very real sense, you need each other."

Tears welled up in my eyes, but as I turned to my mother for support she averted her gaze. I stomped out of the room and up the stairs, where I threw myself on my bed and pounded the pillow with my fists. Damn you, Robert Clifton. Damn you to hell.

Chapter 7

Early November 1823
Adam

It was already half after two o'clock in the afternoon, and I was still waiting. My one o'clock appointment seemed inconsequential to Mr. Grayson, whose office door remained closed and had been since before I'd arrived at ten minutes to one. The clerk wrote busily in his ledger, blotting and sprinkling sand here and there but barely looking up when I coughed or moved about. He'd done his duty—the clerk—entered the office and informed the proprietor that Mr. MacPhail had arrived. Now he ignored me—a shabby, angular young man with a ledger under his arm—obviously not a regular client.

Outside, Reading City bustled with late autumn activity—harvest time and the markets full of pumpkins, squash, turnips, rutabagas. Feeding myself was no problem now. I could easily get a day's work and earn enough to keep myself in food for a week with no worries about spoilage. With my knowledge of iron making, I could have a full-time job at any of a dozen furnaces, but this wasn't where I wanted to be. My heart already lived in that remote Juniata River Valley, making iron at Etna Furnace. All I needed was someone to listen—someone with some influence—someone with rich friends.

The door to the office opened and a portly gentleman stepped out, nodded to the clerk, and strode across to the door. As he passed through the bare room, he turned, gave me an appraising glance, and stepped out. There was something familiar about him, but search my memory as I would for where or when our paths had crossed, nothing surfaced.

As the man closed the door behind him, the clerk rose and entered the inner office. I waited, trying to buoy up my flagging hopes. Not one of my strengths, patience. I liked action, liked things to keep moving, liked immediate responses. Not to be, this day, though. The clerk didn't return for a full ten minutes, and when he did, he approached with a dour expression.

"I'm afraid Mr. Grayson won't be able to see you this afternoon. Something unexpected has arisen. I'm sorry."

Disappointed, I rose, lay my ledger on the clerk's desk, rubbing my hands together to warm them. "May I, then, have another appointment? Tomorrow, perhaps?"

The clerk shook his head. "This new thing will take Mr. Grayson out of town. To Philadelphia, I'm afraid. He won't be back for some time."

I didn't believe the clerk, not for one moment, and the helpless feeling that washed over me threatened to erode my resolve. Who was I to think they might listen to me? Who was I, indeed? Used to disappointment and expecting nothing more, I picked up my ledger and moved to the door.

Out in the street, I looked up and down, trying to decide where to go next. I'd come to the city this morning, had a fruitless meeting with my uncle, Charles McManamy, eaten a lunch of two carrots and an apple under a tree in the park along the Schuylkill, and now been disappointed again in my quest for investors. It was discouraging, to be sure, but each time I allowed my enthusiasm to waver I pictured Etna Furnace, sitting alone in the barren hollow, waiting for revival. I was to be its savior. Not willing to give despair a foothold, I wandered down the street to a public house, where I hoped to slake my thirst and renew my resolve.

Inside, the barroom was quiet in the mid-afternoon lull. Two old men bent over a checkerboard, nursing tankards of ale, while another member of their class held forth to anyone who would listen about his adventures in the revolution. His voice was loud, so the choice not to listen was no one's to make. Once my eyes got used to the dimness, I recognized the man from Grayson's office seated by a window on the other side of the room, one arm sprawled across the back of an empty chair.

What impelled me to it, I couldn't say, but I approached. "Is this seat open?"

The man nodded and looked up as I sat down. "You've a familiar look about you."

"As do you. I saw you in Grayson's office, but couldn't place you. What business are you in?"

"The fur trade. I buy and sell beaver pelts for the hat makers." The man frowned. "I know you from somewhere, but..."

"That's it! My father was a hatter. You probably sold to him. Laird MacPhail."

"MacPhail? Sure. You were just a bit of a boy last time I saw you. Stephen Bratton." He smiled and offered his hand. "Your father still working here in Reading?"

"No. He died when I was twelve. Left my mother with seven of us to raise. Since I was the oldest, she apprenticed me out to an ironmaster at the Birdsboro works."

"Iron, is it? Tough business. Lot of ups and downs. Still in it?"

I nodded, looking toward the barmaid heading for our table.

"Oh, excuse me, but can I buy an old customer's son a drink? What's your pleasure? Ale?"

Grateful for the offer, I pulled up a chair as Mr. Bratton raised a hand. "Two more, here!"

"Must have been hard on your mother, raising all those little ones alone."

"Yes, I guess that's why she remarried a year or so later. Needed someone to provide."

The barmaid brought two tankards of ale, and Stephen Bratton laid a coin on her tray. "You don't sound very happy about that."

"No. He wasn't much of a man. Beat her and the other kids. Nothing I could do. I was too far away, and she never complained. I got the news from my little brother."

"That's often the way of it. Man wants a woman, but not the baggage that comes with her." Well dressed, Stephen Bratton had the look of a prosperous businessman, confident and familiar with the ways of the world.

Painfully conscious of my threadbare state beside this world-wise purveyor of pelts, I wished I had enough money to buy a second round, but if I were to offer, it would take me down to nothing, and I didn't want to put aside my quest and go to work. I sipped my ale slowly, eyes on my companion, thinking.

"What are you doing now, young man?" The question was all I needed to set me off on a sincere and persuasive discourse about the iron industry and all its promise.

Bratton's laugh was loud and deep. "You're a quiet one, but get you talking about iron and you come alive. Like me and beaver pelts. Good to meet a man so taken with his job."

"Oh, I don't have a job now, sir. Not that I couldn't get one. I could, but I don't want to spend my life working for someone else. I want my own furnace. Be an ironmaster. I'm trying to raise money to buy a furnace in the west and put it back in blast. It has everything: ore, limestone—and lots of woods for charcoal."

My enthusiasm had Bratton leaning forward, listening. "So you think you can make a go of it when the present owner failed? How do you think to do that?"

"Yes, sir. I learned all the latest techniques at Birdsboro. I can bring the furnace back into blast and start making iron in the spring if I get some backing."

"Yes, but you'll still have those high transportation costs eating up your profits."

I looked down at my hands, moved to silence by this dose of reality. "I know about that, sir. But there has to be a way. You've heard talk of the Pennsylvania canal, haven't you?"

Stephen Bratton smiled. "Yes, the state legislature voted on it just recently. It'll go that way—up the Juniata Valley from Amity Hall to Pittsburgh. If it's ever built, you can ship either way—east or west—Pittsburgh or Philadelphia."

I nodded, unable to contain my excitement. "I know. I want to be ready—producing my own iron for either market."

Bratton sat back in his chair, eyeing me with a strange new interest. "And you're having trouble raising the capital for this venture? Who've you been talking to?"

A sigh escaped me. "Hardly anyone, sir. Look at me. No one even wants to talk to someone as poor as I am. But I've got a head for this business. All I need is some backing. You'll see. I'll make a go of it."

Bratton smiled, rose and picked up a clay pipe from the mantle. As he lit it and sucked a few deep draughts to get it going, a thoughtful, far away look came into his eyes.

"Money. Hard to come by these days, but I think you might have something promising here. Once the canal's built, you'll be sitting in the right place to make it pay. Problem is, getting from here to there. That canal'll take a long time to materialize. You'll have to get established and stay afloat until it does."

"I know that. But I can live on very little. All I'll need is enough to pay my workers. There's a huge market for iron goods, especially in the west. There's already a forge right on the property. We can make iron goods to sell to the local folk to sustain ourselves in the beginning. The area is growing fast because the charcoal burning clears the land—makes it ready for farming."

"All right. I want to hear more, as long as you can provide the facts and figures."

"I've got all that right here." I took the ledger book from the table and opened it. "There it is, sir. It's all there. If you show this to your rich friends, they'll be ready to jump at the chance. They'll listen to a successful man like you, where they'd dump me in the nearest trash barrel."

With the book spread out on the table before us, we talked and figured for more than an hour. Though Bratton was interested, but non-committal, I felt my speech increase in speed and volume in my desire to convince him.

"Hold, there, boy! I'm not deaf. Just give me some time to mull this over. I've got other things on my mind right now, so just hold your horses. I have to take care of a family matter which..."

He stopped in mid-sentence, as though an idea had struck him. "Are you married, MacPhail?"

I shook my head. "Completely unencumbered, sir. That's why this would be so simple. I could live on almost nothing and put all of my energy and profits back into the furnace."

Bratton peered at me over the rim of his tankard. "Man needs a woman around to gentle him. You ought to think about taking a wife."

"Wife? Why, sir? It would just complicate my plans."

"Not necessarily. Might smooth the way for you, if the right woman were available. Maybe one with more than looks and charm."

Bratton sat back in his chair, watching me fidget, uncomfortable under his steady gaze.

"But, sir, I've no prospects. No hope of any woman wanting to share this adventure with me, poor as I am."

Rising abruptly, Stephen Bratton strode to the counter and dropped a coin in the innkeeper's hand. He motioned over his shoulder for me to follow and, like an obedient child, I did. Outside, Bratton led the way around back to the stables and called for his horse. "Got a loaner for my friend here?" he asked the liveryman.

A horse was produced—rather a likely-looking one—and I soon found myself riding beside Stephen Bratton out of town. Within two miles we came to a tidy farm on the banks of Tulpehocken Creek, orderly and well cared for. The house was large and imposing, built of red brick, a chimney at either end. Bratton pulled up in front, dismounted and turned his horse over to a tow-headed youth in rough overalls. "Keep that one warm and happy for our guest, Jake," Bratton said with an air of familiarity.

"Is this your house, sir?" I asked, getting down from the horse, feeling a little stiff even after so short a ride. I wasn't used to horses.

"It is."

I looked around the farm, struck by the obvious appearance of wealth, not ostentatious, but certainly a comfortable way of life. Beaver pelts must pay well.

Stephen Bratton led the way through the front door into a wide center hall that separated a parlor to the right from a large dining room to the left. The furnishings were quality and comfortable, not enough to frighten one into speechlessness, but as we entered the parlor, speechlessness took hold. Seated on a divan, holding an embroidery hoop and a needle, was the most beautiful young woman I'd ever seen. Dark hair pulled back, braided and wound above her ears, soft brown eyes, full lips parted in a hint of a smile.

"Elinor! Come, girl. I've brought someone to meet you. This is Adam MacPhail, a promising young ironmaster from the west."

I colored at the exaggerated account of my accomplishment, stood there dumbfounded, holding my hat, painfully aware that I didn't look the part Stephen Bratton described.

The young woman rose and smiled a quiet smile, extending her hand. Her beauty was rich and classic, but her energy level seemed not to match. It was almost as though she'd been ill and was convalescing.

"Good day, Mr. MacPhail. Papa, shall we call for tea?"

Her soft, gentle voice was musical, like spring water tumbling over rocks. I stood transfixed, barely able to mumble a greeting, twisting my hat in my hands.

Elinor Bratton. Oh my God! Beautiful. Just beautiful.

Chapter 8

Mid November 1823
Adam

Within a few weeks, Stephen Bratton had gathered investors enough to purchase the Etna Iron Works and send Mr. Crissman on his way. I watched the process with awe, delighted at the prospect of getting my chance to restore the furnace and run it. Show what I could do. Turn a profit and then some. I went about Reading City in something of a daze, unable to fathom my good fortune. Mr. Bratton was matter-of-fact about the whole business, but for me it was miraculous.

The following Sunday I was invited to the Bratton home for dinner. This time I rode a horse provided by Mr. Bratton for my extended use, along with a stipend to provide for my immediate needs. I bathed, shaved, had my shirt laundered and my coat and trousers brushed, turned out the best I could—with little hope of impressing the young lady, but doing my best, just in case.

Elinor Bratton appeared in a fashionable gown, looking every bit as beautiful as she had on Thursday, and just as languid. We sat at table, across from each other, Stephen Bratton at one end and his wife, Alice, at the other. Mrs. Bratton spoke little, concentrated on her plate and sighed now and then, a well attired middle-aged woman with something on her mind. Mr. Bratton tried to carry the show, making jokes and commenting on the cooking, but the other members of the company seemed distracted—concerned with some unnamed preoccupation. I sat quiet, unsure of my place or my purpose.

The dining room was large and simply appointed, with cream-colored walls and windows heavily draped in a brown brocade. A crystal chandelier hung in the center of the ceiling, adorned with candles lit by lowering it on a delicate, gold cord. The room looked ready for a gala dinner party, even though we were only four.

"You mark my words, ladies, this young man is off to make a name for himself." Bratton pushed away from the table and lit a cigar, offering one to me, which I declined. Instead I lifted a glass of claret and toasted, "To the ladies here present."

"Hear, hear!" my host enjoined. "Where would we be without the ladies?"

Not used to genteel female company, I struggled with feelings of unease, watching Miss Elinor Bratton for any sign of boredom or conversely, any sign of interest—in anything. My lack of self-confidence allowed the conversation to lag, though I did my best to contribute.

After the meal, the company withdrew to the parlor, where Mr. Bratton called, "Who's for a game of Whist?"—a request which surely deserved a response, but Mrs. Bratton only picked up her embroidery and started to sew, while her daughter sat down in a window seat, gazing into the garden. I looked around, perplexed, unsure whether to join in the call for a game or go stand by the young woman and gaze out the window with her. I did neither. Instead I stood rooted to the spot, surely looking as uncomfortable as I felt. It was clear Stephen Bratton was at odds with these women, and my presence seemed something of an intrusion. I was relieved when he offered me an invitation to withdraw.

"Come, Mr. MacPhail. Let's leave these ladies to their preferences and adjourn to the library, where we can discuss business."

Eager to return to a more comfortable world, I followed Stephen Bratton out of the room into the adjoining library, where he motioned for me to be seated and poured each of us a generous draught of brandy. I welcomed the warm, relaxing effect of the drink and settled into the comfortable chair, glad to be removed from the scrutiny of such a beautiful, but obviously disinterested, young woman. I was, in spite of myself, falling in love.

I looked around the tastefully appointed room, admiring the grand collection of books. "You must be quite the reader, sir."

"What?"

"The books, sir. So many. Do you read a lot, then?"

"Oh, those." He waved a dismissive hand. "No, I don't read much at all. The books are there for décor—or to impress those who do. My wife reads some, and my daughter."

I took another sip of brandy and let my eyes wander over the titles, all stamped in gold on leather spines. If they were meant to impress, they certainly did the job.

Stephen Bratton was not long in getting to the heart of the matter. "I suppose you're wondering what motivates me on your behalf, young man. Well, you deserve to know that, at least. It isn't all business, I fear. My daughter has been the victim of an ... ah ... indiscretion—left with something of an inconvenience. She and her young man—well, you know how easy it is to get carried away on a lovely summer's day ..."

I had no idea how easy that would be—not in my wildest dreams had I ever imagined bedding a woman I wasn't married to. Many did, I knew, but it was beyond imagination for me, not from any religious constraint, but from a lack of confidence in my own ability to attract and woo even the plainest of young women. My knowledge of iron making stood alone on the list of my expertise, while the social skills didn't even deserve mention. I sat, sunk deep into a wing-back chair, looking out at Stephen Bratton, my mind trying valiantly to encompass the revelation before me. Elinor Bratton, beautiful child, used to all the comforts I knew so little of, was in a fix so far beyond my capacity to conjure, I could only sit and stare.

"The child is due in February. There it is. There's nothing for it but to go forward. I want her married when it comes. No bastard in this family. She's against it now, but she'll see the light soon enough. Now you, you've come along at just the right time."

"I? How does this have to do with me, sir? Surely you don't expect..."

"I won't force either of you. I just want you to know what needs to be done. My daughter isn't in a state to decide for herself, and you—well, there's the matter of Etna Furnace. You do want to acquire it? Run it? Own it some day?" Stephen Bratton took a long sip of brandy.

I felt the brandy taking hold and I rose and set down my glass, overwhelmed with the desire to escape from this situation while I could still control my actions.

"Oh, no, sir. I mean, yes, I do want all that, but I can't let her be forced into marrying me. She's so young and beautiful, sir. Way beyond my station. I can't."

"Listen to me, MacPhail. She'll get over this and be fine. The shock of her predicament has taken her over for the present, but when she comes to her senses, she'll see the reasoning here. She needs to be wed, and soon."

Those words set me to pacing, hands clasped behind my back. "This is too much, sir. The money, the business plan, all tied up neatly, but not without complication. I should have known there'd be a reason for your generosity. But what will *she* say? How will she find *me?*"

"You worry too much," Bratton replied, taking another draught of brandy. "She's just a woman after all. It'll all be taken care of. A quiet wedding—a generous gift to get you started. You can go back and get the furnace in blast. Start producing iron come spring. The child will fit in nicely with your other circumstances. No one need know the details."

I stopped pacing and turned to face him. "I can't."

Bratton put down his glass. "MacPhail. I know I seem a tyrant to you now, but this is the best offer you're ever going to get. Stop dithering over it and take it before I lose patience and withdraw my support."

"I'm sorry, sir. I need time to think. I must go."

"Tomorrow noon. That's when I need your answer. After that, it's too late."

I picked up my hat from the hall tree, found my way to the front door, and let myself out without taking leave of the ladies.

The November afternoon was bright and crisp on the ride back to Reading City, my head spinning with the notion of being married at all, let alone to such a beauty. I wanted her, loved her already, so every aspect of the offer was to my advantage. But what about her? Would she ever be able to love me? How would she find Etna Furnace? I didn't even know the condition of the house I'd be taking her to. How could I ever expect her to learn to love me or the life I would impose on her? The whole idea seemed unfair. But what choice did she have if she didn't want to spend the rest of her life as a soiled woman?

The horse seemed to know its way, and I let it follow the track while I slumped in the saddle wrestling with unfamiliar emotions. As I came to a creek, I stopped and got down to scoop up water for a drink. Then I took off my hat and sat on the bank, letting the unseasonably warm sunshine bathe me in its crisp light. I knew I should be elated, full of joy at my good fortune. It wasn't that I didn't like the girl. How could I not like—love, even—one so fine, so far beyond what I had ever thought myself worthy of? Here was opportunity of every sort standing right in front of me. Why couldn't I just jump at it?

The horse blew at me, shaking its bridle. It wanted to get back to the livery—if I didn't mind. I got up slowly and swung up into the saddle, wondering what Elinor was thinking. Had Bratton yet told her what was in store? I couldn't blame her if she refused. Couldn't see why she wouldn't. Paired up with a lean and homely stranger, sent off to a wild part of the country, expected to adjust to whatever came along. Very different from all she probably expected—sudden and tragic and not at all what I guessed she would have chosen for herself.

I turned the horse toward Reading City and rode on in silence, contemplating my options, which were few. For me this wasn't bad in any way I could think of—a chance to restore that old furnace, make it work, run an iron works and make a success of it. Where else would I ever get such a chance? And then the other: the chance to wed a beautiful girl; even a soiled one was still beautiful. Anyway, out there in the wilds, no one need know about our arrangement. No one need know the child wasn't mine. So why not?

I didn't have anyone waiting for me—had never, in fact, even kissed a girl. That sent a chill through me. What if she found me wanting? What if she spent the rest of her days hating me and our life, pining for the lover she'd lost? What if she turned into a shrew and made my life miserable? In that moment, business seemed utterly simple compared to this. Making iron. No problem at all. Making a woman happy? Something else entirely.

My room at the inn in Reading City was spare and plain, everything I was used to, comfortable with, in fact. I went up as soon as I arrived, foregoing supper, and lay down on the bed with my boots on, staring at the painted board ceiling in the waning light. My head ached. Maybe it was the brandy I wasn't used to. The room seemed to spin slowly above my head. I reached down to touch the floor—hold on—slow down the spin. The next I knew it was morning, and late morning at that. The sun was long up, but dark clouds obscured its light. Outside, a drizzle of rain made Reading City dismal to behold and a match for my mood.

I rose and brushed my hair with my fingers. Since I hadn't undressed, I picked up my hat and left the room almost as I'd found it the night before. I still had no appetite, so I passed by the boarding table and stepped out into the rain with no real idea of where I was going. I walked down Penn Street toward the Schuylkill River, hands in my pockets, hunched over against the damp and cold.

"Hi! MacPhail! Adam MacPhail!"

Jonathan Pitt, one of the other journeymen from the Birdsboro works hailed me. I turned and greeted him with a nod, glad for a familiar face. "Jonathan."

"Where you off to?" Jonathan clapped me on the shoulder.

"Nowhere, really. Just taking a walk."

"What, you don't have to work?"

I shook my head. "Not today. You?"

"Got off to bring the ironmaster's wife to shop. Bad day for it, though. Rained all the way in and doesn't look like it plans to stop anytime soon."

"Got time for a draught?" I felt like being companionable—more like I didn't want to be alone.

"Just about. Lady'll be another half hour or so. Getting fitted for a dress, she is."

I led the way into a public room and found a table off to the left beside a window. The rain kept coming down in a steady drizzle, showing no signs of abating or even changing pace. The room smelled of damp wool and wet leather.

"What you up to these days?" Jonathan asked when we'd been served our tankards of ale.

"Getting ready to go out west—Huntingdon County—to run a furnace out there." I heard myself say it as though it were accomplished. "Getting married, too."

Chapter 9

Late November 1823
Ellie

It was a quiet wedding that Saturday near the end of November. Just my parents, the minister, my best friend and cousin, Alice Jo, her husband, Thomas Cadwallader, and a few others, carefully selected for the respectability and news-spreading promise they lent. From upstairs in my room I could hear my mother mingling among the small company, no doubt offering her guests a smile and a nod and a quick explanation of the necessity for hurry.

"Oh, yes. Elinor and Adam are old friends. Adam is an iron-master—to the west somewhere—Huntingdon County, I believe. Business forces him to return there right away, but, bless them, they *would* be married before."

"Right as rain! Right as rain," my father boomed. "This young man is bound for the future, and Elinor is determined to go there with him. You know how these young people are—impatient to get on with life."

I'd spent the morning in tears, resisting at every turn, even refusing to wear the gown Mama had acquired in such a rush for me. My mother did all she could to console, cajole, and prevail upon me to accept my fate. I was having none of it. Such a sham.

"How can you join him in this conspiracy, Mother? How can you abandon me without a care?" Tears coursed down my cheeks, but my mother, whether by preference or lack of any alternative, sided with my father.

"Now, now, Ellie. It won't be so bad. This young man will probably succeed in the iron business and provide well for you."

"Provide for me? Is that all you think I should marry for?"

"Not all, my dear. But let's not speak of the rest of it."

I threw the veil I was trying on across the room, picked up the bridal gown, dropped it on the floor, and walked on it—slid it around as though wiping the boards clean.

"Ellie!" My mother was not above raising her voice if she thought it could alter my behavior. "You must stop this at once. It's time you grew up and understood how the world works."

"Oh, I understand how the world works, Mama. It works for you and Papa and Robert Clifton. Not for me."

Turning to the door, my mother placed her hand on the knob. "You will come to accept this, Elinor. You must. You're fortunate that this man is willing to marry you. Your life could be so much worse." She closed the door behind her, leaving me awash in tears, none of which did any good.

Then Papa appeared at the door, exhorting me to get dressed and make my appearance like the lady I was brought up to be, under the promise—or was it a threat?—of unspecified rewards.

"What, Papa? Will you buy me fine clothes if I go on with this sham? Or a new horse? A carriage, perhaps? What do I care for that? Why don't I have any choice?"

"You're a woman, my dear. This is how it is. Now get dressed and let's get this over with."

Dumbfounded by this reversal of fortune, this betrayal of my birthright, I stared him in the eye. "Would you really, Papa? Would you turn me out and leave me to fend for myself?"

He turned away, picked up the veil, laid it on the bed. "Worse has happened, my dear. You must think of others. Your poor mother is beside herself with disappointment. I, too, am saddened."

"You're only saddened to lose face with the Cliftons. I'll bet you'll be back in their good graces by spring, once I'm tied up in a neat little package and sent off to the west, where I won't be an embarrassment anymore."

"Now, Ellie, you must listen to reason. Some day you'll thank me for this. You wait and see."

"Thank you for manipulating my life without a care for my preferences? Not likely, Father. Or should I bow and call you Lord and Master?"

I picked up a book and hurled it, hitting him squarely in the paunch, knocking the wind out of him. He doubled over, holding onto the bedpost, wheezing. "Good God, girl! You be the death of me yet!"

"Good is what I say. And welcome!"

"Get dressed. I'll be back in five minutes, and believe me, if I have to, I'll carry you down to the minister!" He marched out the door and joined my mother, waiting for him in the hall.

"How did she get so willful?" he asked.

To me it felt like disownment, exile, abandonment. Standing in the middle of my bedroom, wearing a dress made for someone else, hastily altered for me, I ran my hands over my distended belly, contemplating an empty, loveless marriage to a man I would not have considered three months before. I looked out the window at the browning lawn, the trees bare of leaves, and saw my life—cold, lonely and without hope.

Adam MacPhail appeared for the ceremony in the same suit of clothes he'd worn to meet me, brushed and pressed, but still bespeaking their lowly origins. He stood, nervous and pale, hands hanging limp at his sides as Papa and I approached. Did I feel him hesitate as my father ceremoniously placed my hand in his? The minister pretended not to notice, going on endlessly about the sacred institution of marriage and a wife's duty to love, honor, obey. Not sure I could last through the droning, I stiffened my back and stared at a spot on the wall above the minister's head until he turned to me and asked if I took this man to be my wedded husband. I choked on the words—wiped my eyes on my handkerchief, tucking it up my sleeve, and forced myself to lay my hand in his. Calloused, hardened by manual labor, his hands stood for all that was base and low about Adam MacPhail. I shrank from his touch.

Adam spoke his vows softly, his voice so low none could hear but the minister and me. "In sickness and in health, to love and to cherish for as long as we both shall live." I chanced to look into his eyes for just a moment as he recited the words. There was nothing there—not even a hint of what he was thinking or feeling. I was walking into a cave without a lantern, my fate lost in the darkness beyond the light.

The desire to run away was overwhelming. I turned and glared at my father, seated beside my mother on a straight-backed chair, hands folded across his ample stomach. What right had he to sentence me to life with this man and no hope of redemption? What right, indeed? Was my sin so ruinous? Or was my first sin the worst—the sin of being born female?

The realization slowly dawned that my father saw little choice in the matter, and I had less. Adam MacPhail, however, could have walked away in a trice, but he stayed, holding my hand, stumbling and oafish, through this sham of a ceremony. I wondered at his ability to settle for leftovers when he could just as well have found some pretty and pure young thing who would worship at his feet in gratitude for his making her his own. I wouldn't do that. Not now. Not ever.

Oh, yes. He needed the money. That was it. A penniless dreamer who thought he could bring a derelict furnace and forge in the wilds of western Pennsylvania back from the brink of failure. He was used to leftovers. Didn't blink an eye at them. Furnace or female.

Chapter 10

Late November 1823
Adam

The company lingered a short while for tea and dainty cakes, ordered from Reading City, while the Brattons moved among their guests with relief and their best effort at cordiality. Stephen poured the brandy liberally and toasted his daughter and me. We stood awkward and uncomfortable at the fete, showing no sign of affection, not even a glance. How could there be? The guests, if they sensed any peculiarity, discreetly ignored it. My bride and I went through the motions of a brief reception, smiling and nodding our way through the introductions, without speaking to or acknowledging one another. Once the guests had departed, Stephen Bratton relaxed his bumptiousness and invited me to the library to 'go over some business', while Elinor disappeared up the broad staircase whence she had come.

The business turned out to be an envelope of money, enough to buy the whole Mt. Etna operation, making the furnace and its environs the property of the Mt. Etna Iron Company, owned by a group of investors, including Stephen Bratton, executor. There were other documents naming me, Adam MacPhail, ironmaster and outlining my duties, as well as my compensation for carrying them out.

Taking the money and the papers, I placed them in an inside pocket of my coat, bought new for my wedding. It was wool, and while I knew it was not the most fashionable cut, it would still serve for the kind of winter I expected to face. I turned to Stephen Bratton.

"Sir, I can't thank you enough for this opportunity. I promise, you won't be sorry."

"I've faith in you, young man. I've entrusted a great deal to you, but I consider myself an excellent judge of character. You've passed muster so far. And my daughter—well, go make a home for her and build up the iron works. It's the best thing you can do to assure me that I've done the right thing."

I shifted my weight from one foot to the other, uncomfortable with what I knew should come next. "Shall I stay the night here, then?"

"Of course! My God, man. I wouldn't want the public to know anything is amiss. I'm saving face—for her, for us and for you. You'll sleep in her room. What happens there is up to you."

I stood immovable in my discomfort for so long, Bratton took pity on me. "Here, you need some fortification," he said, pouring a generous draught of brandy for each of us.

Sensing my reluctance to retire, Bratton made conversation. "How old did you say you were?"

"Twenty-seven, sir."

"Yes. Yes. Well, Elinor is young—just seventeen, but I always say you can't start them too young. Train them up in the way they should go."

"Is she—was she very much in love with the other fellow?"

"How should I know?" replied Bratton, annoyed. "How does anyone know what's going on in the female head? Especially young ones."

He sat down at his desk and rummaged through the drawers. "I'm sure she thought she was, but I'm also sure she has no idea what love is."

I watched and listened, contemplating what to do next, glad to have the formalities over, but left with this very awkward, empty space of time. I would have liked to ride back to Reading City, but since that was out of the question, I would just as soon stay here in the library. Trouble was, Bratton wasn't going to brook my shyness forever. I had to leave sometime.

50

Bratton busily rummaged through his desk drawers until he found what he was looking for: another envelope. He pushed it across the desk to me. "Wedding gift. Don't know what kind of living conditions you have out there, but she's used to having things nice. Do what you have to do to make her comfortable."

"Yes, sir. Thank you, sir."

"And stop calling me sir. I'm your father-in-law. It's Mr. Bratton now—or Stephen—whichever, I don't care." He closed the desk drawer with a bang and stood up, facing me, as though challenging me to come up with any excuse to stay downstairs.

I stuffed the second envelope into my coat pocket and turned to go.

"You can take the wagon and team when you leave. They've got a lot of miles left in them. And Elinor's little mare. She'll need it there." He crossed the room and stood looking out the window into the dark night, hands clasped behind him. I took that as my dismissal.

"I'll be leaving early, then. In the morning. Need to get back and settle things up as soon as possible."

"Tomorrow, then. Good night."

There was no one about when I came out of the library into the quiet house. I started up the stairs, then remembered I didn't know which room was Elinor's. I turned back.

Bratton anticipated my problem and caught me at the door. "First room on the right at the top of the stairs."

When I entered, the room was dark. I could barely see Elinor in bed, under a thick feather tick. I stood by the window in my coat and tie, not sure where to go or what to do. I decided to keep my clothes on. This wasn't my idea of a way to start a marriage, but then I had no idea of how to start a marriage, so I was left to guess. I looked around the room, dimly lit by moonlight, and made out a horsehair settee against one wall. I turned toward the bed and whispered, "Are you awake?"

There was no answer for about ten seconds, then a tiny whimper.

"Don't worry. I won't hurt you. I just wanted a quilt or something to cover up with. I'll sleep on the settee."

She rose and lit a candle, carrying it to the closet, where she opened a trunk and pulled out another feather tick. Handing it to me, she looked at the settee and said, "It's too short for you. You'll have to bend almost double to even lie down."

"That's all right. I'll be fine."

Without another word, Elinor crawled back into her bed and pulled the feather tick tight up around her. I wrapped the other tick around my body and lay down on the floor. It wasn't any use trying to sleep. I knew I couldn't. After an hour of lying there staring at the ceiling, sure Elinor was awake, too, I started talking.

"I'm sorry about your situation. You father just told me you're only seventeen. I thought you were at least eighteen."

No response from the bed.

"I'm twenty-seven. This is all new to me. All I've ever done is work in an iron works. Apprentice, then journeyman. I grew up in Reading. My father was a hatter. He died when I was twelve. My mother remarried." I went on as though she might be interested. In case she was, I hoped anything I might tell her about myself could bridge the gulf that separated us.

"What about you?" I waited for a reply, but none came. I raised myself up on one elbow. "We might as well try to make the best of this. We're bound now. Bound for life."

A sob escaped the feather tick nest. I waited. Maybe she'd be ready to talk after she'd had a good cry. I turned over on my stomach and leaned forward on my elbows. "I know it's not a good start, but people change. Times change."

"I'm never going to change." The words came out from under the feather tick in a whisper.

"Never? You have to. It's a rule. Nothing ever stays the same, especially not a woman's mind."

Now she threw the tick back and sat up. "You think because you bought me you can make me love you, but you can't. Robert's the only man I'll ever love. So you might as well know that from the start. Don't talk to me about change. The only change you'll see in me is, I'll get skinny again after the baby comes."

"Bought you? I didn't ... never mind. I won't bother you any more. You can go to sleep now."

She lay back down and pulled the covers up again. I turned over on my back and stretched out long on the floor. The room was silent for some time—long enough for me to think she might have gone to sleep. Then she sat up, threw the tick back again and spoke in a loud whisper, "And another thing! You think you can take me out to the howling wilderness while you try to breathe life into some old broken down furnace. I'm staying here. You'll fail and be back soon enough. Wait and see."

I got up off the floor, stood up to my full height. "That's enough of that kind of talk. I'll make it work. And even if I don't, I won't come back here, so you've got to get used to the way things are. We live in Huntingdon County. I'm an ironmaster. You're my wife. That's all."

She shrank back in the bed, pulling the feather tick up around her again. Soon I heard sobs, wretched, wrenching sobs coming so hard they shook the bed. I heaved a heavy sigh and rolled over. No, to hell with this. I picked up my tick and lowered myself down on the bed. A sharp kick let me know I wasn't welcome. I pushed her over to her own side, pulled up my feather tick, and went to sleep.

Chapter 11

Late 1823
Ellie

That first night in my parents' house I bade Mr. MacPhail sleep fully clothed on the settee in my room, and had I not been preoccupied with my own troubles, I would have found it amusing to watch him try to fold his long legs and arms to fit. He chose the floor, from which he made halting attempts at conversation but soon capitulated in the face of my stubborn silence. Later, in frustration or discomfort, he actually crawled into the bed beside me but made no attempt to touch me or to persuade me otherwise, perhaps because his entry was met with a swift kick to the middle of the back. In the morning, he rose early, pulled on his boots, and left in silence to tend the horses.

I rose at my leisure and took my time getting dressed. A knock on my door interrupted my deliberate dallying, so I opened it after some moments and found my father standing there, looking impatient.

"How dare you hurry me? I'm leaving you and mother and everything I know, and you can't wait to push me out. Some father you turned out to be!"

"Now, Ellie, you wait. He's a good man. You could do worse."

"Bushwah! He's a floundering oaf, and you know it. Don't try to sweeten the situation now. You've ruined my life."

He stepped back and let me pass through the door without another word.

"And another thing. I'm taking books—as many as can be loaded into the wagon. I'm sure you'll not miss them."

Downstairs I found my mother waiting at the breakfast table, but I gave her to know I had no intention of eating. She pointed to the window where I could see my bridegroom—his coat a shapeless article of wool with no distinguishing characteristics except that it was undeniably warm—loading my trunks on the wagon.

"Tell him to bring more boxes for my books," I ordered. "I want as many as the wagon can hold."

Father excused himself to the barn, soon emerging with three wooden packing crates that he brought into the library. "Which ones do you want?" he asked, looking around the room with a sigh.

"All of them. I don't care which. Just pack as many as we can carry."

Adam joined him, and they filled the crates and hauled them out to the wagon while my mother and I stood watch. I felt fully justified in demanding anything I wanted from them, given that, as far as I was concerned, this was the terminus of our relationship.

Amid protests from my mother about how hungry I would be before noon, I wrapped my cloak around me and followed my father and my husband to the front door, both of my parents full of admonitions and cautions—but no apologies.

I heard warnings from my father about how treacherous the roads would be if snow came today, and solicitations from my mother about my trunks and the goods stowed inside, but not so much as a "Take care, dear daughter," or "Write to us when you get there." No. Not even a "We'll miss you."

My new husband escorted me to the waiting wagon, heavy laden with my trunks and the crates of books. Papa had been generous. He gave us a team, Rex and Brownie, to pull the wagon and let me have my little mare, Dancer, tied up behind.

Our farewells were brief and dry-eyed. Still unable to quell my anger at my father's high-handedness, I gave him a curt nod as Adam helped me up to the wagon seat. To my mother I offered an over-the-shoulder wave with my gloved hand. The thought that I might never see them again crossed my mind but was not enough to soften my heart. I think now I could have been more affectionate in my departure but, given my state of mind at the time, it's doubtful.

We set off into the cold, misty morning, moving slowly through the snow toward our destiny. Mr. MacPhail spoke little, only asking after my comfort and talking softly to the horses as they picked their way along the slushy road west. Our way took us to the inn at Palmyra by evening, where we stopped for a welcome warm meal and a room for just the two of us—no three or four to a bed as in the common rooms. My bones ached from the jarring of the wagon over ruts and clumps of frozen snow that littered the road. It would have been a hard journey even in summer and in the best of health, but this was close to unbearable, and it didn't make me feel any more hospitable toward my husband.

New to long distance travel, I had to be shown how to get on with only cold water for washing and no mirror at all. But my interest that night was not in my face, but in the aching and creaking of my bones. I insisted that Mr. MacPhail build up the fire in our room to a blaze and sat with my toes almost touching it, wrapped in my heavy wool and velvet cloak. I went to sleep dreading another day of jolting and bumping along in that wagon. I don't know whether my husband suffered as I did or not. He slept on the floor without protest.

He was patient, Mr. MacPhail. He didn't bother me that night or any other on the way to Etna Furnace, and even though I felt minor sympathy for his having to sleep on the floor, I turned to the wall and slumbered most comfortably. The next morning, when I awoke with the light rays of dawn, he was already gone—out tending the horses again, I guessed. Breakfast at the inn was ample, and I found myself hungry enough to enjoy it for the first time in weeks. Mr. MacPhail was generous to share his fatback with me and to confine himself to corn meal mush. The innkeeper's wife had gotten wind of our newlywed status and gave her approval in loud pronouncements to all present. Toasts and laughter accompanied good wishes and knowing glances at Adam. It made me blush, but Adam merely smiled and nodded in acceptance of the cheerfully offered bouquets.

The second day's travel was colder and even bumpier than the first, and I heard myself complaining—it bordered on bitter—quite often as we jolted along to Harrisburg and turned north up the Susquehanna toward the crossing at Amity Hall. My humor faltered, and though I really did try to contain it, the anger of the past week descended on me. The colder I got, the meaner I felt.

Suddenly I burst out. "Why did you agree to this?"

"Agree to what?" he returned.

"To this. To marrying me. To bartering for a wife. Don't you have any pride?"

It was a stinging attack, but Mr. MacPhail didn't wince. He turned his level gaze on me, his blue eyes steady. "I didn't think I had a choice."

"Yes, you did! You could have turned around and walked away. Now look. You've ruined both our lives."

"It seems to me you took care of your part of that before I came along." He said it mildly, but it stung nonetheless.

"Don't preach to me!" I almost screamed at him. "And don't think that just because my father handed me over to you that you can treat me like chattel."

"You can't know what I think, Elinor. Please don't presume to read my mind. If you're interested in my thoughts, ask me, but don't chide me for your own interpretation of something you know nothing about." His calm, gentle manner piqued my anger even more.

I turned away as he snapped the reins over the horses' rumps, bringing to an end the only conversation we would have that day. The inn at Amity Hall was lively and full of noise, talk, laughter, clinking spoons on pewter plates, a bit of a song now and then. I went to bed as soon as I'd eaten, but my new husband stayed, deeply engaged in conversation with two other men about something they called Juniata Iron, spoken of with a reverence I thought reserved for the church pew.

The third day was no more comfortable than the first two, but my belly was getting used to the jostling, and the weather, while not giving over to sunshine, warmed up a bit. We were now traveling along the Juniata River, a body of water I'd never heard of before but which was to become as familiar to me as my right hand. Its beauty was not lost on me—even in my distraught state of mind I could appreciate that this was, in its own way, a magnificent and promising part of the world. I did not express such feelings to my husband; indeed, I spoke very little to him throughout the day, and he spoke even less to me. My thoughts were focused on how we would proceed with this arrangement. For me, at that juncture, physical union was beyond the realm of possibility. I guessed with time we could learn to be civil to one another, but intimacy such as I had known with Robert Clifton was out of the question.

We slept that night at an inn near Waynesburg and woke to a sky more gray and threatening than any we'd seen. I would have given up on travel until the weather cleared, but Adam rose early, as usual, and went out into the cold morning in the same clothes he wore to our wedding, indeed the only clothes I'd ever seen him wear. I sighed and dressed as warmly as I could, picked up my portmanteau and followed. It seemed I had married a stubborn man.

Chapter 12

Early December 1823
Ellie

The weather worsened as the day wore on, and we made our dogged way along the river through falling snow and falling temperatures—to say nothing of my spirits, which fell faster the farther we traveled from home and everything I knew. Anger seethed beneath the surface, looking for any excuse to erupt. None presented itself, but I was not to be cowed by silence and indifference.

"Humph!" I growled.

Mr. MacPhail drove on as though he hadn't heard.

"Humph!" Again. Louder.

Still he continued to drive, encouraging the horses along the now slippery track, looking neither to the left nor to the right. "Soooo, Brownie. Take it easy, boy. We're soon there."

It was the only hint I had that we were nearing our destination. We edged around Huntingdon, a passable looking town, and when Mr. MacPhail turned the horses across the river and stopped before a likely looking store, I hoped we were through traveling for the day. But alas, he only stopped to buy candles, mumbling something about our needing them that night. I looked back, wistful, as the lights of the town slipped from view in the waning afternoon light, somewhat taken aback at these signs of civilization so far removed from any place familiar to me. We continued on for an hour or more, passing a humble but inviting looking inn standing near the river, where a spritely little stream poured in. In this wilderness and cold, dank weather, any shelter was a treat to the eyes.

"What's that?" I asked, unable to mask the yearning in my voice.

"The hamlet is called Water Street. That's the inn where I stayed when I first came up here."

"Oh, can we stay there tonight? I'm cold and tired. It doesn't look like much, but I don't care. Just shelter. Any shelter."

"We haven't far to go."

My husband clucked to the horses and turned them south along the track as though he hadn't noticed my emotional state. It was getting dark and the snow was far from letting up, but Adam lowered his head and kept on going.

I turned and watched the inn disappear into the leaden twilight, wondering why we didn't stop, longing for nothing more than a warm fire and a hot meal.

Within something more than another hour we passed a huge, imposing mill near the mouth of a creek standing dark against the background of even darker woods and turned off on a narrower track. A little farther along, Adam pulled the horses up in front of a two-story stone house, set on a hillside across the creek, desolate in the darkness. He got down without a word, walked up the steps to the door, and put his shoulder to it. The door creaked open, admitting a clump of cold, wet snow to the plank floor. He turned and motioned for me to come.

"Wait! What is this? Why did we pass a perfectly good inn to stop for the night in a stone hovel?"

"Because this is home," he said.

"Home? Home? How am I supposed to live in a place like this?" I flounced down on the seat, pulled my cloak tighter, and stared into the thick, snow filled woods.

Without a word, he turned and entered the house, closing the door behind him. Soon a light shone through a window to the right of the door. A few minutes later I saw, or rather smelled, smoke from the chimney. The door opened and Mr. MacPhail reappeared and clumped down the steps, ignoring me in favor of the horses. He unhitched all three and led them gently around beside the house, where there must have been some kind of shelter.

I sat on the wagon seat, shivering, and waited for his return, expecting to at least be addressed and offered help. I was not. He walked heavily around the side of the house, stomping the snow off his boots, without even a word or a look in my direction. By now it was completely dark, but this state of affairs was apparently of no concern to Mr. MacPhail, for he set about unloading the wagon, carrying my five trunks on his shoulders, one by one, up the steps and into the house. I watched in disbelief, waiting in vain for him to take notice of my plight and offer relief. I was shivering so my teeth chattered. I wrapped my cloak closer around me and waited.

When he'd finished unloading the wagon, books and all, Adam mounted the stairs one last time, stomped the snow off his boots again and let himself in. I sat there in the freezing cold for another quarter hour feeling sorry for myself in the extreme and gathering my spite. When it was clear my husband did not intend to rescue me, I climbed down, mounted the stairs, slipped on the snowy doorstep, and fell in against the door. It opened with a thud and I landed in a heap at the feet of the man to whom I was now permanently tied.

I would have given myself over to tears, but my husband made no move to comfort me, so I rose and took off my cloak, found a peg by the door, and hung the wet, shapeless mass to dry. I looked around in the dim light of a single candle, afraid of what I would find.

The downstairs was one room, not large, but adequate for a small family, and almost devoid of furnishings, the center occupied by a rough plank table, crudely made and none too steady, a far cry from the kind of furnishings I was used to. A stone fireplace took up one whole end wall, with two low three-legged stools pulled up before it. Ignoring my effort to gain his attention—nay, his sympathy—Mr. MacPhail took a seat on one of the stools and pulled it closer to the fire.

In the corner, left of the fireplace, was a steep, curved stairway that served as entrance to the second floor. Despairing to find out what my bedchamber might be like, I gave the first step a stomp to determine its sturdiness, then climbed. Without a light I bumped my way up into the darkness, feeling along with a hand on the rough stone outer wall.

I peered into the blackness and, lifting my damp and sodden skirt, climbed the steep stairs into the dark room. What kind of man was he, anyway? One who would rather sit by the fire than help a lady, to be sure. I groped my way through the dark to a rope bedstead standing alone against one wall, but without light I was lost—unable to find a tick or a pillow. There was a second room, smaller and colder than the first, but entirely too dark to explore, so I turned back to the dim light offered up from below.

"Mr. MacPhail!" I shouted.

"Yes, ma'am."

"Kindly bring up some light and my trunks," I ordered.

"I'll do that on the morrow, ma'am. It's too dark and too cold to prepare a bed tonight."

"Well, where do you expect me to sleep?" I demanded.

"Thought I'd make a pallet here in front of the fire."

"On the floor? Surely you don't expect *me* to sleep on the floor." I almost added "in my condition," but thought better of it.

"Yes, ma'am, I do."

I raised my booted foot and stomped hard on the floor. No response from downstairs. I stomped again. Harder.

My eyes were used to the dark by now, and I could make out the bed, the sole furnishing in the outer room, offering no comfort, for even the ropes were unstrung. There was no option. Sleep here and freeze to death or let my keeper win this battle. With a swish of my damp skirts, I climbed down the stairs in a temper, determined to make him pay.

Chapter 13

Early December 1823
Adam

I knew I'd have my hands full through the winter, setting the furnace to rights and getting everything ready to start in blast in the spring, so the sooner I could get started, the better, and now, with a pregnant and unwilling wife, who knew what trouble might await?

The situation with Elinor was awkward, to say the least, so my inclination was the less attention paid to that side of things, the better. I guessed I wasn't the first man to come to the rescue of a maid in similar straits, but that didn't make it any easier. I was married now, to a stranger—a riddle you might say—and I was off to prove myself in more ways than one. God help me.

We traveled as far as possible each day on the road, and though my companion rode along all wrapped in sullen anger, my prospects were such that it was hard not to be light-hearted, and before long, I was whistling softly as we rode. The pocket of my waistcoat bulged with the packets of money and legal papers. I looked forward to telling Crissman he was off the hook, free to go, unencumbered. The wedding gift from Bratton was generous enough to keep us for a couple of years if the furnace didn't prove profitable from the start, as I knew it wouldn't. There'd be wages to pay, production costs, and transportation costs.

Indeed, I might have left Elinor with her parents for the winter and brought her to Mt. Etna in the spring, when the sun was bright and the flowers bloomed. My single-minded focus on business blinded me to her side of things. At any rate, her reaction to our first sight of her new home in the gloom of an evening snowstorm was disastrous. Unable to think what else to do, I chose to ignore her tantrum and go about the business of warming the house and unloading the goods. We were off to a worse start than I thought possible, and, with no experience whatever in dealing with women, I seemed to make things worse at every turn.

Ellie

When I awoke that first morning, the house was cold and empty. The fire had all but gone out and my bridegroom, after spending the night curled up in a piece of wool no more respectable than a horse blanket, was nowhere to be seen. I rose from the nest of feather ticks I'd foraged from my trunks and wandered around the barren kitchen in the early morning light, hapless and hungry.

I found a wooden keg of flour, some salt and a little corn meal, but only the barest of utensils, and when I turned to put wood on the fire, I found the wood box empty.

Just then the door opened and Mr. MacPhail entered carrying a dead rabbit, which he deposited on the plank table with a thud.

"What do you expect me to do with that?" I asked.

"Skin it, cut it up, and make a stew," he replied as though I should have had the good sense to know what to do with a dead rabbit.

"Skin it? Not I, Mr. MacPhail. Cook it, maybe. But skin it? No, sir! Besides, how am I supposed to know anything about cooking? We always had help." I moved to the side of the table to face him. "What is this anyway? A frontier hovel? How do you expect me to live here? Cooking wild game and living in a house so small I can't turn around and without so much as a ladle to my name."

He stood by the table, his fingers resting on the rough wood, studying me in silence. When he spoke, his words came slow, even, measured.

"I don't expect anything of you that I don't expect of myself. This is what we have, Elinor. All there is." He picked up the limp carcass, holding it in his left hand. "We can rage against it or we can make the best of it. I can't make you like it, but I hope someday you will. I can't make you anything you don't want to be, but I hope someday you will at least want to be my wife."

His grave face, his intense blue eyes made me shrink from his gaze, almost, but not quite ashamed of my outburst.

"Until then I won't coddle you, spoil you, or cater to your every whim. We've a hard road, and it will take the will of both of us to make this work. There's a bright future here, but it'll take dedication and years of toil. I'm willing. Are you?"

I sat down on a stool near the fire, and buried my head in my lap. "I don't know. I don't know. This is so unfair. If I'd known you were bringing me to this, I would have..."

Hearing the door close, I looked around and found both man and rabbit gone.

I rose and wandered about the room, thinking on his words. Since I'd never heard so many of them come out of his mouth before, I'd not thought him capable of so much verbiage. But the words caught me, gave me pause, for there was no malice in them, no blame, just a matter of fact assessment of the way things were. I could rage against my fate all I wanted. Adam MacPhail would not be moved.

I looked around the barren room, thinking of Robert Clifton—richer, more handsome, better educated, more polished than the man I was bound to. Bitterness flooded over me, and anger again at my father for putting me in this predicament. Surely, if he'd known the conditions I'd be subject to he'd not have bargained this for me. Surely, he would have looked around for a better match. Surely.

In five minutes Mr. MacPhail was back with the bare, beheaded rabbit carcass, which he slapped onto the table and quartered with a practiced swing of an ax. Then he picked up an oaken bucket from beside the door and disappeared again. I watched from the window as he waded through the snow to the spring, about fifty paces from the house. He soon returned with the water, poured half of it into the kettle over the fire, and deposited the quartered rabbit, then turned toward the door again.

"Wood," he said, and, carrying the same ax he'd used to butcher the rabbit, went out the door once more into the cold, snowy landscape.

All the while I looked on in silence, sure I wouldn't offer help but unsure how to stay out of the way. Once the wood box was replenished, I moved to stir the stew with a long-handled wooden spoon, one of the few utensils to be found. In a short time my bridegroom re-entered the house with an armload of vegetables—a turnip, three carrots, two potatoes, and a small cabbage—deposited them on the table and proceeded to cut them up with his knife.

"I can do that," I offered in a small voice. It was the first I'd spoken since his early utterance.

Without a word, he lay down the knife and stepped aside. I took it up, a weapon more suited to skinning a bear than cutting up vegetables, and made an awkward effort to maneuver them into manageable chunks.

"Where did you get these?"

"Bartered them from the miller's wife."

"Miller's wife?"

"Yes."

"There's a miller, and he has a wife?"

"Yes. You're not as far from civilization as you think."

Once the stew was started, Adam showed me how to mix bread and set it to rise with something he called 'starter'—also garnered from the miller's wife. He instructed me on keeping the fire up and how to use an alcove to the side of the fireplace as an oven. Then, without any breakfast, he announced that he had business at Water Street and turned for the door. I resisted the urge to ask to accompany him to this singular symbol of civilization, too proud to ask for anything, given our condition of enmity.

"Is there a store at Water Street?" I asked, conscious of the need to fill the larder and add to the sad array of utensils.

"Of sorts. But my business will take me to Huntingdon, probably tomorrow. Make a list of your needs and I'll see what can be done."

"Make a list? With what? On what? Shall I scratch it on a rock?"

Looking decidedly nettled, he stalked out the door, slamming it with a thud that caused snow to drop heavily off the roof.

Chapter 14

December 1823
Adam

The next day, after tending to the supply of water, food and wood, I took Elinor's little mare, Dancer, and rode off to Water Street to deal with George Crissman. After putting the horse up in comfort, I entered the inn, where I expected to find my client. I was not disappointed. The one-time ironmaster sat in his customary place by the window, grog in hand, looking bleary-eyed and not at all coherent. When I approached, he leaned back and looked up as though looking upon a stranger—one who might be prevailed upon to buy a round. He smiled an unsteady smile, wiped his mouth with the back of his hand, and said, "What ho, now? What have we here? A traveler! From the east, I presume. A little grog, now? Maybe a game of chess? A little wager, perhaps?"

I sat down at his table, looking hard at him as the foggy reaches of his brain produced a memory. "Mr. Crissman, surely you remember me?"

The man scowled, wrinkled his brow with the effort.

"Just a few weeks ago. We went up to Etna Furnace together."

He waved a dismissive hand. "I told you I was done. That's all over now. No future in the iron business. Don't want to talk about it any further." Crissman was making his slow way back to lucidity.

"I've news, sir. Let's adjourn to your home, where we can speak in private."

"My home? Why, we can just as well talk here. There isn't anything to talk about anyway."

I rose and faced him squarely. "Your home, sir. This is no place to conduct the kind of business I'm about."

Crissman rose from his chair slow and deliberate, took his time settling up with the innkeeper, and stepped out into the dooryard in no hurry to comply with my strange request.

Not given much to patience, especially in business, I resisted the urge to grab the old man by the coat collar, turn him around, and kick him in the pants. We arrived at the stable, and while I readied my horse Crissman haggled with the livery boy, something about how much he already owed for board. The old man finally relented and dropped a few pence into the boy's palm and waited for the horse to be brought around. Then we rode out of the dooryard and turned toward Alexandria.

Crissman's house sat in the middle of an open field, once an elegant lawn with a tree-lined drive. The house looked forlorn and dilapidated, the evidence of its former glory now only peeling paint, rotting roof, shutters askew. We rode up and left the horses at the railing, entering through what had once been a well-crafted front door. Inside, the house was cold. No fire anywhere. Crissman evicted a cat asleep on a divan in the parlor, then pulled open the heavy, velvet drapes of a bygone era. "Now, what is it that can't be discussed anywhere but here?" he demanded.

I pulled the packet of papers out of my pocket. "Here, sir, we have the wherewithal to pay off all of the Etna Furnace debts and make you a free man again. We can settle up with your creditors and the county in short order. Once the debts are paid, the property will be owned by the Mt. Etna Iron Company, a group of investors from Berks County. You will be debt free, free to call off the sheriff's sale and go on with your life, wherever that leads you."

Crissman looked at me through still-bleary eyes, comprehension slowly dawning. "You mean I won't owe anything to anyone? None to nobody?"

I couldn't suppress a smile. "None to nobody. You won't own the furnace or any of its environs anymore, but the creditors will all have been paid." I patted my breast pocket. "I've the funds with me right now."

Crissman held onto the edge of a table for balance. Head down, he thought it over for only a few seconds. "Where do I sign? How do I get the money?"

"We'll go to Huntingdon and hire a lawyer to write up the agreement. You don't get the money. You'll provide the records of indebtedness and I'll dispense the funds directly to your creditors. Once you've signed the agreement and provided the list of debts, you'll be free to go."

Crissman grabbed me by the sleeves and shook me hard. "God, man! How I've prayed for this. To be free of that damned furnace and all its problems. Take it and be damned. You'll see how it is. You can't make any money there. You'll see."

Stepping back from his grasp, I folded the papers and returned them to my inside pocket. "It's too late to take care of everything today, so I'll be here tomorrow morning at ten. We can ride to Huntingdon and finish it with dispatch." I turned and let myself out the front door and crossed the dilapidated porch to pretty little Dancer. I mounted and rode back to Mt. Etna along the Juniata, aware of the river rolling ever eastward toward the mighty Susquehanna but thinking only of furnace and forge and my unhappy bride.

My thoughts focused mainly on the plans and details of getting the furnace ready for blast. When I did think of my wife, it was with curiosity, a full measure of bewilderment—and a little hope.

The next morning at about eleven o'clock, Crissman and I rode up to the Huntingdon offices of Jonas Whittaker, Esq., Attorney-at-Law, on Penn Street, not far from the courthouse, and by mid afternoon everything had been accomplished, the papers signed and the documents filed. That was that. Now I was more than anxious to take myself on up the track to Mt. Etna where my future lay. I dismissed George Crissman's invitation to stop for a draught and, with a wave of my hand, mounted my horse and rode out of town, quietly relishing my new status as ironmaster.

When I arrived at Mt. Etna I stopped by the mill for a few minutes to look up Jefferson Baker, the miller whose kindness had lightened my burden a month before.

"Halloo!" Baker greeted me. "You're back! What'd you do, get old Crissman drunk and get him to sign it over to you, debts and all?"

"No. The debts are paid. The furnace is now owned by a group of investors from Berks County. I'm to run it for them."

"Got your work cut out for you, then. I wouldn't want the job, but you're an iron man. Maybe you can get it going again."

"It's what I intend. I'm here to stay."

"You're going to need work crews to start right away cutting wood for charcoal. Takes a while to do that job."

I nodded. "It's number one on my list. Know any colliers?"

Baker tilted his head toward the little cluster of workers' log houses about a quarter mile down the track. "One or two down there, but you'll have a time getting the squatters out."

"I haven't even been down there yet, but if there's any able bodied workers, I'll be glad to hire them.'

Jeff Baker raised an eyebrow and sighed. "Good luck. They ain't used to working for anybody since Crissman went under, and they've turned damned independent."

"We'll see," I replied. "We'll see."

"Looks as though you've brought yourself a wife along. My woman noted that yesterday. Doesn't miss much. She going to be happy living out here so far from everything? Women can be hard to get along with if things don't suit them."

Distracted by thoughts of hiring workers, I dismissed his doubts. "She'll have to be. As you say, I've got my work cut out."

Baker shook his head. "Wouldn't want to be giving advice, but it's been my experience that keeping a woman happy takes some attention. Don't get so caught up in the work that you forget about her."

I let that advice slip by without a reply. "Evening, Baker. I'll see you tomorrow."

Chapter 15

December 1823
Ellie

He was gone for the rest of that day, coming back at night and leaving the next morning again, intent on his 'business'. Left alone to brood on my condition and bleak situation, I exercised my perceived right to feel sorry for myself. But as I unpacked my trunks and went about trying to make the hovel resemble a home the knowledge that my fate was in my own hands, not just his, slowly dawned. If life was to be anything but unbearable, I would have to adjust. But not just yet. I would still indulge my need to nurse my hurt pride for a while, at least.

Once his business in Huntingdon was concluded, Mr. MacPhail spent long hours out in the snowy countryside, walking in long strides, inspecting the furnace, which sat across the race not far from the house, and sizing up the timber that covered the surrounding hills. It wasn't until a few days later that he took me for a walk to show me the furnace and its workings, and, around the bend just beyond the furnace, where Roaring Run emptied into the branch, the mill itself, standing tall against the sky with the miller's house across the track. We'd passed it the first evening but, being in a bit of a state, I hadn't noticed.

Now I found it impossible to contain my delight. "Oh, thank God we aren't the only human beings in this God-forsaken place!"

"Far from it. There'll be people aplenty around here once we get this furnace up and running."

"When can I meet this miller and his wife?"

"Tomorrow. At church."

Delighted, I hurried home to root through my trunks for a dress to wear to church. I found one, a dark green frock of fine wool with puffed upper sleeves and fitted arms, trimmed down the back and hem of the skirt with beaver fur. I had a lovely green bonnet, also trimmed in beaver, to go with it, and my Sunday cape, black wool, lined in red velvet. All the latest fashion. Papa had sent me to Reading City last summer to be fitted with a winter wardrobe in anticipation of my impending marriage. I was more than ready to present myself to whatever local society assembled at church.

Sunday dawned bright and sunny, melting the snow and leaving a light smattering of mud in the path. The church, a pitiful log structure without any pretense of sanctity, stood along the riverbank a half mile or more from our house. The walk there was pleasant on the arm of my husband, still dressed as usual in what were now apparently the only clothes he owned. On the way we passed through the little village of Mt. Etna, with its crude, one-and-a-half story log cabins and two or three larger ones signifying skilled status. This, then, was to be the source of workers for my husband's venture. There was no one about, the folk having already departed for church, but thin curls of smoke from some of the chimneys gave notice of habitation if not prosperity.

I wondered how we should behave in public. Like a plain old married couple? Well, yes. But only as necessary to keep curiosity at bay. If my husband was to be the ironmaster, his station would be set, as would mine. That much I knew. But backwoods etiquette was not in the realm of my experience, so I resolved to watch and learn.

We arrived with a few minutes to spare before the circuit-riding preacher from Huntingdon rode up and led the flock into the house of worship. As I smiled and nodded to those standing around, it became painfully clear that I was overdressed. Not one other woman wore anything but the homeliest of frocks, made of homespun cloth and fashioned after the simplest style and covered by crude, home-knit shawls that they held close against the cold. I'd chosen my wardrobe out of ignorance, but that was not apparent to my new acquaintances. Though they smiled and nodded back at me, they moved away as soon as the opportunity presented itself. I'd offended on my first outing.

The church, like everything else I'd encountered at Etna Furnace, was barren and crude: rough pews, backless log benches, no windows, no pictures to adorn the walls. The Reverend Mr. Burns, sent to us under the auspices of the Huntingdon Presbytery one Sunday per month, was a dour, humorless man, given to long sermons and short smiles. There was, however, one small comfort in the building: a stove. Round, iron, and radiating the luxury of warmth.

"Where did that come from?" I asked my husband.

He shrugged. "Probably from one of my predecessors. Maybe his wife refused to come to church unless it was warm."

"Bless her."

The stove did render the rude building almost cozy, making me wish it were in our house instead of the stone fireplace. We sat in the front pew to the right of the aisle, a place reserved for the ironmaster, an honor I found almost humorous in its pretense. Following my husband's lead I took my place. No back on our pew, either.

The Reverend Mr. Burns rose to speak, clearing his throat and fidgeting with his written sermon. He read to us, every word, in a low drone. I followed closely for the first forty minutes or so, but the warmth soon made me drowsy, and I so wished for a back on our bench so I could relax and...I caught myself just as I began to doze off.

I looked at Adam for a reaction, but he sat tall, looking straight ahead as though intent on the sermon. I took my cue from him, imitating his pose until I felt myself nodding again. Adam pinched my arm, making me start, but I regained my poise for the rest of the sermon, which lasted for two more hours. I counted myself grateful that we had the services of the Reverend Burns on only one Sunday a month.

Upon dismissal the company stood about, apparently waiting to make the acquaintance of the new ironmaster and his wife. Though usually taciturn, Adam managed to muddle through the introductions, but I felt the stares of the women of the company even as he introduced me.

These were common folk from common stock. They knew nothing of style or fashion, indeed, very little even of comfort. My attire set them aback, made them self-conscious, even maybe a bit jealous.

A forge man's wife, a heavy-set woman with three double chins, looked me up and down. "We'd no idea we were getting so fine a lady here at Etna Furnace." Her demeanor signaled contempt.

"No idea at all!" another chimed in. "If I'd a knowed, I'd a wore *my* velvet gown."

"Or your silks, but this ain't the weather for silks," said another.

"Too much mud!" said a third. "Gonna be a hard life for her here."

I stood helpless as all possibility for friendship vanished before my eyes. I'd given these women reason to despise me, intentional or not. So here I stood, looking fine and friendless. Then, from the back of the group a tall, blonde woman a little older than I stepped forward.

"Oh, stop it, you old biddies," she said. "Give the girl a chance. She'll measure up. You'll see." She took my hand and turned to face them. "There's not one of you wouldn't wear just as fine a dress if you had it."

The group dissolved at that, nodding and talking among themselves, but showing no malice toward my savior. Indeed they seemed mollified by her jocular manner.

"I'm Lindy," she said, offering her hand. Lindy Baker. Short for Melinda. My Jeff's the miller, so we'll be close neighbors. I'd meant to pay you a visit before this, but I've a little one sick. Didn't want to pass it on. Oh, and don't mind them." She indicated my critics who had now formed a semi-circle on the other side of the dooryard. "They'll warm up once they get to know you."

I gave her a weak smile and felt her squeeze my hand in return. At least here was one ally.

Chapter 16

Winter 1823
Ellie

December turned cold and colder. Mr. MacPhail was gone most of the time, out riding the neighborhood, rounding up a team of workers to rebuild the casting house and something called a tuyere room. I found him single-minded, purposeful, and unwavering in his drive to create an iron works out of this backwoods disaster. Otherwise he was kind but not effusive, always polite but restrained, leading me to wonder if there was even a shred of emotion in him.

As for me, my condition was becoming impossible to hide, and since no one knew about the suddenness of our marriage, they assumed the child was Adam's and took it as a given that ours was a happy relationship with a long history.

Left alone most of the time, I set about making the dismal abode as livable as I could with what meager tools, supplies, and furnishings I had. In the first week I asked my husband to hire a carpenter to plane and smooth the table top, build us a bench for one side of the table and four chairs—proper chairs with backs on them—for the ends and other side. Then a corner cupboard for storing dishes—I'd brought a set of china from my mother's ample supply—and a divided bin for flour and corn meal.

I took great care in unpacking my books, holding each one in my hands, smelling the leather, caressing the pages. The carpenter built sturdy bookshelves along one wall of the bedroom, under the eaves, where I could see them and take joy from the adventure and enlightenment they promised. As soon as he was finished, I placed each book carefully on its shelf, planning the order in which I'd read them. I looked forward to reading each one, some for the second time, and adding to the collection as the opportunity arose. Adam took little notice of them other than to ask if I had, indeed, read all of them. He didn't show any interest in reading himself; indeed, he showed no interest in anything except his damnable furnace.

I'd no experience cooking over an open fireplace. Indeed I'd very little experience cooking at all, as my mother always had kitchen help and took pride in her own cooking, so I was considered a nuisance in the kitchen. As such, I'd never bothered to learn. Necessity set new parameters for me, and I learned by doing. Within a few weeks I could place a decently respectable meal on the table, and I found my courage in dealing with wild game.

Almost every day one or another of the neighbor boys appeared at the door with a dead squirrel or duck—sometimes even a turkey—to offer. Adam bartered for garden goods and the root cellar was soon well stocked, as long as one didn't tire of carrots, potatoes, turnips, beets, cabbage, or onions.

As for the bedroom, once my five trunks had been carried up and set along the wall opposite the bookshelves, I swept the floor, polished the windows, prevailed upon Adam to string up the rope bedstead, and arranged my feather ticks upon it. I unpacked three colorful braided rugs my mother had insisted I bring, feeling more at home because of their familiar presence.

My husband said little in those early days, for we spent little waking time together because he left most days at first light and didn't return until dusk. Always respectful of my condition, he asked how I felt, if I needed anything, or if he could help me with the chores. I let him carry water from the spring and keep the wood box full but did most of the rest for myself.

His attentiveness might have been looked upon as preliminary to intimacy, but my demeanor gave him notice that advances in that direction were not welcome. He continued to sleep downstairs by the fire, and while he rarely approached me with any hint of affection, I made a practice of simply turning away, thus avoiding any further inconvenience. I knew I couldn't hold him off forever, but I was pretty sure my condition would warrant Mr. MacPhail's celibacy for at least the foreseeable future.

Indeed, the man was so preoccupied with getting the furnace up and running that he directed almost no attention toward me at all. Not that I cared. Christmas came and went with no exchange of gifts or affection and, given the state of the weather, no interaction with our neighbors, who must have pictured us contentedly tucked up, whiling the winter away. I was awash in homesickness, remembering my parents' bountiful and generous Christmas parties to which all the best of Berks County society were invited, but I made a valiant effort not to show my anguish in front of Adam. He'd had enough of my peevishness.

We two simply shared the cabin and its resources as two strangers thrown together by fate, slowly, warily watching one another for any sign of commonality. There were few. He was a poor but well-trained iron maker, ambitious but unassuming, completely unschooled in the social graces, and without the slightest polish or interest in acquiring any, and I was a very young, very spoiled, soiled dove, with no options but to make my adjustments, whatever they turned out to be.

I continued to rage against my fate those first months, left to my own adjustments by my husband, until finally I decided to give up my anger and try to make the best of it. I didn't see any alternative, and though I felt used, cheated, and cast aside, I knew it mattered not a whit to anyone but me.

While I certainly didn't find Mr. MacPhail attractive in any way, he seemed, nonetheless, kind, gentle and even-tempered, not at all volatile like Papa. He was at all times quiet-spoken and hard to read. He showed no passion for anything but making iron, especially if he could make it cheaper, faster, better. If, indeed, he was insulted or angered by my refusal to acknowledge anything like wifely responsibility, he showed it not at all.

I busied myself around the cabin, making curtains, piecing a quilt from some of the clothes I realized too late should have been left in

Berks County, preparing clothes and blankets for the baby, which quickened more with each passing day. I read in the afternoons by the light from the only window in the bedroom. Reading soothed me, calmed my agitated soul, transported me to other times and places. Looking back, I would say it saved my sanity if not my life.

In the absence of other distractions, I turned my attention to this child, pinned my hopes upon it, made up names and personalities for it. If a girl, she would be Alice Jo for my best friend and cousin at home. If a boy, he would be Robert for his absent father. Robert Adam, perhaps, for both of his fathers, but Robert for certain.

As January passed into February, the prospect of giving birth alone here in the wilderness loomed fearful, so I was more than relieved when, late in the month, there came a knock at the door. I rushed to open it, delighted at the prospect of company, and found Lindy Baker there holding a heaping basket of food and other goodies on her arm.

"Hello, Missus. Thought I'd be neighborly and bring some treats. Is your husband about?" she asked as she stepped inside.

"No. No, he's off overseeing the ore mining. Won't be back until dark." I welcomed her in and closed the door.

"Brought you some apple butter," she said, placing a small crock on the table. "You have any apples put by?"

"Yes. Adam bartered some from one of the colliers. They're in the fruit cellar."

"You know how to make sauce? And butter?"

Embarrassed by my inadequacy as a cook, I shook my head, opened the crock, and sniffed the contents as Lindy unloaded her basket on the table. A mince pie, four apple fritters and another crock—of stewed peaches. I marveled at such abundance here in the wilderness.

"Oh, thank you, Lindy! I'd no idea one could eat so well out here."

"Life here ain't so bad. You'll come 'round. Anyway, there's plenty to be had. You just have to know what to do with it. Come spring you'll put in a garden, and next fall you'll have all you can store put by. I know where there's a good apple tree, and we can pick berries all summer to make jam."

She looked around with a critical eye. "Little bit spare, ain't it?"

I sighed. "Yes, I'm afraid I've come here unprepared. My vision of the place was skewed by little experience outside of Berks County."

Lindy's smile lightened my heart. "You'll come 'round," she repeated.

Her gaze eventually fell on my protruding stomach. "This your first, I guess. How soon, do you think?"

Nodding, I ran my open hands over my swollen front. "Maybe another month or so. I'm not exactly sure."

"Looks more like sooner than later to me. Have you a cradle ready?"

"Not yet. Maybe a trunk at first."

"Clothes?"

"Some. I've been sewing." I lifted a stack of nightgowns from a shelf by the fireplace. One thing my former life had prepared me for—sewing. I could sew as fine a seam as any, so my child wouldn't want for clothes.

Lindy examined them with a smile. "Better have more than that unless you want to wash them every day. Lots of linen, too. I hope."

I showed her a stack of neatly folded cloths, ready for use.

"Guess that'll have to do," she said, reaching into her basket and bringing out a beautiful, soft, blue woolen shawl. "Here you go. Cover up for Mama and babe." She draped it over my shoulder and I rubbed the soft wool against my cheek.

"Did you make this yourself?" I asked.

"Yes. I like to knit by the fire before I go to bed. After the young'uns are asleep and my man gets to snoring. Thought you could use a late Christmas gift."

Touched by her kindness, I looked away.

"Now, don't get all dewy-eyed on me," she said. "Wouldn't want anyone to think I was soft-hearted. Out here, a soft heart can leave you alone, hungry, and full of regret."

My loneliness and ragged emotions caught up with me then, and I turned to this one and only friend with gratitude tinged with sadness.

"Now, now. It doesn't mean that much. Just a shawl is all."

"It isn't that. It's just that ... I'm so unhappy here. I don't think I'll ever get used to this place." My chin quivered and I shook my head in despair. "I'm afraid to have my baby here. I want to go home!"

Lindy's arms fell around me, pulled me close, rocked me back and forth. "I thought as much. This is a tad different from what you're used to. Men don't see how that matters, but women do. You'll be all right, sweetie. I'll take care of you when your time comes. Once the baby's here, you'll be so busy you won't have time to be lonely."

"You'll take care of me? You know how?"

Lindy laughed aloud. "Sure do. I've delivered more than twenty so far and only lost one. Haven't lost a mother yet. You'll be fine."

I let myself lean against Lindy's shoulder, comforted by her presence and the thought that here was someone to care for me.

"Besides, your man'll help. Only reason men aren't more useful is they don't know what to do. We'll train him."

From that day on, Lindy Baker was my friend, my ally, my advocate, my confidant. I'd never have made it this far in life without her. She was a child of the back woods, born on a farm near Alexandria, married at sixteen. Now, at twenty-eight, she was the mother of five and the solid pillar around which her family revolved. Tall, faded blonde, brusque in her manner but kind in her heart, she was just the friend I needed to help me through those early years. For Lindy, life was tough, but there was no use fretting about it. Just get on with it, and don't go expecting too much. You'll just buy yourself disappointment.

Chapter 17

Early 1824
Ellie

February came along cold and dreary. Every morning I thought my time would come that day, and every night I went to sleep with the burden still inside me. My complete inexperience with birthing had me sending Adam for Lindy at every little pain. In she'd come, hands full of clean rags, a basin and herbs tucked under her arm. She'd take one look at me and turn on her heel, hollering, "Not yet!" over her shoulder.

The month dragged on and my condition weighed me down in more ways than one. I wanted it to be over. Up to then I hadn't given much thought to the baby I was carrying—as a person, I mean. For me it was a problem, a nuisance, the cause of my misery. But as my time grew near I began to think of it as a child, an extension of myself, an ally in a strange world.

February gave way to March, and the skies, cleared by blustery winds, looked brighter and more hopeful. Anxious for the birth, I felt inside a glimmer of joy for the sunny weather, cold though it still was. I must have counted wrong, for this baby was taking its time about making its appearance and weighing me down in the process.

"Must be a boy," Lindy counseled. "The late ones always are."

I secretly hoped it would be a girl—a child like me—someone I could relate to, understand—company for me in this wilderness.

On the seventh day of March, I awoke to a blue sky and bright sunshine. My back ached, but embarrassed by three false alarms, I got up, dressed, ate breakfast, and sent Adam out with assurances that today would be just another day of waiting. He showed concern for me, even though the nagging thought in the back of both our minds was that the child wasn't his. We went about our public lives as though all was well and normal. Inside the little stone house we continued our dance, unfamiliar, clumsy, guarded—watching each other from a distance, observing and drawing conclusions about this mate that fate had thrust upon each of us, trying to discern its nature.

By noon my pains and discomfort assured me this *would* be the day. I thought I could get to Lindy's house without faltering, but once I set my feet on the track to the mill I knew I needed help. I started out walking as swiftly as I could, holding my distended abdomen with both hands. The pains were regular and increasing in intensity, but still about fifteen minutes apart. I should be able to reach Lindy's between pains, but the way seemed longer than I remembered, and my cloak seemed heavier. I got about halfway there and lowered myself down on a stump to rest. A sudden spasm gripped me with an intensity I'd not felt up to then, bending me over in pain. I must have cried out, for even though the mill was barely in sight, I heard running footsteps and felt someone lift me from the stump.

"There, girl. You shouldn't be out and about in your condition." It was Jeff Baker, Lindy's husband. He turned to their son, Joel, who'd accompanied him on the run. "Go get Ma. Hurry!"

I'm told they carried me back to our cabin, where Lindy set out her midwife's kit, watched, and waited. Jeff sent Joel out to find Adam, but before long he was back, alone, panting from the run. The pains were too close and too intense for me to be aware of the comings and goings, and Lindy kept close, calm track of my progress. Giving birth, like everything else in my young life, was something with which I'd no experience, and had it not been for Lindy's calm assurances, I'm sure I would have screamed and thrashed in pain and desperation. As it was, Lindy's demeanor had the desired effect of soothing and lulling me into believing that, as she said, "If this were as dangerous as all that, there wouldn't be so many people in the world."

Lindy kept encouraging me, telling me it wouldn't be long now, giving progress reports. "It's crowning," she whispered. "Just a few more good pushes, and you'll be done." Her confidence in the birthing process buoyed me up for the final push. Suddenly it was over. The baby came sliding into her outstretched hands, all bloody and slimy and squalling.

"It's a boy." Lindy held the child up for me to see while she counted fingers and toes and looked him over for any defect. "He's perfect," she pronounced.

That's the last thing I remember until I awoke with a tiny wrapped package in the crook of my arm, mouth wide open like a baby bird mewling for nourishment. Lindy stood by smiling down at me. I lay on a pallet before the fire while Jeff and Joel reconstructed my bed nearby.

"You can't sleep on the floor, and those steps are too steep and narrow to navigate with a babe in your arms," Lindy told me.

She helped me put the child to my breast and instructed me on the best way to hold him and when to switch breasts. I obeyed without question, relieved to be free of my burden, sore though I was. The child was robust, full of energy, and came, as I soon learned, equipped with a mind of his own and a powerful set of lungs.

"You did fine for the first time. One of the quickest births I ever attended. Barely got you back here when he made his appearance. It's a good sign for the next ones if the first comes easy."

Next ones. I was in no way ready to contemplate any 'next ones'.

Chapter 18

Winter 1824
Adam

Within a few days it seemed Elinor had made herself comfortable in the house, swept it out, wiped the windows, set me to cleaning out the chimney. Pleased by her willingness to make it a home, I tried to respect her wishes and do what I could to make the little house comfortable for her. Her trunks yielded feather ticks, bed linen, cloth for curtains, and some braided rugs, all of which, I noted, made the house more colorful and homelike. Noted—but did not comment upon. Many such thoughts passed through my mind but, given to reticence as I was, few of them even reached the ears of another. Still, Elinor's efforts at making a home pleased me, even her curious interest in reading and her insistence on bringing all those books along from Berks County. She learned to cook a passable meal in short order, so in these ways my needs were met.

Her condition gave her leave to deny me my rights as a husband, but I gave her time to adjust to the changes in her life and made no demands. The child, she said, was due in February. With so much work to do at the furnace, I didn't give much thought to her needs as long as she didn't burden me. We lived like a brother and sister, sharing a roof but not a bed. Still, the days flew by with getting the raw materials lined up for what I hoped would be an April blow-in. The child, I was sure, would come in due time.

Many, if not most, of the former employees of Etna Furnace had moved on, forced by the need to support their families. One morning, soon after our arrival, I ventured out in search of whatever workers, skilled or unskilled, were still available. The five cabins of the village looked uninhabited, but closer inspection revealed pale wisps of smoke rising against the barren trees and here and there a scrawny child peering out a window. The only other structures, the collier's and head forge man's houses, two-storied and sturdily built, showed more promising signs of habitation: a pile of wood stacked against the wall beside the door and a well-worn path toward the necessary out back. As I approached and knocked on the door of the first, I heard a muffled growl, then clumping footsteps approaching the door, which was opened by a short, bandy-legged, broad-shouldered curmudgeon holding a ferocious-looking dog by a rope collar and peering at me through narrowed eyes. "What's yer business?"

"I need a collier. You able?"

"Able as ever." The man let go of the dog's rope, releasing a tail-wagging, slavering mongrel almost as big as he was. I stepped back, but not before receiving the face-licking of my life. The dog, Nero, was notorious at Etna Furnace for his prowess as a watchdog and his willingness to forgive and embrace a stranger upon closer inspection.

His master's smile revealed a row of teeth worn down with clenching a pipe, and brown eyes set deep in a weathered face. Hitching himself up to his full five-foot height, he set his shoulders back and asked, "What're yer needs?"

"Enough cords to make charcoal all next summer and keep yonder furnace in blast indefinitely."

The smile spread wider, squeezing the brown eyes almost shut. "Work, is it? Real work? Who's gonna put her in blast?" He stepped back to scrutinize me. "You? Know anything about iron?"

"A little. I need somebody to reline the furnace, rebuild the bellows. Set her to rights. Anybody around here can do that?"

Now the man was out on the broad porch in his dingy long underwear shirt and rugged, baggy pants, suspenders wide over his shoulders. He reached out a work-toughened hand. "Mathias Corbin.

Collier. Know my business. Get a crew together in a day or two. Where're we cutting?"

I motioned to the ridge above us, opposite the furnace. "Start up there and work your way back. The less hauling the better for now."

Mathias Corbin's eyes scanned the surrounding woods. "You the new owner? I heard talk they was a new owner."

"Not me. A company from Berks County. Bought the whole operation—furnace, quarry, ore bank, woods. I'm the ironmaster. Learned my trade in Berks. We should be able to make it work this time."

Corbin winked. "Aye, if ye can stay out of the ale house, maybe." He looked toward the furnace. "Been a long time idle. Guess you know the troubles with gittin' bars to market."

"Yes, I've heard. We'll see. That canal they're talking about will change things."

"Huh. We can hope. Meantime, I guess we can mine the ore and quarry the limestone to get her in blast. Hope for the best."

"We'll depend on the local markets right away, get bars to market any way we can, and hang on until the canal comes through."

"*If* it comes through. Gov'ment ain't something I like to depend on."

"Yes, well, I hope you're wrong about that. A canal would make all the difference around here."

Mathias Corbin nodded and hooked his thumbs behind his suspenders. "Hoped I weren't a fool to stay after Crissman give up. Knew somebody'd come along. You're a right welcome sight for these tired old eyes."

Having a good, experienced collier fortified me. One problem solved, I turned to the next. "Right now I need skilled furnace people. Someone to re-line her and rebuild the bellows."

"I'd wager you'd go right back where you come from. Them's the ones knows how to rebuild 'em. Berks County or Chester."

I winced. I should have known the skills needed to put the furnace to rights would be scarce locally. My mind raced back to Berks County, the many furnaces up and running by the hands of the select few who knew how to build them, line them, lay the hearths, mend the bellows. "Yes. I know the ones you speak of."

My impatience to get started now led to delay. I'd have to send for skilled labor, and it might take months to get anyone up here. I slapped my thigh with my gloves in exasperation. God! Was it always going to be like this? Progress like the route of an ant? But I couldn't let frustration take hold, couldn't let my lack of experience with some aspects of the operation slow me down. I knew iron making. The rest would come—some with trial and error. Some with common sense advice from others. I would persevere.

Turning back to Mathias, I addressed my next problem. "Come spring we'll need a seasoned crew. Where have all the workers gone?"

"Anywhere they could find work. Over to Royer. Upriver to Cove Forge. Down to Barree. They's some that knows the trade here and there. Put out the word. They'll come."

"Right. Can you get enough men to help you through the winter? There's leftover charcoal stored in the coal bank to last until fall, if I'm lucky. So you need to cut and stack all winter so you're ready to burn come summer."

"No problem, that. Farmers is bored in the winter. Like to get work when they can." The rough old codger rubbed the stubble of his chin.

My eyes wandered to the little line of cabins over Corbin's shoulder. He followed my gaze, waving his arm at the forlorn looking cabins. "These here's not but squatters. You'll have to git 'em outta here b'fore spring. If you don't they'll cut down every tree, kill all the game and blame you for their woes."

I surveyed the barren row of little cabins, four of them, the farthest one a double long duplex. "Who let them in?" I asked.

"Who was to stop 'em?"

"Any able men among them?"

"A couple. Some of 'em's worthless, though. Too lazy to do aught but make whiskey and babies."

I turned away to give a good, long look at the bleak little community. To call it derelict would be charitable. The cabins weren't that old, but just a short time unmaintained and the weather had taken its toll. This wasn't my realm of experience. I'd come to make iron, not quibble with ne'er-do-wells about who had a right to live where.

As I stood talking to Corbin, the doors to a couple of the cabins opened and two or three scruffy looking men wandered out, barely dressed, partly in homespun, partly in deerskin. They stood at a distance, mumbling among themselves, and were soon joined by a couple more and one or two women. Uncomfortable with their scrutiny, I kept up my talk with the collier, mindful of their presence and curious as to their intentions.

I knew I had to deal with these plug-uglies, like it or not, so I stepped off Corbin's tiny porch and strode over, feigning an air of more confidence than I felt. I stood tall and surveyed the congregation of squatters.

"Good day." I spoke loud enough so that the shy ones standing behind doors could hear. "I've come up from Berks to put this furnace back in blast. I'll need wood cutters, miners, and quarry workers aplenty. If you've a mind to work, you can start by helping Mr. Corbin cut wood. There's wages—and these houses for shelter. If you work, you can stay. If you don't work, out with you."

The assembly stood back, wary, watching, looking like they hadn't had a good

meal in some time nor recent acquaintance with soap and water. Dirty, ragged, and used to their condition, they formed a semi-circle, staring wordlessly as though absorbing my words through ear wraps.

"Corbin will keep your day log. If you work you stay. If you lag, you go."

One man stepped forward, bolder than the rest, a round-shouldered slouch wearing deerskin leggings and a homespun shirt that looked like it'd been made for his father. "What's the pay?" he asked, looking around at the company as though expecting to be feted for his boldness. His hair was long, brown, and matted, his beard tobacco-stained. Sinister brown eyes, barely visible above the beard, challenged me to prove my right to authority.

"Fifty cents a day and shelter." The figure was well within the bounds of a fair wage. "Later, when more skilled jobs come up, the pay will be comparable."

The man leaned back and spat a stream of tobacco juice that missed my foot by inches. Then he grinned and turned to the woman—his wife, I assumed—who stood inside and behind the door. "Fifty cents a day'd barely keep me in powder and shot. Nor tobacco." He looked around the group, sly and self-congratulatory, as though he'd bested me and wanted recognition for it.

"Take it or leave it, man. That's the bargain," I said, trying not to let my impatience show. Who was this squatter to challenge me, anyway?

"S'pose I could give it a try," the man countered, raising his chin in a defiant gesture. He moved from the back of the crowd and extended a dirty hand. "Simon Trethaway, at your service, sir." Everything about him spoke of sloth and insolence. I shook his hand, doubting that our relationship would be either long or fruitful.

"Happy to make your acquaintance, Mr. Trethaway. You others decide what your pleasure will be. Stay and work, or move on."

With that, I plopped my hat on my head, put a foot in the stirrup, and mounted my horse, fully hoping that I'd made an impression as a competent and businesslike manager. I turned the mare toward the mill. Looking about the wintery gray landscape, last week's snow having melted I noted the trees, the hills, the rock outcroppings, even the sky, all blended into a monochrome of gray. This time of year a covering of snow would be welcome. Somehow a white world would seem more in balance, more welcoming than the everlasting gray.

Mathias Corbin was quick to gather a crew and start cutting and stacking wood for the long process of producing charcoal for Etna Furnace. That, at least, gave me a sense of accomplishment. We'd have our own charcoal by next fall. Within the next two weeks I'd hired miners and quarrymen to provide ore and limestone, teamsters to haul the raw material to the furnace, and made the rounds of the local farms to assure a steady supply of food for my workers once the furnace was back in blast. Now my attention turned to furnace and forge.

Chapter 19

Early 1824
Adam

In this way the days rolled by: Christmas, a long, cold January, an even colder February. Elinor seemed, if not content with the business of keeping house, at least resolute, freeing me to tend to the endless details required to get the furnace back in blast. It seemed easier to let the days follow one another than to address the intimacies, or the lack thereof, in our lives. I believed in the power of time to take care of just about anything, and did not believe in the power of talk to take care of much. I asked after her health, helped her with anything strenuous, and watched with curiosity as her girth expanded. She'd said February, but here was March already and no child. I wondered every day whether I should stay within calling distance, and I usually did, but Elinor seemed not to want or need my presence. Other matters were pressing, and I gave myself over to them, hoping not to be blamed for it later.

In early March, I rode upriver to Cove Forge, where iron making was in full swing. I stood by and watched, aware of every nuance, every small distinction that made one forge different from another—and every commonality as well. My heart quickened at the sight of men working in unison, skilled and precise, and the sound of the trip-hammers pounding Juniata Iron into bars, the finest in the world, to be transported over the mountains to Pittsburgh and thence to the whole Northwest Territories.

I approached the forge man and introduced myself. The man stopped long enough to point to the gray stone mansion that was the master's house. "He'll be in there," he yelled over the din of pounding iron.

The forge master was Noah David, late of Scotland, a man of few words and meager hospitality. His housemaid admitted me into a wide hall and pointed to a closed door to the right. "Mister's in his office. He'll open the door for you when he's ready."

Sitting on a bench in the center hallway, looking in wonder at the array of oil paintings that graced the walls, I tried to visualize such opulence for my own home some day. Here were portraits of family members and landscapes, some with the familiar look of the local countryside, others with a foreign look of a rugged land I took to be Mr. David's homeland. I waited for ten, fifteen, twenty minutes, conscious that my errand to gain knowledge of the local work force and its level of skill, while important to me, might not be of any urgency to my host.

The door was finally opened by a tall, graying, bewhiskered man in his late forties, dressed in a tailored coat and trousers of the finest wool and cut, carrying himself as one who knows his station. "Mr. MacPhail. Yes. Come in."

I entered, hat in hand, and waited for the invitation to sit, which was not forthcoming.

"I hear you're getting ready to put the Etna works back in blast."

"Yes, sir. We hope to get her blown in by April."

Noah David's expression gave away no hint of approval or disapproval, no emotion at all. "I welcome your operation. I can use all the pig iron you can produce, if you need time to get your own forge going. There's plenty of market for all the producers around here, and if you hadn't taken on the task of revitalizing Etna Furnace, someone else would have. I gave the matter some consideration myself, but I'm busy enough here. No need to buy trouble."

"I'm sure we can find ways to be useful to one another. Share freight operations, for example." I was still standing, waiting for my host's sense of common courtesy to surface.

"Fair enough. That would prove beneficial to both of us. Now, where did you say you learned your trade?"

"Berks County. The Birdsboro Works."

"Yes." He nodded. "Fine operation there. Did you happen to know Ira McClendon?"

I smiled. "Yes, sir, I did. I was apprenticed to him for five of the fifteen years I spent there. Mr. McClendon taught me everything I know."

"Then you should know your business, Mr. MacPhail. You've been taught by the best. Have a seat, man. What can I do for you?" Apparently my credentials had passed muster.

"Is there anyone local I can call upon to reline my furnace? I could send back to Berks, but I'm in a hurry and I'd rather use local skill if it's available."

"Bedford Furnace. Orbisonia. They've got the most experience around here. I hear they've got a man up from Chester County working on their furnace right now. You could probably hire him when he's done there."

We spent the next half hour in deep conversation about the Etna operation, its assets, and the reasons for its failure.

"In the main," Mr. David maintained, "it was the freight. Always the freight. Iron making and forging are complicated businesses. Freight should be the least of our worries, instead of our downfall. It doesn't take that much skill to drive a wagon or lead a pack train. But getting my bars to market has always been the greatest challenge."

"Yes, but don't you think that will all change once the canal is put in?"

Noah David cleared his throat. "I've very little faith in politicians. They're full of promises but short on action. They can start a project one day and give up on it the next. Don't count on them, my boy. Hope, but don't set your store by the prattling fools."

His assessment was right, I knew, but I still believed my salvation he building of that canal—and the sooner the better. The maps showed it passing right by Etna Furnace. It had to happen if Etna was to revive and thrive.

Noah David rose and shook my hand across his wide, walnut desk. "Welcome to Cove Forge and the Juniata Iron industry, young man. Our fortunes are bound together, no matter the outcome. If I can be of help in any way, let me know."

I thanked him and took my leave, stopping to watch the forge operation on my way out. The sound of the trip-hammers, the ringing of hammer on iron, quickened my blood. I couldn't wait to hear those sounds at Mt. Etna. I forded the Juniata River on horseback and turned down the trace toward home, my head spinning with the possibilities. I had to get to Orbisonia right away to catch that furnace man. Tomorrow might even be too late. As I rode through the woods near my furnace, the sound of axes, the smell of fresh-cut wood, and the sight of men cutting, trimming, dragging, and stacking heartened me. I stopped to talk to Mathias Corbin, who was standing along the track with a woodcutter sharpening his axe. "Good day, Mr. MacPhail."

"How's it going, Corbin?"

"Right well, Mr. MacPhail. Plenty of laborers lined up. More coming every day. We'll have maybe fifty cords stacked by the middle of next week."

"Hire them on, Corbin. We can't have too much charcoal at the ready."

"That I will, sir. Long as there's money for wages, I'll keep a full force in the field. Tate says he's mining ore as fast as he can, and the quarrymen started last week. Next thing you know, we'll be ready to make iron."

I nodded and spurred my horse along the road toward home, anxious to make preparations for the ride to Orbisonia. On the way I passed a wagon loaded with limestone from a nearby quarry. Pulled by four oxen, the flat-bedded freighter lurched heavily up the hillside above the furnace to the charging bridge, its presence gladdening my heart. It was happening. Every day I made a little more progress toward the goal of getting the furnace ready to produce iron. I wanted to tell Elinor about it. Share it with her. See her glad to think t maybe this place I'd brought her to wasn't the hell she thought it was after all.

As soon as the house came into view, I could tell something was amiss. Smoke billowed out of the chimney, more than usual, the mud in the dooryard was trampled into mush, and two of the Baker children played in the nearby woods, shouting as they pelted each other with cat-o-nine tails. I put up my horse, curious at all the activity, and entered the house by the front door. Elinor was not alone. Lindy Baker, Jeff and Joel stood around the bed they'd apparently brought down from upstairs. In it, pale and tired, lay Elinor, a baby in her arms.

Chapter 20

March 1824
Adam

I had to admit I'd given little thought to the advent of this child. My mind had shut it out, to be honest. I stood there now, looking at the tiny, red-faced bundle, wondering what I should do, what I should say. Social necessity required that I act overjoyed in front of this company, so I caught myself in the midst of surprise and changed my demeanor, hoping no one noticed. I leaned over and kissed Elinor on the forehead, whispered my joy at becoming a father, and asked after her ordeal. Did I feel her withdraw from my touch? Then I spoke with feigned enthusiasm about how beautiful and robust the babe was and what a relief it was to have help so close by.

"What will you call him?" Lindy Baker asked, proud of her role in bringing him to us.

I looked to Elinor. There'd been no talk of names.

"Robert," she replied. "Robert Adam MacPhail."

So she would brazenly name the child after his father, as though that shouldn't be an affront to me, and add my name in the middle as an afterthought, even though I would be the only father this child would ever know! I wouldn't have expected to call him by my own name, but something other than the name of his errant father would have been less grating.

I nodded and stepped aside so Lindy could minister to mother and child. Jeff Baker motioned me outside.

"Good thing you got here before dark. I was set to go out looking for you. What possessed you, man, to be so far afield when the need arose? Women don't forgive that, you know."

He took out his pipe, filled it from a leather pouch, and sucked a flame to life. There was no smoking around the mill, what with all the dust in the air, so Jeff took advantage of the opportunity for an afternoon pipe when it arose.

"Yes, I know, but she assured me this morning it was all right." With no knowledge of how a new father should act, I stood by watching my friend's smoke curl lazily up until the wind caught it and whisked it away.

"Next time, keep yourself close. You never know how it's going to go. Lindy's good. Knows her business. But you never know."

Abashed, I contemplated the remote possibility of a next time and looked to the weather to relieve me from scrutiny. "Might be another snow squall in the offing."

Jeff nodded. "You glad to get a boy?"

"Oh, yes. Wouldn't know what to do with a girl." That much was true.

"You learn. With two of them and the three boys coming on, Lindy and I expect some relief from the everlasting work. Get more going as soon as you can, man." He winked.

"You know that's not a problem," I countered, saying what was expected—my contribution to the masquerade.

To be sure it *was* a problem and would continue to be for some time. Now how would I be able to get away tomorrow to ride to Orbisonia to engage an expert to reline the furnace? I had to go. It couldn't wait. What if the man was packing to leave right now? I wrestled with the choices: the need to take advantage of expert help while it was available or the expectations of others that as a new father I should be enthralled with my wife and child and put everything aside to spend time with them. I knew what the immediate company expected of me, and I also knew what delay could mean to my budding operation.

I excused myself from Jeff and re-entered the house, where Lindy was packing up her kit in anticipation of returning home.

"Lindy, may I speak with you?"

"Sure enough," she replied.

I looked around the room, from the sleeping woman to the babe, to the midwife and back, my uneasiness showing in knit brows and tight lips.

"She's asleep. We can talk," Lindy assured me.

"I've got business in Orbisonia. Tomorrow. I can't put it aside. Can you...?"

Her face showed her bewilderment, but her voice gave the lie to it. "Yes. I can tend to things here for a few days. She won't want you around, anyway. Nursing a babe takes some getting used to. Go on, then."

Relieved, I grasped Lindy's hand in gratitude. In truth, I had no idea how to deal with this whole situation and was just as happy to be going away for a day or so. I knew I shouldn't be. Knew I should act the happy husband and proud father, but acting was not in my realm of experience. I could test a flow of iron and know exactly how to adjust the bellows or how much limestone to add for flux, but when it came to women, this woman in particular, I had no idea how to proceed. In fact, I had no idea what I would have wanted to achieve had I been able in the first place.

Orbisonia won out, and the next morning the little mare trotted down the track toward Water Street, Huntingdon, Mt Union, and Orbisonia. I arrived in the early evening, close to dinner time, stiff and sore from the long ride. To my relief, I wasn't too late to engage the services of Thomas Langley, whose work at Orbisonia was almost finished. Langley promised to start at Mt. Etna the following week. The whole trip took two days and gave me time to think about the woman—hardly more than a girl, really—whose fate was now in my hands, and the child—somebody else's child—every man's harrowing fear. I was alone in this, like a man set adrift on the high seas with no sail, no oars, no charts, no help in view.

As I returned, my mind abuzz with the work to be done in anticipation of Mr. Langley's arrival, I was distracted by Mathias

Corbin's hail as I passed the work site, where he had a crew engaged in cutting and stacking logs.

"Good day, Mathias. What is it?"

"It's Simon Trethaway, Mr. MacPhail. Comes late or not at all, leaves early, and stands around leaning on his ax most of the time. Lazy good-fer-nothin'. Bad for morale for the other workers to see him gettin' away with it. Time you run him off."

I knew I'd have to deal with squatters eventually, but up to this point I'd been too busy or too reluctant to take them on. At first it seemed Trethaway would fall into line like the others, but Corbin insisted he was no good and had warned me time and again about dealing with him. The men resented him, but no one said much because he was given to rants and threats. Taking him on meant a fight, and most were more interested in minding their own business. That meant the responsibility for dealing with him fell to me. I knew it, but it was the one part of my job I disliked to the point of ignoring it.

"Bad example," Corbin said. "Ye can't allow 'em to live for free while the others work, sir. That's buyin' trouble."

"I know. You're right. I'll see to it."

"You can see to it right now. He's to home today and drunk, so they tell me."

I wasn't ready to jump right in and put the whole family out into the cold, but I promised to take care of the matter soon and rode on.

Back at our house, Elinor and the baby seemed to be doing well, and Lindy pressed my hand, assuring me that they were, indeed. I pulled up a stool beside the bed and took my wife's hand. I wanted to say something kind and meaningful, but no words came. I was glad to have the birthing over with, glad she had weathered it well, glad the child was healthy, but I couldn't find the words, so I smiled and told her I had hired a man to re-line the furnace and that would mean getting it in blast on time.

Her reaction was to turn away, lift the child and inspect his underclothing. Lindy, looking on, closed her eyes and shook her head. I accompanied her outside to thank her for rescuing me, but she turned an angry scowl.

"If I'd known you'd come back with nothing on your mind but furnace talk, I'd not have agreed to watch over them. You're bargaining with the devil, sir. You're late for the birthing, then you leave right after, and now you come home and instead of talking sweet you talk about your damned furnace! Are ye daft, man?"

I stopped in my tracks, abashed, uncertain and unprepared for a comeback. "I, er—I didn't mean..."

"It's been my experience that all men can be stupid some of the time and some men can be stupid all the time. You certainly lean for the second." Lindy wasn't one to mince words, no matter who she was dealing with, and while I didn't consider her beneath me in any sense, it was still disconcerting to be lectured like one of her children.

Now, as I walked her out the lane and over the little bridge toward the mill, I was confronted with more trouble in the person of Mrs. Corbin, the collier's wife, strutting at me, red-faced, tight fisted and full of anger.

"You!" she hissed. "You've got to get him out of here. Right now!"

I turned my attention to her, dismayed at this show of unfettered rage. "Who, Mrs. Corbin?"

"Simon Trethaway, that's who. The man is a menace to all that's decent. Not fit for human company. Drunk, lazy, good for nothing. Lets his spawn run wild. If you don't get rid of him soon, my man will."

"Yes, ma'am. I'll look into it." I said, struggling to maintain a calm demeanor in the face of this vexation. It was beginning to look like there wasn't a woman in the village who didn't revile me.

"Look into it all you like. Just get rid of him. That's all." She turned on her heel and strutted back down the road, pulling her shawl tight around her shoulders as though suddenly aware that it was still March.

Lindy took advantage of the situation to laugh. "You're getting it from every angle, sir," she said. "Best you mend your ways and be quick about it."

I sighed. "Thank you, Lindy. I'll work on it."

Chapter 21

March 1824
Adam

Uncomfortably sure I couldn't put it off any longer, I mounted Elinor's little mare, still saddled from my return from Orbisonia, and rode toward the village, hoping my approach on horseback would lend weight to my authority. At Trethaway's door I stopped and gave a shout.

"Trethaway! Come out!"

The door remained closed, and I sat astride the mare, a shiver shaking my shoulders. Whether it was the cold or a desire to avoid the coming conflict, I couldn't say.

"Trethaway! Open up!"

Slowly the door opened and a boy of about eight years, Zach was his name, emerged—dirty, ragged, hair matted and clothing askew. He stood in the doorway, eyeing me with suspicion.

"Is your father about, boy?"

"Aye."

"Could you ask him to come out?"

"Aye."

But he stood there, eyeing me still, moving not at all.

I waited. "Could you get your pa for me?"

"Aye."

Suddenly the door was flung wide and Simon Trethaway appeared, giving the child a rough shove, daring me to interfere.

"What's yer business?" he growled, holding onto the doorjamb, obviously drunk.

"My business is to ask you to leave this cabin for someone who is willing to work."

"Work, is it? I work. Work harder than any, and for what? This shack and a meager wage."

"Corbin tells me you don't pull your weight."

"Corbin? You listen to what that old bastard says? If he knew anything about cutting wood, I might be inclined to work for 'im. All he knows is how to crack the whip and berate the workers. I pull my weight and then some. Ask anybody."

"I'm sorry, Trethaway, but you've been warned before, and now it's time to settle up. I'll give you until tomorrow dusk to be gone. You can collect your wages from Corbin after you've moved out."

Simon Trethaway reached behind the door and drew a long rifle to his shoulder. "Go on with ye. I ain't going nowhere. This here rifle is loaded and ready. You want to move me, ye'll have to do it by force."

"Come now, Trethaway. You can't be willing to resort to guns to get your way. If you shoot me, you'll hang."

"Be worth it."

"I'll be back tomorrow to oversee your move." With that I turned the mare and rode away in the direction of the mill, my back crawling with the awareness that Trethaway held me in his sights every step of the way.

That evening, I rode back over to Corbin's to enlist his aid in removing the Trethaways. There were five children—all scrawny, uncombed and unkempt. Simon's wife was as slovenly as he, and I anticipated a job putting the cabin to rights after they were gone. The work crew would knock off early to be on hand when the deadline came. If Trethaway wanted to resort to shooting, there'd be plenty of loaded guns awaiting him.

I wasn't exactly afraid of the man, for he was reputed to be a blowhard, given to threats and wild talk but no real action, so I proceeded with my plan to evict him, cautious but not cowed. As I rode off the next day to see to the departure of the man and his goods, Jeff Baker hailed me.

"Going to kick Trethaway out on his ass, are you?"

"Don't have much choice. He's squatting and refuses to work, causing trouble among the other workers."

"Pity the wife and babes."

"I do, but a man has to take responsibility for himself. I doubt they'll starve. All he's getting from me is a dry place to sleep. Otherwise, he takes care of his own."

Jeff looked thoughtful. "You know he comes from a halfway decent family."

"Really? Where?"

"His old man owns about three hundred and sixty acres across the river on Tussey Mountain. Warrant for service in 1812."

"Why doesn't he live there, then?"

"Bad blood between him and his brothers. They got tired of his laggard ways, same as us, so I guess they run him off just like you're doing."

"Well, my only interest is that he get out of my cabin, off my property. Beyond that, he can do as he pleases."

"Good luck getting him off without a fight. And check your place good once he leaves. He might leave a present or two for the next tenant."

As I expected, Simon Trethaway sat on a stump in the yard, his rifle across his knees, while his wife and children gathered up their meager belongings and loaded them into a wagon borrowed from the head forge man. Once that was done the whole family stood about the yard, looking angry and sullen. The oldest, a youth of about ten, rifle in hand, stared threateningly in my direction. The second, not more than eight years, hid behind a brush pile with a slingshot, watching and waiting. Two more boys, a six-year-old, scrawny towhead I knew only as Lem and the dark-haired, dark-eyed boy named Jude, who favored his mother, watched from the porch of the next cabin. A little girl of about two stared silently from her mother's arms.

Concerned that Trethaway would push the situation to violence, I noted at least three rifles standing at the ready by cabin doorways. Apparently I had the support of the rest of the settlement. The show of force wasn't lost on Trethaway, for, though he continued to hurl threats and insults, he and the whole brood carried out their possessions and threw them helter-skelter on the borrowed wagon.

The loading didn't take long, and once it was done I asked Trethaway where he planned to go, but his response was only a glare and shrugged shoulders. "What do you care? You just turned me out without a pot to piss in. If that's how it is, I can always find work at a better place. Wouldn't have been so bad here but for your lack of gumption to run the place right."

Knowing in my gut that any further conversation would lead to naught, I let his insult go by.

He mounted the wagon, waited for the children to pile on, and turned around, heading off to the south while the other workers watched to assure themselves that this was, indeed, a departure. The Trethaways, defiant in their humiliation, stared silently out the back of the departing wagon. I called to the father, to offer one last effort at consolation.

"You can come back at your will. All you have to do is earn your keep."

"Oh, I'll be back. Ye can count on that. But not to work fer the likes of you. Ye ain't heerd the last of me. Not by a long measure."

Chapter 22

March 1824
Ellie

I lay in the bed Jeff Baker and Joel had dragged down from upstairs, relieved of my burden but still in a disarranged state both mentally and physically. Baby Robert lay in the crook of my arm, his dark head nestled into me. Life seemed different now. Everything had changed. I felt my maternal instincts awaken and welcomed the responsibility placed on me, but I still felt dismay and even revulsion at the thought of my husband and the knowledge that he was more interested in getting someone to re-line his damned furnace than in taking any kind of proper care of me.

When he returned from Orbisonia, I bid him as cool a welcome as I could, given that Lindy was still there. I managed civility but nothing more, turning away from his every advance and focusing my attention on the baby. We might have to work harder to keep up appearances outside, but here we needn't carry on the masquerade.

He came back into the house after Lindy left, standing dumb before me. He appeared to have something to say, but no words came. I gave him ample time to speak, but when he didn't, I did.

"Fine caring-for you gave me. I could have delivered all alone here but for the Bakers. And then you turn around and leave the next day as though I were an afterthought, not important enough to warrant your attention. I know you wanted no part in this, and that's what you deserve. No part whatsoever."

"I had to go or miss the chance to engage an expert," he stammered. "Besides, Lindy took better care of you than I could have."

"You're right about that."

Standing there, hat in hand, looking down at the floor, he mumbled something about being sorry, to which I replied, "Piffle. Sorry is it? You've a sad way of showing it."

He shuffled his feet, head down as though in deep thought, but he did not reply to my tirade. The baby uttered a feeble cry, enough to draw my attention away, and then I heard the door close. Let him go. He was happiest when he could get away and tend to his beloved furnace.

Alone in the room with the baby, I picked him up and held him close. Try as I might, I couldn't shake the feeling of despair that lurked in the corners of my mind. I wished I were home with my mother to care for me, sleeping comfortable in my old room, all my needs met. Wished I could see Robert Clifton once more—present him his son and see him turn to me with love in his eyes. It would all have worked out if only my father hadn't interfered. I imagined Robert thinking about me, wondering about our child, sad beyond measure that he'd lost me. Now here I was in this miserable house in the middle of a howling wilderness, lonely, alone and sad, with a man I could barely abide. What hope was there for me now? What hope indeed?

Adam

Driven to distraction by all the areas of life I knew nothing about, I turned my attention to that which I could control, or at least thought I could. Thomas Langley appeared on schedule the following Monday and proceeded to inspect the furnace. He turned to me with concern.

"It's more of a rebuild than a repair. This furnace has been let set too long. I'll have a time of it to get at the relining, and the bellows are really beyond repair."

"Are you sure? I looked them over and thought a good patching job would do."

"Aye, for a short fix, but if you intend on producing iron non-stop for any length of time the bellows will only last you a few months and you'll be fixing and patching and interrupting your production."

"Right, then. Go ahead and do what needs to be done."

Langley took a room at the collier's house and spent the next three weeks relining the furnace and laying a new hearthstone. I watched with impatience as the stocks of limestone and ore kept coming in to be stored at the top of the stack, ready to produce iron.

I was as fidgety as a child at church, watching every move, mentally calculating how much more time the repairs would take. Finally, around the end of March, Langley gave me his bill, packed his saddlebags and mounted his horse for the ride back to Chester County. All was in readiness for the production of iron.

Elinor had stayed out of the way of the repairs and devoted herself to caring for the baby—Robbie, as she called him. When she heard Langley was leaving, she took an interest in when he would go and what route he would take. The evening before he left, she invited him to dinner, a surprise to me, so soon after her confinement.

"Mr. Langley, sir, do you expect to pass through Reading City on your way home?" she asked, clearing away the dishes.

"Why, yes, ma'am. My route will take me right by the Birdsboro Works, and I have friends there, so I'll stay over a night or two."

"May I give you a letter to carry? My parents live just a couple of miles this side of Reading City on the Lebanon pike. You'll pass right by their farm before you get to Reading."

"Anywhere near Squire Cliftons place, Brighton?"

"Why, yes, right next door. Do you know the squire?"

"Know of him. Not an intimate acquaintance, mind."

"Well, I would appreciate it if you could deliver a letter to my parents for me."

She seemed excited by the prospect, but I was surprised when she returned with not just a letter, but what looked more like a packet for Langley to carry. Addressed to her father, Stephen Bratton, the packet contained, I presumed, the announcement of the birth of her child, but I was puzzled as to what else she could be sending, given her ongoing resentment toward both her parents. She handed the packet to Langley, I gave over the cash owed for his work, and he rode to the Corbin's for his last night at Etna.

Standing in the dooryard of our house, I looked questioningly at Elinor. She avoided my eye, pretending to busy herself with inspecting the flower bed left in disarray by the last tenant.

"That seemed like a large packet to be sending to your parents." I said it abruptly, clearly curious.

"Yes. I had a lot to tell them."

"Only them? Did you enclose a little note for the Cliftons, too? Did you think they might be interested in hearing about their grandson?"

She rose from the flowerbed and confronted me. "And why would they not?"

"Maybe because they don't want to believe they *have* a grandson. Or was it Robert Clifton you wanted to reach?"

She stood before me, defiant, hands on hips. "Perhaps."

I felt my anger rise. "I would prefer that you never make an effort to get in touch with him again."

"I'm sure you would."

"Like it or not, you are my wife. He had his chance, and he dropped you by the wayside. Don't delude yourself into thinking he has any regrets about that."

Now her emotions rose to the fore. She turned away, groping in her apron pocket for a handkerchief. Seeing her distress brought immediate feelings of sympathy and regret, but my anger over her desire to reach her former lover still rankled. I turned and walked to the stable, saddled my horse, and rode after Langley. I caught up with him at Corbin's house, where I knew he would want a good night's rest before embarking on his long ride.

He was quite surprised to see me so soon after his departure. "MacPhail! Did I forget something?"

"No. But if you don't mind, I'd like to retrieve the packet my wife sent with you."

Langley looked puzzled, but he fished the packet out of his saddlebag and handed it to me. I thanked him and returned to my horse without so much as an adieu. Along the track I stopped, dismounted, fished a candle out of my pocket, and opened the packet. The letter to her parents was routine: the birth of the child, his name, her delight in him. There was little else—no description of the countryside, no news about the progress of the furnace, no mention of me.

The other letter was addressed to Squire and Mrs. Clifton. It, too, was routine, but inside of it was a third missive, addressed to Robert Clifton. My hands shook as I read the lines. She told him of the birth of his son, his namesake, describing the child in great detail. She spoke her joy at bringing forth his child, at having this living token of their love, at the happy memories she still treasured and always would, of loving him. I folded the letter and sat for a long time deep in thought. I knew this was how she felt, but I hoped time would have dulled her affection, that she would eventually adjust to the reality that was our life. But here was evidence that my hopes were baseless.

I lowered my head on my arms and sighed. What could I do? I burned all but the letter to her parents, placed it back in the envelope, and remounted my horse. At the Corbin house I hallooed and waited until Langley came forward. As I leaned down to hand him the letter, I thought I noticed a knowing look in his eyes. Yes, it was hard to keep people from making assumptions. "Would you deliver this for us?" I asked. "My wife has changed her mind. She removed some of what she wrote." Langley nodded and returned to the house.

From that day on I gave myself over even more to the production of iron. The blowing in took several days, but finally the furnace was ready to produce iron. The first blast was an occasion for celebration, and I gathered all the workers—there were about twenty-five by now—and we watched the first pour of molten iron into the pig shaped forms at the base of the furnace. A cheer went up from the workers, and I opened a keg of whiskey for the celebration. My dream realized, I poured myself into the development of the Mt. Etna Iron plantation. Managing the business took all of my energy and taxed my skill, but I was, for all intents and purposes but one, a happy man.

Chapter 23

Ellie
1824

Robbie's birth granted a new direction for my life. Fate might have decreed a loveless marriage for me, but I had this child now—helpless, beautiful, and attached to me. Not Adam, but me. I needed to protect him, soothe him, nurture him through life. I did not expect Adam to love him or even care at all about him, so I would fill the void. I would be everything to Robbie, and he to me.

I know it sounds selfish, but I so despaired of ever having love in my life that loving this child made me glad in my independence from Adam. I could live with him, cook for him, keep house for him, but I had my own anchor, and Adam could come or go with no consequence to me as long as I had Robbie.

Winter was just breaking up when he was born, and by the time both of us were settled in, the thaw had begun. I welcomed it, for the winter had rendered me almost immobile except for church services, which, while they served to break the monotony, served little other purpose. The women of the village eyed me from a distance, wary that I should turn out to be as they already assumed, haughty and aloof. All, that is, except Lindy, whose ready laughter and easy manner lightened my heart.

I tried to make an excuse to drop by her house for a visit at least once a week, more often if I could manage it. With five children and,

I soon learned, another one on the way, Lindy went through life with a less than meticulous attitude toward keeping house. She cooked, baked, sewed, and gardened, but cleaning engaged her only when it became so critical that she could find no other excuse. Then she dived in with a zest not to be matched in any of her other endeavors and scattered the dust and dirt to the four corners of the house, where it would lie in wait for her next conversion to cleanliness.

Light-hearted Lindy had her whole brood as allies. All five children loved to frolic in the meadows, wade in the run, pick wildflowers and berries, build dugouts in the woods, or fish in the river at her side. They made quite a sight, heading off to adventure like a troop of soldiers sorted by height, Lindy in the lead with a babe on her hip. In return, the brood helped with the chores to free up their mother for fun. Joel tended garden, Emily helped with the sewing, little Phoebe loved to cook and was encouraged in that pursuit by her whole family as Lindy's cooking left something wanting. Fortunately, Jeff Baker was an easygoing, patient man who accepted his wife's careless disregard for convention with the same acceptance he had for everything else. As long as no one was hurt by it, what harm could there be?

Having been raised by a tight-lipped, devotee of irreproachability, I found Lindy's light-hearted take on life refreshing and welcomed her lightness of being. On a winter's day Lindy would rather go sledding than clean. In summer she'd rather pick berries than sweep floors, and she'd rather jump in the branch for a swim than pick berries, and she'd rather swim in the nude, yelling and laughing, than just swim. That was Lindy, the perfect antidote to my careful restraint.

I adjusted to motherhood with grace; Robbie was a delightful baby, full of giggles and with a disposition to mischief. I enjoyed him to the further exclusion of Adam, who made no attempt to alter our relationship after the incident over the letters. He went about his life and I went about mine, our charade undetected by our neighbors. In a small way, I was proud of our deception. No one knew that Robbie wasn't Adam's child, and that despite Adam's having taken to my bed, we still slept as though there were a board between us.

That came to an inevitable end when Robbie was about seven months old. I'd held off any advances until then, but I sensed that I couldn't expect to continue the practice forever. A man is a man in spite of my wishes. I knew my self-imposed celibacy would inevitably come to its logical conclusion, and I knew I would have to yield when resistance was run through. My intention was not to participate, but to allow him his right. He exercised that right for the first time one October evening not quite a year into our marriage, without preliminaries or promises. It wasn't so bad, really, his asserting his claim as a husband. Memories of my time with Robert Clifton surfaced and danced in my brain as Adam satisfied his need, but those memories were not without bitterness for my shame. Adam was a gentle and undemanding lover, so I made up my mind to accept that part of my fate and returned to my sleeping babe resigned to my role.

Adam

Elinor was taken with this baby. Gave him all her time and attention, cooed over him, coddled him, generally treated him like a little crown prince while I stood back, audience to the alliance. Her attempt to communicate with her former lover had diminished my hope of ever having anything but a mutually agreed upon truce between us.

I made no advance upon her for some time, even though my needs grew to the point of self-gratification with regularity. Elinor seemed happy in her own world, and try as I might to warm to her, I was so dismayed to know she still held love in her heart for her spurner, I let the situation ride for almost a year after we were married.

When it became more and more heavy upon me, shut out of her affections as I was, I made the decision to press my case—indeed my right.

It was October, a bright, clear evening, the sky alive with stars, a sharp coolness in the air that told of colder nights to come. Winter was standing in the wings, ready to move back again, welcome or not. Etna furnace was producing—indeed had been producing iron by the ton since mid April. I'd succeeded in getting the operation back up,

112

had even shipped iron over the mountains by pack train to Pittsburgh and been rewarded with a respectable profit. I'd been patient up to now, given Elinor every benefit, watched her bond with someone else's child, saw her try to reclaim her old love, and stood back from demanding my rights as a husband.

This evening, my patience exhausted, I asked her if we could take a little walk. She glanced at the child, sleeping in his cradle beside our bed, which up to then had remained downstairs in the corner of the room away from the fire.

"He'll be all right. He's sound asleep We won't go far."

She followed with a show of reluctance, as though she'd guessed my purpose. I had no intention of forcing her, just of persuading her of my need—indeed, my right—but I could feel her resistance as we walked along the track that led to the horse barn and beyond.

I reached for her hand, and while she let me take it, she held mine not at all. To remind me that she preferred the shelter of the house to walking in silence in the chill of the evening, she said, "Let's not go too far. Robbie might awaken."

I stopped, turned, and looked down at her. "There's something we need to talk about."

"Yes, I know. You've been patient."

"Indeed. But now..."

She nodded, eyes on the ground. Taking her other hand, I leaned forward and kissed her for the first time on the lips. She drew back, but not away. Heartened by the warmth of her lips, maybe not yielding to mine, but giving way by some measure, I dropped her hands and reached for her, enfolded her in my arms, felt her small body press against me. "I need you, Elinor. I need you to be my wife."

She spoke not a word, only stood while I held her, caressed her hair, spoke soothingly to her. Quickened by the promise of fulfillment, my hands shook and I felt myself given over to long-postponed lust. We stood near to the barn door, and I led her in, searching in the dimness for the ladder to the hay mow. I urged her up the ladder before me and followed unsteadily, my hands still shaking. She lay down in the hay, resolute but without passion, and I bedded her, taking care to be gentle, not to let her know that I was less experienced than she. I took my just rights as a man, brief and without reciprocation. She didn't resist, but neither did she participate with ardor. It was as though she had become resigned to the inevitable in acceptance of her duty. For that brief moment I didn't care. I'd done it. Taken her. Made her my own. From now on, I would have my just station as a husband. I wanted—needed—to say so much, but there was no love or feeling in her assent. Only resignation.

It wasn't what I wanted, hoped for, dreamed about. I wanted to be welcomed with warmth and affection, but I would accept what she was willing to give for the present. I still hoped we would one day love one another in the fullest sense, aware that our beginning had been sad, rough, even desperate. I'd been patient, more so than any other man I knew would have been, but I'd given her as much time and patience as I had to give. Now life would take its course, whatever that happened to be.

Most men didn't bother themselves about their marriages. As long as the house was clean, the food cooked, the linen washed and the bed warm, they were content to continue their pursuit of making a livelihood. But those others had had the advantage of attraction, courtship, infatuation and consummation, the natural order. Having had none of these but the last, I pondered the depth and breadth of our relationship and found it wanting, knew she did, too, but had no notion of how to fix it.

Chapter 24

Summer 1826
Adam

The furnace operated with little change throughout the summer, fall, and into the next winter. I was learning the business side of iron making, and while I was masterful at creating the product, the other aspects of running a furnace challenged my every skill. The little village was expanding rapidly, and new housing was needed to accommodate the growing number of workers. I authorized the building of a plank dormitory near Corbin's house for the single men, and soon saw the necessity for a company store, as the nearest was at Yellow Spring, and I felt bound to provide for all of my tenants' needs. Farm labor was procured to produce food for the workers, and stock, barns, a blacksmith shop, a school—every accommodation to make the operation self-sufficient—became my responsibility.

My days were filled with decisions, orders, operations, and relations with and among my workers. We were a mutually dependent community where functioning smoothly was in everybody's best interest. They worked for me, and I worked for them. So it was with great joy and anticipation that we learned around the time of Robert's second birthday that construction of the Pennsylvania Canal from Harrisburg to Pittsburgh had actually been authorized by the state legislature. Contracts were to be let immediately—not soon enough for me—because New York had long since completed their Erie Canal reaching all the way across the state from Lake Erie to Albany on the Hudson. Pennsylvania had to catch up before New York took all the business away. So a sense of urgency pushed Pennsylvania's legislature into action. I was delighted when, on July 4, 1826, ground was broken at Harrisburg for the canal that would change our lives and guarantee our prosperity.

One morning that summer I was on the road to Huntingdon, the county seat, when I veered from my purpose to visit the Porter Limestone Quarry downriver from Fox Run to satisfy myself that it was being properly managed by Geordan Evans, a foul-mouthed and foul-tempered Welshman who, while running a capable operation, had been reported the object of hatred by his workers.

I stopped before Evans' office shanty and dismounted, dismayed by the sounds of shouting coming from within, and hurried up the steps to see what was afoot. My knock went unanswered for a full minute while sounds of shuffle and struggle continued to the accompaniment of grunts, cries, and obscenities.

"Evans! Open up!" I shouted, already in a state over whatever violence was taking place inside. When the door wasn't opened in response to my call, I put my shoulder to it and broke my way in, sending the quarry foreman sprawling to the floor. Across the room stood a youth of about fifteen, bleeding from his mouth, his hands in tight fists.

"What's going on here?" I demanded.

Evans rose and pulled himself to his fullest height. "Naught, Cap'n. This lad was insubordinate is all. I were about teaching him a lesson."

"That's a lie," cried the boy. "He sent my pa to his death yesterday. Sent him to die in a blast—he knew the danger, but he sent him anyway."

I looked from one to the other. "Go outside and wait for me," I told the boy. When we were alone in the shanty, I turned to Evans. "What's your story?"

"The old man were a drunk. Come to work drunk, didn't know what was going on half the time. He wandered down there where the charge was set after the word went out to lay low. I can't be blamed for the man's lack of judgment and good sense."

"Are you sure the word was loud and clear?"

"Look, Cap'n, I been working quarries since I were a lad. They're dangerous places. You gotta have yer wits about ye or pay the price."

I listened, aware of Evans's reputation for harshness, and wondered about his tale and the motive, if there was any, behind it. I wasn't long in finding out. By the time I got outside the shanty to talk to the boy, he'd been joined by four or five other laborers, all anxious for my ear. But my eye was drawn to one in particular—tall, dark, and slouching on the fringes of the assembly, wary-eyed and lantern-jawed. It was none other than Simon Trethaway, whom I had neither seen nor heard from in almost two years. As the men crowded around, each eager to tell his version of events, Trethaway kept to the rear, avoiding my glance but intent upon hearing every word.

"Evans says the old man were drunk, but he weren't. He were deaf from years of working around blasting. Evans knew it, sure as Ned. Everyone did. Man can't hear the call to lay low. Why send him down where the blasting was?" Spoken by a tough looking quarryman, powdered all over with rock dust.

"Yeah, he knew all right, but he didn't care a mite. Wanted to get rid of the old man, he did." That was one of the older men, bent and wizened from years on the rock pile.

The youth, wiping the blood from his face, held up skinned knuckles for my inspection. "He had it in fer my pa ever since he asked to marry my Aunt Tess, Pa's sister, and Pa told him no. My aunt's right pretty, but a little slow, you might say. Pa were her guardian, and we all know how Evans would have treated her after he quenched his lust."

"Yeah. Yeah," Trethaway stepped up now to contribute his take on things. "Everybody around here hates the bastard. He'd kick a dog and shoot his mother or shoot a dog and kick his mother, wouldn't matter which." He moved back a little from the group, eyeing me warily. I wondered how or why he'd been hired on again in one of my operations, but attributed it to the far-flung nature of the iron business. Quarrymen didn't often talk to the colliers, miners, or forgers. Each had his own domain, sometimes far-flung from the central operation.

I listened to their stories, head down, trying to parse out the truth. "I hear what you're saying, but it doesn't add up to proof that he did it intentionally. A man wandered too close to a blast. Evans says he was drunk; you say he was deaf. Either way, you can't prove Evans did it on purpose."

"Don't have to prove it. We know it, is good enough." Trethaway again, keeping the anger aflame.

Drawn by the commotion, more workers wandered up, each eager to have his say, bringing Evans out of the shanty waving his arms in rage. "Git back to work, you lazy bastards! This ain't no holiday. We got rock to cut and haul. Git back to work."

I waved the others away and singled out the youth at the center of the fight. "What's your name, son?"

"Mike. Mike Morgan. I know I can't prove it, but I'm sure he aimed to get my pa killed."

"Yeah. That's right. Everybody knows Evans had it in for Old Morgan." Trethaway still hung back so as not to miss anything, trying to keep things stirred up.

It was clear; Mike Morgan saw Trethaway as a friend and ally. That alone was cause for alarm in my mind. The boy glared at the shanty where Evans still stood in the doorway overseeing the dispersal of the crowd. "I swear I'll kill him some day."

Dismayed, I replied, "Not this day, Mike. Not this day. Get back to work. I'm guessing your mother needs your wages. We can't look into a man's heart and find intent just because we know there's malice. I'll keep an eye on Mr. Evans, but I can't discipline him on just your word."

"Aye. I know, but I'll get him, Mr. MacPhail. You mark my words. I'll get him."

I left the youth awash in grief and consternation—and with the knowledge that I could do little else. I entered the shanty once more and confronted Evans.

"There's a lot of discontent around here. They say you're too harsh. What say you?"

"Oh, hell, they always got something to whine about. Never mind them. Long as they drag the rock out of here, that's all I care about."

"What about that man Trethaway? I ran him out up at Etna for being a laggard."

"No doubt about that. A laggard, a thief, and a rabble rouser. Don't worry. He won't be here long. I'll run his ass out before the month is out, like as not."

"Well, try to get your job done without starting a revolt, now, hear?"

"Yes sir, boss, I hear."

The notion that Mike Morgan was quite possibly right in his assumptions about Geordan Evans nagged at me as I rode on to Huntingdon. I had deeds to file and ore rights to record, which took most of the afternoon. My business attended to, I returned by way of Water Street and stopped by the inn for a draught.

The innkeeper, Matt Blakely, was by now well known to me, and we engaged in general conversation when I happened by. Still puzzling over the situation at Porter Quarry, I wanted to see what I could uncover.

"What do you hear from the quarry?" I asked.

Matt stopped wiping a glass and looked at me with questioning eyes. "What about it? You mean that Paul Morgan fellow who got himself blowed up yesterday?"

I nodded. "What's the story?"

"They're saying it was bad blood between him and Evans. Just jawing, far as I can see."

I nodded and turned to scan the populace for a familiar face. I found one, Noah David of Cove Forge, sitting alone at a table by a window. His wife of twenty-odd years had died during the past winter, and I hadn't seen him since the funeral.

"Mind if I join you, Mr. David?" I asked, pulling up a chair.

"Not at all, sir. Have you had dinner? I was about to order."

I sat down and raised my hand for the barmaid. "Two more here, and dinner when you've time." I turned to Mr. David, glad for someone to talk to. "How goes it?"

"Good enough. We're getting along. The girls are helping out in the house, and, of course, Thomas and Roger are a great help at the furnace and forge."

With eight children, four still at home, the man had his hands full just keeping them fed and clothed. His two oldest sons ran the furnace and forge, leaving him free to manage all the hundreds of other details. The youngest, a lad of twelve, accompanied his father almost everywhere, and he wasn't long in showing up at Noah's elbow, asking for a penny for a cake.

I felt sorry for the man—left without a wife and with four under-age children to raise, but he seemed to be taking it in stride. I guessed the children were old enough to take care of themselves with the help of their two married sisters living not far away in Williamsburg. Still, it must be a heavy burden. An ironmaster had so much responsibility; I was learning how much he needed a helpmate to carry some of the weight. As I mused on that, David turned the conversation to business.

"How's your operation going?"

"Well enough, I guess. How about you?"

"We're producing about seventy-five tons a month. Not bad, but if we don't find a faster, cheaper way to get it to Pittsburgh soon, those Westmoreland furnaces will have all the business."

"Yes, well, I'm still hoping for the canal to materialize. Seems like progress is being made."

David leaned back in his chair. "Don't count on it. Don't count on it for years. You'd better be ready to ship iron over the mountains the old-fashioned way for quite a while yet. Eight, ten years, maybe."

In the midst of this conversation, and to my relief, we were joined by a giant of a man, tall and broad, who stepped up and greeted us, waved an arm over the crowded public room, and asked if he could take a seat.

"Sure, Adler. Always good to share a drink with a sawmill man. How's business?" Noah David seemed to know everybody, no matter where he went. "This is Adam MacPhail of Mt. Etna. Adam, Mark Adler up from Alexandria."

"Oho! MacPhail! Yes, I've heard of you. Just this afternoon as a matter of fact."

I rose and shook his hand. "That's interesting. What have you heard?"

"Heard there was a little set-to up at Porter Quarry today. Good thing the foreman holds a tight rein. Accidents happen. Blame gets placed. Trouble follows."

"You mean Evans?" I asked. "Think they're being too hard on him?"

I found it difficult to come to any conclusion when talking with either workers or management. Such a wide gulf separated them. My hope was to be fair to both sides, but sometimes the balancing seemed impossible.

Adler continued. "Looks like the workers got to have something to whine about or they ain't happy. Man can't force a good day's work out of 'em without they conjure up some evil purpose to it."

"So you think Evans was doing right?"

"Just doing his job. That's about all ye can expect. These louts have no notion of how business works. Think they can work or not and still get paid. You need to come down hard on 'em, sir. That's what."

"I guess I'll leave that to Evans."

Adler sat down and we were soon engaged in devouring a pot roast dinner. As we ate, I found myself returning to the puzzle of keeping peace between management and labor.

"Funny how there's always two sides, huh? Each side sure they're right? All I want to do is get the iron out, and all I hear about is who's busting who. What's a man to do?"

Adler rubbed his chin. "All I know is, them that's got skill don't mind to work. Them that ain't spends all their time looking for ways to skin you. You gotta have managers that can make 'em toe the line, or you'll go broke with trying to keep 'em happy."

We finished our dinner amid small talk of the weather and horses, with no further mention of the canal or labor problems. Outside, Elinor's little mare awaited. I was ready to go home.

Chapter 25

Summer 1828
Ellie

In the years to follow as our friendship grew, Lindy and I would sometimes take a day for ourselves, leaving little Robbie in the capable hands of the collier's wife, Mrs. Corbin, and Lindy's younger children with the older ones while we would walk out along the river carrying a picnic hamper to give ourselves over to the joy of a few hours of freedom. On one of those occasions, when Robbie was about four, Lindy turned serious.

"You know I'm with child again."

"Really, Lindy? Number seven already? Aren't you tired?"

She lay on an old quilt we'd brought along, looking up at the cloudless blue sky. "To say the least. I love the lovemaking, but the result is beginning to wear on me."

"I guess it would. I can't think what seven children would be like, and yet there are those with ten and twelve."

Lindy screwed up her face into a scowl. "Not me. This is it. No more than seven."

I looked askance at her. "How are you going to keep Jeff happy and set the limit at the same time?"

"They tell me there's ways. Tonics you can drink to get rid of it. Other things, too. Every old woman has a remedy."

"Like what?" I couldn't see myself resorting to any of these, but looking at Lindy's life full of noisy, rowdy children and unending work I could see why she might think about it. So far I'd escaped a second pregnancy and counted myself lucky.

"Goose quills, so I hear. If you get to know women like I do with the midwifery, you'll hear many a plan once the birthing is over. What's your secret?"

"Secret?"

She nodded toward my belly. "Nothing in there since Robbie, and he's four already. Are you barren, or do you have some secret means of preventing it?"

I colored, embarrassed. "No. I..."

"Come on, Ellie. Some women have those wads they stick up inside, and I hear there's an herb tea you can drink. I've even heard of some kind of cover the man can put on, but I wouldn't know where you'd find such a thing."

I frowned at this introduction to a topic I'd blithely disregarded up to now. "I really haven't done anything like that. Adam is just . . . not very demanding." I said it hesitantly, in a quiet tone, my eyes downcast.

"Hah! You're lucky. Jeff is always in the mood. Can't keep him away for more than a day or so. Hence, seven kids in fourteen years."

I gave myself over to silence, drawn in by the image of a man wanting his woman so much. I despaired of ever having such a relationship with Adam. His needs seemed disarmingly easy to meet, and that was all right with me, but my thoughts wandered back to Robert Clifton's ardor in the orchard at Brighton. A shiver fluttered through me, and I pulled my shawl closer even though it was a warm day.

Lindy leaned back on her quilt and smiled. "Never mind. Anyway, I think a woman should have a plan for spreading the babes out and keeping the numbers down. Give her body a chance to recover and mend itself. I see a lot of broken down wombs in my line of work. I just thought maybe you had some secret of your own."

We lay on a high bluff overlooking the river. Below us, on the track, two men carrying a wooden case and a metal tripod walked along, oblivious to our presence.

"What do you think they're about?" I asked, relieved for a reason to change the subject.

Lindy rolled over and got up on one elbow. "Looks like surveying equipment. Maybe they're tracking the route of the canal."

"Oh Lindy, won't that be fine? A canal! We can get on a boat and go for a ride to Huntingdon, Williamsburg, or Hollidaysburg and come back in the same day."

"What fun!" She laughed, seeming to have dropped the earlier subject, to my relief. "Your Mr. MacPhail's going to be rich!"

I smiled to myself and nodded. I thought she might be right, even though the prospect seemed pretty far in the future.

Lindy's curiosity about my avoiding pregnancy became moot when just a few months later I found myself with child again. There would be five years between this one and Robbie, too long for them to be very close. In my mind I would always separate Robbie from Adam's child, or children, as the case may be. Despite the circumstances, Robbie was a child of love, at least on my part. I still dreamed of Robert Clifton, wondered about him, whether he was at all curious about this son of his growing up in the wilds of Huntingdon County. All of that had to be put aside now that I was carrying Adam's child. I felt no bitterness. Adam was kind and considerate, and ours had developed into a relationship of mutual consent if not mutual love. Indeed, we never spoke of love. It didn't exist for us.

I must admit my father wasn't *all* wrong in his choice of Adam MacPhail to rescue me, at least as pertains to his business acumen. He was soon making a success of Etna Furnace, as evidenced by the growth of the village, the new company store built last fall to serve the needs of worker and owner alike, the huge stone barn where a hundred mules, not horses anymore, but mules, abode. The blacksmith shop across the road from our house kept three men busy every day shoeing mules and horses, while the forge over near the village on the bank of the Juniata produced cast iron kettles, plows, tools, even stoves for an ever-growing community.

With the impending success of Etna Furnace, my thoughts turned to the need for a proper manor house, suitable to the needs of our now growing family, but my husband was quite satisfied with our little stone house and saw no need to change our abode. Adam was already talking about repaying my father and buying a controlling interest in Mt. Etna Furnace Company. My preference, fueled by my lingering resentment over the way my 'situation' had been handled, was to put the money into a house that would stand as testament to our station in life, not to mention my own pride. We might be living on the wild edge of civilization, but we needn't perpetuate the image.

I had to insist on the enterprise. Adam, happy to stay in that small stone house forever, was always so preoccupied with the daily operations that he barely saw the need for better living conditions. My determination to live in a new, larger home suited to our social status caused him to consider for some time before he would relent.

I drew up a rough plan and Adam presented it to Mr. Holder, a stonemason who worked in association with Mr. Gregg, a builder. Mr. Gregg kept in his employ both rough and finish carpenters. It was the latter whose work I most hoped to impress.

In the midst of all the other ongoing improvements, our home took shape, an imposing edifice built of Pennsylvania limestone from our own quarries. Four windows and a door across the first story, five windows across the second. Four huge, high- ceilinged rooms, two downstairs and two up, astride a central hall, eight fireplaces, an ell expansion which housed the kitchen and servants' quarters above. I had to admit that Adam had been right to place his fortunes in Etna Furnace. It grew and changed before our eyes from a poor, neglected undertaking to a thriving, bustling community of workers all dedicated to producing Adam's revered Juniata Iron.

Chapter 26

1829
Ellie

The construction of our home began in the spring, painfully slow in my eyes, and continued through the fall. I watched every move the carpenters made, passing my approval on every detail. There was the joy of anticipation, the planning and buying of furnishings, floor coverings and drapery, the pride of moving into our own mansion. Adam, ever reluctant to spend money, allowed me this indulgence, but enthusiasm for the venture eluded him.

As far from civilization as we were, even the smallest complement had to be imported in the same freight wagons that hauled our product to Philadelphia. Even though Pittsburgh was closer and a more booming market, its frontier character made the Philadelphia trade more attractive, to me at least. The return of a train of wagons from the east meant a Christmas-like joy of discovery, opening every crate to unpack the treasures within, and it wasn't only me. Everyone in our little village benefitted from the arrival of shipments of foodstuffs and dry goods from the east to stock the shelves of our company store. Every wagon train brought us closer to the life I'd left in Berks County.

Work on our home progressed nicely, and just before Christmas we moved out of the little house and into the mansion, suited to my perception of a proper home, even finer by any measure than the one

I'd been raised in. There were still details to be attended to: paintings, table linens, china, and porcelain. But my joy was undiminished by such minimal shortcomings.

The pack trains kept coming and going, though they slowed or almost stopped in the winter months. That was a time for relaxation and reflection, when Adam could review his accounts, tend to furnace repairs, build up the stocks of raw materials, and await the spring rains to swell the river. On the swollen waterway he shipped his iron bars on big, wooden arks built for the one-way trip downstream to the Susquehanna and on by way of the Columbia railroad to Philadelphia, or down the Susquehanna and the Chesapeake all the way to Baltimore.

Our mansion stood back from the river, on the flat land across the track from the poor little church we still attended every Sunday. Compared to the other buildings on the plantation, the house was imposing, yet still in keeping with the style of other ironmasters' houses. I was delighted with it, already comfortable in my role as the master's wife. Adam, on the other hand, never fully settled into the role of Ironmaster. He was too busy *being* the ironmaster to think of himself as exalted or above his workers. Indeed, he saw himself as their partner, not their overlord.

That first Christmas in our new home made a beginning toward healing the breach between Adam and me. Our child was due within the month, strengthening the tie that grew so haltingly between us. We celebrated the season by showering Robbie with gifts and enjoying a sumptuous Christmas dinner, prepared by our newly hired cook, Mrs. Gwynn, an overweight, red-faced Welsh woman whose skill in the kitchen would be our lifelong delight. She made plum pudding, German kringle, and Irish stew with equal skill.

That year we established our custom of inviting the workers to stop by the manor house on Christmas day for gifts of oranges ,candy and nuts for the children and a small cash bonus for the workers. They trooped in throughout the afternoon, dressed in their very best, rough though that might be, shining clean, and full of good wishes. The men received a draught of Adam's best whiskey, and the women contented themselves with joining in singing Christmas carols as I accompanied them on the new pianoforte, brought with painstaking care all the way from Philadelphia.

It was a delightful afternoon in which I felt the stirrings of friendship, which until that time had been rationed for me. A smile from Mrs. Billington, the founder's wife, now happily situated in the stone house we had relinquished. A request for my recipe for plum punch from Mrs. Appleton, the head forge man's wife. Even an invitation to join the church choir, only just forming up, along with the hint that I could accompany them if the church could ever afford an organ.

After an especially rich Christmas dinner and an afternoon of cheer, I retired to my bedchamber, feeling very much as though I'd overindulged. But it wasn't long before I knew that this was no case of indigestion. This was labor. I rose from my bed and opened the chamber door to call Adam to my bedside. He arrived promptly from the parlor below, where he had been watching Robbie ride his new 'Hobby Horse', his face flushed with concern.

"Is it time, Ellie? Is it time already?"

A full month early, I could tell this wasn't to be the easy delivery I'd had with Robbie. "Could you send for Lindy, please?" I asked.

By the time Lindy arrived with her kit, her daughter Emily at her side, I was in the throes of full labor, and somehow this didn't feel right. It was early, but the spasms were wrenching. Lindy calmly went about her vigil, all of her equipment set out on a table beside my bed. I labored through the night, sweating and crying out in pain and fear that this child was somehow not going to make it. My fevered brain conjured up outrageous reasons for it. I hadn't wanted it, didn't love its father, thus causing a difficult delivery, or perhaps, even worse, some disability, disfigurement, or even death. My strength wore down as the night progressed, and in spite of Lindy's calm reassurances, I knew something was wrong.

Lindy had assured me all was well, she could see the crown of the baby's head, but that was hours ago. No matter how hard I pushed, she didn't report any progress. By five o'clock in the morning I lay back, exhausted, afraid for both of us now.

"Lindy, what's stopping it? If you can see its head, what's stopping it?"

Lindy looked haggard and tired, but she still tried to reassure me. "I've seen this before. You push and you push and then all of a sudden, here it comes."

Suddenly, as though bidden, my body gave a great spasm and I felt the child's head move down. Lindy grabbed and held it, exhorting me to push just once more so it could pass. I did, but to no avail. There really was something holding it back.

Lindy began to minister to the baby, ignoring my questions, intent on keeping it alive.

"Oh, Mommie, it's blue!"

That was Emily, unable to control her dismay.

"What? What? Lindy, tell me."

Lindy straightened up. "Em, give me the knife. The cord is wrapped around its neck. It's choking."

I lay back and gave way to tears. I wanted this baby more than I'd realized. Wanted it for Adam, to make up in some measure for my disdain, my lack of affection, my cool demeanor. Now it was not to be.

I could hear Lindy working, holding the tiny head in her left arm while she maneuvered the knife with her right hand. Suddenly there came a whimper, then a lusty cry. Thank God! My baby was alive.

The rest of the delivery was routine once the offending cord was cut. The child, another boy, was washed and wrapped in soft flannel before his father was called to my bedside. I held him close, to comfort him for his rough entry, and looked him over carefully to assure myself that he really was all right. He was perfect, though smaller than Robbie had been, more delicate in his features, and with the penetrating blue eyes of his father.

When Lindy called Adam into the room he came slowly, almost reverently. He knelt beside my bed and looked at his son's face for the first time. Then he looked at me, struggling to express his joy. "Oh, Ellie, thank you. Thank you."

I was taken aback at his reaction, feeling some regret for directing all my wrath at him, wishing I could somehow make myself care. But how do you summon feelings of love?

"What shall we name him?" Adam asked.

"You should name him. He's your son."

"How about Laird? Laird Bratton MacPhail? After my father and your family. Would that suit?"

I managed to eke out a weak smile. "Yes, it would. It would suit very well."

Part Two

1831–1834

Chapter 27

Summer 1831
Ellie

Work on the canal progressed rapidly, winding along the Juniata River from its confluence with the Susquehanna, passing through town after town, bringing with it the promise of prosperity and diversion. Adam, so delighted by the prospect of cheaper transportation of blooms, fairly walked on air. I was cheered by it, but for a different reason. It meant goods would be more readily available for the company store and for our own pleasure. I could get velvets, silks and brocades, silver candlesticks or fine china, just like in Philadelphia. The very thought put a smile on my face.

Excitement was in the air as the digging drew close to Mt. Etna, and I wandered out of an afternoon and watched the men labor to dig the canal basin. Irishmen, 'fresh from the old sod,' as they liked to say. They were a strange lot. Hard-working, hard-drinking, hard-fighting, musical, devotedly religious and profane. They camped alongside their work, eating hearty, drinking hard, and swearing in the most creative ways. Their demeanor made Adam squirm, made me laugh, made six-year-old Robbie strut about in imitation. Laird was too young to find them interesting, but I did. Drawn to the canal basin almost every afternoon, I watched the steady swing of the pick and heft of the shovel and listened to the musical sound of their brogue.

One in particular struck my fancy, broad shouldered, with a twinkle in his green eyes and a ready smile. I picked him out from among the workers on the first day. He was young—a little older than I, I would guess, and very handsome. Charming, witty, quick. Everything Adam was not. I knew I shouldn't, but I felt myself drawn to the man, this Timothy Judge, who swung his pick and glanced over to see if I was watching those muscles flex. Oh, I was watching, indeed. The ripple of the muscles in his back when he worked shirtless, the way he rubbed the back of his neck when he took a water break, the way he looked at me as though I were naked. There was no pretense at propriety with Timothy Judge, only crackling sparks in search of tinder.

I found an excuse to wander down by the canal basin almost every day, rain or shine. They still worked in the rain, mind you—and in the sun and in the wind. I carried Laird, a wriggling, squalling, wrenching lad, set upon the idea of walking by himself. I stopped and let him down, pretending to be completely preoccupied with watching him, but my eyes strayed to the workers, searching for Timothy, singling him out. Once I'd found him there was no turning away. I was glad most folks were busy with their daily lives so there was no one around to watch me let myself sink into lust. It'd been so long since I felt even the slightest twinge of desire. Adam asked little of me, and I accommodated him with little enthusiasm and no passion at all. But this. This Timothy Judge set my blood to running.

He was fresh, that one. Nothing shy or retiring there. He caught my eye and smiled when I arrived, stood where I could see him unobstructed, took off his shirt and dug half naked. I could barely take my eyes off him. He must have felt my gaze burning into his flesh. He turned, looked at me over his shoulder, and winked. My heart fluttered, aching for the chance to touch him. Really, Ellie, I told myself. You should be ashamed. I knew I should, but I wasn't. My attention was riveted on his strutting, flexing, utterly captivating brawn. And he was funny, too. Told loud jokes to his fellows and got them laughing almost to tears. He mimicked speech and movement with ease, remarkably able to catch the nuances of both.

I must have spent close to a month watching, making excuses to be out on the canal bank, scheming for ways to make my visits look legitimate. By then the work had progressed beyond the Etna Furnace property following the Juniata River's winding way upstream toward Williamsburg. I had no business wandering that far from home. It became harder to construct a reason for being there, and yet ... I was by now in the throes of a full-on crush, unable even to think like a sensible woman, my head turned by admiring glances and soft-spoken compliments.

Then, one afternoon while wandering in the woods in search of wild strawberries, I heard a twig snap and turned to see who was there, hoping it might be the object of my headlong rush from sensibility. It was. Tim Judge stood about ten feet behind me, leaning against a tree, one hand in his pocket, the other holding a sprig of timothy up to his lips. He smiled. I smiled.

"What are you doing out here today?" I asked.

He took it as an invitation and came forward, dropping the sprig of timothy as he came, his eyes leveled on me. "I could ask you the same question."

I took a step back as he approached, mindful of the need for propriety. "I'm picking berries. The wild strawberries make a fine jam."

"Aye, so I've heard."

His voice was melodious, with a slight tremor that made the hair stand up on the back of my neck. "Would you like some?" I held out the basket, unmindful that there were only about a dozen berries in it.

Tim reached in and took one, keeping his eyes on my face. "Now, what are you really doing out here, and where is that screaming banshee you call Laird, is it?"

"Asleep. He's napping, and cook promised to get him up if he awakens. He usually sleeps for an hour or so."

"And the other one? The lad you call Robbie?"

"Oh, he's gone snaring rabbits with the workers' children. Fancies himself quite the woodsman."

Tim Judge gave me a knowing look. "So you come out here to pick berries in the only free moment you have, now?" He took the basket from my hand and hung it from the branch of a gnarled apple tree, then turned and brushed a leaf from my shoulder.

His touch set me afire. I longed to reach back and touch him, swoon into his arms, feel the fire of his kiss, but no. Not this time. With a monumental effort, I held myself under control, chattering about strawberries and asking about the dig; how it was going, and why wasn't he working this day?

He took another step closer so that he didn't have to reach anymore—just raise his arm to touch me. I shivered in my dress, despite the warmth of the sun on my back—shivered at the thought of being held, loved by this man. I reached for the basket, but he grasped my wrist and held it tight. I looked around to see if anyone was there, but we were alone. My heart pounding, I searched his face, full of fiery anticipation of the kiss I knew would come.

We stood like that for a long moment—gazing into each other's eyes—unable to turn away in spite of the very real chance that someone might happen upon us. Then Tim abruptly let go of my wrist and turned away. "I ought to know better," he said. "This is the way to hell, Mrs. MacPhail. The straight and sure way to hell. Let's go our ways and forget about this."

I nodded, abashed, and stepped back. "Yes. Yes. We must remember who we are and where we are. We can't indulge ourselves so. I'm a wife and a mother. I must go now. I'm sorry, Mr. Judge, is it? Yes, well, I'm needed at home right this minute. I'm sure baby Laird is awake by now."

He stepped aside and let me pass, my skirt brushing against his trouser leg as I did so. I smelled his scent, urgent, manly, and wondered how I could ever walk away from him again.

The path wound back to the house, about a half mile, just enough to gather my composure before entering the back door into the kitchen. Cook was leaning against the work table peeling apples for a tart. She barely raised an eyebrow when I put the scant basket of strawberries down. "Not so many this year," she observed and kept on peeling. "I think Laird's awake. I heard him talking to the curtains a while ago."

I smiled at that and entered the room off the kitchen that we used as a nursery during the day. Laird stood holding onto the iron crib bars, giving them a good shake. His round little face so different from

136

Robbie's that I wondered at the way babies had of taking after one another or not. This child of mine and Adam's was taller and leaner than Robbie had been, and more amenable, as well. Laird would be the peace maker, the diplomat, the care taker, while Robbie, at six, already showed signs of the lack of consideration for others and an aversion to hard work that would characterize him for all of his life. He was already the most adept person at avoiding labor I had ever met, except, perhaps, for his father. I picked up Laird and changed his diaper, then carried him into the kitchen, where cook was just putting the apple tarts to bake.

"Land, let's get out of here," she said, red-faced. "This kitchen is hot enough to melt me to butter."

"It was your idea to make apple tarts," I chided her.

"Yes, I know, but Mister loves them so."

I marveled at her willingness to suffer discomfort in order to please. Such altruism was not in me.

I took Laird out on the lawn and put him down to play. He didn't like the feeling of the grass against his bare feet, so he adopted a high stepping gait to avoid the tickly stuff. I laughed at his antics, partly in relief at my narrow escape from certain disaster.

Chapter 28

Late Summer 1831
Ellie

Once unleashed, my desire would not be stayed. I tried to keep away from the canal digging, telling myself that they would progress rapidly toward Williamsburg and soon be gone. Out of sight, out of mind, I told myself. But those insolent green eyes, the tilt of his head, the gentle teasing curve of his lips would not let me go. Still, for me at least, my thoughts were only those of a young woman's crush. What was going on in Tim Judge's head was another matter entirely.

He took to wandering the woods in the evening after work, appearing near our house like a ghost in the mist, drifting in and out of sight. At first I thought it was my pent-up desire trifling with me, but one evening, after I'd put the boys to bed, as I sat on the wide front porch, gazing out over the canal ditch toward the river, I saw him, bold as brass, walking along the canal bank, a brash smile turned my way. He lifted his hand in a jaunty wave, turned his head toward the river, and was gone down over the bank in a trice. I bested the impulse to wander out and meet him among the wild phlox blooming like a pink mist along the water. Instead I rose and entered the house, where Adam sat on a carpeted platform rocker, reading by lamplight.

I smiled warmly at him, picked up my embroidery, lit another lamp, and sat down opposite to restore my composure. Try as I would to dismiss him, the image of Timothy Judge accompanied my every thought until, yawning, I put down my embroidery, mounted the stairs, and went to bed, only to fall into restless dreams.

The next day, after too little sleep, I was agitated, unable to concentrate, short with the children. My thoughts fluttered around the coming evening, the wistful hope that he would appear again. I told myself it was childish, impossible, improper, unthinkable, and then I thought about him all the more. Evening couldn't come soon enough, would come too soon, wouldn't come at all. Robbie pestered me to take him swimming, and, thinking it might get my brain readjusted, I consented. I left Laird with cook, and we walked hand in hand to the riverbank, Robbie chattering all the way about his prowess as a swimmer, I, lost in the dream of being loved by Timothy Judge.

As we approached the riverbank, we heard shouts and laughter, which, to my relief, came from Lindy and her troupe, swimming, splashing, swinging out and dropping from a rope, enjoying the delights of an afternoon on the water. Robbie and I joined them, welcomed with shouts of, "Watch this, Mrs. MacPhail!" and "Hey, Robbie, come here. I'll watch him, Missus!"

I settled myself beside Lindy on an old quilt she'd laid out and took off my shoes and stockings, wriggling my toes in the warmth of the sun. Lindy languished on her stomach, arms clasped in front of her, a wide brimmed straw hat shading her face.

"Sorry to disturb you," I began.

"No harm. It's just as restful having somebody to talk to. How've you been?"

"Well. And you?"

"At least I'm not pregnant! Thank God for that small favor. But wait. I might be by tomorrow. Jeff had that look in his eye this morn."

I laughed. "You know you love it, Lindy. It isn't all Jeff!"

"I know," she chuckled, rolling over on her back. "Be nice if you could just go at it without a care."

I laughed again. So different from my point of view. I wondered what it might be like to lust after my husband, to tingle at his touch, to wait expectantly for him to join me in bed. Lindy knew all of this and more, I suspected, with only the fear of another baby to hinder her abandon. I shared that fear as well, but it wasn't balanced by the joy.

Lindy rolled back over to face the riverbank, her eyes scanning the group of children splashing and swimming. Suddenly she pushed herself up on her hands, looking past the children to the other side of the river.

"What's *he* doing here?"

"Who?"

"That bog-trotter."

I looked across and saw him, Tim Judge, big as life, standing on the far bank, his hat tilted forward, hands in his pockets. It gave me a turn to see him so bold. "Oh, him? Isn't he with the work crew?"

"Should be. It's a digging day for sure, but I don't like the look of that one. Seems to be hanging around here a lot."

My heart set up a tattoo in my chest. "You've seen him before?"

She nodded. "My Jeff thinks he's for stealing anything he can lay his hands on. We don't need that. Got enough of that kind already. No need to import it."

I sat up and watched as Tim wended his way among the trees away from the river. "Why do you think he's a thief?"

"They all are. All they know how to do is steal and drink and fight. Jeff says he'll be glad when the canal's dug and they get out of here."

I listened in wonder at her assessment of the canal diggers. To me they seemed a rowdy bunch, but hard working and full of fun. I'd never heard such talk about them before.

"Popish, too," Lindy went on. "First thing you know, they'll be bringing the Holy Father, or whatever they think he is, over here to run things. Fine kettle of mackerel that'd be."

It was a kind of awakening to hear such anti-Irish talk in connection with Tim. I'd known a few Irish back home, mostly stable men and servant girls. They seemed all right to me. Poor as dirt, but nice enough.

"They're all right by themselves, but get two or more of them together and you'll have a brawl and go up against any one of them and the rest'll gang up to defend them to the death. No sense. No manners. And don't get me talking about the drink." Lindy spoke louder now, rising to a sitting position.

"How do you know so much about them?" I asked, curious as to what prompted her tirade.

"What's the matter with you? Haven't you been watching them while they're here? How much do you have to see before you know they're scum? And that one." She thrust her head toward where Tim had disappeared among the trees. "He's the worst of the lot for fighting and lollygagging. Think I'll tell Jeff to report him for laying off work and snooping around decent folks."

I rose and walked barefoot to the edge of the water, wading up to my ankles in the soft, giving gravel. I turned and motioned to Lindy to join me, but she was busy folding her quilt and collecting her chicks around her. I called Robbie and he waddled up, wet pants hanging down to his knees. "Mama, can't we stay?" he asked.

"No, dear. Laird will be awake, and cook has more to do than watch him." I took his hand and led him up the path to the little arched bridge over the canal ditch. Looking down into the raw scar snaking its way along the river, I thought how soon it would be full of water and boats bringing the world to Etna Furnace and maybe taking some of the world away. I let Robbie run on ahead and walked slowly, my mind on my conversation with Lindy. I felt naïve and silly now for entertaining romantic notions about a man I barely knew. I reminded myself, that, happy or not, I was a married woman, the wife of the ironmaster, with a place in the community. There on that picturesque little bridge, I resolved not to let the likes of Timothy Judge turn my head ever again.

Chapter 29

Summer 1831
Adam

Summer was upon us, and the canal was progressing nicely—digging through our property on the way to Williamsburg, Hollidaysburg and beyond. They told us we could have water in it by next year, though I was afraid to let myself believe it. I made my rounds, watching every step of iron production with attention to how it was done and thinking, always thinking about how steps could be saved, operations simplified, work made easier. I monitored the comings and goings of ore, limestone and charcoal, sending wagons here and there, observing the founder as he directed the workers as they fed baskets of ore, stone and charcoal into the mouth of the furnace. I checked the air from the bellows, inspected the molten iron as it poured out into pig-shaped blobs at the base, and watched the trip hammers at the forge pound the iron into bars.

The nighttime was most romantic for me: the soft, red-orange glow against the night sky, the constant rumbling of iron wheels against gravel, the shouts of the workmen intent on their tasks. They worked two twelve-hour shifts, six days a week. We banked the furnace on Saturday nights, but it roared back into production after Sunday midnight, keeping the iron flowing until, after months—nine, sometimes as many as twelve—we had to shut her down for repairs.

We were fortunate if we could go that long without a shutdown. I knew iron furnaces were notoriously plagued by work stoppages from all manner of irregularity. Too much of one element, not enough of another, improper heating, chilling, blockages—any of these could bring production to a halt and require another blowing in. We tried to time the shutdowns to the winter, when travel was hard anyway, but sometimes the fates had other ideas, and floods, accidents, or just plain hot weather dictated our production schedule.

One morning as I stood in the charging house watching fillers tote baskets of charcoal, iron ore and flux to the tunnel head atop the stack, my attention was drawn to a youth riding up the road from the river in a holy hurry. I didn't recognize him, but it was a sure guess he had something on his mind as he rode right up the ramp to the charging house. I stepped outside, brushing charcoal soot from my pants.

"Mr. MacPhail?"

"Yes. What is it?"

"I come from Porter Quarry, sir. There's trouble down there. You gotta come."

"What sort of trouble?"

"It's Foreman Evans, sir. He's gone. Disappeared. No explanation. No by your leave. Just gone. No trace. There's them that thinks he's been murdered."

I thanked the lad and invited him to rest by the creek and water his horse. His ride back to Porter could wait while I changed my clothes and saddled my horse to join him. I walked back to the house, some distance farther than the old house had stood from the furnace. Ellie had insisted on leaving the old house as a residence for our manager, and I saw the wisdom in it.

Our new home stood proud in the flat along the river, like a bastion of stone. I imagined it standing there for two hundred years or more, solid, sheltering our descendents, proud founder of a lasting lineage. I seldom let myself think like this, prideful and vaunty, but for the time being at least the iron business was good.

Ellie was sitting on the front porch, looking out over the canal ditch at the river, her a book in her lap. I still felt an emptiness between us that I was sure she shared. I wished it weren't so, but, as my mother used to say, "If wishes were horses, beggars would ride."

"I'm off to Porter Quarry. They tell me Evans has disappeared. Can't fathom it, but that's what they say. I'm going down to see."

"That Mr. Evans they're always complaining about? The mean one?"

"Well, I'm not sure he's mean. Just a hard taskmaster. At any rate, I'll probably not be back until supper. I may even ride on down to Water Street and have dinner at the Inn. Haven't heard any gossip in a long time."

"There's bound to be some if Mr. Evans has really disappeared."

"Yes. Look for me when you see me."

I changed my clothes and walked out to the stable, where I asked Emmet Leeper, our old groom, to saddle a horse for me. "Mrs. MacPhail's little mare will do."

It was taking me quite long to get ready, so I guessed my young messenger was probably getting anxious. It was my habit to walk everywhere about the plantation, to ride only when distance demanded. It kept me in touch with the operations to be seen by the furnace, by the forge, by the smithy, by the store, in and out of my office on the store's second floor. I liked that. Made me feel a part of things.

The ride downstream to Porter Quarry took a little less than an hour. On the way, the youth spouted the theories aloft. "Some say he must've got drunk and fell in the river. They're looking for him to turn up down to Alexandria in a day or so. Some say he just left. Didn't want to work here no more."

I found that idea difficult to hold onto. The man would at least have collected his wages.

The lad continued with his theories. "Tomorrow be payday. Some say he's waylaid the paymaster and made off wi' the money afore they'd got wise to 'im." He glanced sideways at me, testing my reaction to this bit of fable.

"I spoke with the paymaster this morning. The payroll was delivered to Evans's office, safe and sound yesterday afternoon. Besides, it isn't cash, it's scrip, unless the workers requested cash,

144

and few do." I did give some thought to the possibility that Evans had made off with it, but that didn't fit with whatever else I knew about the man.

We rode along in silence, each weighing his own theory, but my judgment was that Mr. Evans had just gone off on some personal business and would turn up soon, probably before I got there. I was wrong.

In the quarry yard we tied up our horses outside the foreman's shanty. I went in and looked the place over. Nothing seemed amiss. The payroll was locked in the safe, untouched, the desk awash in papers, mostly orders and invoices. The calendar on the wall had notes scrawled on the days of the week indicating deadlines and shipments.

A group of men greeted me as I emerged from the shanty, each anxious to tell his own version of events. "Ain't nobody saw him since yesterday noon," one of them assured me.

"We got no i-dee where he went," chimed another. "No i-dee, but we're damn thankful."

"No more of that," I warned. "Keep your venom to yourself. We'll have to investigate further. Anyone been to his house?"

"Oh, yeah. No sign of him there. Just some dirty clothes is all."

I searched the group for a familiar face and found one, young Mike Morgan, who'd been fighting with Evans a few years back. "Take me there?" I asked.

Morgan nodded and turned toward the dusty, gray gravel road that led in and out of the quarry. We were quickly joined by Simon Trethaway, falling in step beside us as though he'd been invited. I nodded to him.

"My i-dee is that he met some foul play for the shabby way he treated folk," Trethaway offered.

I ignored the remark, having heard it so many times before, preferring to talk to young Morgan rather than this do-nothing. Indeed, I wondered why he was still employed at all. There was something about Trethaway that made my skin crawl.

"Don't you have work to do this morning?" I asked him. "Am I paying you to crack and load rock, or to gad about making up tales?"

He bristled. "I was just tryin' to offer assistance. Might know a thing or two, is all." He dropped back along the path and stopped, apparently affronted by my reference to his lack of dedication to an honest day's work.

I didn't care if he was affronted or not. I didn't like him and wanted no show of confidence or trust in him in front of young Morgan or anyone else.

Except for the self-appointed theorists and gossip couriers, the quarry operation seemed to be going along as usual. I could hear picks and shovels and shouts, the rumble of wagons loaded with rock. Morgan and I picked our way around huge boulders to the road and followed it past tall oaks, their leaves laden with fine quarry dust.

"What are your thoughts on this, Morgan?"

"Nothing would surprise me. You know how the workers felt about him."

"Some of them, yes, but if there was as much hatred as you seem to think, I should have heard of it."

"Begging your pardon, sir, I let you know a long time since."

I rubbed my chin, thinking this was still probably just an easily explainable event. Not a crisis, to be sure. "Yes, you did, but I thought it was mostly your problem with him, not everyone's."

"Everyone wouldn't have wanted to see him dead, but it only takes one, sir, and if you ask me, that Trethaway you just bullied would be high on the list."

"Really? Why so?"

"Evans had it in for him. They was always at each other over something. I heard Evans was gonna give him the boot along with his pay today. If Trethaway wanted to do him harm, he had plenty of chance."

"You're awfully sure he's met with ill fate."

Mike Morgan nodded. "I see it that way, sir."

We arrived at the small stone cottage, set back from the road by a narrow strip of grass. Our approach was greeted by a big, scruffy-looking dog on guard, barking loud enough to be heard at the quarry. The front door was ajar, I assumed from others looking for Evans that morning. Inside, the single room was in fine disarray, clothing draped and scattered over chairs and the floor, the bed unmade, a chair turned over, a half bottle of whiskey and a dirty glass on the table.

I picked up a shirt from the floor, looked at what might have been blood stains on the front and sleeve, righted the chair, and placed the shirt over the back. I was beginning to wonder if there might be something to this. But beyond the shirt—and the stains could have been something other than blood—berry juice perhaps—there was no evidence of anything having happened. I wandered around the cottage, inspecting everything I could see, but saw nothing amiss. Just an untidy room in need of a cleaning and a dog in need of its master.

"Anybody feed that dog today?" I asked.

"Nah. All's afraid of it. Can't get close. Growls if you look at it."

"Well, find something and put it out for him. He'll eat when we're gone."

Mike Morgan moved to comply. He opened a cupboard and found nothing but a sack of flour, some salt, coffee, and corn meal.

"Where did he take his meals?"

"Made the rounds. Workers' houses. Expected to be treated like a guest. Every night a different place. We all had him at our table."

I frowned at this. "Every night? Never ate at home? Where'd he eat last night?"

"I don't know. We can ask around." He looked away, noticeably uncomfortable.

His discomfort aroused my suspicion. "Leave the dog. He'll catch himself a rabbit. Let's go back to the quarry and see who hosted Evans last night."

"Last meal, more like."

I ignored the dark reference and walked back, my head full of questions. The workers might know something, or not, but it was a sure thing if they did, they weren't about to tell me.

We returned to the shanty and soon drew another gathering. In spite of these interruptions, work continued as usual and the call went out to take cover for a blast. We entered the shanty, followed by a half dozen others, each eager to air his theories. The blast shook the little building half off its foundations and interrupted conversation for a good three or four minutes while we waited for our ears to stop ringing.

"Anyone know where Evans ate last night?" I asked.

"Down to Water Street," someone said. "Saw him ride off on his horse around dusk."

"Yeah. The inn. Went there about once a week. To slake his thirst."

"I thought someone said no one had seen him since yesterday noon."

I looked around at the assemblage, waiting for some explanation.

"That were Jonesy. He don't know what's goin' on. Not right in the head, he is. Don't set no store by what he says." The speaker was a short fellow, hair white with quarry dust, blue eyes looking out through a powdered face.

I saw Simon Trethaway slouching outside in the shadow of a machine shed, watching but definitely avoiding my gaze.

The group all seemed anxious to agree that Evans had gone to Water Street, so I decided to head on down to see what I could gather from the tavern crowd.

As I mounted my horse and turned her nose north, I heard more speculation. "Prob'ly won't never find him. Lots of places to lose a body around here. Could be blasted to bits by now." The speaker was Simon Trethaway, grinning widely until he caught my eye, then turning away. I rode to the inn with uncomfortable thoughts, uneasy with the workers' talk. If, indeed, they had done away with my foreman, how could I rein them in? If they had the power to depose my leaders, what power had I?

I arrived at Water Street in the late afternoon and immediately sought the ear of Matt Blakely. The innkeeper saw everything and kept it to himself unless he knew you well. Fortunately, my operations had increased his business and made him willing to talk.

"Come in here around seven o'clock. Sat over there in the corner, his reg'lar place. Ate and drank hearty and left around ten. Didn't talk to nobody. No games, no girls."

"Not much to go on," I observed.

"Find his horse yet?"

"Not that I know of. The quarrymen are full of theories, but if they actually know anything, I'm not going to get it out of them."

"Looks like they met him on the way home and did the deed. Prob'ly took the horse and sold him."

"Could have, but I'm not convinced he's dead. He might have just gone off or met with an accident or fallen off his horse drunk."

"See anything of him on the way down here?" Matt asked, raising an eyebrow.

"I think we'd better send out a party to search the route. He might be lying in the canal ditch with a broken neck and a lame horse."

"Yeh. You get the quarry workers to do that. They'll find him if he's to be found." There was a cynical edge to Blakely's voice.

I took my place at my customary table by the window, remembering how this room had looked to me that night eight years ago when I sat in the same place talking to old Crissman. How life had changed. Achieving my dream of being an ironmaster brought with it a whole new set of problems. My meal was served, and I ate watching the clientele come and go, eating, drinking, playing cards, discussing the news of the day, which included the story, rumors flying, of my lost foreman.

Geordan Evans was not only gone, he never turned up again. The mystery of his disappearance cast a pall over the operations at Porter Quarry. The workers had hated him and were glad he was gone, but if they knew his fate, they had no intention of revealing it.

After about a month, the constable closed his investigation and put away his files. I was never again to feel completely in control of the Porter operation, haunted as I was by the knowledge that things could happen beyond my control. I promoted one of the senior quarrymen to foreman, and the threats, loose talk and angry accusations stopped, but the speculation over what happened to Geordan Evans never did.

Chapter 30

Fall 1831
Ellie

If I thought just resolving to put Timothy Judge out of my life was all that was required, I was wrong. Even though I stopped going out of my way to watch the dig, and even though I made every effort not to wander away from the house alone, and even though I tried to lose myself in domestic duties, he could still steal into my thoughts and run over my best intentions.

But I was some months away from having seen or heard from Mr. Judge when I was awakened one night by the sound of a violin playing softly in the woods near our house. A light sleeper, I was immediately alert, my ears straining to guess the direction of the serenade. Next to me, Adam slept soundly, unaware of the soft strains wafting in on the night air. The children, too, would not awaken, but I feared, without knowing why, that Mrs. Gwynn might also be a light sleeper. The music continued for perhaps a half hour or more, ebbing and flowing on the breeze, lulling me back to sleep in a tranquil dream.

I awoke the next morning troubled by the memory of the music. Had I dreamed it? If not, who would be about playing a violin alone in the woods on a dark night? Try as I might to dismiss the notion, I couldn't help thinking it might be Tim Judge. The dig had moved on to Williamsburg, and I no longer saw him wandering about in the woods, but somehow his presence lingered. I felt as though he was watching me, contemplating my every move, following me with his eyes. Away from the house, I would feel a presence and turn but see no one. Still, I felt the need for caution lest my watcher know my inner most secrets.

In the kitchen, Mrs. Gwynn had not only heard the violin serenade, she'd concocted a theory to explain the phenomenon. It was the wood nymph of Welsh legend, trying to lure a lover out into the woods for a tryst. I shuddered at the thought of how close to the truth she might be, unable to dispel the idea that Timothy Judge was playing with me. I went about my day, caring for the children, ordering stores, even helping Mrs. Gwynn make blackberry wine. I'd never helped in the kitchen before, but Mrs. Gwynn was always glad for company, and her teaching ways set right with me. We baked an apple crumble for dessert, and I took just a little pride in presenting it to Adam after dinner.

He seemed distracted that day, not awake to my pronouncements, but he managed to wolf down the apple crumble with no trouble at all. We'd reached a satisfactory place in our lives, neither sublime happiness nor hollow dissatisfaction. We maneuvered around each other, neither hostile nor harmonious, a mutually acceptable unspoken accord, devoid of either passion or devotion. I'd begun to suspect that this was how most marriages ended up, but I still felt cheated of the few years of so-called bliss that I imagined others had but could not conjure for Adam and me.

The modest success of the Mt. Etna Iron Company took the edge off my resentment of him. We were, after all, comfortable if not rich, and though I felt no particular affection for my husband, I no longer saw him as my enemy. In fact, that summer we succeeded in planting the seed of another child, whose advent would be in the New Year, and whose gender, would, I hoped, be feminine.

As the summer wore away toward fall, I thought I heard the violin once or twice again, but with the breeze blowing through the trees, I couldn't be sure. Others thought they heard it, too, but no one ventured out to investigate, choosing instead to enjoy the soft, sad music and leave the explanation to the wind. When Mrs. Gwynn persisted in thinking it was her wood nymph, I teased her that it might be a summons to her, as she was the only unattached female in the village.

In the fall, Lindy and I ventured out for some bittersweet, taking her three youngest along to gather black walnuts. I loved the nip of the fall air, clear and biting in its promise of colder weather to come, and the acrid smell of dry leaves, finally letting go in response to receding sap.

"What do you think, Lindy? Will we be riding a canal boat to Hollidaysburg by this time next year?"

"Like as not. They say the ditch is way past Williamsburg almost to Duncansville at the foot of the mountains. There's to be a portage railroad to carry the boats up over the crest. Who ever heard of such a thing?"

"Adam says they'll be able to ship our bars to Pittsburgh as soon as it opens. Won't be long now." I stifled a giggle, just thinking about it. "Look how far we've come in just eight years! Not even eight yet! I'd never have believed it."

Lindy smiled a little ruefully. "I liked it the way it was," she said. "Change is hard for me."

"Oh, but Lindy, this is good change. It brings the world to our doorstep.'"

"I know, but..."

"But what?"

"But I'm afraid for these young'uns. My Joel is eighteen already and always talking about going west. Sometimes I wish I could stop time and keep us just the way we are right now. I like us this way."

"Don't you want them to have a better life?"

"My life ain't been so bad. I got all I want. Me and Jeff and seven young'uns. Never lost one. Hope I never do."

"In this day and age, you're lucky to have seven healthy children. Think of those babies up in the Children's Cemetery." I turned my face toward the burial plot on the hillside above the furnace, newly established as a final resting place for workers' children whose young lives could be so easily snuffed out by illness or accident. Hardly a house where tragedy had never visited.

"Oh, I know that. Seen enough birthings to know the chances. Not many families get them all born and raised without losing one or two. Maybe I'm selfish, but seeing them getting close to grown gives me a turn."

I couldn't quite put myself in Lindy's place. My boys were seven and two. I couldn't conceive of them being grown and ready to go out into the world. It seemed like forever away.

"Well, maybe they'll all choose to stay right here. Young folks talk about going off in search of adventure, but they don't all go, and sometimes the ones that go come back."

Suddenly I perceived movement out of the corner of my eye. When I looked, there were just the trees. No one. But a moment later I heard a twig crack and turned to look hard into the woods. I thought I saw the shadow of someone climbing the ridge nearby. Lindy, lost in speculation about the uncertain future, didn't seem to notice. Maybe it was just some of the local boys out snaring rabbits. Still, I felt uneasy. I hadn't seen Timothy Judge since summer, but every time something unexplained happened, I thought of him. Surely he was long gone from Etna. I was just being silly. But I couldn't get him out of my mind.

"We'd best get back," Lindy announced, picking up her basket of bittersweet. "You kids bring the walnuts. We'll have a shelling party this week if you get more. Maybe Friday night."

The children cheered. Any excuse for a party suited them—and their mother. They picked up the basket and ran on ahead, stopping here and there to gather more green-hulled walnuts. I followed behind, picking cockleburs out of my skirt. As we stepped carefully from rock to rock crossing Roaring Run I realized I'd left my bonnet tied to a low hanging branch.

"Lindy! You go on ahead. I left my bonnet. I'll go back and get it."

"I'll wait here," she replied.

I stepped carefully back over the rocks and sprinted up the path we'd just come down. When I arrived at the clearing, my bonnet was still hanging from the limb, floating gracefully in the autumn breeze. I rushed up and picked it off the tree, and as I was putting it on, a piece of paper fluttered to the ground. I stopped and picked it up, curious. How did that get in my bonnet? Had Adam put it there without my notice? I unfolded the paper and read:

Love Thee, Dearest? Love thee?

Love thee, dearest? Love thee?
Yes. By yonder star I swear,
Which through tears above thee
Shines so sadly fair;
Though often dim
With tears, like him,
Like him my truth will shine,
And—Love thee dearest, love thee?
Yes, till death I'm thine.
Leave thee, dearest? Leave thee?
No, that star is not more true;
When my vows deceive thee,
He will wander too,
Adored of night,
My veil his light,
And death shall darken mine
But—leave thee dearest? Leave thee?
No, till Death, I'm thine.

~ Thomas Moore

I read, then looked around to see who was near, but only the breeze rustled the last of the leaves, and I stood alone. Shivering, I pulled my shawl about me and tied my bonnet under my chin. Who? Who indeed? Then far away, along the river I heard it again. The mournful, sad strains of a violin.

I hurried back down the path, hoping to reassemble myself before rejoining Lindy. But, to my relief, she and her brood had gone before, giving me time to calm my fevered head. I stepped out of the woodland path onto the gravel road that led past the furnace and the smithy to the mill and on toward the village. As I passed the mill I waved to Lindy, sorting black walnuts with her children in the yard.

"Here, want some of this bittersweet?" she called.

"Oh, yes. I almost forgot." I stepped under the huge sycamore that sheltered their cottage and picked my share from the basket.

"Got your bonnet, I see. You look flushed. You all right?"

"Oh, I'm fine. Just rushing to try to catch up."

I made my excuses and continued on my way home. The poem burned in my dress pocket. I took it out and read it again as I walked. It had to be Timothy Judge. And the violin, too. What *was* he about?

I arrived back in the village in time to gather the boys from the collier's wife and herd them home with a promise of pumpkin pie from Mrs. Gwynn.

"Pumpkin!" cried Robbie. "My favorite!"

"My faborite, too!" added Laird.

Chapter 31

November 1832
Adam

By the end of this year we were producing about six hundred tons of iron annually, and the store was selling castings as fast as the forge could mould them. The canal was fast approaching, and my fortunes could only grow with that, so I wrote to my father-in-law to inform him that I would pay off my final debt to him and the other investors within another year. Mr. Bratton's response was to ask after Ellie and the children—a third, Alyssa, had joined us in the early spring. The Brattons had never met their grandchildren. Except for brief letters announcing their births, Elinor chose not to keep her parents close.

The canal was set to open in November, with plans made for a gala celebration on the twenty-eighth. We waited all day in impatient anticipation for the first packet boat to arrive at Mt. Etna from Huntingdon on its way to Hollidaysburg, peopled by a number of canal officials and ladies and gentlemen of note. For us, it was a day of wonder. I don't think I ever really believed that a canal would materialize out of the years of political maneuvering—hoped, but didn't really believe—but here it was. It meant unprecedented prosperity for Etna Furnace. I had to smile at that, remembering the tall, skinny awkward youth who had had the audacity to believe he could make this operation work. The past nine years had tested my mettle, what with the inevitable ups and downs of the iron business, but I now felt like a seasoned veteran, able to handle whatever the fates had in store.

For Elinor, the canal meant another step toward bringing civilization to our doorstep. She didn't speak so much of Berks County any more. Huntingdon County was becoming as sophisticated and cosmopolitan as anywhere else, and Elinor, while she couldn't bring herself to acknowledge that fact, was still, I was sure, inwardly pleased with our progress.

The day of the canal opening dawned cold and gray with a hint of snow in the air. Not to be discouraged, we spent the day in busy preparation, hanging bunting across the front porch, setting out tables for an evening feast, and hailing our workers as they enjoyed the holiday. Groups of young boys ran back and forth along the towpath, each vowing to be first to spot the packet boat as it rounded the bend a quarter mile downstream. Late in the day some even ran back along the towpath as far as Fox Run to be positioned to race along beside the boat and dodge the prods of the mule drivers. It was a day-long party with food and drink aplenty, which induced one or two vigorous or perhaps inebriated young men to jump into the cold waters of the canal in celebration. It was only about four feet deep, so not terribly dangerous, just cold. Our children, Robbie, now eight years old, and Laird, three, watched the party from the porch, excitement in their eyes. Baby Alyssa would not remember this day, but she would be told about it so often she'd think she did.

"Can't me and Laird ride the packet to Williamsburg with you?" Robbie begged his mother.

"No, dear. It will be too late for either of you to stay up. We'll take a ride on one of the later boats and go to Williamsburg for a day. Perhaps we can do our Christmas shopping there next week."

Robbie showed his disappointment in downcast eyes and a decided pout.

"Don't worry, Wobbie. We'll get to go." As usual Laird strove to pacify his older brother.

Near dinnertime Ellie and I took a walk around the plantation, greeting our workers, passing the time, and handing out small commemorative coins stamped with the date and the image of a canal boat. The children grasped these with enthusiasm, competing with one another to collect the most.

"Did you ever think we would have come this far in nine years?" I asked Elinor as we walked.

"No. I must admit I had no faith whatsoever in this whole endeavor." She smiled, holding baby Alyssa close against the gusts of November wind. "My father would be proud of his keen foresight." The touch of irony in her voice wasn't lost on me. "Certainly, it could have been worse."

Encouraged by her words, I bent down to look into her eyes. "You really mean that?" I asked.

"Yes, I do. At the time I couldn't see a future at all for either of us, but it's turned out not to be as bad as I expected. Maybe I'm just getting used to it, but I don't hate it here anymore."

For the first time in our marriage, I felt a tiny spark of hope. We did not live at odds with one another, but ours was a marriage of acceptance, at best. I still wondered if the time would ever come when she'd look upon our union with not only acceptance, but love.

Along the path to the furnace near the boat landing below the mill we met Jeff and Lindy Baker, their seven children, scrubbed and polished, trailing after them. Joel was as tall as Jeff now, with Emily looking quite comely as a seventeen-year-old. Phoebe, too, was blossoming into a beauty, giving their mother pause to think that these three at least were hovering on the edge of the nest, ready to fly at the least temptation.

"Your brood is about to test some wings, Lindy," I said.

"Aye, don't remind me. Every day I see the signs."

"Better hold on tight to Em. I think she's taken with that young man."

The company turned to see Emily smiling shyly at a tall, slender, blond youth standing at a distance near the edge of the wood, leaning on his rifle.

"Who is he?" Ellie asked, craning her neck to get a better look around Jeff.

"Don't you recognize him?" Lindy asked. "Lem Trethaway." Her scowl left no question as to her opinion of the young man, but Emily was already moving away from the group, intent upon a liaison.

"Trethaway?' Ellie asked. "Simon Trethaway's boy? I thought they were long gone from here."

"No such luck," Jeff Baker told her. "They never went far, but we're sure to hear a lot more from them in the future. Seems Simon's father died and left the land on Tussey Mountain to his oldest surviving son. That'd be Simon."

Rubbing my chin, I frowned. "How'd Simon get to be the oldest surviving son? He had at least two older brothers."

"Both died young, so I hear. One in a hunting accident and the other got killed when a tree he was cutting down fell on him."

I shook my head, frowning even more. "Sounds like Simon did all right for himself."

"How fortuitous," Ellie added, rolling her eyes.

As we spoke, who should appear, poling a boat across from the other side of the river, but Simon Trethaway himself, accompanied by his wife, both of them decked out in fashionable new clothes. They reached the shore and climbed out, careful not to soil their unaccustomed finery. As they moved up the bank to where we stood, Trethaway offered his hand and led his wife up to the track, a gesture of elaborate and deliberate gallantry, designed to impress. I hadn't seen him since that day some time ago when Geordan Evans disappeared down at Porter Quarry. Now, out of politeness, I smiled and offered my hand, but Trethaway ignored it and did a little strut.

"Don't go trying to be all nice, MacPhail. I ain't fergot how you run me off back in the day. Got me some land and a new job, so I won't be needin' no how-de-do from you."

"I heard of your good fortune. I hope it turns out well for you. What sort of job will you be doing?"

"Lock tender on the canal. It'll be up to me to get them boats where they goin'."

Obviously proud of his newfound respectability, Simon Trethaway walked along the canal bank with an air of importance, his buxom wife on his arm, decked out in ribbons and ruffles, smiling a gap-toothed smile. We watched him swagger and strut, round-shouldered, hail-fellow-well-met, as though he'd arrived at his destiny, intent on relishing his status as landowner and canal authority.

I cringed at his antics but pushed him out of my mind. No need to let the likes of him get into my head on so fine a day. Besides, there was nothing to be done but accept his situation, however he'd acquired it. I had designs on some of that land across the river. The ore deposits alone would keep my furnace busy for years, to say nothing of the timber, which years of cutting had sadly diminished on our side of the river. But I doubted any negotiations with Trethaway would end in my favor, so I put the matter aside for the present.

Now I turned to Elinor, noting her eyes on the backs of the retreating couple. Her distaste showed as she reached for Lindy's hand. "Don't worry about Em, Lindy. It's just a young crush. It'll pass."

Lindy shook her head. "No. She's the same age I was when Jeff Baker turned *my* head. I know the signs. She's already gone."

Elinor frowned and walked on, her head down, lost in thought. I noted her distress at the realization that children grow up much faster than you expect, and, once they do, there's little you can do to deter them from their chosen course. She looked around for Robbie, who'd scurried off with a group of boys to drop maple leaf boats off the canal bank and run along shouting bets and boasts on whose would get to the lock gate first.

We'd butchered a hog for the canal opening, and my collier, Mr. Corbin, tended the roasting over an open pit. The warmth from the coals and the aroma of roast pork welcomed us as we gathered for supper at long tables arranged on the lawn to accommodate the crowd. The ladies of the village had prepared so many dishes for the table, it was impossible to taste all of them. After dinner with the whole village, including more distant neighbors and some uninvited guests, we retired to our front porch to await the packet boat. With all the excitement of the day, both Alyssa and Laird were ready for bed, so Ellie tended to them while I watched Robbie climb the porch railing, swing out and jump to the ground, climb back over and do it again. Suddenly a shout arose from the canal bank.

"Here she comes!"

With that all citizens of the village gathered on the canal bank, yelling and cheering as the boat made its way slowly around the bend in the darkness, light showing from its windows and torches burning aloft. Men and women sat on chairs on the roof of the passengers' quarters, bundled under thick robes, smiling and waving. As the vessel approached its canon roared, answered by a salute from the guns of our local populace, who'd formed a ragged line along the canal bank. The cheering was accompanied by a pieced-together band: drum, fife and trumpet, giving out with the improvised strains of Yankee Doodle.

Elinor joined me and we walked to the bank where the boat was drawn up for us to board. We climbed to our chairs atop the cabin, covered our laps with woolen robes, and felt the wonder of transportation beneath our feet. The ride was long with the slow movement through the locks, but the awesome technology held us in rapt attention.

Along the way, country people had gathered despite the cold and darkness, awaiting the marvel, cheering endlessly as we passed. It was indeed a day of joy and fellowship such as comes along only once in a lifetime. At Cove Forge, near Williamsburg, we were joined by Noah David, wearing a black top hat and cutaway coat in the latest style, with a strikingly beautiful young woman on his arm. Elinor gave him an appraising glance and whispered that she hadn't seen such a dandy since leaving Berks County. I smiled at her willingness to acknowledge our progress.

Once the boat reached Williamsburg, the party was in full swing. The community band was out in force, making our little effort at Mt. Etna look almost piteous. The canon boomed and the veterans of the War of 1812, assembled for the occasion, responded with a volley of their own. There was music and dancing, food and drink in the square long into the night, and Elinor and I stayed until almost dawn, milling among the crowd, greeting friends.

The dancing and celebration kept on until the sky lightened with the promise of the new day with an accomplished Irish fiddler playing rounds and lively Irish jigs to the accompaniment of a piano that'd been brought out to the street for the occasion. The fiddler seemed entranced as he played, faster and more melodious as the night progressed and the people danced and called for more. A handsome lad, his eyes flashed in merriment as he capered around the square, challenging every lady to dance. One by one they came, drawn by the joyful sound, dancing, looking into his eyes as he played them away.

We stood with Noah David and his new, young wife at the edge of the festivities, but the fiddler would allow no one to abstain, and he danced right up to our group and fixed his eyes on Elinor. We all clapped to the music and shouted encouragement to Ellie to dance, and dance she did, with a vigor and sense of rhythm I'd never seen in her. She picked up her skirts and danced a sprightly jig, moving to the music, her eyes bound to the eyes of the fiddler.

A sight to behold, this talented young man using his music to excite, then soothe, then romance. As the night drew on toward morning, he changed the tempo to a soft, sad song, wafting through the night air, lifting the heart and soothing the soul. It sounded vaguely familiar to me. I couldn't tell where I'd heard such pining beauty, but I knew I had. Somewhere.

Chapter 32

December 1832
Ellie

Timothy Judge playing his violin (the locals called it his fiddle) at the canal opening celebration unnerved me completely. Up until the moment we reached Williamsburg the day had been joyful and full of promise for all. But seeing Tim playing in the town square, relishing his role as the center of all attention, the recipient of praise from all quarters, discomposed me in the extreme. I tried not to stand too close, tried not to meet his eyes, but as the night wore on and his attentions more insistent, I felt my resolve eroding.

I think he might have been drinking, he was so enraptured, caught up in his music as though possessed. But when our eyes met, I saw excitement, captivation, spellbinding seduction smiling back at me, inviting me to dance, daring me to follow. So nettled was I by his brashness, I moved to the rear of the crowd and tried to take up conversation with a woman I recognized but hardly knew. Not to be deterred, Tim wound his way, playing and laughing with the crowd, to where Adam and I stood. I could not keep clear of him; he held the gathering enthralled, and with the help of ample quantities of whiskey flowing from every tap, no one but I was aware of his insistent fixation on me. As the night waned, I found resistance more elusive, and when he came close, try as I might, I was seduced again and again by his eyes until I felt helpless to struggle against him, carried away by the insistent, pulsing rhythm.

Finally, when his relentlessness would no longer be denied, I gave in, stepped forward and danced, hoping to satisfy his thirst and settle my nerves. He never touched me, playing his violin all the while, a fast moving reel spilling through the square as he led me hither and yon, unable to do aught but dance, our eyes fastened in secret magnetism. People roared and clapped the rhythm as I spun and whirled, my breath coming in short gasps until, exhausted, I fell to the sideline and Tim swung away to tempt another with his magic.

Having given way, at least in my mind, to wanton lust, I wanted now only to be alone, to lie down and sleep, to linger no longer in the public eye. I turned to Adam, who was quite taken with my performance, and asked that we retire to the home of our friends, the Neffs, whose house at the edge of the Big Spring was opened to accommodate overflow from the town's only hotel.

We excused ourselves from the Davids, walked up an almost deserted High Street to the Big Spring, which lay sparkling in the dawn's early rays, and crossed the bridge to the Neff mansion at its edge. Both of us tired and in need of rest, we spoke little as we undressed and slipped into the bed so neatly turned down for us. But I lay awake long after Adam's even breathing told me he was asleep, my heartbeat slowing as long as I kept thoughts of Tim Judge at bay but quickening as the breeze brought the sound of the violin wafting up from the square.

Chapter 33

December 1832
Ellie

Upon our return home the next day, I pushed all thought of Timothy Judge from my mind, determined to lose myself in domestic pursuits. I enlisted the help of two of the iron workers' daughters to give the house a good cleaning for the holidays to come. We undressed all the beds and hung the feather ticks out to air while we dusted and swept and scrubbed the whole house. All the while I disciplined myself not to think of the events of the canal opening, even though I couldn't keep myself from stopping to watch every time a canal boat passed our front lawn. The novelty would wear off soon enough. For now it was great entertainment.

True to my promise to Robbie, I arranged to take the two boys to Williamsburg a week later to visit the shops on Front and High Streets, where, to my dismay, as we disembarked from the packet boat, Tim Judge, stripped down to his shirt, wet with sweat, even on a cold early December day, unloaded freight at the dock. Intent on his work, he seemed not to notice me, so I swept past him, turning my head to the side in hope of not being recognized, and indeed thought I was successful until I heard that Irish brogue whisper my name.

"Ellie."

I turned and smiled. "Why, Mr. Judge. How nice to see you again. I thought you'd be long gone from Williamsburg with the canal finished."

"Aye, you would. But I like it here. Decided to stay and cast me lot along the Juniata."

This was disconcerting news, for if Tim Judge lived anywhere close, it was cause for my discomfort. I needed distance between us, space to help strengthen my resolve.

"Did you enjoy your dance, now, Mrs. MacPhail?"

"Oh, yes. It was quite a nice evening, didn't you think?"

"Aye. I did indeed."

His eyes met mine, locked until I turned away to tend to Laird's crooked buttoned jacket.

"Will ye be comin' to town often now, Mrs. MacPhail?"

"I don't think so, Mr. Judge. The boats will bring much of what we need, and my husband can carry a list when he comes to town."

"I see, Mrs. MacPhail. I was wondering, do ye still go out walking among the bittersweet in the fall?"

"I've already got mine for this year, so no." I felt my heart pounding in my chest, wondered if he could hear it, too.

"Ye'll be about gathering holly and trailing pine for Christmas, I'd warrant. There's a fine stand of holly on the hill above yer house. I've seen it. T'would be a great place to gather some, come Saturday morning."

"I wouldn't know about that, Mr. Judge. I'm terribly busy with my household chores."

Robbie and Laird fidgeted and teased, impatient to get to the shops, so, grateful for the excuse, I took leave of Tim and we trooped up the street to Walker's Store. As I shopped I tried to concentrate on the boys and their Christmas gifts for their father. Robbie selected a cast iron horse and wagon, which pleased him mightily, while Laird wanted to buy Adam a handful of cigars. I took motherly note of the contrast between the two, one still very attentive to his own wants and needs, the other ever considerate of what would please someone else.

Upon leaving the store we wandered down the street to the shop of Mrs. Patterson, purveyor of yarns, cloth, and notions for dressmaking. I took more than reasonable time making my selections in hope of avoiding another meeting with Mr. Judge. I selected a soft fabric, maroon wool, for my Christmas dress, and added yarn in a rich shade of gray for a wrap. That should keep me busy through the coming days.

When it was time for the next boat to leave, I gathered the boys close and enlisted each of them to carry a parcel. Rosy-cheeked and exhilarated with the shopping expedition, they munched cinnamon buns as we watched for the packet boat. Tim Judge must have been occupied elsewhere, for he did not appear as we waited on a bench beside the landing. My relief at that set of circumstances lasted all the way home.

Chapter 34

December 1832
Ellie

Saturday morning. Saturday morning. It was all I thought about for the rest of the week. I wouldn't go, of course, but thinking about it was harmless enough. All the while I pondered what might happen if I did, wondered how I could ever resist Tim Judge's advances, keep my wits about me, preserve my good name. By Friday all the housecleaning had been done and Mrs. Gwynn was half finished with her holiday baking, done almost entirely with Adam in mind.

"Mister likes the snails," she'd say, referring to a walnut cookie she prided herself on, "and last year I could hardly bake enough kringle to keep him happy."

"That's because you'd bake another kringle as soon as he finished the first. You're going to make him fat."

"Time was when he could have used it, but now he'd better go easy."

It was true that Adam had filled out nicely in the years we'd been at Etna. Gone from lanky and awkward to solid and mature, grown a beard, and looked the role of the ironmaster, though I still took issue with his wardrobe. Try as I might, I could not persuade him away from the canvas pants and loose linen shirt of a common worker as opposed to the appropriate attire for an ironmaster. I took every opportunity to call his attention to Noah David's style and taste, but to no avail. Adam owned but one suit of dress clothes, black broadcloth, which sufficed for church and all other social occasions. Otherwise, he clung to what he was used to, the common attire of a working man.

As much as I dreaded it, looked forward to it, feared it, anticipated it, Saturday morning came soon enough, and with it a cold wind and a snow squall. With every intention of staying in the house, I busied myself with cutting out the new Christmas dress. But by ten o'clock, I could resist no longer, telling myself that I would just go out and turn Mr. Judge away to keep him from freezing to death in the hope of my appearing. I took my warm cloak from a peg and announced to Mrs. Gwynn that I was going out to fetch some holly and wouldn't be long. She looked out the window at the blowing snow with a raised eyebrow, but I pretended not to notice and let myself out the back door.

In the cold, gray morning I felt a haunting loneliness and deep longing for comfort as I trudged along up the hillside to the holly trees which stood in a little grove near the top, just under the brow of the hill. Observing the shining leaves and red berries from afar, I felt a surge of Christmas spirit, associated with children and carols and merriment. I even hoped, momentarily, that Tim Judge might have changed his mind and would fail to appear. But no. He stepped out from under the boughs of the tree as I approached, his head cocked to the side, a smile playing around the corners of his mouth.

"I *thought* ye'd want some holly. Here, I picked some for ye."

I took the holly from his outstretched hand and held it close, in spite of the sharp, pointed leaves. "Why did you come here? Why the music in the woods at night, the poetry, why? Didn't we settle this some time ago? Isn't this the road that leads straight to hell?"

"Aye. It does. I canna tell ye otherwise. But I canna leave it alone. Canna leave you alone."

"But you must. I'm a married woman. I have three children. I can't just give myself over to lust."

"Oh, so it's lust is it? So you feel it, too? It's not just *my* dream?"

"I feel it, too."

He stepped toward me, but I stepped back. As he reached for my wrist, I dropped the holly to the ground. He pulled me to him, wrapping me in his arms. Feelings I hadn't known since Robert Clifton bedded me in our orchard flooded over me, pulling me along with the tide. Before I could wrest myself free of his grasp, Tim kissed me hard on the mouth and I responded with a passion I never expected to feel again, indeed had never felt with Adam.

"Tim, no. No. We mustn't."

"I know, but I can't help meself. I love ye. Have loved ye ever since I came here digging and saw ye on the canal bank, watching. Believe me, I know right from wrong. But I can't get ye out of my mind."

"Then you must move on. You can't stay here with this hanging between us. You said yourself..."

"I had to come. Can't stand being without ye. It'll be such a long winter. I must have ye, Ellie. There has to be a way. Come away with me. We could go west and they'd never find us."

The word west brought me to my senses. West. The promised land. The start-over place. The solution to everyone's problems. The hoped-for end of everyone's dreams.

"No, Tim. No. What about my children? Do you think I could ever leave them? How could I? I may not be in love with my husband, but he's good to me and a good father. What better could you offer me?"

"Love! My God, woman, can't ye see? Your life is passing by without love in it. Love is all there is, really."

"Maybe, when it only involves you and your beloved, but there is more at stake here."

"Aye. I know. But there has to be a way for us. I know ye love me. I can feel it in your touch, see it in your eyes. Ye want me as bad as I want you. Oh, Ellie, come with me. Come with me."

I wrested free and stood a few feet away, my heart beating fast, my brain clouded by his pleading. I knew the truth of it. Knew one of us must be strong enough to resist, but my will was weakening, standing there in the cold snowy woods, wanting nothing more than to be folded into his loving arms again. Tim smiled an endearing, lopsided smile, and reached for my hand.

Now he kissed me again, an urgent, searching kiss that grabbed me, pulled me along, made me want to let go of all inhibition and yield. Suddenly a shot rang out in the snow-blown woods, shocking us back to reality. We pulled apart, listening, watching. Nothing. Someone was hunting nearby. Had they seen us? Tim stepped warily away, turned in the direction of the shot, watching the woods with steady eyes. A deer, mortally wounded, stumbled and fell at the crest of the hill about a hundred yards from where we stood. The hunter, seemingly unaware of us, tracked up to it and knelt by its side, took out his knife and slit its throat.

We watched in silence as Lem Trethaway let the animal bleed out onto the snow, then deftly cut open its belly and gutted it. Intent on his task, he didn't look in our direction, but I couldn't dispel the certain knowledge that he'd seen us. I barely knew the youth beyond the fact that he and Emily Baker were sweet on each other, but I knew him as a Trethaway, no recommendation of discretion or integrity.

In spite of every effort to control my fear, I began to shake, standing there in the snow. Tim sheltered me with his arm and led me silently back under the Holly tree, where we could still see Lem but he couldn't see us. Sobered by this turn of events, unsure what should come next, but ever diligent to my responsibilities, I whispered that I shouldn't go home without the holly. Tim shook his head.

After some time, standing close under the tree, we ventured out and started down the steep hillside, putting as much space as possible between ourselves and the hunter before we stopped, still under the cover of the woods and said our good-byes.

"Please don't come back, Tim. Don't stay here. Be gone before we bring disaster down upon us."

"I can't promise. If that lout saw us and talks, ye may have need of me yet. I'll do me best to leave ye alone, but God help me, I love ye." The snow matted his hair, making him look young and plaintive, like a waif with neither home nor hearth.

"Go. Go now. I'll go back for my holly and see if he's gone. Please, Tim. Go now."

"One last kiss."

We looked around and saw no one, so I stepped back into his arms for that last sweet and tender kiss that set me to shaking again and Tim to trying to comfort me, holding me tight once more before releasing me and turning away. I watched him slog downhill through the ever-deepening snow, wet and clinging to his shoulders like a mantle of cotton, wishing beyond hope that I'd never met him.

Chapter 35

1833
Ellie

For the rest of that winter Timothy Judge gave over coming round, playing the violin in the woods at night, and leaving poetry for me to find. That close call with Lem Trethaway scared both of us into discretion. I wondered every time I saw Lem whether he was a witness to our tryst or not, sometimes sure he looked at me with knowing eyes, but when I met his glance, he looked away like the shy boy he mostly appeared to be. I avoided him at every opportunity, intent upon giving him no further reason to betray me if indeed he needed any.

When summer returned, bringing freedom and abandon, Lindy and I continued our berry picking adventures, accompanied by a laughing, yelling, squabbling rabble; her children and mine. The berries were just an excuse to spend an afternoon together and catch up on all the local gossip. Intent on our mission to keep Mrs. Gwynn busy for days producing pies and jams and jellies, we crossed over the river in two rowboats and wandered up the slope of Tussey Mountain, laden with picnic basket and berry pails.

I knew Lem Trethaway lived somewhere nearby in a cabin long abandoned by his father in favor of the lock tender's house, and I chose a wide route to avoid the possibility of running into him. Ever since winter I'd been vigilant to avoid crossing his path. We passed

within a few hundred feet of the rude log cabin where he was said to
live with just his hound and his gun and a whiskey still out back, but
all appeared deserted. I knew Lindy had concerns of her own about
Lem Trethaway, but we passed in silence, each attending to her own
set of fears. When Lindy spoke it was clear she'd been pondering the
attraction between Lem and Emily.

"Wish I could get her away from him," Lindy sighed. "Can't talk
to her, though."

"Oh, Lindy, maybe she'll get tired of him. Girls do, you know."

"Not my Em. She's steady. Lord knows, she sees some good in
him, but I don't. All I see is Trethaway, and Trethaway means
trouble."

We arrived at the berry patch and lent ourselves to the task of
filling our pails to the brim with luscious black raspberries. All four
children, Robbie and Laird with me, and Lindy's three youngest,
Lane, Jared and Jenny, ate berries as fast as they picked them,
enjoying a rare treat, but being of questionable value as help. We did
manage to fill our pails, and once finished with the berry picking we
spread out our quilt on the ground and unloaded the picnic basket.
Mrs. Gwynn had packed an especially good lunch of cold chicken,
cold baked potatoes and bread and jam. We called the children back
from their explorations in the woods and sat them down around the
quilt amid protests of "I'm not hungry," "I hate cold potatoes," and
"Can we go play now?" until Lindy and I cut them loose just to save
our sanity. Relishing relief from childish protestations, I lay on my
back, staring up at the cloudless blue sky when Lindy brought me up
short.

"Remember that Irish canal digger who used to roam about the
woods after the dig had moved on?"

Careful to sound vaguely uninterested, I murmured, "Uhm?"

"You know. The handsome one who used to sing sometimes when
the crew was camped for the night."

The memory of Tim's clear, crisp Irish tenor flooded over me,
made me miss him again. "Oh, that one. Yes. What about him?"

"Oh, nothing. Just talk, that's all."

"What kind of talk?"

"I hear he's still around Williamsburg, loading freight on the canal boats. You'd think he'd be long gone by now."

"I wouldn't know."

"I hear he's quite the lady's man. Anyway, Jeff says he's signed on with Corbin now to cut wood. Must be he's tired of lugging crates and bales."

Suddenly I was annoyed with the flies and the hot sun and the talk. I rose to my feet, called the boys in again and looked to Lindy. "Shall we wrap this up?"

Not quite ready to return to the old routine, Lindy rose reluctantly and stooped to pick up the quilt. "What's got into you?" she asked.

"Nothing. Why?"

"Just seems like you got all huffy when I was talking about that Irishman. What's his name?"

"I wouldn't know his name. Why should I?"

"Humph. Seems like it matters some to you is all. You were fine until he came up."

"I have no idea what you're talking about, Lindy. I just got annoyed with the heat and the flies. Let's go down to the river and soak our feet."

Lindy didn't need a second invitation or any excuse to go swimming. She gathered the berry pails and I followed with the folded quilt and the picnic basket. The children ran ahead, reached the riverbank, and were wading in the clear waters of the Juniata before Lindy and I had cleared the glade.

I sat down in the shade of a big old sycamore and took off my shoes and stockings. Robbie and Laird were already stripped to their waists, pants rolled up, wading and splashing, laughing and shouting. "Mama! Watch this!"

"Mama, make Wobbie quit spwashing."

"Can we swim under the bridge?"

Lindy looked around, determined that we were alone, and proceeded to strip down to her shift. Always shy of any appearance of impropriety, I contented myself with soaking my feet. Not Lindy. She stepped back from the stream, got a running start, and jumped full bore into a deep pool. The children, delighted with her antics, swarmed around her, yelling and splashing like forest nymphs. I sat alone on the river's edge, soaking my feet in the cold water, lost in thoughts of Timothy Judge, disturbed that hearing anything about him gave me such a start. I had to get free of this man before it was too late. Why did he stay around? Why take work even closer to my home? Why not move on? Why, indeed?

Neither hope nor fervent prayer was to spare me the distress of seeing Tim Judge again, for within a week of learning that he'd signed on with Mr. Corbin as a woodsman I found out that he'd taken a room with Mrs. Askey, a widow woman living up the hollow from the furnace. Apparently, Tim was intent on continuing this disastrous course that could lead us nowhere but, in his own words, to hell.

Determined not to yield, I made myself take the long way around when I heard the crews cutting down trees and was more then relieved when their work took them deeper into the forest, where I didn't have to hear the constant clash of ax against trunk. I stayed close to home, never going anywhere alone, giving any gathering of workers a wide berth. Somehow I managed to emerge at the end of the summer with not a single sighting of Mr. Judge. I still thought about him incessantly, but his boldness in taking work right under my husband's nose rankled me. He was too brash, too bold, too resolute. While I struggled to maintain self-restraint, he seemed intent upon placing temptation squarely in my way. One of us would have to yield. One of us.

Chapter 36

1834
Adam

Running an iron works keeps a man occupied day and night. While the making of iron is complicated, dealing with people—workers, overseers, managers, wife, children, neighbors—is even more so. I found myself spending the major part of my time tangled in and pondering how to deal with these day-to-day quandaries. Take Simon Trethaway, for example. Yes, I'd run him off in the early days, and justifiably so, but his emergence as a landowner and wage earner for the canal company put him in a more respectable light, at least in his own mind. He did a passable job as lock tender, kept the boats running on schedule, but that was the extent of his respectability. Still prone to nettle me, he couldn't resist making brash and insulting comments designed to provoke, challenge, and hurt.

I did my best to overlook these attempts to bait me, but it did irritate, all the same. I wanted to approach him about buying some of his land over on Tussey, but I put it off for some time, unwilling to plant the idea that he could hold sway over me. I wanted to try to mend the rift my running him off had caused, but whenever we met he invariably eyed me with suspicion and came at me with remarks designed to cut.

Sometime the second year after the canal opened, I sought to approach him on the matter of timber, always a problem for a furnace which ate up an acre a day—to say nothing of the forge, which devoured almost as much. I didn't think he'd be willing to sell any land unless he was in extreme distress, but ore, timber or quarrying rights might tempt him. I decided to approach him at his house, which proved to be my first mistake. I might have expected a cool reception, but it turned out to be even less cordial than I'd anticipated.

I arrived in the early afternoon at the lock tender's house, a small stone cottage provided by the canal company, already showing signs of seediness from lack of care. I found the porch empty of all but a few chickens and knocked on the doorframe, the door standing wide open. Inside the house was a table littered with dirty dishes, an upturned pot, crusts of bread, and some half-eaten corn cobs. No one answered my knock, so I turned and looked about the yard. Here were more signs of a slovenly lifestyle: a broken down wagon with a missing wheel, a weedy garden, chickens ranging wherever they pleased, leaving their waste on the porch, the steps and the walk.

"Halloo!" I called, hoping to rouse someone from somewhere.

"Halloo, yerself."

The response came from the river bank, where a congregation of Trethaways stood about watching young Jude labor to land a huge carp. Not wanting to interrupt the process, I stood to one side and watched with everyone else. The whole Trethaway family stood ready to offer a full complement of advice and derision as the youth played the fish endlessly in hope of tiring it sufficiently to drag it up on the bank.

"What's he going to do with it?" I asked one of his brothers, the oldest—Luke, I think.

"Feed it to the dogs."

I looked around at the collection of hounds, skinny, lop-eared, and flea-bitten. The Trethaways didn't bother to feed them, just let them wander in search of their own food. It was a wonder there was a live chicken in three counties, except that killing a chicken earned a hound a severe beating, so the penalty made its way into those thick skulls and the chickens were thus spared. Other game provided by the boys, a groundhog here, a possum there, a raccoon on occasion, made up the remainder of their fare. That and whatever table scraps were left after the family had dined. For anything else, the dogs were on their own, and from the looks of them, the pickings were slim.

After a half hour of playing the carp amid a chorus of advice, heckling, and profanity, the boy lifted it from the river, proud of his feat, and threw it into the weeds for the dogs to fight over. The entertainment done, I singled out Simon Trethaway, standing among his four sons, ragged, unshaven, slack-jawed, and shifty eyed, no longer the well-dressed land-owning quasi-gentleman of canal opening day. When his eye met mine, I discerned a hardening and girded myself for the assault.

"What have we here? A gentleman! An ironmaster," he said with exaggerated respect. "To what do we owe the honor of a visit from our esteemed ironmaster?"

"Good day, Trethaway."

"G'day to you, sir. And how can we serve your needs this fine day?"

"A word would do. A word in private, if you please."

"And what if I don't please? What then, Cap'n?"

"Well enough. I can take my business elsewhere." I was intent upon standing my ground, aware that to show any sign of weakness would seal my fate.

"Now, now, Cap'n. Don't take offense. I was just funnin' with ye. What's life worth if we can't have a little fun, eh?"

I looked around at the assembled company of rough-hewn forest louts and decided that this was neither the time nor the place to talk business. I shouldn't have come here myself—should have sent a lackey. "If you wish to hear what I have to say, you can find me at my office in the store building any afternoon at three."

"And why might I want to hear what you have to say, sir, if I may ask."

I shrugged. "You may or may not, as you wish." With that I turned and walked back up the path past the squalid dooryard and on to the towpath, feeling I'd made a point. I made a silent wager with myself that it wouldn't be more than a day before Trethaway appeared in my office.

I was right. The next day, at about ten minutes past three, my clerk entered with the information that Mr. Simon Trethaway awaited in my outer office. Resisting the temptation to keep him waiting, as he would have me, I asked the clerk to show him in.

"Good afternoon, Mr. Trethaway. What can I do for you?" My intent was to keep the interchange formal and businesslike.

"Do fer me? It was you wanted my time, Cap'n. So what's yer business?"

"Oh, yes, that. Well, I was wondering if you were interested in selling the timber rights to, say, a hundred acres or so. Needn't be the best land. I'm talking about the higher ground, up near the crest."

"You be talkin' about the best of me timber."

Disconcerted by his clear grasp of the situation, I nodded. "Maybe not the best, but good timber, yes."

"And good ore, Cap'n. Good ore up there, too."

A level stare passed between us. This was not going to be easy. Much depended on how badly Trethaway needed or wanted money. I wasn't dealing with a dullard here, no matter that his appearance belied that fact.

"Are you of a mind to sell?" I'd thought this over beforehand and felt it best to get on with the negotiations before my adversary had time to adopt some outrageous posture, so I slid a prepared offer across the desk to him.

He shrank from it, giving it wide berth—as though afraid to touch it. "I, ah, ahem, I, ah, would need to share it with my, ah, solicitor, if you will."

It dawned on me like a punch in the gut: the man couldn't read. Like many of the local folk, he hadn't had the benefit of schooling. But I was wary of the advice anyone else might put in his head, afraid that he'd get even bigger ideas about the value of his ore and timber.

"No need, man. Look. It's completely straightforward. I'm offering you twenty-five cents an acre. Twenty five dollars for a hundred acres, and you get to keep the land. Nice tidy sum."

Now his wiliness came to the fore. "Seems to me it be worth more to you than that. You stand to profit by the iron that comes of it."

Never having dealt with him before, I realized I was up against a clever negotiator. Ignorant and illiterate, maybe—but a deal maker, nonetheless. "Make me a counter offer and we'll see if the price is right."

"Tell you what, Cap'n," he said, rising from his chair. "I'll get my solicitor to draw ye up an offer and then we'll talk."

Realizing that this was going to be at least as difficult as I'd anticipated, and probably more so, I rose and waved him off. "Suit yourself. My offer stands as is, but there's plenty more land about."

"Not as close as mine, Cap'n. Those transportation costs will wear ye down. Mark my word." He turned and walked out the door into the afternoon sunshine, a hitch in his step and a sly smile on his lips.

Stepping out on the second floor balcony, I watched him slouch down the track to the boat landing to pole across the river to his lock tender's house, wishing I didn't have to deal with such a lout. It disrupted my day and my disposition to the extent that I gathered my papers and told my clerk to close up for the day. The walk home was short, but it served to soothe my conflicted nerves.

As I happened to pass by the mill on the way home, Jeff Baker hailed me. We walked away from the noise of the stone grinding, the wheel turning, and the run making its mad dash to the river. Jeff looked tired as he pulled out his pipe and lit it up. He crossed one arm over his chest and rested the other elbow on his forearm, pipe to his mouth, obviously concerned about something.

"What's on your mind?" I asked, expecting a business problem— some farmer couldn't pay his tab, or the grinding stone wearing down—something like that.

"Simon Trethaway is what."

"What about him?"

"He's selling whiskey to the furnace men and the colliers. Notice how some of them have been falling off the job lately?"

Not wanting to appear blind to the obvious, I nodded. I hadn't seen anything that concerned me, but then Jeff lived a little closer to the workers than I did. "Where's he getting it?"

"His own still across the river. You know, Lem lives in that cabin over there, tending it. Shows up every Saturday with a new supply and the old man sells it to all comers."

"I see. Like father like son, huh?" A thought flashed through my head and was gone. How our Robbie seemed callous, disregarding other peoples' feelings, always looking for a way to get out of work. Like father like son, indeed. But, then, I didn't know much about this Robert Clifton, whose legacy I was raising. Still, the only thing I knew about him wasn't good.

"That the same one of those boys your Emily is sweet on?"

Jeff drew on his pipe, letting the smoke waft above his head to mingle with the cool clear air. "Yeah. That's him."

"You talk to her about it?"

"Sure. Only she don't hear very well when it comes to Lem."

I winced. "They never do. What about Lindy? Has she tried?"

"Ain't no common ground between them these last months. Lindy flat out despises Lem Trethaway, and there ain't no hiding it. My only hope, and it's a slim one, is that she might listen to you or Mrs. MacPhail. Missus and Em was pretty close when Em was little."

Knowing I'd be inept at talking over a delicate subject with a pretty young woman, I immediately passed on the prospect to my wife. "Sure. Ellie can talk to her. I doubt she'd pay *me* any mind, but she might hear a word or two from Ellie. One thing certain, Ellie has no time for Lem Trethaway."

Jeff nodded, then shook his head. "Girl gets it in her head to fall in love with somebody, ain't much good talking will do."

We stood contemplating life's challenges for a while, I concerned with the selling of whiskey to my workers, Jeff concerned with the impending loss of his daughter. My opposition to the reckless consumption of alcohol was well known. There was no place else to get whiskey except at my store, and the sales there were strictly controlled. My workers were expected to appear at church on Sunday and work on Monday showing no sign of the slightest intemperance. Drunkenness on the job was grounds for immediate dismissal. The idea that Simon Trethaway was producing and selling whiskey to my workers provoked my wrath even more than his failure to bargain on the ore and timber rights.

Sensing my dismay, Jeff tapped his pipe on the heel of his boot and slipped it back into his shirt pocket. "Thought somebody ought to let you know," he said.

I left Jeff to his thoughts and retraced my steps past the mill and the blacksmith shop to my office above the store. I needed to consider this situation carefully. Come up with a plan that would rid me of the nuisance that was Simon Trethaway. I thought the best way to handle him was through a third party—my lawyer, or perhaps the canal company—on the issue of selling whiskey to my workers. In truth, I had no desire to have further negotiations with the man. It was clear he nursed his hurts carefully and was in no hurry to declare a wound healed.

Chapter 37

Spring 1834
Ellie

Spring came late that year. It was cold well into May, giving rise to old wives tales predicting a bountiful harvest. It was neither here nor there to me. I was preoccupied with my family; that and keeping my distance from Timothy Judge. Though I struggled to dismiss him from my mind, he still stole into my thoughts, giving me no peace. One afternoon, to escape my brooding preoccupation, I walked to the mill to see Lindy, who'd stuck close to home through the winter, her hibernation a burden to me.

She greeted me at the door looking like she was near the end of her tether. "I'll be glad to see spring really come," she told me. "The dampness makes my bones ache."

"You need to get up and get out, Lindy. Keep those bones moving."

"Not sure I want to anymore," she replied. "Life ain't what it used to be."

"How's that?"

"Our Em is gone. Gone off with Lem Trethaway last Tuesday to Huntingdon to get married by a Justice of the Peace."

"Oh."

"Oh is right. I talked myself hoarse about how no Trethaway I knew ever amounted to anything, but she couldn't hear it. Kept saying

184

Lem was different. Not like the rest of 'em. I should have kept to myself. Maybe I pushed her into it."

"I doubt that. Truth is, keep an eye on her waistline. She's probably with child already. That's usually what prompts a hurry-up marriage." My thoughts inevitably returned to my parents' home in Berks County and the chagrin my own pregnancy had caused. At least Emily didn't have to deal with the dilemma I had.

Lindy was not to be consoled that day. Motherhood had always suited her so well, better than any of the other responsibilities life had handed her, but now she felt defeated. "I wanted more for Em than this. I wanted her to marry up, not down."

"Marrying up is no guarantee of happiness. Maybe she and Lem will make something of their lives."

Lindy wiped her hands on her apron, head down as though studying the weave. "As if that ain't enough, Joel is still talking about going west. West. West. That's all I hear. What's so bad about right here? Right here, where your family can help you and support you?"

I had my own concerns that day, and going to see Lindy had been my plan to put them aside and focus on more pleasant thoughts, but Lindy's state of mind worked to bring me down even lower. I saw the need to take my leave before I, too, sank deep into the morass.

"I just wanted to dig some irises from in front of the mill. I needed some to fill in around my window wells," I told her.

"Help yourself." She turned away, rummaging through her sewing box, as though intent on her mending.

"Now, now, Lindy. It just seems bad now. You'll get used to it. At least she hasn't gone far."

She picked up a shirt to mend and measured her thread, keeping her face turned away from me. "I know. I'm just being foolish. It'll all come right in the end."

I smiled. "Yes, now that's my old friend talking. It *will* all come right in the end."

I let myself out and went around the corner of the mill, where I hailed Jeff. "Could you find me a shovel? I want to dig up some irises before they bloom."

Jeff nodded and reached for a shovel stored behind the door. "Been talking to Lindy?" he asked.

"Yes. She's not herself today."

"Can't blame her. I've been of a mind to go over there and drag Em back home myself."

"Don't even think about it, Jeff. It'll bring about more trouble than you ever bargained for. I don't know Lem any better than the rest of the clan, but I wouldn't want to provoke the wrath of any of them."

Jeff followed me around to where the irises stood tall against the rugged stone wall of the mill and dug them for me, his face betraying worry.

Sensing that, I did my best to steer him away from the problem at hand. "I should have dug these last fall, but it slipped my mind. I guess they'll catch on all right now."

Jeff didn't seem to hear me, standing back and looking across the river, rubbing the back of his neck. "Kids. Don't know nothing. Won't listen to nothing."

I dropped my irises into a bucket Jeff provided and turned to go home.

"It'll be all right, Jeff. It'll work out."

I picked up the bucket and started on my way, mulling over Lindy's troubles and my own. I was past the mill but not yet to the village when something made me glance up into the woods. There, not thirty feet away stood Tim Judge, grinning like he expected to be welcomed.

"I thought ye'd never look up," he said. "Come to me."

I looked around, satisfied that we were alone and, leaving my bucket of flowers by the path, went reluctantly to his outstretched arms.

"Tim. Tim. We've can't do this. We've got to be strong. I don't know why you keep staying around here. You should leave and give us both some relief."

He smothered my words with a kiss, holding me tight against him. I struggled to loosen his grip, but encircled by his strong arms, I was helpless.

"I know all you say is true, but I can't help meself, Ellie. I can't live wi'out ye. I've tried. God knows I've tried. It's been such a long winter."

"Then leave, Tim. Get yourself away from here before we're both doomed."

He loosened his grip and I stepped away, determined not to be trapped again. "Here," he said, handing me a crumpled piece of paper. "Sir Thomas Moore again. He says it all."

I took the paper and stuffed it into my apron pocket. Turning back to the path, I retrieved my bucket and walked fast—almost ran— toward home. Before I entered by the kitchen door, I stopped in the dim evening light and read the poem.

Quick! We Have But a Second

Quick! We have but a second,
Fill round the cup while you may;
For time, the churl, hath beckon'd,
And we must away, away!
Grasp the pleasure that's flying,
For oh, not Orpheus' strain
Could keep sweet hours from dying,
Or charm them to life again.
Then, quick! We have but a second,
Fill round the cup while you may!
For Time, the churl hath beckon'd,
And we must away, away!

    See the glass, how it flushes,
Like some young swain's lip,
And half meets thine, and blushes
That thou shouldst delay to sip.
Shame, oh shame unto thee,
If ever thou see'st that day,
When a cup or lip shall woo thee,
And turn untouch'd away!

Then, quick! we have but a second,
Fill round, fill round while you may,
For Time, the churl, hath beckon'd,
And we must away, away!

~ *Thomas Moore*

I crushed the paper in my fist, fully intending to burn it in the kitchen stove, but somehow it was still in my apron pocket that night when I undressed. I took it out, read it again and, smoothing the damp paper flat, placed it in a book beneath the first poem.

Chapter 38

Summary 1834
Ellie

For the next three months I did my best to keep busy tending to family and home, ever diligent in my quest to avoid seeing or hearing about Timothy Judge. I turned to Adam to distract me, but he was too preoccupied with business to notice my dispirited state. I tried to lose myself in reading, but inevitably the stories brought Tim to mind. I longed for someone to talk to, someone to listen to my wretched feelings, someone to help me through this dilemma. I was disconnected, adrift, longing for the support of one wiser than I, afraid my resolve would melt and lead to disaster.

Lindy. Yes, Lindy. Even though she was still in the throes of sadness over Em's marriage, I invited her over for tea, not expecting pity or indulgence, but, perhaps, understanding.

"What? Tim Judge? That Irish swell?" Her first reaction was anger and disdain that I should be so foolish as to even entertain such a notion. "What can you be thinking, you, the wife of the ironmaster?"

I sat across from her in our dining room. It was Mrs. Gwynn's day off and the children, mine and Lindy's, were playing in the side yard. I'd made us a cup of tea, and we sat near the window where we could monitor their play, but our conversation held sway.

"I know. I know. I'm a fool to ever have paid him any mind, but I'm so lonely and so unhappy, I don't know what to do."

"Lonely? Unhappy? What have you to be lonely or unhappy about? You've got the best life any of us could imagine. Mr. MacPhail cares for you. You've lovely children, a lovely home, enough money to buy France. What in the world?"

The story came tumbling out, everything from my love affair with Robert Clifton to the sad and loveless marriage arranged by my father for his convenience, not mine. My everlasting resentment about not having any say in the matter. Lindy sat, slacked-jawed, in rapt attention, shaking her head in disbelief.

"My God, Ellie. Why didn't you just refuse?"

"Looking back, I don't know. If I'd refused, I don't know where I'd have gone. My father wouldn't have let me stay and bring shame on him."

"Really? Would he have turned you out?"

"I think so. Thought so then. Anyway, what's done is done. Here we are, ten years later, with three children and a prospering business but no love in my life."

"The very reason why you should be happy with what you have. Most people don't get a quarter of what you've got, and if they had, they'd be forever grateful."

"I think I'd be all right—not happy, mind you, but able to accept things as they are—if it weren't for Tim Judge coming into my life, refusing to be turned away. I love him, Lindy. I can't help myself. I love him. He's everything Adam is not. Music, poetry, romance, things Adam has never thought of."

"How far has this thing gone, Ellie?"

"Not that far. A few kisses and declarations of love. I'm trying to hold him off, but it isn't easy."

Lindy turned away in disgust. "Your trouble is you think being happy is all there is. It isn't. You could be happy as a bird on the wing until reality sets in, and it will. Say what you will, Mr. MacPhail is a good man. He's done right by you, and he doesn't deserve the humiliation that would go with your following your whims. Put Tim Judge out of your mind and get on with your life. Why, I've even a mind to go see him myself and let him know which way the sun sets.

Shame. Shame on both of you for even thinking of acting on your basest urges."

It was the rude awakening I needed. I'd always known what I *should* do, but the emptiness in my life made it easy to give myself over to dreams and fantasy. When the struggle was only inside my own head, it seemed that Tim and I could somehow make our love work. But in the light of the judgment of others I saw the length and breadth of our temptation and its consequences. Talking to Lindy turned me back to the path of righteousness. All that was left was to persuade Tim.

So I made a point of watching where the wood cutting crew was working, when they started, and when they ended their workday. I found reasons to be close to the path to Mrs. Askey's boarding house around quitting time. I made up excuses for being away from home near the dinner hour—Lindy was still in distress and needed me, or I'd gone to the church to practice the piano and lost track of the time. Finally, after several attempts at waylaying Tim Judge, I met him on the path one evening in early September, alone.

His greeting gave me pause as he reached to take me into his arms, shaking my resolve. "Oh, my love, I'm so glad to see ye. It's been so long," he breathed into my hair. "Oh, just to see ye, to hold ye again, makes me weak."

Slowly, patiently, I forced myself to back away, to lay out the perimeters of our relationship, to make sure Tim believed that I could never yield to him. I told him that Lindy knew and would tell Adam if she saw me fall.

"Why did ye go and tell her?" he demanded. "Don't ye know she'll hold it up to ye later? And why lead me along for a couple of years if this was the end ye had in mind?" He pounded his fist against his thigh in exasperation. "Ye've broken my heart, so ye have, and fer what? So ye could run and hide behind the skirts of the miller's wife? Don't ye care for me at all?"

"No, Tim. No. I do care about you, but I know this is impossible, and we've got to move on. I'm sorry I needed help to get through this, but it's the only way."

"Only way? Why? Because yer afraid of going against convention? I told ye we'd go away. Make a new life for ourselves. Oh, Ellie, don't. Don't do this to me."

"I must, Tim! We'd be alone and penniless, trying to start over. And what about my children? Surely we have to consider them."

We argued, wrangled, contradicted one another in contentious struggle for almost an hour before Tim, subdued by reason over passion, stalked away down the path, his shoulders set, his face like stone. I waited another twenty minutes before I turned toward home with a heavy heart. As I sneaked in the kitchen door I could hear my family at the dinner table, playing a word game with Adam. Taking the back stairs, I ascended to our bedroom and lay down on the bed. Sometime later I heard the door open and close. Adam, looking for me.

"So this is where you are! I sent Laird up here to find you, but he must have forgotten what he came for. Why didn't you come down to dinner? I've been worried."

"I'm sorry, Adam. I have a headache. I should have told someone, but I just gave way to it."

He asked no more questions, but turned and let himself out into the hall without a backward glance. I wondered whether he believed me, but, unable to think clearly about anything, I gave myself over to sleep. I would deal with it in the morning.

Chapter 39

Fall 1834
Ellie

Autumn descended upon our valley and I was again engaged in the gathering of apples, black walnuts, bittersweet. Lindy usually came along, but this day she'd been called across the river to Emily's bedside. Her time had come. Lindy being the only midwife around, came by the responsibility for delivering her first grandchild in full stride. I felt a pang of apprehension when I heard that Em was in labor. It seemed early, but I pushed it aside and went about my gathering. Laird was with me, but Robbie, getting more independent by the day, was off with some of the workers' boys doing whatever boys did in the woods in the fall. Once in a while I could hear war whoops off in the distance, telling me they were still at it, whatever it was.

We completed the apple and nut harvest, having filled all the baskets Laird and I could carry, so we set out for home, planning to ask Mrs. Gwynn to make apple butter the next day. Suddenly Laird asked, "Who's that man over there, Mama?"

Turning, I came face to face with Timothy Judge. We hadn't seen one another in the months since our breakup, and my heart caught in my throat when I looked at his face, thinner and somehow gaunt.

"Why, Mr. Judge. How nice to see you again."

"Aye, and you, Mrs. MacPhail. I see ye've a right strong helper with you today."

Laird beamed up at him, proud to be recognized as a right strong helper.

"Yes, this is my son, Laird. How have you been, Mr. Judge?"

Tim's eyes had a distant look, and his smile, when it flashed, lacked the old mischief. "I'm well, Missus. Well enough." His speech was clipped, lifeless.

"I'm happy to hear that. We like to keep our workers healthy." Turning to Laird, I explained, "Mr. Judge works with Mr. Corbin cutting wood."

"Not any more," Tim interrupted. "I've taken me over to Yellow Spring to clerk in the store and care for the horses. I was just back to Mrs. Askey's collecting me things."

"Oh," I replied, surprised, but relieved to know he wasn't in our employ anymore. Yellow Spring wasn't far, but it was in a direction that would give me less risk of seeing him.

"The inn over there needs a handyman, so I'll do that along with the clerking—for me board. The owner is getting along. Says if I work hard for another, oh, say ten years, I might be able to buy it."

"Oh, Mr. Judge, how nice for you."

"Aye, me wife thinks so."

Stunned silence greeted that revelation. I must have stood immobile for almost a minute, my eyes searching his face for any hint of a joke. Laird looked up at me, wondering, I'm sure, what was wrong.

"Wife? I'd no idea you were married, Mr. Judge. When did this happen? Who is she? Do I know her?" I breathed deep, struggling to keep my voice steady, unquavering.

"Aye, you do. Nancy Confer. It *was* a bit sudden. Just a week past. Seems I was disappointed in love, broken hearted, I was. Driven to the drink by blighted hope. Nancy came along at just the right time and made me forget the other. I'm better now."

I couldn't tell if he'd said better or bitter, but it was certain his intent was to hurt me. I tried to shrug it off, feigning delight at his good fortune. "Oh, how fine. Yes, I do know Nancy. A lovely girl. I hope you'll be very happy."

"I'm sure we will, ma'am. She's to help with the cooking and cleaning at the inn. We'll get on well. True love, you know. Nothing like true love."

As though to rescue me, Laird jerked on my sleeve. "Mama, I have to pee!"

I excused us and picked up my basket to move on, but not before Timothy Judge called after us, "I wish ye happiness, Mrs. MacPhail. Happiness and love!"

I walked away, hurt, angry, beside myself with indignation. Silence enveloped us, my son and me, as I struggled to deal with my emotions. Jealousy was one, to be sure, but also humiliation, anguish, shame. Laird trekked along beside me, lugging his basket of black walnuts, silent, but childishly aware of my consternation. Shifting his basket to his other hand, he reached for mine.

"It'll be all right, Mama. You'll feel better soon." The same words I used to comfort him after a bad dream or a scraped knee.

As Laird and I passed by the mill on our way home, Phoebe Baker, Lindy's seventeen-year-old daughter, hailed me. "Mrs. MacPhail, my mama needs you across the river. There's trouble."

I raised my hand to shade my eyes and looked across the river, as though that could tell me anything. "What trouble?" I asked.

"Baby trouble. She sent me to get you, but you weren't home. I waited and waited. I was just going back when I saw you coming."

"What sort of baby trouble?" Strange for Lindy to send for me, with my limited knowledge of birthing.

"It won't come. Emily's about dead from exhaustion, and the baby won't come out. Mama don't know what to do."

"Here," I said, handing her my basket of apples. "Take Laird and these up to the house. I'll go right away."

I broke into a run, tearing down the rocky bank to the river's edge where a skiff waited with a long pole. I stood in the middle of the boat, my skirts dragging in muddy slime, and poled the boat as I'd seen others do, careful not to lean over too far or to dig too deep. I was amazed at my prowess as a navigator, but with no time to indulge in self-praise, I beached the boat and ran up the trail the quarter mile to Lem Trethaway's cabin.

It was a rough place, bark still on the logs, roof shingles mossy and beginning to curl. Smoke came from the chimney, made of sticks and mud, a throwback to the last century, with little comfort to recommend it.

I pushed the door open to a scene I hope to never see again. Lem sat on a crude bench with his back to the wall, his face haggard. On the bed, Emily lay in bloody sheets, her face gray, her eyes blank, her chest barely moving when she breathed. At the foot of the bed, Lindy sat on a three-legged stool, her head on her arms. When she saw me, she dropped her hands, shaking her head in despair.

"Help me, Ellie! I don't know what to do. I've never run into such as this before."

Here was the voice of experience, the voice of wisdom, of assured, rational decisionmaking calling on *me* for help. How was I to know? What was I to do? I took Lindy's hand and led her away from the bedside, sat her down on the only other chair, a rocker Lindy herself had given to Em. Then I moved to the woman, hardly more than a girl, who lay helpless before me. What to do, indeed?

"Lem, go to Williamsburg for the doctor. Hurry, now. He'll know what to do."

Lem looked blank at me, but rose to obey, his eyes returning to his young wife, lying helpless amid the bloody quilts.

"Do you have a horse?" I asked.

He shook his head, pulled on his coat anyway, and waited for further instructions. He stood there like a bumpkin, rooted to the spot, unable to think or bring himself to move.

"Get over to our house and take one of our horses. Go on, now. Get to town." I spoke with such authority that a second later the door opened and closed behind him.

I turned to Lindy, aghast at the state of the room, the bed, and its occupant. "Lindy, let's get her out of that bloody nightgown and change the sheets.

"There ain't no more. I've already changed them twice." Her voice was tired, hopeless.

"Phoebe will be here in a few minutes. We'll send her to my house for clean sheets and a nightgown."

Remembering that Phoebe would have no way to cross the river, I pulled on my cloak and rushed out the door and down the trail to Simon Trethaway's house beside the canal.

"Halloo!" I called. "Halloo, Trethaways!"

Simon's wife, Caroline, stepped into the doorway. "Whatcha want?"

"Send one of your boys up here. We need him. Emily's birthing."

"Whatcha need a boy for that?"

"Just send him!"

The woman disappeared inside the house, and a few minutes later the youngest boy, Jude, emerged, eating a big chunk of cornbread. I marveled at the youth's appetite at a time like this, but was grateful for his strong, young back.

"Go catch up with Lem. Get to the other side and tell Phoebe Baker to go to my house to get clean sheets and nightgowns. Bring her back as quick as you can. Hurry, now."

I returned to the cabin and pulled the stool around to sit by Lindy, reflecting on how little qualified I felt to do anything beyond arranging for clean sheets, which would have nothing whatever to do with the outcome.

"Lindy, is there anything you want of me? I mean, if you direct me, maybe I can help move things along."

Lindy's voice was dull. "Naught. The baby's breach. Coming into the world turned around. I tried and tried to turn it, but nothing worked." She glanced over at her daughter, so pale and wan, lying deathly still. "It's probably dead by now anyway."

"Oh, Lindy, no. It can't be. You wait and see. The doctor will know what to do."

"Near to forty babies I brought into the world, and you'd think I'd be able to save my own grandchild."

I patted her hand. "I'll warm some water and we can wash her. By then the sheets should be here." With no other thought than to pass the time until the doctor arrived, I put the kettle over the fire and looked around for a basin. I removed the bloody sheets and lifted the child bride to the table while her mother turned the quilt on the bed to hide the blood. With the warm water, I bathed Emily's frail, young body, looked around, and found one last clean nightgown and slipped it over her unresisting form. I'd never been this close to death before, and I wondered at how calm and still it was. I could barely tell she was alive, so uncertain that I looked to Lindy more than once for reassurance.

As I lifted her to return her to the bed, Emily let out a sigh, soft and gentle, but final. I knew she'd gone. I looked at Lindy with eyes that couldn't hide the truth. She lowered her head, her shoulders shaking as I lay her child down for the last time. I turned to comfort my friend, feeble though my efforts were. We cried together in the darkening cabin, I for the tragedy of life lost too soon, she for the tragedy only a mother can know.

The funeral was held at the church in Mt. Etna, the body lying in a wooden coffin fashioned by Lem. The child, dead before its mother, lay in the crook of her arm. Both looked at peace, Emily's long, strawberry-blond hair drawn over her breasts, giving a soft resting place for the baby. Lem stood watch over the two of them, dazed, his face showing no emotion. Even though I still feared him, I grieved for his loss. But Lindy, the old sassy, fun-loving Lindy, was gone from us. In her place stood an empty shell, no life, no emotion but grief everlasting.

Chapter 40

Fall 1834
Ellie

Home from the funeral, I tried to drown my own sadness in work, took on the Christmas preparation and the canning of the last of the pumpkin with a heavy heart. I held my own children closer, hoped that any new life would come to us without loss. Watching Lindy and Jeff grieve increased my love for them and made me appreciate all that was mine. I'd had no time to give to my feelings about Tim Judge, but now those feelings receded in the light of true tragedy.

The next week I took the packet boat, alone, to Williamsburg to do some errands, visit my friend Alice Neff, and shop for some household needs. As I stopped in front of my dressmaker's shop, a side door opened and Tim Judge and his new, young wife stepped out. I gasped in recognition.

"Why, Mr. Judge, how nice to see you again."

His eyes registered surprise at seeing me, but he merely nodded. "Mrs. MacPhail."

"Is this your new wife, sir? I'd heard you were married."

He looked away, then back at his wife, disconcerted by my presence. "Yes. Nancy, this is Mrs. MacPhail. Ye remember her—the wife of the ironmaster at Etna Furnace."

The young woman smiled and offered her hand, which I shook warmly. She was a beauty, no doubt about that, her eyes a deep blue, her blond hair peaking out in curls from under her bonnet. She looked up at Tim with love in her eyes, sending a chill all the way through me. With no idea who I was, nor that I, too, was in love with her husband, her greeting was warm and cordial, just as mine was cool and deceitful.

I took my hand away, smiled, nodded to Tim, and stepped around them to my dressmaker's door. I wanted to get away. Farther away than was reasonable, given the circumstances. I wanted to leave Williamsburg, Huntingdon County, the whole state of Pennsylvania. I'd been easily thrown off balance again by Timothy Judge, seeing him, meeting his new wife. And I thought I was past all this. Enough.

Not long after that unpleasant meeting I found myself with child again. Perhaps another girl to even up the sides. My sympathies were with Alyssa, lest she be called upon to adjust to three brothers. The newcomer was due in spring again, and by this time, my fourth pregnancy, I was used to the routine, knew what to expect. Adam, as ever, was pleased at the prospect of another child, always proud of our growing family. Still, we spoke little of intimate things. Most of our conversations involved the furnace, workers' problems, or the neighbors. There was never talk of love, not even at our most intimate moments. Still, with Lindy's critical eye on me, and mindful that there is much in this world weightier than my problems, I tried to be satisfied with what I had. Adam was kind, undemanding and certainly an able provider, and I told myself that Tim's marriage had freed both of us from peril.

Chapter 41

1835–37
Adam

Simon Trethaway continued to harass me, bent on his unwavering course to bring me woe. My efforts at compelling him to stop selling whiskey to my workers came to naught. The canal company sent a man to speak with him, but that warning fell on deaf ears, as did the second and the third. I looked for some legal recourse, but none presented, unless some tragedy were to give us an opening. I'd tried to deal with the situation from my end, ordering the suspension or firing of workers who came to work under the influence—or didn't come at all because of drink. But this policy brought about dissatisfaction among the workers for its inherent unfairness. Simply put, some people could hold their liquor better than others and thus avoid detection, and some people had been drinking for so long, they knew how to conceal it, while others, new to the vice, might be caught and summarily released on the first offense.

So with no other recourse, I wrote another letter to the canal company, demanding this time that Mr. Trethaway be fired. I knew such an action would bring down wrath upon me, but so did too easy access to whiskey. Anyway, my frustration with Trethaway drove me to extremes.

Elinor advised against getting him fired, fearing retaliation. I understood her trepidation, but I couldn't have my operation threatened—or even slowed—because of one man's lack of character.

The canal company took swift action, and within the month Mr. Trethaway was deprived of his home and his livelihood, to say nothing of his short-lived respectability. Now I was in for it. I knew he would keep producing and selling whiskey to all comers, so I put it out that no workers were to cross the river between dusk and dawn, except in company of a work detail, but, of course, enforcement of that edict was almost impossible and I soon had to let it lapse.

Aside from my tribulations with Simon Trethaway, life continued with modest prosperity and, despite the ups and downs of the economy, Etna Furnace produced a respectable profit. Ellie was carrying another child, all of ours were whole and healthy, and I was beginning to look toward the prospect of one of our boys, either Robbie or Laird, growing into the business. At twelve, Robbie showed little interest in iron, preferring instead to think about horses—the faster the better. Laird, on the other hand, even at seven years, followed me everywhere I went, listened to all of my conversations and frequently offered words of child-like wisdom in support.

I felt a need to be fair to Robbie—not show any prejudice toward my own son—but as they grew it became difficult to maintain equilibrium in my relations with them. Never had two brothers been more different in appearance and in temperament. Robbie would always be the choice for handsome, and he could charm the harshest critic into singing his praises. I'd never met his father, but I guessed the child favored him, as I could see little of his mother in appearance or demeanor. But Laird would be the choice for character. Even at a young age he showed grown-up consideration for others and was unfailingly kind and fair, always fair.

Our new baby came toward the end of April, a calm and beautiful girl child whom we named Bethany, followed in a short two years by her brother, John. The children were all fine and healthy, adding to my satisfaction with my lot in life. When John was born I tried to show Elinor my appreciation for this gift, another child, by bringing home a new, young mare, as her little lady, Dancer, was aging.

Besides, the old horse would make a nice, safe riding horse for the children. Ellie's response was puzzling and less than appreciative.

"A horse? What made you think I wanted a horse?"

"I don't know. Dancer is getting old, and..."

"Well, yes, I guess it is needed, but it needn't be mine alone. I have little desire to ride."

I dismissed her testiness as related to her recent confinement, but as the weeks rolled by I saw little progress toward recovery of her normal humor. As in the past, I wondered but did not venture to ask, unready to withstand whatever wrath she might feel free to dispense. Ellie had never lost her spark, or her willingness to call a liar a liar or a drunk a drunk. She continued to refer to her own father as "that Berks County Bastard." Earthy talk for one who, in all other pursuits, presented herself as a lady. For as long as she continued to see her father in this light, I assumed that my stock had risen no higher than his. Ellie could hold a grudge.

Then, one sunny afternoon in June, I was pleased to see her astride Lizbet, the new mare, riding up Pole Cat Hollow toward Yellow Spring. Good to see her out and about, but I wondered at the direction she took. It'd been a long time since she'd seen Lindy. I wondered that she didn't ride over there for a visit with her old friend.

When next I saw her, she came riding back slowly, almost slumped in the saddle, pale and wan, as though the ride had taken away all her energy. She listed to the side, barely holding the reins and I called for the stable boy to catch Lizbet and put her away, and stood by to help my wife to her bed.

"What is it, Ellie? You look worn out. Is something wrong?"

"No, no. I'm all right. I just need to lie down for a while. I rode too far. That's all."

I led her to the kitchen door and called for Phoebe Baker, who'd been enlisted as a housemaid, to help Mrs. MacPhail to her room. Phoebe rushed to her aid, and Elinor leaned on her arm as they proceeded into the hallway and up the wide stairs. I didn't see Ellie again until I retired at eleven o'clock that night. When I entered she was sitting up in bed, reading.

"How are you feeling?" I asked.

"Better now." It was a terse, clipped response.

"What do you think it was that upset you? Something you ate? Or just too much exertion?" I wondered at that because, even though baby John was only four months old, Ellie had always bounced back quickly after giving birth. This time was different.

"What upset me, what always upsets me to the point of distraction, is you."

Taken aback by this sudden attack, I cast about for some injustice, some indiscretion I was guilty of, but could think of none.

"Why, Ellie, I don't understand. What have *I* done?"

"You've done the same as you've always done. Nothing! Nothing to show me affection. Nothing to lighten my load. Nothing but run your damned furnace without a thought for me!"

Now, caught in the quagmire of emotion, I cast about for a refuge from the onslaught I knew was coming. I'd always so neatly avoided it—found some reason to be gone, to be busy. Ellie rarely challenged me directly, preferring to keep me guessing with veiled criticisms and vague references to imagined slights.

"Affection? Show you affection? How does a man do that when his wife keeps an invisible wall between them? Makes him ask, nay beg, for his rights as a husband? I ask you, how?"

It had never occurred to me that Elinor needed me for anything. She'd made her feelings clear at the outset and hadn't given me cause to think they'd changed. Now I was not only dumbfounded, but angered by her cornering me like this.

"If you had anything in your heart but making iron, you'd know my needs. You'd see how lonely I am and how sad. You'd comfort me instead of going about your business as though nothing else on earth mattered."

"I don't understand, Elinor. Once you told me you would never love me, so how do you expect me to care for you?"

"That was then!" She shouted the words and pulled the coverlet up to her shoulders, turning away to the wall.

I stood by the bed in complete bewilderment. What did she want? How to please her? How to make amends for whatever wrongs she conjured against me? It was too much to decipher. My old feelings of inadequacy in dealing with her rose to the surface, and I turned and walked out the door. I slept in the parlor, wrapped up in a cotton quilt borrowed from Mrs. Gwynn, wondering how far I'd come in more than twelve years.

Ellie

It was all a silly venture from the first. I'd been feeling so low since John's birth, I couldn't seem to find joy in anything. Even reading offered no relief from the sadness that enveloped me. The children bothered me with their bickering and squabbling. I'd cut back on my visits to the nursery, preferring to let Phoebe Baker take care of things there. I nursed the baby without pleasure. I hadn't seen anything of Lindy since he was born, and I judged her to be in the same low humor she'd been in since Emily died, to say nothing of Joel's constant talk of moving west. I needed to be lifted up, not pulled farther down.

Now nothing seemed right in my world: no happiness, no joy, nothing to look forward to. Such ill humor led me to thoughts of Timothy Judge, whose path and mine hadn't crossed in more than two years. I didn't even know if he was still clerking at Yellow Spring. Maybe I'd been too hasty in cutting ties with him. What if he still felt something, the same as I? In my desperation, I dreamed that we might somehow grab some happiness before it was too late.

Such a low state of mind nurtures old hurts. My anger at Adam surfaced again, and I felt the need to punish him for his emotional neglect, his never-ending focus on making his damnable iron and nothing else. I returned to thoughts of our first days, full of rancor and bitterness toward all of them; Robert Clifton, my father, my mother, Adam. Once again I gave myself over to rekindling old hurts that, if carefully tended, would surely break out, burst into flame.

So in this distracted state of mind, I ventured out to Yellow Spring to call on Timothy Judge. The new horse was difficult, more than a handful to manage. It took all of my horsewoman's skills to keep her on track, so by the time I arrived, I was disheveled and sweaty.

The store at Yellow Spring served the local trade, the boarders at the hotel, and wayfarers on the toll road. I'd been there so seldom, I didn't know what the inside looked like, so when I entered I made my way toward the back of the store, thinking the counter was there. But it was to the right in the middle of the side wall, and I must have looked a fright wandering around lost. Tim Judge was waiting on a customer and didn't interrupt his business to serve, or even acknowledge, me. I stood there, hot, tired and sweating, on the verge of a swoon, for a full five minutes. When that farmer was finished with his purchases, there came another. Waiting gave me time to consider what I was doing there. What did I expect to happen? Finally, Tim Judge and I were alone in the store, the smell of raw wood, cotton cloth, salted meat, and iron kettles mingling around us.

"Well, what brings ye here, my lady?" Tim smiled a mocking smile. "Are ye lost or found, is it?" He was thinner and looked older than I remembered. His hair hung limp over his brow, and his leather vest showed sweat rings under the arms.

"I... I wanted to talk to you. See how you've been."

"Sure, it's fine, I've been, my lady. Fine indeed. And yerself?"

I hesitated, looking around for who knew what, uncomfortable with my mission. "I'm well. Do you like it here? Working here, I mean."

"It's a living. A man needs to make a living, what with more mouths to feed all the time." He stood back from the counter, arms crossed, watching me.

"More mouths?"

"Four now, my lady. A lovely daughter and a set of twins—boys— and a babe born not a week ago."

"Oh. And your wife? She's well, I trust." Startled and caught up short by this news, I struggled to regain my proper demeanor, remember my station.

"Aye. Well and keeping her beauty. I chose well with that one." Now he stepped up to the counter, hands on the edge, his attitude almost mocking. "Is there anything I can do for ye, ma'am? Ye look tired—almost unraveled. Can I get ye a drink of water?"

"No. No thank you. I must be going. It was nice to see you again. I just thought that maybe..."

"Maybe what?" Tim asked in a tone edged in a jeer. "Ye haven't told me what brings ye here."

"No. No. It was nothing. I must be on my way."

He watched me struggle with embarrassment, his posture almost lordly, his eyes never leaving my face. "Ye had yer chance, my lady. Ye passed. Now it's too late."

I snapped my riding crop against my skirt, turned and hurried outside, untied Lizbet, and tried to mount her without a mounting step. She started to walk away with me hanging onto her mane and the saddle. I held on, dragging my feet in the dust, crying for her to stop. The door to the store opened and Tim Judge stepped out, watching, but not moving to help. I regained my footing, yanked on Lizbet's halter, almost dragged her over to the porch, and mounted from the second step. Tim watched with apparent amusement as I struggled to seat myself.

Mortified beyond embarrassment, I rode off down the road at a clip, full of hatred for I knew not whom. Tim, yes, but Adam, too, for being such a lout of a husband, and for my father again for putting me in this hateful mess. Unable to give voice to my extreme distress, I raged, as well, at the system that bred it. To be subject to such humiliation merely because I was a woman, while the men involved did as they pleased, without a care for me, was the ultimate insult. I arrived back at Etna, my face covered with dust, my clothes sticking to me. I wanted to die.

From my bedroom I asked Phoebe to bring water for a bath. The warm water soothed me somewhat, but, aside from nursing baby John, I kept everyone else at bay for the rest of the day.

By evening I was ready to take Adam to task for what I saw as purposeful neglect. I wanted to yell and swear and throw things. Everyone in my life seemed bent on ignoring me, taking me for granted, using me, humiliating me, directing me. So when he entered our bedroom I unleashed a torrent of hateful, angry words, without caring where they fell or how much they hurt. Adam's reaction was to leave me to my wretched state and sleep downstairs. Damn him.

Chapter 42

Late 1837
Adam

One day life was good, the next life was not so good. When I found myself at the not good stage, I had to admit I liked the good better. Running a furnace was complicated when times were good. When times were bad, it was impossible. 1837 brought a downturn in business that threatened our very livelihood. Orders were down. Prices were down. Costs were up. Workers complained, misbehaved, stirred up trouble, and generally made me and themselves miserable. Inventory piled up, rusting on the canal bank, and nowhere to send it. People and animals needed steady work and purpose, and I seemed able to provide neither. All of a sudden, being the ironmaster weighed heavy on my shoulders.

It was a difficult state, accustomed as I was to at least modest success. The question was, shall this situation pass or is the iron industry doomed? Demand for everything had fallen off, as though the whole country were dying on the vine, while English imports sold unabated. Why couldn't people see the value of Juniata Iron? Why didn't congress place a higher tariff on English imports? Why, indeed? I tried to maintain good humor, but my fears managed to get the best of me, especially when confronted by the likes of Simon Trethaway. Though long ago fired as lock keeper, he still manufactured whiskey aplenty and, try as I might, I couldn't find a way to stop him from selling it to my workers. Now, when times were hard, his business was booming. Men drink when in despair.

Trethaway had moved his family to a new cabin farther up the mountain from the river and, while they didn't mingle much with the local folk except to sell them whiskey, they seemed to support themselves well with hunting and keeping a garden in addition to the still. Young Lem continued to live a bachelor's life in his cabin across the river from the village, minding his own business and causing no concern, but he didn't sell whiskey anymore. His brothers took care of that trade.

One December morning, a few days before Christmas, I was riding to Cove Forge to talk things over with Noah David when I encountered Simon Trethaway and his youngest son, Jude, on the track, driving what looked to be a new wagon. I nodded and tipped my hat in polite but reserved recognition, determined not to engage in conversation.

"What, ho, neighbor MacPhail." Trethaway gave me a put-on jovial greeting.

"Good day, Trethaway."

"Off to town, are ye?"

"Only to Cove Forge."

He maneuvered his horses to block my way. Stuck between the horses and spiky apple trees overgrowing a fence, I hesitated, not wanting to urge my mount into the trees.

"Things be not so good in the iron business now, eh?"

"Things could be better."

"Aye, they could, so I hear. But my business, now, my business is boomin'."

I turned my horse's head to try to reverse direction, but Trethaway urged his team alongside, closing any escape route.

I rose in the saddle, looking past the wagon and over the driver's head. "If you don't mind, I've business at Cove Forge."

"Don't mind a bit, Cap'n. Yer free to go as ye wish. Just want a minute of yer time is all."

"For what purpose?" Irritability showed in my voice.

"Why to cetch ye up on the news of the neighborhood, Cap'n. Since ye were so quick to deprive me of my livelihood as a lock tender, I'm thinkin' to make yore life a bit hard in return. Sold my ore rights to Colbert at Springfield Furnace."

I swallowed hard, trying to maintain my equilibrium in the face of this deliberate provocation. "Well, t'was your right."

"Aye. You bet it was. And I'm bound to keep selling whiskey, too. Can't nobody stop me. Just thought you'd want to know."

"Yes, well, it may seem convenient for you now, but one never knows how things can change."

"Is that a promise, now, or a threat? Don't push me, MacPhail. Some as has, has paid the price. I ain't one to fergit a grudge. Talk to that there Evans fella from Porter Quarry." He squinted at me, his face full of venom. "If ye can find him, that is." He spat his tobacco juice in my direction, landing a splat on my boot. "Mind me, now, MacPhail. Ye'll be lucky to come out of this panic with the pants to cover yer ass!"

He cracked the reins over the horses' rumps and moved ahead, clearing the way for me to go. I dug my heels into my horse's side, nudging him into a slow walk, and as the wagon passed me I noticed the boy, Jude, peeking out over tailgate. Thin and scrawny, he looked like he could use a good bath and some hearty soup. Apparently, prosperity wasn't accompanied by cleanliness in the Trethaway household. I nodded to the boy despite my outrage at his father, and he turned away without responding. I wondered how he saw the old man—whether he was yet capable of critical appraisal of his roots.

When I arrived at Cove Forge, Noah David was as full of bad news as I was, and commiseration was no comfort. We both wondered if and how we could weather this decline. In an effort to steer the conversation away from our troubles, I told him about my encounter with Trethaway.

"I passed Trethaway on the track. Says he's sold his ore rights to Colbert."

David stopped. "He has, has he? Well, that's bad news for you, and we've nearly used up the good ore around here. Some of these local ore banks are nearly worthless, the ore's so low grade. We'll be hauling it from farther and farther afield. Why didn't you offer him more?"

"Didn't give me a chance. There's bad blood there, you know. I had to run him off from working for my collier, and then I got him fired from the canal company for selling whiskey to my workers."

Mr. David let out a sigh. "Whew. You've sewn the seeds of your own destruction, man. That one's a bad one."

"I don't see how I could have helped it. I agree that he's mean. Right now he as much as told me he had something to do with Geordan Evans's disappearance down at Porter Quarry."

"Now that's interesting. Old crime. No one looking any more. Must feel pretty safe to be running off his mouth about it."

I nodded. "No hope of justice at this late date."

In addition to my business troubles, things at home had gone from bad to worse. Ellie was pregnant again, and I feared a repeat of the dark cloud that had enveloped her after John's birth. She was seldom happy, not openly angry, but surely not satisfied with her life. I had just about given up those hopes I'd nurtured early in our marriage that it would somehow come to a happy state. So I managed my troubles by old habits of being gone and staying long from home. There was always a willing companion at the inn at Water Street, ready to engage in a drink or a card game or just talk.

Chapter 43

Late 1837
Adam

I returned home from Cove Forge, amid bursting energy and chatter centered around plans for Christmas. I hadn't the heart to tell our brood that money was tight or that they might have to curtail their Christmas wishes. Their excitement served to push me into a false hope that somehow things would improve in time for a glad holiday.

Most likely to be disappointed was Robbie, who, at almost fourteen, was old enough to understand our circumstances—but by temperament not even slightly moved to alter his demands. The rest—Laird, Alyssa, Bethany, and little John—could be satisfied with small things, and even less if they knew of our dire straits. But Robbie wanted a horse—not just any horse—one he'd had his eye on for some time, a big bay with a reputation for high spirits he'd seen but never ridden at Yellow Spring. On hearing about the horse, his mother voiced concern that it might be too high-spirited for so young a rider, and I watched the whole turn of events with a hand on my pocketbook. I tried to talk to the young man but found him wholly intractable when it came to his own desires.

"Robbie, times are hard. Have you not seen the stacks of iron bars on the canal bank? The idle furnace? We must economize for the present."

The boy smiled his most charming smile. "But I can still have my horse, huh, Papa?"

It was as though he hadn't heard a word. "I really don't think we can manage it this year, lad. Maybe next year."

"I was going to ask for a new saddle, but . . . of course, the horse will come with one, won't he?"

"No, I don't think so. Saddles are dear, too, Robbie. You really should give this whole matter more thought."

Oblivious to all arguments to the contrary, Robbie went on with his plans and expectations for Christmas.

I turned to his mother, hoping to garner her support for my frugal resolutions, but no. As usual, she couldn't bring herself to say no to Robbie, even when his demands surpassed the reasonable.

"Oh, surely we can afford to buy him the horse he wants. Horses don't cost that much."

"But this one's a wild one. You said so yourself. Maybe we should wait until a better match comes around."

"I can't bear to disappoint him, Adam. He wants that horse so."

I turned away, my hopes dashed. Ellie simply could not bring herself to deny Robbie anything he wanted. I should have expected that.

So it was on the day before Christmas, having been assured that Elinor had presents to meet the needs and desires of the other four children, that I set out for Yellow Spring just after noon to meet the owner of Old Hickory, after the nickname of the hero of the Battle of New Orleans and president of our country. The man was Timothy Judge, an Irishman brought here to help dig the canal who'd decided to stay.

I'd some experience with his kind, since many of my workers were of like origins. In my mind, the Irish were an interesting people, full of emotion that expressed itself in fighting, singing, poetry, fancy oratory, drinking, and little else. But if they knew anything in this world, it was horses. So I expected to get a good horse from Mr. Judge, who'd been breeding and raising them for a few years at Yellow Spring, and, so I'd heard, wasn't averse to racing and betting in the bargain.

The conversation went well at first. I told him I had a thirteen-year-old who'd had an eye on one of his horses, and Judge seemed amenable to a deal. Then, for some reason, he seemed to hesitate, waver in the dealing, and asked, "Aren't you the ironmaster over to Etna?"

"Yes, I am."

"And this boy you're buying for, is it young Robbie who spends more time looking over my horses than he does earning his keep?"

"I would guess that's right."

"Well, now, Mr. MacPhail, is it? Yes, I know the very horse you speak of, and I have to tell ye, that horse is special. Worth a lot to me he is, both as a race horse and at stud. I wasn't looking to sell him for some time, sir. He's too valuable."

I listened to his speech, melodious and hypnotic. What is it that makes a people speak with such a lilt, such a rhythm to their words that they give one's ears pleasure at listening even while they quash your hopes? How does it happen that all speak with a single cadence that marks them as a people the moment they open their mouths? I couldn't say, but I found myself watching the man's lips move in wonder at the lilt and swing of his words.

"What would it take to make him Robbie's?"

"Oh, at least two hundred and fifty, now. No less than that."

Two hundred and fifty dollars for a horse? What could the man be thinking? "I wouldn't be willing to pay more than a hundred, and I'd be overcharged at that."

"Nay, sir. He's worth every penny. I can sell him any time I want, and no questions asked. It's two-fifty, so it is."

"Well, let's have a look at him."

Mr. Judge led the way along a path out back of the store to a stable where half a dozen horses breathed steam into the cold air. All were good, sound horses, like kings held for ransom in a lowly stable. I wondered at this crude Irishman's ability to acquire such fine animals on what had to be a meager salary. Following him to the last stall, I drew in my breath at the beautiful animal before me. Big, strong, proud, he nickered at Judge, shaking his gracefully arched black mane.

216

I took a step forward and reached for the horse's head, but he shivered and pulled away, stamping in nervous irritability. Now I was annoyed. Not only was this Irishman overcharging me, but the horse wasn't gentle tempered. This one would be a handful to work with and, knowing Robbie's lack of self-control, I could foresee trouble. The horse whinnied and pawed the ground, skittish. I stepped back.

"Well, thank you, Mr. Judge. I appreciate that this is a fine animal, but I don't think he's a good match for our son. Too self-willed for a youth to handle. Perhaps I'll see you again about another one. This one is not for me."

Tim Judge held the horse's halter and backed him away as I turned and walked out of the stable. "Sure, and ye'll be being sorry for passing the opportunity, MacPhail. I'll merit ye already are."

Strange thing to say, but I nodded, tipped my hat and let it go by. The ride home through Polecat Hollow was cold in the December wind. I stabled my horse and entered our house through the back door, hoping to find some baking going on in the kitchen. I wasn't disappointed. The air was alive with the smell of bread, cookies, and pies. Cinnamon, ginger, nutmeg and sugar intermingled, tickling my nose. Ellie and all five children were engaged in helping Mrs. Gwynn roll, cut, decorate, bake and set to cool all manner of sweets. I reached for a sugar cookie, smiling at all the activity.

Ellie returned my smile, a rarity for her, and called my attention to Alyssa and little Beth, busily sifting sugar over the next batch. I motioned to her to step into the dining room.

"What is it?" she asked when we had retreated to the quiet space.

"It's that horse. The owner wants too much for him."

"How much is too much?"

"Two hundred and fifty dollars."

She drew in her breath, dismayed. "Well, can't you bargain with him?"

"I tried. I'm afraid he's adamant. Not anxious to sell, for one thing."

"Who in his right mind would expect to sell a horse for two hundred and fifty dollars?"

"Mr. Timothy Judge. That's who."

She was visibly disturbed. I couldn't tell if it was the name that set her off or a delayed reaction to the high price. "Well, who does he think he is? And who does he think he's dealing with?"

"He knows who I am. I guess he's just not that interested in selling the horse. Says it's worth more to him in a race or at stud. But I have to tell you, Ellie, I'm relieved. That horse is far too much for Robbie to manage."

Ellie turned away, looking out the window, wiping her floury hands on her apron. "Nonsense. You'll just have to pay it," she said. "We can't disappoint Robbie."

"What? Pay more than twice what the horse is worth to placate Robbie? No. I can't do that."

She turned on me with fire in her eyes. "Well, we'll see about that. Robbie wants that horse and we can't disappoint him."

I stood dumbfounded, watching her stalk back into the kitchen, hands on her hips. What? What was going on here? Why didn't anybody but me realize how serious our situation was?

Chapter 44

Christmas 1837
Ellie

So. Timothy Judge thought he could cheat my husband and deprive my son of his heart's desire to get even? To punish me for breaking off with him? We'd see about that. I left the children in Mrs. Gwynn's care and hurried upstairs to collect all the money I had, a hundred and twenty-five dollars, saved from my father's wedding gift. With that I returned to the kitchen and sent out to the stable for my mare to be saddled. When Adam asked me my business, I hedged, saying I had to see Lindy about some Christmas plans and would return in about an hour. I wrapped my wool cloak around me and rode off up the Polecat Hollow road toward Yellow Spring, my mind awhirl with angry thoughts.

My arrival at Yellow Spring was greeted by three skinny, long-eared hounds walking stiff-legged around my horse, barking like all possessed. The store had a seedier look about it than I remembered—like someone was keeping store, but not really *keeping* store. I slid down from Lizbet's back and mounted the steps, fire in my eyes. Tim Judge, waiting on a customer, looked away and concentrated on adding a row of figures on a brown paper bag when he saw me. I strode right up to him, jostled the other customer out of the way and addressed him across the counter.

"You have a horse for sale, do you?"

"Why yes, I do—sort of."

"What do you mean, sort of? It's that big Bay. The one you call Old Hickory. And I won't pay more than a hundred dollars for him. Anything more would be a travesty."

Tim looked toward the other customer, a local farm wife with a long list in her hand. She stepped aside and wandered to another part of the store where she stood fingering the fabric lined up in bolts. Tim turned back to me.

"Oh, ma'am, I am sorry, but Old Hickory isn't for sale." He was leaning over the counter right back at me, hands braced on the edge, eyes level with mine.

"He's for sale all right. Everything's for sale to the right buyer."

Tim leaned back just a bit. "Well, the right buyer would have to come up with a princely sum, I'm afraid."

"What princely sum?"

"Two hundred and fifty dollars, cash money."

"You're a fool. Nobody around here has that kind of money—and if they did, they wouldn't spend it on some unbreakable demon horse."

"Who says he's unbreakable? He's halter broke already and will be ready to ride by spring. Besides, he's worth more to me than all the rest of them put together, so I'm not all that interested in selling him."

I glared at him, a worthy adversary, and decided right there that I would stop at nothing to get what I wanted. If Tim Judge thought he could push my husband around and disappoint my son, he'd ill considered one aspect: me.

"I'll have the horse. It's for my son—for Christmas. I'll take him with me right now."

"Ye know the price. I've already had dealings with your esteemed husband, and he hightailed it out when I told him it were two hundred fifty dollars. And that's firm, m'lady."

"I've a hundred dollars here with me right now. Take it or leave it."

Tim's lower jaw thrust out and his eyes glared into mine. "I believe I'll have to leave it now."

I looked around the store. The farm wife, uncomfortable witnessing our exchange, made a quick exit out the front door.

"There. Ye've made me lose a customer," Tim said.

"All right, I'll give you a hundred-twenty-five, and not a penny more."

I watched him consider my offer, the corners of his mouth turned down. How had I ever found those lips inviting?

"No, m'lady. I ain't budgin'. Two hundred fifty it is."

"Fine. Where's your wife? Does she know about me? About how you courted and flirted and tried every way on God's earth to woo me? How you only married her out of spite to get even with me?"

Now he stepped back and placed his hand on the counter, poised as though to jump it. I ducked my head in anticipation of decapitation, but Tim just stood there, lips tight, eyes ablaze with anger.

"And yer husband? How would he like to know the same? And you the fine lady. Ironmaster's wife?"

We stood glaring into each other's face, the wooden counter between us. Tim's face was drawn, white around the lips. I marveled at how one could love a person, lust after them, be willing to give up everything for them, then learn to loathe and despise them in the same lifetime. Nothing colder than a dead love.

"Look, Tim. I know your employer, Mr. French. One word from Adam and he'd send you, your wife, and all your children packing. You have a soft life here, keeping a store and some horses, but you could be back grubbing in a quarry, or worse, at one word from me. So think about it."

Tim's hands dropped to his sides, a look of resignation on his face. He hesitated, then sighed. "Looks like ye've had the best of me, Mrs. MacPhail." He drew out my name in a sing-song way that told me I'd won, but made me wonder at the cost.

Nervous that he'd change his mind and renege on the deal, I thrust the hundred and twenty-five dollars at him and turned to the door. Suddenly, in three steps, he came round the end of the counter and reached for me, grabbing my wrist, his eyes narrow slits in his distorted face. "Ye'll be sorry now, Missus. Sorry for threatening me. Sorry for cheating me. Sorry in ways ye've yet to imagine."

I wrenched my arm free and turned to go. "Tell your groom to bring him around. I'll inspect him before I buy."

"That would be me. I'm the groom and the trainer and the stable mucker all in one."

I waited on the porch steps, Lizbet's reins in hand, while Timothy Judge strode to the stable and returned a few minutes later with Old Hickory, a big, muscular Bay stallion, resistance written all over him. My son had a good eye for horseflesh, I'd give him that. This was a champion in every way—spirited, willful, fast and competitive. I mounted Lizbet as Tim handed me the lead, and I spurred my mare into a brisk trot, leading the manliest of horses behind.

Our arrival at Etna was greeted by shouts and cheers from the children, whose eyes lit up as they saw the unmistakable air of superiority with which Old Hickory carried himself. I sought Robbie among them, smiled, and handed the lead to him. "Merry Christmas, son."

Adam stood in the background, solemn and silent, apparently put out at what he perceived as my willfulness. I slid to the ground and handed my reins to Emmett, our groom, and walked, tall and proud, to Adam's side. "There. It's done. Robbie shall have his Christmas, and you shall not be cheated."

"That depends on how much of a bargain you negotiated." He moved farther away from the children, his eyes questioning. "That's a lot of horse for such a young boy. You'd have done better to have taught him to temper his desires. This just makes him think it's his right to have anything he pleases."

It wasn't the first time Adam and I had traded words over Robbie. The boy's place in my heart was sealed. None of the other children could touch me as he could. I simply could not deny him anything, and this rankled Adam who, I must admit, sought to be fair in his dealings with all of the children.

"I talked Mr. Judge down to a hundred and twenty-five dollars," I told him, a trace of pride in my voice. "At least I didn't let him cheat me."

Adam turned away, embarrassed, I thought, that his wife had negotiated a better deal than he could have. Then he turned back. "I hope you didn't promise him anything you couldn't deliver."

That stung. What did he know? Did he suspect my relationship with Tim Judge, or was he just referring to the possibility of other considerations in the trade? Or had Lem Trethaway seen Tim and me once long ago and whispered it into Adam's ear where it stayed and swelled and cankered?

I entered the house by the kitchen door and passed quickly through the center hall and up the stairs to my bedroom. Instead of being satisfied with the deal I'd made and my compliance with Robbie's wishes, I felt anxious and guilt laden. What did Adam know or suspect? How could I find out? Damn Tim Judge for being so bitter, seeking ways to punish me.

My memory wandered to Tim's threats in the bargain. How did he propose to get even? What were the ways I'd not yet imagined? Shaking, I hung up my cloak and smoothed my dress. It was near the dinner hour, and Mrs. Gwynn would soon be ringing the little silver bell in the dining room to call us to table. I wanted more time to think over my situation and to parse out the threats, real and imagined, that plagued me.

Instead I opened my door and crossed the hall to the nursery where the children—all five of them—were washing for dinner. Robbie was flying around near the ceiling, so elated with his horse, but Laird, Alyssa, and Bethany carried on in a more businesslike manner. Little John, standing in his crib, rattled the rails in anticipation of dinner. I picked him up and gathered the others to me, hugged them, smoothed their hair, and whispered loving words in their ears. Robbie stood back from this mothering, his young face set in an expression that told me my motherly overtures were on the wane with him. Already.

I smiled at him over the heads of his siblings, but he returned only a weak smile, as though he'd gotten what he wanted and felt no further need to placate me. I fought the urge to grab him and shout into his face the risks I'd taken to get him what he wanted, the danger I could be in this very moment with Adam's cryptic remark echoing in my brain. Oh, Robbie, surely you appreciate all this. Surely you won't abandon me like your father did.

The thin tinkle of the bell called us to the table, where there was much cheerful talk about the holiday to come and requests for sweets, Christmas carols, and the lighting of the candles on the tree. Agitated though I was, I stayed with the children, sang with them, allowed them an extra cookie each, and tucked them in one at a time, except for Robbie whose manner assured me that he didn't need to be tucked in anymore. One more blow. When the house was finally quiet I joined Adam in the parlor, shared a hot mulled cider with him, and took up my knitting.

The cider took the edge off our interactions, and by the time we went to bed it felt as though we were back to normal and all was well. Adam kissed me goodnight on the forehead, as was his habit, and moved to the settee by the window to read by lamplight for another hour or so. I turned over to sleep, but Adam soon interrupted.

"How well do you know this Timothy Judge, Elinor?" His words sat me bolt upright, set my heart to pounding, and left me breathless.

"Not well at all, why?" I struggled to keep the quaver out of my voice.

"It seems strange that you just rode over there and got him to cut his price by half. How did you manage it?"

I shrugged in an elaborate gesture of ignorance. "I've no idea. I just told him I would pay only a hundred-twenty-five dollars. Said I had the cash with me and he could take it or leave it. Maybe he needed the money so direly he was willing to settle."

Adam's eyes showed no emotion. He nodded slowly and returned to the book in his lap. "A hundred and twenty-five dollars is still a princely sum, and more than should have been paid for a child's first horse."

Fear washed over me. What did he know? What did he suspect? I'd been foolish to put my safe life in jeopardy so as not to deny my son's Christmas wish. Trembling, whether from cold or from fear, I nestled down under the covers, trying in vain to sleep as the snow fell softly on the land.

Chapter 45

Winter 1837–38
Ellie

Christmas morning dawned white and softly cold. All four older children rushed downstairs and into the parlor before the fire was up, never minding that they could see their breath. They opened their presents—a cradle for Alyssa's doll, a baby doll for Bethany, and ice skates for Laird. We then trooped out to the dining room, where the fire burned warmer, and sat down to a breakfast of cinnamon rolls, oatmeal, and sausages. We were barely through when Robbie announced that he was going to the barn to visit Old Hickory.

"Don't even think about riding him yet," Adam admonished. "He's a long way from trustworthy."

"Yes, dear," I echoed. "Emmett will have to work with him for some time before you can expect to ride him."

"Yes, yes. I know. I just want to visit," he replied pulling on his mackinaw and buttoning it close around his neck. The kitchen door slammed as Robbie hurried out to the stable. Not five minutes later we heard the door open again and Robbie's cry. "Papa! Papa! Come quick!"

With my heart in my throat, I ran outside in just my dress with no thought to my comfort. "What?" I screamed. "What? What's happened?"

I followed Adam and Robbie to the broad open door of the stable where I could see the groom lying prone on the floor, blood streaming from his head. Old Hickory stood in his stall, hindmost facing out, blowing hard. Adam and I raced to the stricken man's side. So this is what Tim Judge meant by ways I'd yet to imagine.

Adam took the situation in hand, sending for the doctor in Williamsburg, whose arrival was delayed until past the mid-day mealtime because it was, after all, Christmas morning. In the meantime, I pacified the children with our traditional ritual of preparing for the visit of our workers later in the day, while Adam and Robbie rode to Yellow Spring, Old Hickory in tow, to demand our money back from Tim Judge.

The groom, poor old Emmet Leeper, was carried into our kitchen and placed on a makeshift bed near the fire, where he lay unconscious until Dr. Wiley arrived after noon. The doctor was pale and wan, having been up all night attending to a birthing somewhere up Clover Creek before he responded to our call. I met him in the kitchen, leaving the children in the parlor with Phoebe Baker. Mrs. Gwynn fixed the doctor a plate, which he politely set aside on the table while he tended to Emmett, who lay, gray and unconscious, on the pallet. After a brief, and to my mind cursory, examination, the doctor shook his head.

"No hope here. He may lie for a few days, but he's as good as dead right now."

Mrs. Gwynn's eyes met mine and we both looked away. I felt a wave of panic and despair at what my actions had caused. The groom wasn't young—perhaps fifty—but he'd always been kind and hard working. Adam was especially pleased with his manner and complimented him often on his soft and gentle touch with the horses. Tim Judge must have known the dangers he was exposing us to— perhaps he even hoped the disaster would fall on Robbie. I couldn't believe he'd be so base as to do this on purpose, but it certainly looked that way.

Adam and Robbie returned soon after the doctor's diagnosis, both subdued by the news. "Is he suffering, do you think?" Adam asked the doctor.

"Not likely. Knocked senseless. Probably will never know what hit him."

Adam turned to me, his face grave. "Mr. Judge took the horse back. Here is your money. I hope never to have to deal with him again."

I took the money and stuffed it back into my reticule without looking at him. I couldn't, given that most of this was my fault. I searched Robbie's face for a sign of compassion, but he sat down at the table and stuffed a cookie into his mouth, apparently little moved by the gravity of the situation.

"Robbie, don't you feel badly for Mr. Leeper? It could have been you. The man is seriously hurt. He may die. Don't you have anything to say?"

Robbie shrugged. "Wasn't my fault. I'm sorry, but I wish I still had the horse."

"Robbie wasn't ready to give up on Old Hickory," Adam pointed out. "We're all lucky it wasn't one of us got hurt. Mr. Judge seemed to think it was a result of mishandling, but I assured him it was not."

I shuddered to think of Tim refusing to acknowledge that the horse was dangerous . . . a killer even. I looked at my son, leaning over a plate of cookies, unconcerned and unapologetic, and thought again of his father.

Chapter 46

1838
Adam

Not given to fighting or violence of any kind, I watched the scenario in our kitchen unfold for the next several days, barely able to control my anger. Who was more to blame—my spoiled son, his handmaiden of a mother, or the dastardly Irishman who must have known the nature of the horse long before all this happened? For the first time in my life, I wanted to hurt someone, and as time passed, my anger focused on Timothy Judge. I barely knew him. Corbin said he'd worked for him in the woods for a short time—came in with the canal diggers and stayed. Noah David reminded me that it was Judge who played the fiddle so vigorously at the canal opening. But that was all I knew.

This incident with Robbie and Elinor was disturbing. I saw things in the boy that gave me pause, but his mother remained oblivious to any fault. She was a good mother to all, but it didn't take a sorcerer to see that Robbie held a place in her heart beyond the hope of the others.

Our next child, born the following June, was to be our last. We named him Stephen Edward, a name Elinor proposed—to my surprise—since she still nurtured anger toward her father and had not seen him since our marriage. I agreed to the name with the stipulation that he be called Edward, and so it was. Then, almost as a summons from above, we received a missive from the namesake grandfather informing us of the death of Alice Bratton, Elinor's mother.

I watched my wife for any sign of grief but saw none. Her bitterness toward both of her parents seemed not to have diminished in fifteen years. She showed no interest in returning to Berks County for any sort of remembrance, and I honored her wishes in spite of curiosity about how her father would see his handiwork after time. I'd long since paid off my debt to Stephen Bratton and bought out his investors, so it seemed to me that things had not turned out so badly for Elinor, and so she might have a softening of heart toward them, especially her mother, who had only acquiesced to her husband's wishes. But once the announcement came and Elinor refused to be involved, any prospect for discussion died.

Elinor

My mother died a month ago, and my father saw fit only to inform me of it now. I might have felt something for her, but as usual, my father has orchestrated things to his liking. He wouldn't have wanted me to attend the funeral as, I am sure, the Cliftons would have been among the mourners. He wouldn't have wanted to risk their displeasure at having me, and per chance Robbie, present. Wouldn't want to make them uncomfortable in the presence of their unacknowledged grandson. Well, he could die and rot in hell before I'd give him access to any of my children. Die and rot in hell before I returned his correspondence, visited him, or gave him any satisfaction whatsoever.

I was surprised at the depth of my anger. I didn't think of either of my parents much, but when I did it was not with love, but with lingering resentment. I may have been young and foolish back then, but I did not deserve to be treated like property to be bargained for and bid on. As I re-examined my attitude toward them it became clear that everything I felt about Adam evolved from that, and for once I was sorry for him. All he ever wanted was a stupid furnace to watch over, tend, make his own. A wife in the bargain was almost irrelevant to him. I didn't blame him for it. Adam was unassuming and accepting of whatever came his way. I, on the other hand, had very well-defined expectations of life, expectations that had been dashed on the floor of our Berks County parlor that November day some fifteen years ago.

I may not have felt anything for my parents, but through their reappearance in my life I came to realize that I did feel something for Adam and the life we shared. Five children of his and one of my own, a large and comfortable home, status in the community. It was as comfortable a life as I might have expected from Robert Clifton, even if it did lack passion or adventure. Adam MacPhail had grown on me, steady and predictable though he was. I felt no deep passion, but a quiet acceptance and gentle appreciation for his devotion to me, to our children and to Etna Furnace. He was a good man, after all.

All this and more occupied my thoughts as the winter of 1838 unfolded. The slowed economy kept Adam tense and on edge. He closed the furnace down, 'for repairs and relining' . . . but I knew it was because there were no orders, no work, no money coming in.

When times are bad, people get desperate and difficult to handle. Most of our workers had gardens and access to plenty of game, so there was no danger of starving, but neither was there any hope for a better life. Men stood around the store leaning on the hitching post, hands in their pockets, waiting. Waiting for what? A miracle? Adam didn't have a miracle to his name. All he knew was hard work and hope, and this was how he dealt with the small crises that inevitably accompanied hard times. Some of our workers gave up on the iron industry and went west. This disturbed him because many of the jobs required skill, and skilled workers were hard to replace. As for those who stayed, petty squabbles, bickering, fights, even one or two brawls between the Irish and everyone else, bore witness to the lack of work and hope.

The county's population was changing before our eyes. Where there had been mostly English, German, Scotch-Irish, and Welsh, now more Irish were settling down to stay. There was a feeling that the latecomers were somehow lesser people, especially since they were Catholics. There were no Catholic churches outside the cities, and the presence of a priest could set off whispering suspicion and grumbling unrest.

People like the Trethaways were always ready to heap scorn on anyone they could feel superior to, and while their lives were in no way rich, they took perverse pleasure in calling out the "Shanty Irish" or "Bead Squeezers" or "Popish." Almost any Saturday night there was a guaranteed fist fight or an all-out brawl somewhere around Mt. Etna or Yellow Spring or Water Street, take your pick, and if it was not initiated by a Trethaway, it was a good bet there was one or more of them involved.

So Adam had his hands full as the economy stayed down for more than two years, and I could see the fear in his eyes. Everything he'd worked for, everything he'd ever wanted, stood on the precipice of disaster.

Chapter 47

Summer 1838
Ellie

My steadfast friendship with Lindy Baker continued through all these trials. She never completely recovered from the loss of Emily, but with her other children still in need of their mother, she rallied and put up a good front. Phoebe, eighteen when Emmett Leeper was killed, served us well as parlor maid and nanny. Where Emily had been out-going and popular with the young men, Phoebe was shy and retiring. One summer afternoon after the incident with Tim Judge and the horse, I took myself and baby Edward over to the mill to visit Lindy.

"Well, look what the wind blew in!" she greeted me. "Sit. Sit. I've fresh baked apple dumplings. Have some."

"Oh, Lindy, you always have fresh baking. I don't know how you do it. How've you been?"

Her smile told me she was coping, but no longer the same fun-loving Lindy I'd known. "Things aren't so bad. Jeff is carrying a lot of farmers on credit, but at least he has customers. How's Adam holding up?"

"As you'd expect. Not complaining, but the furrows in his brow get ever deeper. I think this panic will end. In fact, I'm sure it will . . . but he's not convinced the iron business will ever come back. He worries incessantly about English imports. I know it'll come back; we produce fine iron, but these ups and downs may do us in yet."

Lindy laughed. "Spoken like the true ironmaster's wife. Getting used to him, are you? About time, I'd say."

I smiled at that and looked around her spacious kitchen. Ten-year-old Jenny, her baby, played with a kitten near the hearth. She reminded me of Emily—a bright, pretty child with red-gold braids. "So how's your whole brood?" I asked.

"Not so bad. I think we've talked Joel and Chad out of moving west. That's a load off my mind. I hate to be one of those mothers, but I'd feel so afraid for them if they left. There's Indians and weather and poor crops and God knows what hardships out there. Here, a least, we have civilization."

I chuckled at her description of the dangers of going west. People were doing it every day, more and more, and the talk we heard was mostly good. Once in a while we heard stories of disaster, but mostly we heard of good outcomes if we heard at all, which was not certain.

"Well, I'm glad to hear they're cooling off about it. Joel will be taking himself a wife one of these days, no doubt. Twenty-four and still a bachelor? That won't last long. And Chad, what's he? Twenty? My goodness, Lindy, you'll be a grandmother soon enough, I'll warrant."

A cloud passed over her face, initiated, I was sure, by the thought of one grandchild already in the ground. "I guess you're right. Joel's been sweet on that little bit of a thing, Harriet Summers from over in Fox Hollow, since he was just a sprout, and I think Chad has eyes for that Corbin girl, Susannah. Wouldn't doubt that there'd be a wedding or two 'fore this year is out."

Lindy's other two boys, Lane and Jared, clumped in from the mill, pummeling each other, the spring mud clinging to their boots. "Git on with you two, you're tracking up my floor!" Lindy scolded.

"Hey, Ma," Jared announced. "Lem Trethaway's poling his boat across the river. Come see."

"Why'd I want to see that good-fer-nothing? Only if he fell out and drowned," Lindy replied, bitterness in her voice.

"No, Ma. Really. Looks like he's coming here."

Lindy rose and looked out the window. "Go git yer Pa."

Jared gave Lane a shove. "You go," he ordered.

Lane, ever the peacemaker, opened the front door and yelled, "PA! Ma wants you."

"Git on with you, Lane. He can't hear you from here!"

The boy clumped out into the muddy dooryard, closing the door with a thud, and was back with his father in a few minutes.

Lindy stayed at her post by the window until Jeff entered the room. "What is it?"

She nodded toward the scene at the mouth of Roaring Run below. Lem Trethaway tied up his boat and picked his way up over the slippery, mossy rock steps, past the mill, clear to the house.

"What you think *he* wants?" Lindy asked.

As if in reply, Phoebe appeared, coming up the road from our house, wrapped in a wool cloak I'd given her. Lindy saw her first, watched as she and Lem greeted each other like old friends, and then entered the house together.

The chill in the room was palpable as the young couple entered, looking shy and awkward. Jeff stepped forward. "What do you want here, Trethaway?"

Lem looked at Phoebe and reached out for her hand. "Me and Phoebe, uh. Me and Phoebe'd like..."

"To court." Phoebe finished the sentence for him.

"What?" Jeff asked. "I thought we were done with you. First you take Emily, and now you want her sister? No. Not on yer life."

Lindy stepped forward, right up in Lem's face. "Git out of here and don't never come back, hear? You done enough damage around here. I swear if I ever see you in this house again, I'll shoot you myself!"

Lem stood mute, taking in the anger. "It weren't my fault about Em. I done right by her. It weren't my fault."

"It's true," Phoebe assured them. "Lem's a good man. He didn't hurt Emily, Mama. It just happened."

"Just happened! If she'd lived in a decent house instead of that hovel of his, she might've made it. I never did meet a Trethaway was worth the powder. I lost one child to you, Lem Trethaway, but I don't allow I'll lose another."

I rose and stepped toward Lindy, reached for her hand, speaking calmly. "Lindy, don't be so brash. It's clear Phoebe likes him, and he's never really done anything to give you reason to despise him. Not really."

She jerked away, glaring. "Don't tell me what to do with my own young'uns. Phoebe wouldn't have took up with him if she'd been home here instead of traipsing back and forth between your place and ours. That's where he got at her."

"Remember how you tried to keep Emily from him? That didn't work, did it? What makes you think it'll work this time?" Even though Lem Trethaway instilled fear in me that he'd reveal my own past indiscretions, I felt a need to divert Lindy from this path. "Look at him. He's come to you in an honorable way to ask permission to court Phoebe. He's not sneaking around like a coyote on the prowl."

Absorbing my argument, Jeff stepped back, looking thoughtful as the young couple stood hand in hand before the door. His eyes sought Lindy's. "Mebbe . . . mebbe we ought not to be so hard on him, Lin. Em never did complain about him. She was real happy right up until..."

Lindy turned to me in despair, her face distorted in anguish. "See? See what I mean? It ain't worth it to even have them and raise them. Soon as they're growed they want to go off and live their own lives like you don't matter a mite."

I reached out and gathered her into my arms, thinking how she might be called upon to comfort me in the same circumstances in a few years. "You still matter, Lindy. Your children love and honor you as always. It's just that this force is greater. You know that. You and Jeff know that. You can't pick and choose the who and the what for them."

She leaned into me, her shoulders shaking with grief. Jeff moved to put an arm around her and led her back to the table. "We can't, Lindy. We can't afford to lose Phoebe, too. We gotta let her pick her own way."

"Oh, Daddy, it'll be all right." Phoebe pleaded. "Lem's a good man. He just needs a chance to show what he can do."

Lem Trethaway dropped Phoebe's hand and crossed the room to her mother in two strides. "I know you didn't want me for Emily, and you don't want me for Phoebe, either. But I ask you this. Give me a chance. If I ever do her wrong, you can come looking for me with a shotgun. I promise."

Lindy, still in Jeff's arms, turned to face him. "I guess," she whispered.

Chapter 48

Spring 1839
Adam

After more than two years of lean times, the iron business seemed to be picking up. Orders came in from Pittsburgh, our most profitable market, and I was kept busy trying to reassemble my stable of skilled workers. The foundry was in full production, and we were shipping bars as fast as the triphammers could pound them out. The canal turned out to be besieged with problems, but it still provided generally reliable transport, if one overlooked the delays brought on by failing locks and bank cave-ins. I felt more confident than I had in years as we approached the winter. Hoped to keep the furnace in blast for the whole season, maybe into spring, with the demand building up.

Christmas came and went, with a mild December adding to my optimism. Then came January. The storms raged and the snow piled up, but we still kept the furnace going twenty-four hours a day. The hearth and lining seemed to be holding, and I strove, perhaps against my better judgment, to take advantage of the markets to make up for the slow pace of the two preceding years.

February added to the snow levels, and my concern about the approaching spring grew, given the history of flooding along the Juniata. Still, if the thaw was gradual, the river could accommodate the runoff. Around the middle of March a warming trend justified my fears. The temperature rose to the mid-forties and stayed for almost a week. The river kept rising, fed by its swollen tributaries, and along with high water came rain and more rain. The forge flooded first, as it was closest to the riverbank. The tenant house, furnace, store and barn were far enough away from the river not to be in danger except for the raging waters of Roaring Run. As the days wore on and the rain continued, most of the snow was cut away and the river filled with huge floes of floating ice and debris washed from its banks.

I had Corbin gather a crew to monitor the water's rise and try to move as much as possible out of the way. Our home, set back from the river and canal banks as it was and up on a rise, wasn't threatened, but keeping the children indoors with the excitement of the flood was almost impossible. I left that to Ellie, Mrs. Gwynn and Phoebe, but I took Robbie with me on my rounds as he was, at fifteen, old enough to be of help.

The ice rolled along with the current, grinding and crashing into the lock gates as it went. An ice dam formed against almost every lock, and the grinding of the huge blocks of ice against the iron lock gates sounded like the groans of dying men. I rushed from one point to another, assessing the risks and trying in vain to find a way to protect the canal banks, bridges, and locks. Finally, I watched— helpless—as the banks washed away, leaving the structure of the locks exposed, until this, too, was destroyed.

Dismayed beyond description by the damage we encountered when we went out to assess it after the waters receded, I was sure the canal would be out of service for months while the repairs were undertaken. I watched my hope of recovery from the 1837 Panic fade, leaving me to look at perhaps five more years before the return of prosperity. I'd chosen a volatile and undependable business.

One afternoon during the week after the flood, Robbie and I were riding the river's edge looking for salvageable parts—timbers, iron fixtures, lock gates—when Robbie insisted on climbing down the bank at a steep and precipitous point to retrieve his cap, blown off by the incessant wind. The remains of ice chunks lay strewn along the bank, and the boy *would* climb down them to get closer to the water. He grabbed a long stick to catch the cap as it floated by and leaned out with no caution, bringing me to the point of exasperation, warning him time and again of the danger, to no avail.

Suddenly I heard the groan of shifting ice and, when I looked, saw Robbie fall twisted against one huge ice mass, his left foot wedged between it and another. I dismounted and crept down the steep bank to release him, but found the rock of ice too heavy to move. I tried using a sodden fence post as a lever, but broke it off in the process.

Robbie, frightened and in pain, began to cry for his mother.

"I'm doing all I can, son. Don't worry. I'll have you free in a moment." But my optimism was unfounded, for the more I tried to maneuver the block of ice, the harder it pressed against the boy's foot.

"Help, Pa! It's crushing my ankle!" he cried.

After almost a half hour of struggling to release him, I rose and shook my head. "I can't do it alone. I'll have to go back and get help."

Tears streamed down the boy's face, whether from pain or fear, I couldn't tell. I crawled up the steep bank and mounted my horse, riding back along the river as fast as I dared. The first person I saw was Lem Trethaway, manfully poling his boat across the river, the treacherous current carrying him way downstream of the mill. He struggled to get across, straining against the rushing current, and by the time he reached the near bank his boat had been carried a hundred yards beyond the mill. I hailed him as he was tying up.

"Lem! Head downstream. Robbie's trapped between two ice blocks. I need help to get him free."

Lem returned to the boat, raised his pole, and let her drift with the current, keeping to the near shore, trying to steer as best he could in the rushing water. I pointed to where I'd left Robbie and hurried on toward the mill where I begged help from Jeff Baker and his sons, Joel and Chad.

"Jeff, bring your horses and some rope. Robbie's trapped under a block of ice. We have to get him out."

Quick to respond, Jeff called over his shoulder for Joel to harness up the team. I led the way back to the boy, who by now was shivering with the cold and crying in pain. The ice block under him shifted again, pinning his left leg up to the knee, while his right arm and hand slipped into the icy water. When Jeff and his boys arrived, Lem Trethaway was kneeling at Robbie's side, talking him down from screaming panic. Joel and Chad, more agile than Jeff and I, crept down the bank with a rope that they tried to loop under the huge block of ice. They threw the other end of the rope up to us and we quickly tied it onto the harness of the team. The horses began to pull, but the rope slipped off, slapping young Chad across the face. I made my way down the bank to Robbie, reached for his hand, and did my best to comfort him, with little to fuel optimism. It was after four o'clock, and, true to the topography of these ridges and hollows, the sun was already down. It was cold and getting colder, and it looked like this might be a bigger job than we were equipped to handle. Joel and Chad re-tied the rope, only to have it slip off again.

"Hold!" I shouted, raising my hand. "If we keep trying to do this, the ice might shift and crush his ankle to shreds."

Into this mix came the one person I least wanted to see, Simon Trethaway. He'd seen our predicament from across the river and come over on the canal bridge, the only one still intact. All opinion and superiority, he slouched along toward us, his round-shouldered gait in contrast to his barking orders, shoved the Baker boys aside, and immediately proceeded to take over the rescue operation.

"Here. Ye'll never move that block without hurting him more. We got to shove it down, not drag it up. You, MacPhail, send up to the forge for some iron bars. We'll lever if off'n him."

"I already tried that," I replied, anxious to dismiss this unwelcome meddler. "Can't you see? It's wedged against that rock in the river. You'll never move it that way."

"Just get the bars," he ordered, and I looked at Jeff with raised eyebrows but nodded to Joel Baker to go for the bars.

"Take Chad and Lem with you. And bring a wagon. We'll need it to haul him home once we do get him out." I felt the need to regain control of the situation in the face of Trethaway's arrogance.

The three of us—acquaintances, enemies, adversaries—stood about on the riverbank looking down at the trapped boy, listened to him cry for his mother, and tried to assess the best means of rescue. Convinced that Trethaway was wrong about levering the ice back into the river, I persisted in trying to wrap the rope around the ice block in a way that would hold.

It took more than a half hour for the Baker boys and Lem to return, bringing lanterns against the gathering darkness. They were followed by a throng of onlookers, including Elinor and Laird, the smaller children having been left with Phoebe and Mrs. Gwynn. The cold was taking its toll on Robbie, and his wailing had diminished to moans and an occasional call for his mother. Elinor, spurred by a mother's love, ventured down the bank to his side, laying her cloak over him and trying to hold his right side up out of the water.

Her eyes sought mine, imploring me to do more, but I was taxed to my limit with trying to divine a way to release the boy. The iron bars were carried down the bank and one end wedged under the top block of ice. Three men weighed down on each bar, and the block groaned and shifted, Robert cried out in pain—and still the boy's ankle was pinned tight.

Simon Trethaway stood atop the bank, hands on hips, barking orders to the men, who now included his other sons, Luke and Zeke, both of whom were older and stronger than Lem. With so much manpower, one would have thought a mountain could be moved, but not this mammoth mass of ice.

Time after time they tried to loop the rope and drag the ice or pry it up high enough to free Robbie, but nothing worked, and the night was getting colder. The boy lost consciousness after another hour, leading us to fear for his life. I noted frost forming on his right hand and unwrapped my muffler, handing it to his mother. She lifted the boy's hand and tucked it inside her bodice, wrapping the muffler around his head. Her look of despair made me shiver. What would she say if he should die? It would all be heaped on me, to be sure.

Someone built a fire on the riverbank to provide warmth and light to the would-be rescuers, but try as they might, their effort brought no good results. Finally, I came to my wits' end, ready to give myself over to despair. When there seemed no way to extricate the boy, I thought of one more possible solution.

"I think we can get enough pull on the rope if we loop it around the top of the rock, force it down as low as it will let us, and pull the block into the river."

"You're crazy, man. Ye'd have to get into the water to do it, and five minutes in that water would do ye in. Besides, the ice block could fall on the rescuers. What kind of stupid talk is that?" Simon Trethaway was adamant. He threw down the end of the rope and stalked back to the fire.

"I don't know, Pa," Lem told him. "It might be the only way."

"You're as teched in the head as he is if you think that'll work. You been hanging 'round these Etna folk too long. Got you thinkin' dumb as they think."

"I'm willing to try if anyone else is." Lem looked around, but the men present turned back to warming themselves by the fire. The other Trethaway boys stood toward the back of the group, one on either side of their father, muttering in agreement with him.

I looked at Jeff Baker, hoping to find an ally, but he just shook his head. "We'd have four or five corpses in the morning instead of just one."

"I could help." I looked around and saw our young Laird standing at my side. "I'm strong, Papa. I could help."

"You're too slight, boy. The current'd take you. Go back over by the fire. We'll get it done, don't you worry."

Down the bank, Elinor sat on another ice block, a lantern balanced beside her, head on her arms. I pulled a ragged blanket from the wagon bed and slid down to her side, wrapping it around her slight form. She looked up at me with the saddest of eyes.

"Help him, Adam. Please."

I rose and climbed to the top of the bank, looked the company over and resumed my position as ironmaster. "You, Joel and Chad, you tie the rope around the top of the block. Tight now, and down as far as you dare." Turning to the Trethaways, I said, "Whichever among you is up for the challenge can get in the water with me. Tie the other end of the rope around your waists and wade out as far as you can still touch bottom so that if the block falls into the water it won't hit you. Come on. We can be done with this and back home in twenty minutes."

I looked around the company, convinced that this was our only hope. "Elinor! Come up here. You'll be in the way down there."

Not waiting to see who, if any, would follow, I slid down the bank past the prostrate boy and into the water, grabbing one end of the rope offered by Chad Baker and tying it around my waist. The freezing water numbed my legs and feet almost immediately, so that I could barely tell if my feet were touching bottom. Shivering and holding onto the rope, I made my way until I was up to my waist in the swift current, about ten feet from shore, struggling to keep my footing. I turned to look back at the bank, and slowly the forms of three men made their way down into the water. Two men on a rope, Luke and Zeke Trethaway on one and Lem and I on the other, we called for the Baker boys to give us the go. On the count of three, we all pulled on the ropes, and slowly, groaning and sliding, the block moved up and turned over into the water.

"Look out!" I shouted as the huge block of ice upended and came crashing down. Too late. The block snagged on a rock, hovered for a second and crashed down on Lem Trethaway, smashing into his head and driving him under. Frantic efforts to raise him brought no results, and, mindful of the danger to anyone in the water, we pulled ourselves out and lifted Robbie to safety.

Up on the bank, we wrapped ourselves in blankets near the fire as the company stood looking down into the darkness, helpless and silent.

Chapter 49

Summer 1839
Ellie

Our lives would be forever changed by the events of that March night in 1839. The world we knew ended and restarted when Lem Trethaway died in the frozen waters of the Juniata. His father, always fractious at best, became obstinate in his rage against Adam, never passing up a chance to blame, curse or threaten him. All the old hurts resurfaced for Simon Trethaway, nursed through the years to greater significance than when they occurred. I feared for Adam's life and warned him against going out after dark and traveling alone. Simon Trethaway became a menacing presence, lurking in the shadows, living on the mountain but never far from Mt. Etna, looking for a way to avenge his son's death. Adam, horrified by the tragedy and dismayed at the depth of Simon's hatred, tried valiantly to move on, turn his mind to other tasks and make amends any way he could.

I did what I could to support Adam against Trethaway, even took to riding out with him on his rounds, waiting in the gig while he inspected operations or talked with his workers. Adam tried to allay my fears by asserting that Trethaway was all talk, but I couldn't take comfort from that. I carried a book to pass the time and often climbed down to talk with the women-folk while Adam conducted business. This practice brought an unexpected harvest of warming friendships I'd wished for ever since the beginning.

Spring inevitably gave way to summer, and the village returned to normal. Except for Trethaway's unpredictable outbursts. One sunny afternoon in June, Adam and I were driving up hollow to check on the Canoe Mountain ore mining operations when Simon Trethaway suddenly appeared out of the woods on horseback, a shotgun across his saddle, blocking our way.

Adam, ever reasonable and courteous, addressed him as a gentleman. "Excuse us, Trethaway. We've business on the mountain."

Ye've business with me, too, MacPhail."

"What do you want of me, man?"

"Vengeance! I want your life in exchange for my son's!" he shouted.

"Sir, your son's death was a tragedy beyond words—for all of us. But I didn't make him go into the water. He went voluntarily."

"No. He went because he wanted to be looked upon as worthy of that Baker slut. Another one like her sister. He figured to impress you and them so he could marry her."

Adam, his face white, hands shaking, continued his path of reason. "I have no influence on the Bakers, man. He wasn't trying to gain my approval."

"Ye lie!" Trethaway roared, raising the gun. "I should cut ye down right here and now, like I did that son of a bitch of a foreman ye had down to Porter. Thought he could maltreat me and get away with it. Well, where's he now? Same place you'll be when I get through with ye. A Trethaway never fergits a wrong."

Frightened beyond reason, I rose and threw myself in front of Adam. Trethaway cursed and lowered the gun. "I'll catch ye some day when you ain't got no woman to protect ye. Besides, I like watching you squirm and worry over when ye'll see me again." Turning his horse, he rode off up the hillside.

Adam caught me around the waist and settled me back on my side of the seat before he wiped his brow and sighed. "You know, if he wants to kill me, there's really no way to stop him. He'll do it someday."

"He's lost all reason. Isn't there something the law can do?"

"Not unless he actually tries to kill me. Short of that, he hasn't broken the law. Anyway, if I did need the sheriff, I'd be dead long before any help arrived."

"Well, can't you find a way to get him before he gets you? At least carry a gun. I swear, Adam, the man is insane. Everybody knows it, knows how he's been harassing you. No one would blame you if you struck first."

"You know I can't do that."

He snapped the reins and the gig moved on up the track. I sat silent beside him, my heart pounding, thinking that if it were me, I'd find a way to protect myself, whatever it took.

The next day, I walked down to visit Lindy, the first time I'd seen her alone since Lem's funeral. We sat outside by Roaring Run, a cool refreshing mist rising from the water. Lindy didn't try to hide her relief at not having Phoebe tied to Lem, but she did relent some in her remembrance of him.

"I guess he wasn't all that bad. I never knew him to do much of anything except the old man's bidding—run that still for him to sell the liquor. I wonder what Lem ever got out of it. Do you think the old man paid him?"

"I don't know. Ask Phoebe. If anyone knows, she probably does."

Lindy pulled a face. "Don't know as I'd like to ask her anything about Lem Trethaway for a while yet. She's still in a state over losing him—torn between anger at Adam for putting him in danger and pride in Lem's having been brave enough to respond to Adam's call."

I took a deep breath. "Poor Adam doesn't know where to turn. Simon Trethaway won't give him any peace. Says he killed Lem and promises to get even. I worry for Adam, the children, all of us."

The irony of the situation wasn't lost on Lindy. "Old Trethaway sure has a lot of grief for a boy he didn't give a rip about while he lived."

I nodded. Lem had lived a solitary life in that old cabin on Tussey Mountain before and after his marriage to Emily. People thought it was because he wasn't like the rest of them—more decent and upright than his father ever hoped to be. My own brief acquaintance with him had turned out to be of no consequence. He'd apparently kept whatever he saw or didn't see on the ridge behind our house to himself. I was grateful for that, whether I needed to be or not.

"There's more to the story now," Lindy said, pulling her chair closer to mine so I could hear over the creaking of the water wheel. "Phoebe told me last night that she's got Lem's baby growing in her."

"Oh, Lindy! How do you feel about that?"

"Don't matter how I feel. What is, is. Her pa ain't happy about it, but a grandchild is a grandchild no matter what you think. She'll be all right."

"So that's why she asked to be relieved of her duties at our house."

"That and she still blames Adam for her loss."

Poor Adam. One more heap of blame upon him.

The other two Trethaway boys, Luke and Zeke, seemed subdued by the incident—almost as though they realized how close they, too, had come to death and were grateful for another chance at life. Within a few months, both had moved west—some said Iowa, others said Indiana—as though to separate themselves from the stigma of the Trethaway name. The only two children left in the household were young Jude and Caddie, the only girl, who, at eighteen, showed signs of a wild and lascivious nature. Rebellious, sneaky, and mean, Caddie Trethaway's ways stood testament to the old adage about the proximity of the apple and the tree.

Robbie's ankle was broken—smashed, rather—and his right foot frostbitten to the extent that he lost three toes. He would limp for the rest of his life, full of resentment against everyone but himself. As for Lem Trethaway, Robert expressed neither admiration nor respect for him. To Robbie, he'd just been too slow to get out of the way. Now the veil of motherly love began to slowly strip from my eyes, and, not for the first time, I saw my first-born as more like his real father than I wanted to admit: selfish, immature, and lacking in compassion. Deep in my heart I hoped it would pass, that somehow Robbie would grow up and become the kind of decent man he'd been raised by.

My own response to the incident, after being assured that Robbie, though maimed, would recover, was a new-found admiration for my husband's courage and leadership standing out in the face of all the tragedy, bitterness and regret that would follow. I began to see that Adam MacPhail stood above other men for courage and integrity, and as I, too, matured I realized for the first time in my marriage that my father had done well by me, whether by accident or design.

Adam

In the months after the tragedy in the river, I had one encounter after another with Simon Trethaway, all of them angry, threatening and dangerous. He would wait until he saw me ride out alone and follow me, hanging back just far enough to make me aware of his presence but not close enough to exchange words. I tried to go about my business as normal, but Elinor insisted on accompanying me in my rounds, clearly out of fear for my life. I couldn't allay her fears, so I tried to be patient and allow her to feel that her efforts to protect me bore fruit. She even wanted to post a guard at my office door, but I refused to be intimidated to that point.

Trethaway's behavior had been beyond all reason before Lem's death. Afterwards he was impossible. Anxious to look unfazed by his antics, I kept my schedule, attended to business, and made a point of behaving as though his conduct passed without my notice. For me, his threats really did seem empty. The man was always threatening someone, promising vengeance, predicting doom. No one took much of anything he said seriously, and I tried to keep that in mind as the summer wore on with no letup in his menacing behavior.

Besides, I had plenty of other things to worry about. The damage to the canal and the ironworks from the spring flood would take a long time to repair. Business had picked up some, but it was slow, and getting orders out now required hauling the bars all the way to Hollidaysburg to be loaded on the Portage Railroad, bypassing the damaged canal on the Juniata.

Feeling the need for commiseration, I rode upstream to visit Noah David at Cove Forge on a hot July afternoon. His operation was as damaged as mine—and his markets as slow. As I rode into the yard near his forge, I took note of the results of the flood on the canal, still ravaged after more than four months.

"MacPhail!" His hearty greeting raised my spirits.

"I stopped by to see someone in worse shape than I," I countered.

"To be sure, but I hear you've personal problems as well."

"Nothing I can't handle," I responded to wave off concern. "I'm more worried about getting my bars to market. Looks like I'll have to shut down early this year. Furnace needs attention."

David nodded. "Come in and sit down." He led the way to his office, now familiar to me, dark and cool inside the eighteen-inch-thick walls of his stone house. "Sorry to hear about that business with the Trethaway boy. That kind of thing has a way of festering. I lost a young fellow about five years ago. Nice young man—fell into the crusher. His family still hasn't stopped blaming me."

"I know the feeling. Old man Trethaway is all over me about it. Blames me, threatens me, does everything he can to make my life miserable."

The door opened and David's small daughter, Wren, entered the room. "Papa, mama says I can't go berry picking alone. Will you go with me?"

David's face softened as the child approached and sidled up to him, her face alight with anticipation.

"Maybe later, dear. You can see I'm with a gentleman now."

"Yes, Papa. Who is he?"

"His name is Mr. MacPhail. He lives down river at Mt. Etna."

"Mt. Etna? Can I go to Mt. Etna, Papa? Do they have a berry patch at Mt. Etna?"

David set her down on the floor. "Some day, my dear, some day. Mr. MacPhail has children, too. Perhaps you and your Mama can go calling and visit them. Now run along, and tell cook I'd like some of that cabbage soup for lunch."

"All right, Papa, but you have to go berry picking with me this afternoon."

I smiled at the little girl's ability to bring all conversation to a halt and claim her father's attention. A child whose appearance came late in life could often do that. My own brood, while important to me, had not the same ability to stop the world. This was David's second family—the first all grown and married—with a new, young wife and this one child to dote on, he was enjoying this second chance.

"Yes, where were we?" he asked, rearranging the papers on his desk. "You're hauling your bars to Hollidaysburg, eh? Me, too. I'm disappointed in the canal, friend. Poorly constructed, always down for maintenance, corruption in its management. I hear there's talk of railroads coming in. The sooner the better, I say."

"Railroads can come, but it'll be a long time before we see any close enough to make any difference for us. The canal may be messy, but it's here, and we don't really have an alternative."

"If I were a younger man, I'd put my money in railroads. Think of how many iron rails it'll take to run across Pennsylvania. Enough business to carry us to Kingdom Come."

I wanted to take joy in the future prospects of the iron business, but it was subject to so many ups and downs, I'd lost some of my youthful confidence. Still, the prospect of providing rails and iron for locomotives was promising—all very iffy right then, but both David and I had to anticipate the possibilities with enthusiasm.

I rode home feeling better than I had since before the flood. The day was warm, the shade comfortable, and the air alive with the buzzing of honey bees intent on their mission. Suddenly a shot rang out above my head. My horse reared and I held on to the reins as he bolted down the track. Behind me shouts of laughter ripped the air. I didn't need to turn around to know the who and the what of it. I slowed my horse to a walk and continued, looking over my shoulder every so often, but saw or heard nothing more.

Chapter 50

1842
Ellie

Since Adam and Noah David were close friends, it was expected that Noah's young wife, Elizabeth, and I would bind the tie even closer. Elizabeth David was a lovely young woman; poised, well educated, stylish, and beautiful. Her marriage to Noah could not have been anything other than convenience, given the disparity in their ages. He was fully fifty if he was a day, and young Elizabeth about twenty-two when they married. Their only child, Wren, followed her mother's traits to a tee and made a game of winding her father around her finger. She was, nonetheless, a charming child, considerate of others, friendly, outgoing; in short, a pleasure to have around.

Elizabeth and Wren drove up in their gig once a week in warm weather, and we tried to see each other at least monthly in winter. Our children came to consider Wren a cousin, if not a third sister, coming in age as she did between Alyssa and Bethany.

Elizabeth, born and raised in Harrisburg, passed for a sophisticate in our small and backward society. She'd attended Miss Strong's Academy for Young Ladies in Selinsgrove, a Quaker School, one of very few girls' schools west of the Susquehanna, and was deeply devoted to the education of women. She taught Wren to read at an early age and volunteered to teach our two girls and tutor them in the fine arts of womanhood. The girls were quite anxious to be with their friend and to learn how to sew, embroider, and crochet along with reading, writing poetry, singing, dancing, and playing either the piano or the harpsichord. So it was arranged that they would spend two days of each week at Cove Forge learning proper ladies' skills.

I was pleased to be able to offer Alyssa and Bethany the benefits of education and encouraged their efforts, but I made it clear that I expected them to study the classics and to read more than sentimental novels.

Adam was in favor, since the boys had been tutored at home for years. Robbie was already planning to attend the college at Carlisle, and Laird was working hard to follow in his footsteps. They seemed to be growing up at a gallop, while I would have been satisfied with a slow walk.

Elizabeth David became my friend and confidant almost at once, and we spent our visiting hours discussing our readings and recommending works for each other. We read some of Margaret Fuller's work and agreed that much progress was needed in the area of women's rights. Elizabeth was better traveled than I and well acquainted with ideas considered radical in most circles. But when she talked with me about things like getting women the right to vote or own property, I was right there with her. Having someone to discuss such ideas with brightened my life.

While I liked and admired Elizabeth for her accomplishment, my loyalty to Lindy Baker was never in question. The contrast between these two friends of mine was striking. Elizabeth, young, beautiful, sophisticated and well-to-do, always looking for change and excitement, and Lindy, older, wiser, more sensible, accepting of her role in life and satisfied to be who and where she was. Wisely, I never tried to mix the two friendships. They represented different worlds, and I was comfortable with both—seeing the merits of each but leaning neither way.

One afternoon in the mid-forties, as our fortunes were beginning to return after the Panic of 1837 had extended itself, at least for the iron industry, well past acceptable limits, Elizabeth rode up in her gig, driving a fine chestnut mare I hadn't seen before.

"Elizabeth! New horse?"

"Yes, Noah insists upon spoiling me—and if not me, Wren."

"Does Wren ride?" I asked, never having seen the child astride a horse.

"No, but driving a fast gig isn't beyond her."

I laughed. "Such a spirited girl will be a handful for a husband some day."

Elizabeth sighed. "I hope she finds a patient man. Her father has made her impossible and laughs at the prospect of any man taming her down."

She got down from the gig and handed the reins to our young groom, Charles Leeper, son of the unfortunate Emmett. I invited her to sit on the porch and enjoy some cold mint tea. She'd come alone, and I wondered what she'd done with Wren.

"Oh, she's gone to Hollidaysburg with her father for an excursion on the Portage Railroad. They'll stay the night in Johnstown—Noah has business there—and return tomorrow. She'll want Alyssa and Bethany to stay on this weekend so she can regale them with her adventures."

Elizabeth settled into a rocker near mine as Mrs. Gwynn brought out a tray with a pitcher and two glasses of tea made from the mint that grew wild along the banks of Roaring Run. We talked for a while and watched the canal boats float by, enjoying a gentle breeze coming up from the river. It was some time before the real purpose of her visit surfaced.

"Ellie, do you know that Irishman, Timothy Judge, who works the store at Yellow Spring?"

I hesitated. Tim Judge had been out of my thoughts for some time. What interest would Elizabeth David have in him?

"We've had some dealings with him. I don't know him well," I lied.

"Well, I hear from Noah that he's involved in some sort of rabble rousing with the workers. Have you heard?"

I shook my head. Rabble rousing? Tim Judge? Yes, I could believe that. "What sort of rabble rousing?"

"Telling the workers they're underpaid. Saying they could get more money if they quit and went to work for themselves. Throwing about the idea of their starting their own business, town, whole community, with everyone sharing the profits."

"Really? I'd think they'd rather work here where their needs are met, where they have homes and reliable work. Anyway, why would Tim Judge care about the workers? He's barely worked a day since he quit digging the canal."

"I don't know, but Noah says he wants to talk to your Adam about him. He's run him off from Cove Forge twice in the past two weeks for standing around talking to the men when they should be working."

"Why would they even listen to him?"

"Oh, he's a charming speech maker, that one. He talks like an angel, promises the earth and sky, and then goes on his merry way without a care."

"Hmm. Adam hasn't said anything about him being around here. I hope he doesn't get it into his head to bother *our* workers. Adam doesn't like him to start with." I related the story of the rogue horse and Emmett Leeper's death, and Elizabeth shuddered at the thought of a poor man dying because of Tim Judge's carelessness.

I couldn't understand what Tim could care about wages and working conditions for people other than himself, but it seemed he'd taken up the cause. I marveled at how little I'd ever known about the man and counted myself lucky not to have gone too far with him.

"Noah said he was handing out tracts—printed leaflets about some town out near Pittsburgh where all this talk is put into action. A lot of the workers can't read, but others will read to them—or Mr. Judge will, anytime, often without being asked. Noah had to threaten him with the sheriff last Tuesday."

I breathed a deep sigh. The iron business was subject to so many ups and downs, it was hard to keep skilled workers, and we'd just barely come through a long downturn. If we were to survive, we needed the loyalty and dedication of our workers, not someone coming along to stir them up and make them dissatisfied. And why did it have to be Timothy Judge?

Late that afternoon, after Elizabeth had gone home, I took myself over to the mill to see what Lindy had heard. If anyone knew the dirt on Tim Judge, she would. I found her in her kitchen, taking bread out of the oven, her youngest son, Jared, standing around in his underpants, his overalls over his arm.

"Just a minute, Jared. I can't do more than one thing at a time. When I get this bread turned out, I'll mend your pants."

I smiled and reached for the overalls. "Here, Jared. I'll take care of that for you."

Lindy straightened up and smiled. "These young'uns still need a Ma ever once in a while," she noted. "Can do almost a man's work, but couldn't mend their own britches if the needle was made of gold and the thread was twisted silver."

I took the overalls to a bench outside the door where the light was better and threaded up a needle from my sewing pouch. The tear was L shaped and long, like he'd caught it on a nail. The boy waited inside the door as I stitched and double stitched, knowing boys as I did. As I handed the overalls back to him, Lindy stepped out the door and joined me on the bench, fanning herself with her apron.

"Wouldn't take a second call to get me to go down and jump in the river," she puffed. "It's hot and hotter! What brings you over here this time of day?"

"I had some news this afternoon that won't keep until tomorrow."

Lindy's eyebrows went up. "Hmm? What sort of news?"

"Have you heard anything about someone going around talking to the workers about setting up some kind of community where they all share and share alike?"

"You mean besides Simon Trethaway?"

"Simon Trethaway?"

"Sure. He's been at it these many months. I thought you'd a heard by now. Just does it to get under your Adam's skin, I guess, but most folks around here don't set much store by what he says. They know about the bad blood, and they take whatever Simon Trethaway says as bile, anyway."

"Well, it wasn't Simon Trethaway I meant. It was Tim Judge."

Lindy's eyes widened. The memory of my confession about Tim and me came back to her, and though she'd never mentioned it again, it was clear she had no time for Tim. The horse incident had sealed it for her, and I was sure, if Tim Judge even showed his face around Lindy, she'd give him the comeuppance she felt he deserved.

"What's that Shanty Irish trash care about anyone else's living? He ought to tend to his own business, which, if I hear right, is considerable. Must have half a dozen runny-nosed brats hanging 'round that store. Jeff said the last time he was over to Yellow Spring one of them kids had fallen down the old dry well and there was a great to-do about getting her out. Some people ought not to even have children, if they can't watch them better than that."

"I know. Seems as though some folk are better at *making* babies than *raising* them."

"Judge would know that, for sure. No, I ain't heard nothing about him raising Ned with the workers, but I'd sure be surprised if he wasn't in cahoots with Simon Trethaway over it."

The thought of an alliance between Tim Judge and Simon Trethaway set my teeth on edge. "I'm always worried about Tim, anyway, you know. He's unpredictable. I'm afraid somehow he'll try to make something out of what went on between us back in the day."

Lindy looked at me over her spectacles. "Some things never go away, do they? Always come back to haunt you. Well, you can't keep him from it if he wants to do you hurt, but I think enough time's passed so most folks wouldn't make much of it now."

I sighed. "Youthful indiscretion. I can't for the life of me remember what attracted me to him. I'd not even look at him now."

"Be glad for that. You grew up and learned to appreciate what you had. Too bad good sense comes too late for some and not at all for others."

I sat quiet, looking out at the river, thinking about Adam—how angry it made me that Tim Judge would do anything to hurt him or undermine his business. Adam took pride in treating his workers well. He listened to their concerns and tried every way to meet their needs—showed them respect and appreciation at every turn. Damn Tim Judge. "Well, let me know if you hear anything more about either of those plug uglies doing any more mischief. Adam needs to be aware, if he isn't already."

I was mistaken in thinking that Adam didn't know about the alliance between Judge and Trethaway. At dinner that evening he told our children not to engage in any conversation about wages or working conditions with our workers' children, and to be always polite and respectful when talking to the workers or their families. Then, with a weighty look at me, he said, "There are people around who want to cause us trouble by inciting our workers against us. We need to be above the fray. Do not," he said with a meaningful glance at Robbie, "engage."

Robbie, immediately on the defensive, asked, "Who? What do they say?"

"Robbie." I said it with all the parental authority I could muster. "Do not engage."

Adam looked around the table. "Please respect my wishes, children. You'll understand someday." He rose and excused himself to the parlor, where I found him sometime later.

"So I suppose you're wondering what that table discussion was about," he began.

"No. Elizabeth David was here this afternoon. She says Tim Judge is agitating around Cove Forge, and Lindy says Simon Trethaway is up to the same around here, with little to show for it, I hope."

"We can hope. It remains to be seen how many will listen."

I took a deep breath and resolved to do whatever I could to make sure neither of these purveyors of discontent would wreak havoc on our lives.

Chapter 51

Summer 1842
Adam

I tried to keep it from Ellie for as long as I could, but I knew someone would tell her eventually. Simon Trethaway and Tim Judge had been taken in by the utopian movement, reading all about how the poor and exploited should create their own communities, share and share alike. They'd decided to take it upon themselves to further the rights of workers, although it was beyond me to fathom what interest they should have in those rights other than feathering their own nests. It seemed to me right from the start that both men were involved, at least in part, as a way to harry me. Once this alliance was general knowledge around Mt. Etna, I had to warn Ellie and the children to be careful what they said and who they said it to. We didn't need to add to the unrest with arrogance or selfish interest.

Trethaway was always dangerous, but while I didn't wish to be jocular about so serious a situation, it did occur to me that he'd passed up many a chance to kill me so far. Still, nothing deterred him from flinging threats and insults at every opportunity.

Tim Judge was another character altogether. I couldn't get a handle on the origins of his hatred for me, but as time went on, it became more and more clear that he harbored such. The incident over the horse had been unpleasant, but surely not enough to generate such bile. Thinking that he, of the two, would be more likely to listen to reason, I decided to ride over to Yellow Spring and engage him in conversation, so I mounted my horse and rode off alone, something I seldom did since the advent of Trethaway's rage against me. The ride up through Polecat Hollow was uneventful, even though I kept a wary eye on the woods along the way. Upon my arrival I found the place deserted, the store standing wide open, the inn across the road quiet in the afternoon sun—no children under foot, not even a chicken scratching in the dust.

I went around back to the stable, where I heard some signs of life, and there I met Mrs. Judge, looking pregnant, carrying a fork of hay bigger than she was, with little ones trailing after in various stages of undress and want of hygiene. The woman was still young enough to be almost pretty, but eight years of marriage and five children had taken their toll.

"Good day, Mrs. Judge. Is your husband about?"

"Nay. Gone to a meetin' he is. To Hollidaysburg. Says *ye* better get ready, for the storm is about to burst. Upon *ye*, I mean, Squire."

"Squire? How did I get to be a squire?

"Squire, ironmaster, rich man. All the same to the likes of us. So says Tim."

"What got him interested in all this?" I asked.

"Oh he's been readin' through all the long winter months. You know some days not a soul comes in the store. When it's cold and snowy, that is. Then's when he reads and reads and reads. Got him a bunch of books that he reads all the time. He's pretty learned is Tim."

"What does he read about?"

"I don't know, but it sure gets him wrought up. Paces and cusses and pounds his fist. I keep the young'uns away when he's like that. He gets mean."

I looked around the shambles of a stable yard—cluttered with loose straw, broken implements, piles of horse manure—nothing that wasn't broken, scarred, or worn out. Mismanagement and carelessness abode here. Everything I'd thought about Timothy Judge in the past came into focus now as I surveyed his realm. A restless dreamer, incapable of sticking to anything long enough to make something of it. I shook my head and turned away from the used-up woman and dirty, unkempt children.

"Tell him I'd like to see him. He can stop by my office when he gets back."

Raising the hay fork again, the wretched soul nodded and turned to look down at a child clinging to her skirt. Pale and tired, her dress barely hanging from her shoulders, she hefted the forkful of hay over the side of the stall. The look on her face—a look I can only describe as despair—told me that hope had fled long ago and wasn't coming back. It was clear that five children with another one on the way and a worthless husband had drained it from her.

I was back at my office two days later when Mr. Judge entered without knocking or asking leave of my clerk. I looked up, surprised, when he strode up to my desk and leaned over close enough for me to smell liquor on his breath. "What ye want of me, MacPhail? My woman says ye been sniffin' around."

"Yes, Judge. I've been wondering what concerns you about my operation. You've been talking to the workers, handing out leaflets. You seem to think it needs changing."

"That ain't sayin' enough, Master. Yer makin' money on the backs of the poor workers. Gettin' rich while they barely survive. Yer the rulin' class, oppressors, all of ye. We want the workers to band together and take things into their own hands."

"That's all wrong, Judge. Ask any of my workers and you'll see that they're secure, well paid, and content. Anyway, what concern is it of yours even if it were true? You don't work here."

"Sure, and if I did, ye'd be firing me for trying to help the poor buggers."

I had to agree on that score. If firing would rid me of his presence and his influence, I'd jump to it. "What do you want of me, then? And why should I listen to you?"

"It ain't what *I* want of ye. It's what the workers want of ye. They're the voice. I only speak in their favor."

"Who appointed you spokesman? Which of my workers selected you to speak in their behalf?"

"None yet, but they will. Once they understand how exploited they are—how ye take everything from them to line yer own pockets. They'll jump at the chance to control their own destinies, live a decent life without being run into the ground by the likes of ye."

"Run into the ground? You're daft, man. First off, you're taking it upon yourself to agitate for workers who aren't in need, and second, you've no concept of how a business is run. Your actions could destroy the whole operation here. Then where would the workers be? I don't know where your ideas come from, but you're sadly ignorant."

"My ideas come from years of exploitation at the hands of the likes of ye, MacPhail. Digging the whole damned canal, for one thing, and working like a dog cutting trees in these woods for another."

"Well, you're out of that now. Running a store can't be such onerous work. Why start up this agitation?"

"Because it's right. I've been readin' up on it. Robert Owen, Charles Fourier. They call it for what it is—exploitation. The workers ought to own this place and run it themselves. Then ye'd see a better world. Everyone sharing the profits."

That was enough. I rose from behind my desk and stepped up to him, shaking my fist in his face. "You have no idea what it's taken to build this iron works. No idea at all. You came here poor and ignorant, and now you think you've earned the right to tell me how to run it? Get yourself back to your store and don't show your face around here again—or at Cove Forge. I'll run you off myself, if need be."

Timothy Judge glared back at me, fire in his eyes. "Ye'll have yer hands full to stop what I've started. Ye'll have yer work cut out turning me and Trethaway off our track. We've got a plan to change the way things are done around here. Oh, and while yer thinkin' yer so high and mighty, it might interest ye to know that yer wife doesn't share yer opinion of me. She found me mighty attractive back in the day. If ye don't want that spread around, ye might think again about running me off."

He turned and stalked out the door, leaving me standing there dazed and confused. What was he talking about? Ellie? My Ellie? Suddenly the threat of labor agitation faded and the thought of my wife with Timothy Judge invaded my whole being. I restrained myself from chasing him down and beating him senseless. This was too much. I had to talk to Elinor.

I was back in our parlor within five minutes, looking for my wife. I called to her from the foot of the stairs and she descended, looking calm and beautiful in a dress of summer lawn. She came down the stairs smiling—laughing, actually—at something young John had said. I waited in the hall below, my whole being in turmoil.

We entered the parlor and I closed the doors against the household help or the children hearing. "What have you had to do with Timothy Judge?"

Her face fell. She whitened and sat down. "Why? What have you heard, and from whom?"

"From himself. He says you found him attractive back in the day. What day? When and how, Elinor? What is this about?"

"Oh, Adam, no. No. It wasn't what you think. A dalliance. A brief tryst. Nothing more."

My hands were shaking now. I reached for her, grabbed her by the shoulders, raised her to stand facing me. "A tryst? A dalliance? My god, woman, what do you mean?"

Tears streamed from her eyes, dripping down on the bosom of her lovely dress. "I ... I was lonely. So sad. I found him attractive. He lured me into thinking we could...could run away. I didn't. Oh, Adam, I didn't mean..."

Dropping my hands to my sides, I stood mute in the middle of the parlor. It was true. She'd been loved by another man—and not just any man, but the basest and lowest of men. I turned away, unable to quell my trembling. I wanted to hit her—beat her—make her pay for all the years of parsing out her affection, depriving me for so long while she nurtured a fantasy of being reunited with her former lover—and now this. The uncertainty, the insecurity, the emptiness. Any other man would have struck her and gone after him, but I could only think of the furnace, the company, all I'd worked for in the years since we'd been married. I knew she didn't love me. So what? What was she going to do about it? What, indeed.

Chapter 52

Summer 1842
Ellie

The world ended for me that day. Adam coming in the middle of the day, accosting me, telling me that Timothy Judge had told him about us. Told him I had loved him once. And now I stood naked before my husband, the husband I had once loathed and now accepted, respected, even held affection for. What could I say? Beg forgiveness? Make amends? I watched Adam step away across what I feared was a gulf too wide to be bridged. How could I expect him to forgive so much? I cried, but as so many times before in my life, crying did no good.

"Adam, I..."

"Don't speak. Don't try to make excuses or lie or whatever it was you were going to do. Please. Leave me. I need to think."

"It never got that far, Adam. I want you to know that. It was a brief fantasy—a foray into an impossible world. So long ago. I was young and miserable."

"Please, Elinor. Don't make it worse. Please, just leave me."

"No! I won't walk away without making you understand exactly what happened and why. I loath him now, have loathed him for years. He's not at all what I thought. And it's ironic that he should bring pain into our lives after so long. Really, Adam. I harbor no sweet memories. Only regret."

Adam's face, contorted by pain, turned away. He took a step toward the door, but I reached out for him, touched his sleeve, bade him listen. Then I poured out my heart to him as I never had before. Told him how bitterly disappointed I'd been by Robert Clifton's rejection. How sad and angry I was when my father treated me in such a high-handed way, voiced my anger at him for accepting my father's offer without reservation and putting the running of the business before me. I cried and pleaded for forgiveness, even though I knew I'd behaved unforgivably.

"It comes down to this, Adam. Why can you decide for yourself, be the master of your being, while I can't? You always had a choice, but I didn't."

He grabbed my shoulders again and turned me to face him. "Don't try to justify your behavior, Elinor. I've treated you well—done everything for you."

"Everything except treat me as an equal. That's all I want, Adam. All I've ever wanted. To be free—to choose for myself—make my own decisions. Is that too much to ask?"

He sat down in the carpet-covered platform rocker, his head in his hands. I stood before him, anguished, afraid all was lost. Then I knelt at his feet, took his hands in mine, and looked into his eyes, those intense blue eyes that never wavered, never gave way.

"I know I don't deserve forgiveness, but I ask for it now so that we can make something of this marriage. We have five children . . . and Robbie . . . who didn't do anything to deserve for their world to be broken. This was so long ago, and I've never wavered again. Not once. Adam, you must believe me, Tim Judge is nothing to me, and if he thinks he can hurt us with this rabble rousing, we must stand together and face him."

Adam's face was unreadable, his eyes hard. He was thinking about so many things. The company, I knew, and Simon Trethaway, with his incessant threats and ravings, and now Tim Judge, who thought he could use me to gain advantage and get Adam to yield to his demands.

He rose from his chair slowly and turned again to face me. "Stay here, Elinor. I'll tend to this."

Chapter 53

Summer 1842
Adam

I strode out of the house and turned toward the stable, where I asked young Leeper for my horse. Once mounted, I rode up Polecat Hollow toward Yellow Spring, my anger tempering as I rode but my sense of honor undiminished, my brain alive with thoughts of calculated revenge. If Tim Judge thought himself exploited now, how would he like to be without a job or a place to lay his head? I was well acquainted with Thaddeus French, the absentee owner of the Yellow Spring store and inn. It wouldn't take much to persuade him to let Judge go—after all, he was, at best, a poor a manager. French could do better. Or how would Mr. Judge like to spend some time in jail while his wife and children starved by the wayside? The kind of rabble-rousing Judge was engaging in wasn't looked upon with favor in Huntingdon County, and with my business and political connections I could arrange his arrest—have him in jail by sundown. Or how would Judge like to be transported, bag and baggage, to some place, like, say, Oregon or California? Maybe that would be far enough to quiet his noise about my wife.

I rode into the shabby, worn little stable yard behind the store, expecting to find Judge there among his precious horses, but I found the stables reeking of horse manure and not a soul in sight. Just as I turned to go 'round to the store, I heard a whimper from the farthest stall. Barely able to see in the dim light, I followed my ears to the entrance where, in a ragged little circle, the five Judge children stood like stair steps, their faces raised in a dumb gaze. Hanging from a rafter by a hemp rope, their mother dangled, twisting slowly, head cocked at a grotesque angle, her face blue, her tongue protruding from her mouth.

Gasping, I rushed to cut her down, but as soon as I reached her I knew it was too late; she'd done this hours ago. I found a knife stuck in a post and cut the rope, catching the frail body over my shoulder. The children stood watching, dull eyed, stupefied, uncomprehending. I spoke to the oldest, a girl of about eight. "Take your brothers and sisters outside now. I'll see what can be done."

"She's dead, ain't she? S'what she allus said she'd do some day. We was out gigging frogs all morning. That's when she done it."

"Where is your father? Is he about?" I looked around for a pile of clean straw and laid the body out, gently crossing her arms and placing my handkerchief over her face.

The girl shrugged. "Ain't seen 'im all day," she said. "He been gone a lot since him and Trethaway took up together."

"Can your brothers ride?" I asked, referring to the twins, about six years old, who stood behind their sister staring at their dead mother.

"Yes, sir. I can." The taller of the two—and the more likely looking—hitched up the strap of his overalls. "You want me to go to Williamsburg for the doctor? He won't come. I know, cause we went for him when Mama had Linny, and he said no. Said he didn't need no more charity cases."

"No. Not the doctor. Go to Mt. Etna and get the preacher."

The boy took a last look at his mother and climbed up on the back of a broken-down old mare who looked as hungry as he did, dug his bare heels into her sides, and clopped out of the stable. As the other children followed their older sister out the door, I climbed up the side of the stall and untied the rope from the rafter. The rest of the stalls were empty. It looked as though Tim Judge was down to only two horses, one of them barely a nag. Lot of good his reading and ranting had done him.

With nothing to do but wait until the minister arrived, I surveyed the scene around me. The stable, the brick store, the clear, lovely spring, the owner's mansion which served as an inn. It seemed a likely place where a man could get a foothold and build something, but Tim Judge had let it fail. My rage at him returned and with it the shaking and the pain in my gut that had started in the parlor of my home as I'd listened to my wife plead for forgiveness.

A half hour later, when the boy returned with the minister, I was still looking at the frail, pathetic body stretched out in the straw, wondering what would become of her children. Apparently, their father had more important matters to attend to. The minister, Rev. Snyder, a kind, elderly man who had answered the call to our little church a few years before, took one look at the body and backed out of the stable. He went 'round to the front of the store where the children sat, numb and silent, on the steps, and I followed, unwilling to spend any more time with the corpse.

"Come, children. Let's go over to Mt. Etna to see Mrs. Snyder. She's preparing a room where you can bathe and change into clean clothes."

"These is all the clothes we got," the oldest girl explained. "There ain't no money for clothes."

It occurred to me that there was a whole store full of dry goods—bolts of muslin and gingham. Plenty of raw material, but making clothes for the children would have required time, energy, and skill, all of which were apparently in short supply here.

"Oh, don't worry about that. We've plenty clothes to go round," the minister assured them. He turned to me. "I'll have Frank Stalling make a coffin and get someone to dig a grave. Do you know where the father is?"

"No, but I'll wait for him, if you'll take care of the children."

Rev. Snyder handled the grim details with dispatch, returned to the stable, and covered the body with a dirty sheet stripped from a bed in the living quarters behind the store. Then he lined the children up, hefted the youngest up on the saddle in front of him, and bade the others follow him to Mt. Etna.

I watched the sad little column move along the track and disappear among the trees, silent and obedient, numb to the grief that the youngest might never even feel. Left to myself while waiting for the dead woman's husband, I went into the store and sat through the afternoon and evening, alone with my thoughts. No one came around, not even a customer, and I passed the time taking inventory of the stock. Seemed Timothy Judge had neglected that aspect of the business, too. The shelves were almost bare, the flour weevily, the produce wrinkled and shriveled. God! The man didn't take care of anything—work nor family. Again the bile rose in me and I longed to get my hands on him, beat him senseless.

Boredom forced me to wander about looking for something—anything—to distract me from the disaster upon disaster that had made up my day. My eyes fell upon a book stowed under the counter, and I took it out, lit a lamp and began to read. It was by Charles Fourier—all about how people could and should live in harmony, sharing the bounty of the land and their own production. Seems this Fourier had started what he called a Utopian community as an experiment to show the merit of his thinking. I didn't need to see it to know that such an endeavor would never work because there would always be a Timothy Judge or two—too lazy to work but sharing equally in the proceeds, thus angering their fellows and bringing the whole operation down. It might take a while for it to fail, but fail it would, that was clear. How anyone with any sense could entertain such a notion was beyond me. But the appeal of the idea was easy to understand for someone like Timothy Judge, living in poverty and unable to make himself do what it would take to fix his circumstances. The prospect of living in comfort with little effort would be attractive to such as he.

My thoughts wandered back to Elinor and her dalliance with this man. Her words of the morning echoed in my brain. I knew I'd been inattentive—always putting the business ahead of her. But what was all this talk about rights? Everyone knew, women had no rights. Was it unjust? Well, probably, but that was how it was—how it had always been. What made her think she could, or even should, change that? It may not have occurred to her, but men's choices were limited, too and changing the order of things would bring us to chaos.

I dozed with my head on my arms on the rough wooden counter until, around five o'clock in the morning, I was aroused by the sound of an approaching horse. I rose from my chair and waited while the man dismounted and, attracted by the light, came stumbling up the front steps and into the store. Wherever Tim Judge had been, there was liquor in abundance, and he had indulged freely. Now he stood before me, bleary eyed and uncomprehending.

"MacPhail. Ye here to hear more about yer wife and me?"

I took one step toward him, jabbed my left fist into his gut, doubling him over, and caught him so hard in the face with my right that I knew as he slumped to the floor that I'd broken his jaw. I picked up my hat, dusted it off, and plopped it on my head, then stepped over the drunken mass on the floor and walked out the door.

The ride home in the dawning light refreshed me. I felt better.

Ellie

Sitting at home with the children, I was sure I knew where Adam had gone, and prayed that he wouldn't confront Tim Judge. Kind, gentle Adam had never been in a fight in his life, but Tim had—many of them. My fears intensified when I saw a pale and ragged boy ride up to the minster's house, bareback. He looked familiar, but I wasn't sure where I'd seen him. Still, given the direction he'd come from, my apprehensions rose. In a few minutes Rev. Snyder left the house looking unnerved, saddled his horse, and rode out with the child in tow.

Mrs. Gwynn, ever curious about any sort of goings on, crossed the lawn to the parsonage and visited with the Snyder's girl. She was back in ten minutes with a story so ghastly I thought for a moment she'd made it up in some perverse way to tease me. But one look at her face told me that this terrible thing had really happened, and all I could think about was Adam, hurting already, forced to deal with such a tragedy. I waited, hoping he would arrive soon, but when the troop of children and Rev. Snyder returned without him, my fears escalated.

269

What was he doing? Surely he wouldn't go so far as to kill Timothy Judge. Surely not.

I sat through the rest of the day and through the night, distraught, worrying over every possible outcome. But when Adam finally arrived at around six the next morning, he seemed calm, settled, almost serene. He came into our bedroom in the quiet dawn light, approached me in my bed, and reached for my hand.

"Oh Adam, you didn't..."

"No. He's been punished beyond my ability to get even. Now I want to put all of this to rest."

I rose from the bed and stood facing him, holding both of his hands, searching his eyes for lingering bitterness. There was none. Only resolve.

"Ellie, I... I've thought this through. We may not have had the best of starts, but we've weathered so many storms. What we have left is on solid ground. I wish I'd understood you better in the beginning, but at least I think I do now."

He held my hand as he spoke, and I looked into his eyes, so glad that he was all right, I didn't care about anything else.

"If you can forgive me my shortcomings, I can certainly forgive yours."

I smiled into his eyes. "Oh, Adam, how could I not? You always meant well. I was too immature to see that, but I know it's true."

"We'll make this work, Elinor. We will begin again—live another day—put the past behind us. Can we still make a go of it?"

"Yes. I know we can."

"Fine, then, I do not wish to hear the name of Timothy Judge in this house—ever. Now rise and get me some breakfast."

Relief flooded over me, and even though I'd no idea of what had transpired between Adam and Tim, I was grateful for the chance at a new beginning. Mrs. Gwynn usually made breakfast, but this was a hearkening back to the early days of our marriage when I did it all. This time I would do it gladly, willingly, gratefully,

Chapter 54

1843–44
Ellie

In the months to come, Adam and I worked slowly though past slights and trespasses, letting time do its measured healing. We talked more now, more than we ever had before, and about more than just the everyday. Because it was on my mind we spoke often of women's rights and the tiny, burgeoning movement nurtured by the writings of women like the Gremke sisters and Margaret Fuller. At first, Adam was inclined to disagree, reluctant as any man would be to admit he'd been a party to depriving others of their rights, but as he had time to consider it, he admitted that he saw the truth in my thinking.

"Think of our daughters, Adam. If they should inherit a share of the company, what would happen to it?"

"It would pass to their husbands, of course."

"And what if their husbands turned out to be dullards or blackguards or worse?"

His brow furrowed as he considered the proposition. As a father, he'd always held a special place in his heart for Alyssa and Bethany. Both showered him with affection and strove to make him proud.

"I see your point, I really do," he said. "I wouldn't want this to get out, but I'm beginning to understand that women are, as you say, treated like property. I'd want to protect our girls from that."

My smile said all I wanted it to say. "Thank you, Adam. Thank you for listening."

The children were growing up and needed the security our home offered before they should fly. I found myself struggling with the same musings, longings, and regrets that Lindy had experienced before me. Children! Millstones when they're young, delights when they mature enough not to need any hovering, harbingers of change and transformers of life, my everlasting concern and delight.

As a family we now entered a phase that pleased me, one I longed to preserve, even though I knew it could not last. We were such a close knit group, enjoying each other's company, happy in the security that Etna Furnace provided, while around the perimeter of our contentment the future raised its incessant and inevitable presence.

As for Timothy Judge, his children were taken in by local folk, two to Williamsburg, another to Alexandria, a third to Huntingdon, and the last to a home in Hollidaysburg, separated and lost to one another. He continued his alliance with Trethaway, preaching at every opportunity the virtues of the Utopian life, passing out handbills exhorting the 'downtrodden and exploited workers' to join in a great and noble experiment, a 'Utopia along the Juniata to be founded on lands generously donated by Mr. Simon Trethaway for the purpose of establishing God's kingdom on earth.'

The bills described in detail the wondrous, carefree and advantageous life to be had by simply contributing all one's worldly goods to the common coffers and sharing alike in the proceeds. Amidst a great to-do of preparation and planning, the would-be saviors of the poor and downtrodden shaped and reshaped their mythical community, undeterred by the realities of weather, human shortcomings, or diminishing funds.

It actually looked like they might make something of it for a while. People came from far away, mostly from the cities—the locals didn't bother to lend an ear—and willingly parted with their savings, their worldly goods, enthralled with the promise of shared ownership and a peaceful communal existence. Many of them had no experience with the agrarian lifestyle they were embracing, and for some, the sheer effort of planting, reaping, and caring for animals was more than they were willing or able to maintain.

Simon Trethaway made a big show of his donation to the cause and no effort to disguise his delight at the prospect of free labor to clear his land and prepare the soil for farming. There were about twenty families at the start, all full of hope and high expectations, and while we watched with interest, our skepticism, given the character of the two entrepreneurs, held sway. The first winter was harsh. Deep snows and freezing temperatures drove two or three families away at the outset. Still, the recruitment went on and a few more families straggled in. By the spring, crops were sewn, clearing the woods continued, and Adam watched with chagrin as wood that might have made good charcoal was turned into rough cabins reminiscent of times we thought gone by.

In those days, I loved to visit Lindy and hear her go on about the carrying on across the river. "Can't figure what makes folks so ready to believe anything they hear," she mused. "I guess if you don't know them two buzzards, you might be inclined to listen, but how long does it take for the real sitiation to set in?"

"Let's keep watching, Lindy. It shouldn't take much longer." I laughed. Even though both Trethaway and Judge still bore us ill will and did everything they could to turn the newcomers against us, it was entertaining to watch the goings on and speculate on the outcome.

The outcome wasn't long in coming. A poor harvest that second year made discontent inevitable, and when the second winter proved even harsher than the first the hopes and expectations of the community began to erode. Trethaway and Judge traveled farther and farther afield to recruit new citizens for their experiment, while the earlier converts murmured ever louder among themselves.

"Seems to me them two keep on the road so's they don't have to face us at home," one of their number complained to Adam.

"Yeah, stay away so they don't have to face the music," another added. The discontent was mounting.

A few of the women from the commune crossed the river to our store for necessities, but with almost nothing to trade with, Adam had to limit their credit. When by January of 1844 it was apparent that those left were in dire need, a delegation of men from Beulah Land, as they called, it came across to plead their case.

Their spokesman was a sincere and earnest middle-aged man named Thomas Clary. Like the others, he'd given everything he had to the cause, and now it looked as though all was lost. There was no money for seed for spring planting, and even if there were, it was doubtful they could hold themselves together until harvest time. Food supplies were low, and some of the group were ready to give up on what they saw as a lost cause. A few turned out, as predicted, to be lazy shirkers whose very presence contributed to the unrest, but with the founders always absent, there was no one to mediate these conflicts, and the anger festered.

So when Thomas Clary led a destitute-looking delegation into Adam's office, he listened patiently and tried to find ways to alleviate their suffering.

"Why don't you take this up with your leaders?" Adam asked them, moved by their plight but concerned about the effect a rescue might have on our own operation.

"They ain't around to take up with," Mr. Clary replied. "Ain't seen nothin' of them since November or thereabouts."

"What about Mrs. Trethaway? Surely she knows where to find her husband."

"She won't open the door if any of us folks goes around. Says she's got naught to do wi' it."

Adam sighed and rose from his desk. "Come with me. I can let you have only the barest of necessities, but at least you won't starve." He led the way downstairs to the store and directed the storekeeper to extend as much credit as was reasonable.

That took care of the immediate problem, but it was clear that the two founders of Beulah Land would avoid all responsibility as the project foundered. Simon Trethaway stayed away for months, although we suspected that he visited his family under the cloak of darkness more than once, and Tim Judge might as well have been swallowed up by the earth. When Trethaway did show up he was besieged with complaints and demands for restitution, which he dismissed with a wave of his hand.

"Ye shoulda worked harder, me man. Ye didn't put in yer fair share, and now ye want to fix blame on me. How am I supposed to control the weather? Is it my fault the soil is rocky? What do ye mean, I didn't live up to me promises? What promises?"

In the end, their deceit caught up with them, leaving the two entrepreneurs awash in debt and facing the wrath of those whose money they'd pilfered. The two saviors of humanity were so busy trying to quiet their critics and avoid their creditors, they had little time to harass Adam. After only a little more than two years, the much vaunted, highly touted Beulah Land lay uninhabited, a desolate ruin, its adherents scattered to the winds and its miscreant founders at liberty to repeat their mischief if they could find more willing ears.

When spring came, Adam had to refuse to extend credit for seed, telling the men to abandon the Utopian idea and seek work elsewhere. Some packed up what they had left and moved on. A few sought work as wood cutters or quarrymen, but there wasn't enough employment to go around. We watched the little settlement wear down to two or three households and several poorly built empty cabins already starting to rot into the ground.

Beulah Land was finally reduced to one lone inhabitant, a bearded hermit by the name of James Sanders, late of New York State, a shoemaker by trade, who crossed the river about every three months to bring shoes to sell Adam for the store. Strange, taciturn, unsocial, he was a master of his craft, and the shoes he made were worthy of a king. He tanned his own leather and worked it to a soft, pliable state so that his shoes gave comfort even when new.

He'd come into the store and place eight or ten pairs of shoes on the counter and state his price. There was no negotiating, no discussion. If the store manager wanted his shoes, he would pay the asking price or Sanders would gather up the lot and take them back to his cabin. Adam saw the value in the man's fine craftsmanship and directed the manager to pay what was asked. The shoes sold promptly, leaving the manager to apologize to latecoming customers who had to go home empty handed and wait for the supply to be replenished.

Our young John found James Sanders fascinating, sitting outside the man's cabin, watching him work with the leather, awl, and iron last, sewing his shoes as he had learned at the hands of a master shoemaker somewhere in the Adirondacks. John said Sanders spoke very little, allowing him to watch but not interrupt. When he took a break, he would offer John a drink of water from the spring near his door, or a crust of bread he'd baked himself. Sometimes there was cheese James Sanders had made from the milk of two goats he kept tethered on a grassy field behind the house, or perhaps an egg from the coop that housed four hens and a rooster. A garden plot provided a wide variety of vegetables, and James Sanders was a woodsman of the highest order, for he knew every edible berry, herb, root, and twig, and when not working on shoes, he and John would trek the woods in search of the bounty it offered to the knowledgeable gleaner.

A gentle soul, James Sanders had been taken in by the Utopian talk, found Beulah Land to his liking, and stayed after it was abandoned by the rest, modeling his life to a level of independent self-sufficiency our son found alluring. I wondered that John might take to the way of a hermit, but his brother Laird assured me that John would not be one to live alone in the woods, his friendship with Mr. Sanders notwithstanding.

Young Edward, the baby of the family and everybody's darling, showed a personality that endeared him to all. His sisters pampered and babied him long past necessity, and his brothers tolerated him well beyond their patience with any other youngster his age. It was his sunny disposition that made him such a pet . . . a ready smile, a contagious laugh, a propensity for mischief, especially when aimed at his siblings. He worked side by side with his brothers at whatever task they set themselves to, displaying an uncanny ability to imitate both word and mannerism, which set the older boys to laughter at every turn. Young Edward MacPhail was the prince of the neighborhood, charming everyone with a joke or a compliment, never at a loss for either.

So as ours lives continued and mended and knit closer with the passing years, Lindy's brood grew and prospered, as well. Joel took a wife, moved to a farm in the river bottoms at the foot of Fox Hollow, and started a family. Chad moved to Water Street, became the innkeeper's assistant, and grew into the ownership as though he'd inherited it. Phoebe gave birth to Lem Trethaway's child, a little girl who favored her mother and was called Tess, but when Phoebe married Chris Coleman and moved up to the top of Coleman's hill, the little one stayed with her Grandma Lindy, unready to leave the home and grandmother she loved. One by one they grew and left, but in the same way they came back—Joel to bring his wheat to the mill, Chad to court one of the Corbin girls, Phoebe to visit and keep an eye on her mother and her child. Jared, Lane, and Jenny lingered, but they, too, grew up and grew on, leaving Lindy and Jeff to face each other over a barren table where once chatter and laughter held sway.

But Lindy was still Lindy, so nothing daunted her for long. She was still up for a walk in the woods, a berry picking expedition, or a trip up to the cemetery on the hill behind the tenant house to take flowers to the graves of the children there. She quilted all winter, providing her family with warmth and shelter long after they were capable of doing for themselves. She still kept a passable garden and canned, dried, and pickled all the food she could store against the winter.

Our visits now centered around talk of those going west in ever greater numbers. Neither of us could fathom the attraction. Lindy counted her blessings that none of hers ever actually went, while I wondered if I would ever have to face the possibility. At times like this, I thought of my father, alone and aging in Berks County, and wondered if he ever regretted sending me away, thus missing the chance to know his grandchildren, one of life's secret rewards.

Chapter 55

1844
Adam

The troubles over Beulah Land were barely past when one evening there came a heavy knock on our front door. Seated in the parlor, reading the news from Huntingdon, I looked to Ellie with a question. Who came pounding on the front door at such a late hour? Who, indeed? I rose and opened the door to an angry, none-too-sober Simon Trethaway, leaning against the doorway for balance, fire in his eyes.

"Trethaway! Good evening. What brings you out at this hour?"

"I'll tell ye what brings me out," he snarled, letting go the door jamb, swaying dangerously to and fro.

"What brings me out is that good for nothing son of yours. That's what brings me out."

Watching him waver, confused and annoyed by his manner, I decided my best option was to let him say his piece. "Son? Which son is that, my man?"

"The cripple. Robbie. That's the one."

My heart floundered in my chest, knowing how Robbie could try my patience and raise the bile in others with his unfettered haughtiness and insistence on acting the prince.

"Robbie? What's he done?"

"Rutted my Caddie, that's what!" The man pushed his way into our center hall, standing large, menacing, his eyes tiny slits in his red and bulbous face. "Got her with child, he has. Now, what do you say to that, MacPhail? And you so high and proper. What say you now?"

Robbie! What was he thinking? Twenty years old, reading the law at college, a bright future ahead. I'd been considering opening my own rolling mill in Pittsburgh and having him run it. Grooming his brother, Laird, to take *my* place. Now what?

"Caddie? Are you sure? Is she sure? I'd no thought of them even knowing each other, let alone..." I turned to Elinor. "Send for Robbie."

She ascended the stairs, holding her skirts up in her haste. As she disappeared into the children's room, I turned to Trethaway. "Are you sure about this? I mean, are you sure it was Robbie?"

"If my girl says it were he, it were he. She oughta know." His small, mean, belligerent eyes dared me to argue.

Elinor was back downstairs in a minute, her face drawn. "He's not here. Allysa says he goes out at night down the back stairs through the kitchen door. Says he does it all the time."

I turned back to Trethaway, anxious to dismiss him and have time to consider this situation without his ranting in my ear. "I'll see to Robbie. What do you expect from me?"

"Why make him marry her, is what. What else?"

"I see. Well, we'll have to hear what Robbie has to say. We can talk tomorrow over at my office." All I wanted now was to get rid of him—get him and the stench of him out of my house.

"Don't you go tryin' to squirm out of this, MacPhail. I'll have yer furnace and yer house and yer whole operation 'fore this is over. My Caddie's a good girl, and ever'one knows Robbie MacPhail is a rake."

I moved to herd him toward the door before the rest of the children would come down to witness this intrusion. "We'll talk tomorrow. Good night, man."

He turned and waved a threatening arm around the hallway. "All of this. Every last splinter. I'll have it all."

I felt myself move to push him toward the door, but Ellie's restraining hand on my arm stopped me. I stepped aside, holding the oval brass doorknob tight as he staggered past me. "You mark my words, MacPhail. You've messed wi' my family one time too many."

Once he was gone, I returned to my chair in the parlor and sat down heavily. Robbie. Robbie, always pushing the boundaries, considering himself above the rules, caring little for the rights and feelings of others. This kind of behavior didn't surprise me, but Caddie Trethaway? My God, Robbie, what were you thinking?

Ellie spoke first. "Do you think it's really so, or is Trethaway just making it up? I mean, the girl may be pregnant, but . . ."

"Let's wait until Robbie gets home. I want to hear his side of it."

Unable to settle down to rest, we sat up until almost midnight before the sound of hoofbeats told us our son was home. We waited until he'd stabled his horse, heard him sneak in the back way, but I was waiting for him in the kitchen.

"Good evening, Robbie. What keeps you out so late?"

He hesitated, taken aback. "Oh, nothing. I was just over at the Rouzers is all. They had a party for Gerald—to send him off to Ohio or wherever it is he's going."

"Come in the parlor. Your mother wants to talk to you."

"Me? What'd I do?"

"Yes. What did you do? Speculation abounds."

When the three of us had arranged ourselves in the parlor, Elinor took up the quest. "Robbie, have you been friendly with Caddie Trethaway?"

His face whitened, and he swallowed hard. "Caddie? Me? No. Why?"

"Her father says she's with child—by you, he says."

Robbie jumped to his feet. "No! No! It can't be. I've barely even ‍ken to Caddie Trethaway. Everyone knows she's free with her ‍‍rs. It could be anybody. Anybody."

‍Well, her father insists it was you, so what do you have to say? ‍‍t be?"

‍‍ing his head, Robbie turned and looked out the window at ‍‍ world beyond, hands at his sides. He didn't respond

verbally. Indeed it was only a barely perceptible nod of his head that gave us the dreaded news.

Ellie immediately rose and crossed the room to him. "Oh, Robbie, how could you? You know what low people they are! How could you consort with Caddie Trethaway?"

I waited to hear his response. Would he defend the girl? Defend his own actions? Take responsibility? Unfortunately, none of these. He simply turned and announced that he was tired and would talk to us in the morning.

But Ellie, overwrought by the revelation, pressed him. "But, Robbie, why? Why her, of all the girls in the world? You know her father's a danger to your father, to all of us."

Now Robbie turned to her, his eyes dark. "My father? Are you so sure of that, Mother? I've wondered often about my father. He must live somewhere down in Berks County, does he not? Yes, I believe he does. For this man, tall and slender and blue eyed, is no more my father than is Simon Trethaway."

Ellie grabbed his arm, pulled him to face her, as though she could steer him away from the truth. "Robbie, what are you saying? That Adam isn't your father? How can you think such a thing?"

"Enough now, Mother. I've known for some time. I wrote to my grandfather down in Berks County when I was fourteen, and learned the truth."

"Oh, and did he also tell you that your real father abandoned me when he learned of your coming? Would you like to know this man who cared nothing for you? Adam has done everything a real father would do and more, and I won't have you behaving with disrespect toward him."

I stood back from this confrontation, surprised at Robbie's courage in pursuing the circumstances of his birth on his own. It passed through my mind that he might have harbored hope of finding that he was heir to some fortune or other, a motivation that I could easily ascribe to him. I listened as mother and son unwrapped their secrets.

My concern was that Simon Trethaway would find the means of turning this into good fortune for himself. It was certain he cared little for his daughter's honor and even less for the welfare of the coming child. For him it was a happy accident that he could turn to his advantage. I decided that I could think about this better after a night's sleep, so I excused myself and left Elinor and Robbie to work out their differences.

The morning brought another twist of events, for when Robbie failed to appear at the breakfast table I looked questioningly at his mother. She shrugged and continued to eat her oatmeal. I sent Mrs. Gwynn upstairs to roust our son out of bed, but she returned with the news that Robbie wasn't in his bed; indeed, the bed hadn't been slept in. Now I turned to Elinor with wondering eyes. Had she and Robbie come together with a plan last night? To run instead of taking responsibility? I cleared my throat loud enough to catch her attention. I gestured with head and eyes to ask the question. Did he run? "Surely you didn't . . ."

She looked at me, her face grave. She nodded. "Yes, I did."

"But Elinor, how can you allow him to turn his back just as his father did? "

"He couldn't stay here anymore. Don't you see? I couldn't let him marry into that family, give her father even more leverage against you. Robbie deserves a better life than that. And so do you. This will all blow over soon. And I am still not convinced the child is his."

"But he wouldn't have had to marry her. I could have bought Trethaway off. But what is worse, I can't condone his walking away without a care for the life he might have brought into being. The least he could have done was provide for the child's upbringing and education. You, of all people, should know that."

She turned abruptly and stood with her back to me, lowering her head. "We don't know for sure that it's Robbie's child. May never know."

I wondered now whether the same questions had passed through the minds of Robert Clifton's parents some twenty-one years before. But Elinor hadn't been like Caddie Trethaway—known to be easy and willing to accommodate all comers. I felt a passing sympathy for Robbie, given the suspicion that the culprit might well be any one of a dozen or more.

I touched Elinor's shoulder. "Where did you send him?"

"To Berks County. To my father. At least he has one grandfather who'll acknowledge him."

"I'm surprised you can let him go so easily."

She turned to face me again, her face drawn and pale. "I could hardly bring myself to it. A mother has to expect to part with her children sometime, but I wasn't ready yet. I can hardly bear it."

"Will your father really open his home to him? After all these years, I mean."

"I expect he will. Father has always favored boys, excused their shortcomings, bailed them out of trouble, given them every advantage . . . son or grandson."

"This complicates my life, you know. Trethaway is liable to resort to more threats—maybe even get up the gumption to carry some of them out."

I sat at the head of the table as Mrs. Gwynn carried in a huge bowl of porridge from the kitchen and the other five children trooped in to take their places and fill their bowls, chattering and eating with an enthusiasm I remembered from my youth but could no longer call up.

"Where's Robbie?" Laird asked, spooning molasses onto his porridge. "Stayed out too late again, did he?" His knowing smile bore witness to his enjoyment of his brother's devil-may-care lifestyle. More relaxed than Robbie, not so competitive or so ready to find fault—and infinitely more reliable—Laird still admired his brother's ability to turn almost everything into fun and games.

Elinor cleared her throat. "Your brother's been called away."

"Called away? Where?" That was Alyssa, who, at fourteen, held her oldest brother in deep admiration. "Will he be gone long?"

"To Berks County. Reading, actually. He's needed on your grandfather's estate."

"Grandfather? I didn't know we had a grandfather." That was young John, always ready to cast the light of truth upon any situation. "What's his name?"

"Stephen Bratton. We've been out of touch for some time, but your grandfather needs someone to handle things for him now. He's getting up in years."

"Why so sudden?" That was Bethany, carefully buttering her bread and looking across the table at Alyssa with a knowing glance.

I felt the need to intervene. "So, children, if anyone asks about Robbie, just say he's been called away. That's all. Just called away."

Laird continued to spoon porridge into his mouth, voracious, like any sixteen-year-old. "I don't guess this has anything to do with Caddie Trethaway, does it?"

"Why, Laird, it certainly does not. Why would Robbie have anything to do with Caddie Trethaway?" Ellie's indignation did little to slow speculation.

Laird smirked into his porridge bowl. "Oh, I don't know. What *would* a guy like Robbie have to do with a girl like Caddie?"

"Really, Laird! Your own brother! How could you be so harsh?"

Unsettled by the drift of this conversation, I intervened once more. "Let's not give ourselves over to rumors."

That quieted the speculation for the moment, and the children concentrated on their breakfast until their mother excused them. I stopped Laird in the hallway after the girls had gone upstairs to their sewing tasks and the younger boys had gone outside to run along beside a passing packet boat.

"What have you heard, Laird?"

"Nothing. Just that Robbie and Caddie kept company a while back."

"Meaning...?"

"Meaning they probably got to know each other, if you know what I mean," he replied, glancing over his shoulder at his mother, who was still seated at the table.

"Is Caddie known to be free with her favors?" I asked.

"Some, but word was that she was Robbie's girl, so the other fellows backed off. That's what I heard."

So Robbie had, indeed, had a close relationship with Caddie Trethaway. Intimate. Carnal. The truth slowly dawned, awakening my anger at the boy's poor judgment. As Laird turned and left through the kitchen, I looked at Ellie.

"What do you think it'll take to settle with Trethaway?" she asked.

"God knows. It won't be easy."

Chapter 56

Summer 1844
Adam

The next morning, Trethaway appeared at my office before I'd even had a chance to sit down at my desk. When I informed him that Robbie had no intention of marrying his daughter, he exploded into a rant that fairly shook the office walls.

"Won't marry her, won't he? We'll see about that! Where is he? He'll be glad to be getting married after I get done with him."

"He's gone. Had to leave on short notice. Family business."

"I'll bet it were short notice. Just last night, I'll warrant. Where'd he go? I can always go after him. Bring him back. Teach him some manners."

I sat behind my desk, steepled my fingers and exhaled a sigh. "Come on, man. There's no proof that the child is his, but I'm prepared to make him take responsibility—short of marrying her, of course."

"What kind of responsibility is that?" Trethaway calmed right down when the idea of some other kind of compensation arose. "It better be plenty. My Caddie's a good girl."

Letting that comment hang in the wind, I opened my desk drawer and took out a bank pouch. Trethaway's eyes narrowed at the sight of it. Such a man could always be bought, but this time the price was bound to be high.

I opened the pouch and counted out a hundred dollars—more money than the man had seen in quite some time time—but he shook his head, as I knew he would. So went the negotiations until we settled on a price—twice the original offer.

"One stipulation," I told him. "You get the first fifty now, the second when the child is born, the third when it reaches its first birthday, and so on until it is three years old. I'm not paying to support a dead child."

"Naw, MacPhail. I want it all now. No wiggling out of it. I gets it now, or I goes after that young buck and brings him home dragging behind me horse."

That was one threat I feared he just might carry out. I pictured Ellie's face before me, asking me how I could let our son fall into the hands of such a low cur. Funny, I always *had* thought of him as my son. Oh, I won't pretend I loved him as much as my own children, but I did care for the boy—tutored him, played him fair, and was prepared to set him up in an honorable and respected position in the world. If Trethaway ever figured out where he was, it could be disastrous for all of us. Still, I couldn't bring myself to hand such money over to my mortal enemy, so I put him off by standing firm on my offer. Trethaway stormed out, vowing to find the boy and destroy him.

In the meantime, nothing deterred him from spreading the word that his daughter was pregnant by Robbie MacPhail, and the hollows were soon alive with the gossip. Robbie's continued absence fanned the flames, giving Trethaway further incentive for his demands.

He came raging into my office three weeks later, having been put off as long as I could manage, demanding that Robbie return and face the preacher. "I got a shotgun loaded and ready. If he ever comes home, that is. And if he don't, I guess I'll have to take it out of your miserable hide, MacPhail. Either way, my Caddie'll get her just desserts."

"Don't be so rash, Trethaway. Your daughter will get her due. Still, we have only her word that Robbie is responsible, and that is open to question."

"Open to question is it? We'll see what's open to question. Mark my words, MacPhail, if you don't take proper care, it'll be more than money you'll lose." As he glared at me across the desk, I fought the urge to brush him off with a wave of my arm.

"Perhaps we should wait and see if the child resembles anyone else who might have had a hand in it. I'm told Robbie wasn't her only suitor."

I said it deliberately to bait Simon Tethaway, tired of him baiting me. Exasperated beyond my limits, I was ready to withstand whatever barrage he chose to send my way. It wasn't long in coming.

"So that's how it is, eh? I mighta knowed you'd protect that arrogant young miscreant. Well, this is the last time ye'll mess wi' a Trethaway. Ye killed Lem, and now yer spawn's ruint my Caddie. Watch yer back, MacPhail. One of these days, the'll be a musket ball in it." He spat the words, hands curled into fists. "Don't you ever go out alone, man. Don't you ever think I ain't watchin'."

I turned my back and pretended to study a map on the wall, a map of the holdings of the Mt. Etna Iron Company. It seemed an eternity before I heard the door slam and the rumble of his footsteps down the stairs. I found my hands shaking in spite of my resolve to remain calm. The man was all talk, full of threats and false bravado. It was highly unlikely that anything would ever come of it.

My best efforts at ignoring his demands did nothing to calm the air. The constant tension between us increased, every meeting fraught with venom designed to bully and dishearten me. It was all I could do to resist the temptation to take him up on his challenge, to call him out on his threats, and to have it done with. It was only Elinor's entreaties not to be drawn down to his level that restrained me.

Finally, in extreme frustration and contempt for his bluster, I made him a final offer of a handsome sum—subject to some restrictions on his behavior—which he quickly agreed to and then proceeded to ignore once the money'd been paid. I handed the stack of money over to my mortal enemy and turned my back while he gathered it up, all the while blathering about how he had a plan for investing it. I still wasn't sure whose child Caddie was carrying, but now the question was moot.

Chapter 57

Fall 1844
Adam

In the meantime, Caddie Trethaway's girth expanded through the summer and into the fall until one day, without warning, she appeared at our back door, asking for the mistress. Elinor, dismayed by her uninvited guest, met with her in the kitchen, out of earshot of the rest of the household. "What can I do for you, Caddie? Are you in need?"

"Yes'm. I need a place to go. A bed to lie in when my time comes." This was a quiet, subdued Caddie, not the sassy, willful young wench who'd plied her wares along the canal since she was sixteen.

"Surely your parents..."

The girl shook her head. "They done turned me out. Said I were a disgrace to 'em. My pa says I ain't no good and not to bring no bastard home to him. He says you owe me a livin', since it were your Robbie done me in the first place."

Ellie listened in polite silence as the girl unloaded insults, excuses, and every ounce of blame she could muster before breaking down at the kitchen table. A hesitant pat on the shoulder, a cup of tea, and things came right again as my wife probed for the truth behind the histrionics.

"Did they really turn you out?" she asked.

"Yes'm. Said I weren't worth nothing no more. Said I should come to you."

Elinor, torn between her rage at the Trethaway's treachery and fear that the girl was merely playing us for what more she could get, listened in silence as Caddie gave her account of the last seven months, ever since she knew she was with child. While defending her honor to the outside world, Simon Trethaway had berated and abused the girl at home—locked her in a filthy slab shed, deprived her of food, warmth and sanitation, called her every low and vile name he could think of, and even beat her on occasion. Now she sat, bruised and broken, at our kitchen table, begging for shelter for herself and her child.

When Elinor told me about their encounter that evening, I was even more affronted than she, given that I had already paid her father generously and hoped to be done with the matter. But Ellie was filled with cautious compassion for the poor girl as she related the tale to me, and I couldn't help but be touched by her entreaty that this child, so maligned and mistreated before its birth, might well be her own grandchild.

"All right. I see you've been swayed by her pleas. What do you propose to do?"

"I've been thinking about that. The Davids at Cove Forge have need of help right now, and they have that little cottage by the river empty. Perhaps we could get them to put her up during her confinement in return for work after the baby comes."

I wasn't of a mind to approach Noah David on the subject, but I could tell from Ellie's resolute face that my wishes were not primary to this case. "Would you like me to talk to Noah about it?"

"No. I thought I would see what Elizabeth thinks. She's probably the best one to approach Noah. I'll drive down there tomorrow and talk to her."

The result of Ellie's tireless maneuvering was that Caddie should go to Cove Forge for the time being. In late November Lindy was called down to deliver the child, a robust boy with admirable lungs who, grandson or not, wormed his way into my wife's heart with no trouble at all.

Cleaned up and well fed, Caddie gave every appearance of respectability, working in the kitchen at Cove Forge and taking care of her son, whom she named William. A little kindness trimmed her temper and warmed her demeanor to the extent that she came to be thought of in the David household as a reliable and valued servant and young Willy as an 'almost' grandchild.

But Simon Trethaway was on to bigger and better things. Undaunted by the complete failure of his Utopian effort, his new plan for 'investing' my money was to run for the Pennsylvania Legislature. When that news fell upon my ears, I laughed heartily, sure that a man as low and base as Simon Trethaway could never garner enough votes to get elected, but by the time election day arrived I wasn't so sure. Traveling the length and breadth of Huntingdon County, his wagon loaded with casks of his homemade whiskey, he attracted attention any way he could and promised the earth and sky to all who would vote for him.

Away from the area where he was known, he cut a fine figure—dressed in a new broadcloth coat, top hat, wool trousers, a clean linen shirt and stylish cravat (all purchased with my money)—strutting back and forth on the streets of Huntingdon, Mt. Union or Shirleysburg, chewing the end of an expensive cigar, and offering free liquor to all comers.

Twice I saw him climb up on a stump and speechify in grand manner to anyone who would listen. "I'm a man of the people! I know how your lives are, 'cause I've lived it, too. We country folk need a voice in Harrisburg. Nobody else gonna speak for you like I will. You can count on having my ear without fail. I'm your voice. Your good shepherd."

When I saw how the local people thronged around him, drinking liberally from his whiskey barrels, I had to at least entertain the notion that he could possibly win. And win he did.

If I thought Simon Trethaway was obnoxious before, it could in no way describe his demeanor once elected to public office. He handed out favors to all comers in exchange for promises of undying loyalty and provided jobs for his most ardent supporters, including Timothy

Judge, who stood first in line. There was nothing to be done about it, wish as I might that there were.

Once the excitement of the election died down, life at Mt. Etna returned to quiet routine. My workers seemed content with their lot, and prosperity went a long way in keeping them so. The furnace was running twenty-four hours a day. At the forge, three triphammers beat the pig iron into bars to be shipped to Pittsburgh, where Noah David and I had pooled our resources to open our own rolling mill. I was happy to partner with him and help insure success for both of us, as our relationship had grown into something of a bond over the years.

Then, one day in early May, after Robbie had been in Berks County for more than a year, we received a letter asking that his mother come to the bedside of her dying father. Elinor might have been reluctant to comply except that she missed her son and welcomed any opportunity to see him. Without hesitation she packed her trunk and left by coach from Huntingdon, a much less slow and perilous journey than we had made so many years before. She kept in close touch with me by writing letters while she was gone, even to the point of letting me know that she had met the mother of her old paramour, Robert Clifton, news that neither delighted nor surprised me.

Chapter 58

1845
Ellie

I'm not sure I would have undertaken the trip back to Berks County if it had not been that I missed my son. My father's condition did not move me nearly so much as the prospect of a reunion with Robbie. Papa lay abed, in a weakened condition brought on by a fall from the ladder to the hay mow, although why he would undertake to climb one was beyond me. The doctor assured me that his fractured hip would heal but that his age, seventy-two, and his lifelong habits of overeating and devouring alcohol in flagons would make that a very slow process.

Robbie greeted me at the depot in Reading, looking fit, handsome, and very well turned out in clothing I could only describe as splendid. I spent the large measure of my time with him for the next few days, getting to know him again. He'd opened a small business in Reading, buying and selling beaver pelts like his grandfather before him, and he went to his office every day, seeming to have settled down to a more responsible life.

I entered my father's room only out of necessity, spoke to him only in response to his requests, and ignored the constant tapping of his cane on the floorboards demanding my attention. I quickly engaged a neighbor girl, Missy Halloran, to tend to the laundry and cooking, freeing myself from any more than necessary interaction with the old man.

I hadn't intended to be harsh with him. After all, things had worked out better than I'd hoped and I no longer saw my forced marriage to Adam as a scourge. But deep inside I still could not forgive his embracing the idea that, as a woman, I was no more than property to be disposed of as he saw fit. I couldn't help resenting the fact that he considered my sex inferior and himself duty bound to keep me on the straight and narrow path of acceptable femininity.

I took pride in Robbie's business accomplishments, even to the point of talking openly like a proud mother when neighbor women stopped for tea out of courtesy to my late mother. I didn't doubt that my bragging on Robbie would reach the intended ears.

As if to prove me right, one afternoon in late May I heard a gig drive up as I was sitting on the back porch making a plan for that summer's kitchen garden. I roused myself and walked around the side of the house as Mrs. Martha Clifton, mistress of Brighton, mother of my former lover and grandmother to my son, stepped down with the help of her driver.

"Why, Mrs. Clifton, how nice to see you after so many years." My voice dripped with honey. "How have you been? Missy! Bring some tea to the front porch for Mrs. Clifton and me!"

The elderly woman gave me her hand and I walked steadily beside her up the wide front steps to the porch, where we sat down in two wicker rocking chairs, a small table between us. Age had withered her to a sprite of a woman, still bright eyed but only a shadow of the proper lady I remembered.

"I'm surprised you'd come back here after all these years," she began. "I'd think you'd still be angry over the way you were treated."

Taken aback by her forthrightness, I merely smiled, consumed with curiosity about the purpose of this visit. "Ah, here's Missy with the tea. Do you take sugar, ma'am?"

She nodded. "It sounds strange for you to call me ma'am. I'd thought at one time that you would call me Mother Clifton."

I almost dropped the sugar tongs. "So you were opposed to my exile, then?"

"Deeply opposed, but I dared not interfere. My husband was adamant that our son should marry into some established Philadelphia family."

"And did he?" I really was curious about Robert Clifton. Was he relieved to escape my clutches? Or might he gladly have married me, given the chance? For the first time, it dawned on me that Robert might have been manipulated as much as I.

"Oh, yes. He did. The Robertsons of Fairmount. Their daughter, Abigail."

"Ahh." It was all I could muster, confronted with the image of Robert Clifton, scion of the Berks County Cliftons, securing his rightful position in Philadelphia society. All the old stratifications, the knowing of one's place, the privileges of wealth and masculine gender came flooding back to me, long forgotten in the egalitarian wilds of Huntingdon County.

"Life hasn't been kind to my son, I'm afraid. He's had money and social status, but that can't heal heartbreak."

"Heartbreak?"

"Oh, yes, dear. Robert and Abbie have lost three children. There was a fire. So sad. His wife went mad over it. Had to be committed to an asylum. There'll be no more children, so, you see, your son is my only surviving grandchild."

I breathed in slowly, determined not to give her the satisfaction she craved. They hadn't wanted to acknowledge my son until now, but now was too late. "So you'd like to meet him, would you? Make amends? Take him under your wing?"

She sniffed and took a sip of tea. "Why, yes. I think that would be a fine start."

"Why are you asking me? Robbie is grown, able to speak for himself. Why didn't you just go visit him at his offices in Reading? I'm sure he'd be happy to hear that you've declared him worthy."

"Now, Elinor, let's be civil. You were treated badly, I know—sent off to the ends of the earth with that oaf. You have a right to be bitter. But be reasonable. The Squire is gone and I'm getting on in years, as is your father. My son Robert would claim your boy as his son and make him heir to Brighton, as, I am sure, you feel is only his right."

"Oaf! Oaf! You call my husband an oaf, you, the mother of a shirker, a rogue and a user! Please, Mrs. Clifton, leave me. Don't come here offering to raise my son to legitimacy now after having ignored both of us all of his life."

"But, my dear, as you say, we can approach the boy on his own merit. I just wanted to make a mutually congenial arrangement. I don't know why you're so short with me. After all, I was in no position to protest when my husband laid down the law."

I rose from my chair and paced the length of the porch, anger boiling up inside of me. "That's the problem, Mrs. Clifton. You, my mother, all women. We accept second-class status as though it were our due. We don't even speak up on behalf of our children! We let little girls grow up believing themselves incapable of anything but the most trivial of pursuits while we encourage our sons' every ambition."

"Well, that's the way it is, my dear. The way it always has been. You can't change nature."

"It isn't nature that needs changing. It's men's minds! And it won't happen until women dedicate themselves to raising their daughters as equal to their sons."

The elderly woman took another sip from her teacup, set the cup down, and dabbed her lips with a napkin. "I see you've developed some radical ideas. I hope you haven't spoiled Robbie along the way. With or without your blessing, my son will call on him to set things into motion. I must go now. I tire so easily, and incivility wears me out."

I shook my head in despair. The woman and her son would have their way. Robbie would welcome the wealth and status they offered, would revel in being accepted into the family and Philadelphia society. I knew he would, and I wouldn't waste the effort in trying to turn him away from it. Taking Mrs. Clifton's arm, I guided her down the steps and out the flagstone path to her gig. As I turned to re-enter the house, I heard the grinding of gravel as she drove away and wondered why I wasn't thrilled that Robbie would finally regain his birthright.

Back in the kitchen, I was assaulted by the incessant pounding of my father's cane on the floorboards above. It was no time for him to be demanding anything of me. I lifted my skirts and tromped up the stairs, ready to give him short shrift. "What is it now, old man? How can I serve your every need and bow to your every wish?"

Taken aback by my brusque manner, he straightened up in the bed, wincing in pain from the fractured hip. "I was wondering who you were talking to. I could hear you had a guest on the porch. That was all."

His meek manner, so untypical of him, disarmed me. "It was Martha Clifton."

"Martha Clifton? What did she want of you?"

"She says Robert, her son, wants to make Robbie, my son, his heir, now that his other three children are gone."

My father's eyes, watery at best, gazed up at me, questioning. "What? Why? Why now?"

"I just told you why. Since his other three children died in a fire, he has no one, so now he wants to claim my Robbie."

"Oh, well . . . what's he want Robbie to do?"

Exasperated with his lack of comprehension, I pulled the pillow from behind him, fluffed it up roughly, and shoved it back in place. His pain showed in a twisted grimace. "Don't be so rough, Elinor."

"Why not, Father? Do you expect kindness, gentleness, a dutiful daughter after the way you treated me?"

"Treated you how? I gave you the means to make something of your life. To avoid shame and humiliation. What have you to complain about?"

Now my rage erupted, giving me leave to raise my voice in anger. "What have I to complain about? What, indeed? Treated like property, no better than a cow! Given no say in my destiny. Forced to bow to your demands. You old bastard. How dare you ask me what I have to complain about!"

The reversal of our life roles was complete. As the holder of power, I felt the stark contrast of this day over the day in 1823 when Adam MacPhail first appeared in our doorway. Then my father was brash, self assured, unassailable. Now he lay helpless abed, in pain and without even a semblance of authority. I could say anything I wanted to him—berate him, insult him, lash him to death with my words. I stopped, looked into his watery eyes, and sighed.

We regarded each other in silence, my father struggling to comprehend my rage, and I, realizing for perhaps the first time since he treated me with such arrogance, that he really did think he was doing the best by me.

I turned away and busied myself with arranging his toilet items on the washstand. The silence was long and heavy, weighing on both of us. Then, from the bed, came the words I never expected to hear, halting and softly spoken.

"I'm sorry, Elinor. I thought I was doing the best I could for you. I loved you more than I loved life." He closed his eyes, wincing—whether in pain or regret, I couldn't tell. "If I could change it now, I would. I'd let you make your own choices."

His hand smoothed the quilt and came to rest near the edge of the bed.

Keeping my back to him, I lowered my head as I felt the pain drain from my heart. Years of resentment and anger fell away with that simple declaration. Transported back to the days of being my father's only daughter . . . loved, cherished, fawned over . . . I bit my lip and turned to face him. "Oh, Papa ..."

When I turned he was gone. That quickly, that simply, that finally, he slipped away into oblivion. I touched his hand, picked it up, held it to my cheek, but there was no more to say, no more anger, no more blame. That chapter of my life had finally closed. I placed his hand over his chest, closed the shade, and left the room.

Now all I wanted was to speak with Adam. I sat down at my mother's writing desk and composed a letter, telling him of my father's death and asking that he come to Berks County to help me settle my father's affairs. I called for our stable boy to saddle up and ride to Reading, where the letter could be posted and sent by the canal all the way to Mt. Etna. Adam would receive it within two days, and could, I hoped, be there in three more.

Chapter 59

1845
Adam

Elinor's letter arrived on the packet boat and lay on the table when I arrived home from work. Her father had died and, her being the only surviving child, there was much to attend to. I left the five little MacPhails in the care of Mrs. Gwynn and three local girls who worked by turns as housemaids. At seventeen, Laird was capable of taking care of most things, but it was a comfort to have Mrs. Gwynn in charge. The two girls, Alyssa and Bethany, both budding adolescents, were now being tutored by a young Welsh woman, hired at Mrs. Gwynn's behest and generally capable, while the younger boys, John and Edward, sat among our workers' children at the school I'd established just three years ago. It was late May, so I hoped to be back to attend to the boys' summer activities before the term was over.

The trip to Berks County brought back memories, some pleasant, others hurtful, of our wedding trip along the same route. I wondered how Ellie felt about all of that now. Never reticent about her anger at her father, she'd shown no inclination to grant him the slightest indulgence, but I hoped she'd found it in her heart to forgive *me* for whatever transgressions she perceived as mine. Our day-to-day interaction was pleasant, even kind. We'd mended our marriage and come to a state of acceptance—if not complete bliss—but I still held out hope for some expression of caring, of satisfaction with the way our lives had turned out, of love even.

Upon my arrival at Reading I was met by a well-dressed, confident Robbie, grinning with pride at the handsome team of horses that pulled his small carriage. Same old Robbie. Most interested in showing off his possessions and in acquiring more. I shook my head and smiled back, accepting that it was beyond my ability to change him.

Elinor was waiting at her father's home, having held up the funeral for me. The body had been prudently kept on ice in the spring house awaiting my arrival, and once I'd had time to rest and bathe, the neighbors began arriving for the wake. It was a quiet evening of half-whispers, expressions of sympathy, and sniffling into lace and linen handkerchiefs. Elinor bore up well, given that her association with her father had been long strained by his high-handedness and her own willingness to nurture a grudge. The evening wore on, with mourners coming and going until, close to nine o'clock, an elderly woman, regally dressed, entered on the arm of a gentleman I could only describe as short and squat—though elegantly attired. Elinor rose to meet them, extended her hand to the woman and looked long into the eyes of the man.

I knew without introduction that this was Robert Clifton, the bane of my existence, antagonist, rival, competitor for my wife's affection. I stood a little to the rear watching the scene unfold. I couldn't hear every word, nor did I wish to, troubled as I was by this turn of events. I'd not expected the Cliftons to want to mourn with Elinor, and especially not with Robbie, but here they were, acting the gracious and concerned neighbors. Our son rose and greeted them warmly, giving me to wonder if he had established this cordial relationship on his own and for his own purposes. Suddenly Elinor turned to me and held out her hand for mine.

"Robert, Mrs. Clifton, I'd like you to meet my husband, Adam MacPhail, ironmaster at Mt. Etna." She said it proudly, with a hint of self-assurance that spoke of satisfaction with her station in life. I felt my apprehensions fade as I shook the hand of the man whose actions had so dominated my own. Elinor wasn't play-acting for effect. She was signaling to Robert Clifton and the world that she was a woman of attainment, fulfilled, and satisfied with her status.

Clifton nodded, withdrew his hand from mine as quickly as was prudent, and stepped back to introduce his mother. The old woman had an unmistakable hauteur about her, born of years of wealth and privilege. It was clear that these two were used to getting what they wanted and that resistance was a waste of time and effort, giving me to wonder if there was anything else I had that they might challenge me for.

Looking into Robert Clifton's face was like standing behind our Robbie as he looked into a mirror. Robbie MacPhail was the image of Robert Clifton, right down to a cowlick just above his left eyebrow. In stature, walk, gesture, and word it was hard to tell them apart but for age.

After a brief but polite exchange and expressions of sympathy, the Cliftons proceeded to view the remains and take their seats among the other mourners. The formalities of the wake were quickly dispensed with, and the latecoming guests departed as soon as politeness allowed. Robbie, Ellie and I were left alone in the parlor with the dead man, given over to our own thoughts. Mine were of the power of time to alter and mend almost any circumstance. I'd lived in dread of meeting Robert Clifton for years, insecure and uncertain of my own worth. And now, here he was without the power to add or detract from that, just a man, after all.

Ellie

I felt huge relief at meeting Robert Clifton face to face one more time. There he stood, the white knight of my youth, short, rotund, and not at all attractive after twenty-two years. I was even proud of Adam, whose height and stature towered over Robert Clifton like an oak over a barberry hedge. Straight and tall in all ways, not just physical, he would not have left a girl in trouble. He would not have ignored the fruit of his loins until it became convenient to notice him. He would not have gone off to Philadelphia in search of a more advantageous match.

Strange how things you've dreaded all your life don't turn out the way you've imagined them at all. Seeing Robert Clifton middle aged, no more the drake about whom the ducks fluttered, I realized that he was now and had always been just a man. Adam was his better in every way, and I regretted my prolonged idolization, my schoolgirl disappointment at not sharing my life with him. Adam deserved better, but though we often come too late to wisdom, I hoped I still had time to make it up to him, to show him how much I had learned to care over the long years of our marriage.

Sure and steady, Adam MacPhail stood by my side and by our son's side, facing his former competition with dignity. Competition, indeed. I felt nothing for Robert Clifton—not love, not regret, not even a wistful desire to remember. I turned to Adam, placed my hand on his arm, and walked away from my father's coffin and all things past.

The next day's funeral service was a simple matter of going through the courtesies. I stood by the grave as they lowered the coffin, brushed away a tear, and joined my husband and son in the carriage ride back to my father's house, where we set ourselves to the task of deciding how to settle the estate, all of which was now mine in fact, if not by law.

My father's death had brought me up short, made me think that perhaps I'd been too harsh in my judgment of him. He really had only done what he deemed best for me, out of nothing but paternal concern. I felt the sadness of loss, along with regret for my behavior. Some of it. But there lingered a bitterness reserved for all that is unfair and unjust in life, the idea that anyone is less important or less valuable than anyone else. Be it my father's fault or my own—or even the fault of endless generations who accept the world as they find it and make no move to change it—there is injustice aplenty. But for me, no little girl should be raised to think herself inferior to boys, to hand over her sovereignty to father, brother, or husband. I was resolved to do my best to change that, whatever it took. Acceptance was unacceptable.

Back at home in my old bedroom, where we'd spent that first tumultuous night of our marriage, I turned to Adam.

"Thank you for coming. I needed you."

He reached for me and enfolded me in his arms. "It's great to be needed."

"What happens now? With my father's estate, I mean."

"Whatever you want to happen."

I sighed. "I'm not sure I know what I want to happen. Anyway, legally, its yours. I know that. What do you propose? Will you sell it?"

Adam took my hand and led me to the now faded settee he'd rejected as a bed on our wedding night. We sat beside the window, looking out at what had once been my mother's prize rose garden now overgrown with weeds.

"I've been thinking about all of this," he began, "and I want you to know you don't have to come back with me. You can stay here— live here on your own, or with Robbie. The other children can visit. I know you've regretted marrying me. Now is your chance to make the most of the remains of your life."

"Adam! What are you saying?"

"Just that you're free to do as you wish. I won't hold you." He took my hand in his and raised it to his lips. "You've done right by me."

"But, Adam, don't you want me? Have I been so selfish, so malicious that I've ruined any chance for our happiness?"

He rose and turned to face me. "No, Elinor. I didn't mean that at all. I just know how sad our arrangement has made you all these years, and I thought it wasn't too late to give you a chance to manage your own life."

"Oh, Adam, you've misread me. I'm not unhappy. Haven't been for such a long time. I love our life at Etna Furnace. Love our home, our children. I love you. I wouldn't leave all of it for anything. I belong there now."

He reached for my hand again and pulled me to him, holding me close. "Oh, God, how I've longed to hear those words. "I love you. I love you."

We stood in the middle of the room, holding each other, surrounded by memories, bonded by a lifetime together. Finally, I stepped back, smiling at him.

"Oh, Adam, let's go home."

Sovereignty. All I'd ever wanted. Finally I knew my place, and it was not here. It was far away in the wilds of Huntingdon County, at a place called Mt. Etna.

That evening at dinner we discussed the new direction our lives would take.

"Robbie, what do you plan to do now? Stay or go back home with us?" I knew the answer, but I wanted to hear him say it.

"I'd like to stay here, Mother. If you can see your way clear to let me live in this house, I can oversee the rental of the farm land and take care of the details of settling the estate."

I nodded, looking to Adam for any indication that he would oppose such a plan. His slight nod gave me leave to continue.

"You shall have my permission only so long as you conduct yourself like a gentleman. Mr. Clifton and his mother want to negotiate with you regarding their holdings, so I would keep this estate intact for your brothers and sisters. Do you call that fair?"

Robbie nodded. "I've already met with them, Mother. I stand to inherit a much larger estate there, but not until my father dies." He shot a glance toward Adam, almost apologetic, but still guardedly self-congratulatory. "I mean no disrespect, sir."

"None taken," Adam replied.

I knew Adam had reservations about letting Robbie have his head. Early indications had made him consider the depth and breadth of the boy's character. Now I hoped that the distance between this place and Mt. Etna would be to Robbie's advantage. Hoped he'd matured enough to follow the right path. I knew Adam was more skeptical than I, but, bless him, he was still willing to give the boy a chance.

"Then your father and I will start back to Mt. Etna tomorrow. Any papers needing to be signed can be forwarded to me. With you living here, I'm confident the estate is in good hands. And Robbie, don't sell your produce before you harvest. Your Clifton inheritance is subject to the whims and winds of outrageous fortune. Be cautious."

Robbie nodded. "I know, Mother. Don't worry."

By morning all was in readiness for our departure. This time, instead of bumping along on a heavily loaded wagon pulled by a plodding team, we rode in Robbie's fine carriage to Reading, where we boarded a coach for Harrisburg. Better roads made the journey shorter and less jolting, so, after a pleasant night at a Harrisburg inn, we departed the next morning by coach again for Lewistown. There we boarded a packet boat on the canal and rode along in early June sunshine, enjoying the lovely Pennsylvania countryside. Mount Union, Huntingdon, Water Street, and finally our own Mt. Etna came into view. It gave me joy to return, gather my children around, and hear all about their lives in my absence. Adam, anxious to get back and take over the reins of the business, stepped from the boat and strode across the lawn to our house, beaming amid hugs and shouts of welcome from the children, intent on making the most of the remains of the day.

I was content to sit on the front porch watching the boats glide by, drinking my tea and feeling fortunate to be where I was and who I was.

Chapter 60

1846
Adam

Despite the inevitable ups and downs of the iron industry, Etna Furnace continued to prosper, generally improving production each year. I installed a hot blast system soon after the technology became available, and that reduced the need for charcoal—always a problem, as the denuded hillsides bore witness. Our furnace consumed the wood of about an acre a day to produce Juniata iron, to say nothing of the demands of the forge and smithy. The hot blast method improved productivity, so by the early 1840s we were producing twice as much iron as we had at the start. We changed from horses to mules for the heavy hauling and transport, our magnificent stone bank barn accommodating up to one hundred mules at a time.

I'd worked hard for my success, and, while not a proud man, I did look with satisfaction on an operation that employed as many as a hundred and fifty workers, providing for their every need—from food and clothing to transportation, education, even spiritual needs. I loved our little community and the day to day management tasks that made it work. Few, if any, other industries could boast wages as high as ours, as well as housing, gardening space, hunting privileges—to say nothing of a well-stocked company store. No wonder my detractors' utopian ideas fell on stony ground here. I would never have boasted, but I did take quiet note of the rare achievement of such success from humble beginnings.

I was not without my detractors, however, for I was still confronted almost daily with threats of dire consequences for my many 'transgressions' against Simon Trethaway by his ragged band of followers and political aspirants. It seemed that to curry favor from our shoddy and contemptible legislator, one had to swear undying enmity for me and mine, demonstrated by public condemnation and censure, both vocal and written as often as the opportunity arose. First among these critics was Timothy Judge, whose presence in our midst was a continuing annoyance. He'd left Yellow Spring in disgrace, only to surface again in Huntingdon, editor of a small but radical newspaper, the sole purpose of which, it seemed, was to degrade me and mine. I did my best to go about my business ignoring his attacks, for it was beyond my power to quiet his frenetic rants.

In addition to running his rag of a newspaper, he'd been granted the position of local assessor, a political appointment in recognition of his undying loyalty to our esteemed legislator. Judge was responsible for estimating my worth, and therefore my taxes, a responsibility which he accepted with nothing short of delight. Each assessment was inflated beyond all reason, and each time my attorney had to appeal to the county for adjudication, a case which I always won but which cost me in attorney's and accountant's fees.

After a couple years of this, I took it upon myself to confront my bedeviler, not out of hope for relief from harassment, but out of sheer frustration. I happened to be in Huntingdon on other business when I met Mr. Judge walking down Penn Street, attired in a fine suit of clothes appropriate to his station, head held high, cane in hand.

"Mr. MacPhail. Pleased to see ye, and how propitious. I was just finishing up my assessment of yer holdings. Quite a large accumulation of assets, my good man."

I stepped aside as though to avoid contact, tipped my hat, and proceeded to pass him by.

"Hold, MacPhail. Ye'd be best advised not to snub me, sir. I have connections in high places, ye know."

I turned on him, unable to conceal my contempt. "You and your 'connections' can go to hell, Judge. You're not worth my time or my concern. Do what you will. My dealings are honest and fair, not subject to whatever direction the political winds may blow."

"Oh, really, MacPhail? I suppose ye give no care to where the new railroads will run, then, do ye? Yer precious canal is falling into disrepair, and the legislature is not of a mind to prop it up. What will ye do when the railroad bypasses yer operation altogether and yer canal is nothing but a muddy sinkhole?"

"And I suppose you and your 'connections' can promise to support the canal against all comers and influence the positioning of the railroad, all in the name of the people?"

Judge took a step back, appraised me from head to toe and smiled. "Come now, MacPhail, ye know we canna go that far, but your support is needed to keep the legislature looking wi' favor on Mt. Etna."

"I would support a stray dog against your friend, Judge. Or a pig. Either would do me more favor than Trethaway."

"Aye, my friend is right when he tells me that ye're a hard and bitter man."

Hard and bitter might better describe the man standing before me, blocking my way. Fine clothing could not cover up the emptiness in his eyes, green and devoid of feeling. He rocked back on his heels, reloading for another barrage as I launched one of my own.

"How are your children, Mr. Judge? Do you see much of them? They must be growing up tall by now."

Everyone knew that after his children had been taken away, given over to be raised by the kindness of strangers, scattered about the county, he'd never made the slightest effort to reclaim them, provide a home or any kind of sustenance. He was as much a failure as a father as he'd been as husband, storekeeper, utopian founder—or assessor, for that matter—and I took a perverse pleasure in reminding him of that.

His reaction was to step forward, almost touching me chest to chest, and tap me hard against the shoulder with his cane. "They're better than yer sad lot, I can promise ye. At least they've no exploitation of the poor to apologize for, unlike yer eldest, young Robbie."

"Exploitation of the poor? What poor?"

"Why, Caddie Trethaway and her poor bastard son. Done in by Robbie MacPhail."

"How is it exploitation? The woman and her son have a place to live, food on the table, and clothes on their backs. And her father was handsomely paid in money yet to be conferred on her. Where is the exploitation?"

"Aye. Ye think ye can buy anything. Food, clothing, and loyalty, as well. But ye'll see. Yer time is coming, MacPhail. The time fer reckoning. My friend Trethaway hasn't forgotten all the dirt ye've done him."

I'd heard enough. There was no use standing there arguing in the street. I stepped around him and continued on my way, resolving never to be drawn into such useless conversation again.

When I returned home that afternoon I was confronted with a scene of busy preparation. Young Laird had asked permission to take his brothers, John and Edward, along on an outing to Spruce Creek. They would fish in the creek, roam the trails, and camp for a few days. The younger boys admired their older brother and loved to be included in his adventures—especially John, who was anxious to share his knowledge of the woodlands. Laird was a responsible young man, and his days of carefree roaming in the woods and fishing the streams would come to an end soon enough. At eleven and nine, John and Edward were eager for anything that included fishing, hunting—and their older brother. So they loaded up their horses and a pack mule with a tent, fishing rods, food, cots, and their dog, Deuce, so named because he was the image of his father, a border collie full of pee and vinegar and unacquainted with restraint.

They arrived at the banks of Spruce Creek late in the afternoon and proceeded to set up camp. Laird, always the master fisherman, caught them a mess of trout for their supper and they settled down for the night. Deuce, kept in the tent to reduce the possibility of his tangling with a skunk, woke them up around midnight, barking ferociously. Laird loaded up his shotgun and, taking a lantern and the dog, ventured out to investigate. A large, black bear loomed up on its hind legs, pawing the darkness and growling at the menacing dog. John and Edward, unable to contain their curiosity, followed, each armed with a wood club left over from the night's firewood.

The ensuing struggle is difficult to describe, but, as told to me later by John, Laird motioned for the other two to get back into the tent and tried to call the dog away. True to his nature, Deuce ignored all commands and continued to bark, snarl, and growl, all of which served to anger the bear. Laird stood his ground, and, hoping to avoid a clash between the two beasts, let go a single shot into the air. As he stepped back to reload, the bear rushed at the dog and the two were soon entangled in mortal combat.

The other two boys now stepped back out, rushing forward to try to save the dog, but the folly of their mission was soon demonstrated when the bear lashed out with ferocious claws, catching Edward across the left side. Laird, frantic to save his brothers and the dog, took careful aim and shot into the black and tangled mass of bear and dog. There was a sudden silence during which Laird hoped he had wounded or at least frightened the bear into retreat.

Then there came a deep, violent roar as the bear reared up again, the dog lying dead at its feet. Instead of charging the gunman, it swerved toward the stout canvas tent, ripping and rampaging over it like it was paper. Both boys tried to run away as the beast concentrated on ravaging the tent, but their movement caught its eye, and quick as lightening, it chased down Edward again, grabbing him up in one swift swoop of its front paw, dropping him, swiping across his body, picking him up, biting into his flesh, shaking and dropping him again.

Frantically, Laird reloaded and raised the gun once more. "Look out, John! I have to shoot!" he cried.

John got out of the way, ducking down behind some rocks, hearing, but not seeing the shotgun blast again. Then there was silence. Nothing but silence and the blackness of the night. The bear was gone, and, picking up the fallen lantern, Laird lit it again, holding it aloft to see his young brother lying bleeding and scarred on the ground. John ran to the creek for water to wash Edward's wounds while Laird, trembling and crying, entreated Edward to rise, open his eyes, speak, to no avail. The boy was dead, killed by the mauling bear before his brother could get off his shot.

It was an unspeakable tragedy for our family, but more than that for Laird. He would never fully recover from the guilt he carried for not being able to protect his brother. John felt it, too, but his was less intense, more forgiving than Laird's. They brought our little boy home the next day, so overcome with grief that they could barely relate the story. Their mother, at first refusing to believe what they said, crumpled on the front steps of the house, overwhelmed by the worst disaster that can befall a mother.

It was as though the world had ended and we were left. We stared at each other around our dinner table for months thereafter, with little to say and much to grieve. Our Eddie, so full of sunshine and mischief. So promising, funny, and kind. How could we go on? How could we fill the void in our hearts? How could we help Laird? And how could I comfort his mother?

Chapter 61

1848
Ellie

To say Edward's death was devastating to me is like saying rain falls from clouds. My disbelief soon gave way to a heaviness in my heart that wouldn't lighten, wouldn't release me from its icy grip. How could I ever get over such pain? How could I help Laird get over his? It was too much. Too much for anyone to bear, but bear it I would, for I had no choice. I stumbled through day after weary day, blind to everything around me, unable to think, react or even care what else happened.

Alyssa was being courted by a fine young man from a prominent Williamsburg family—Mark Wilsoncroft was his name—but I couldn't share in her joy or get caught up in her plans. Tears would well up from nowhere, unbidden, and engulf me at every turn. I remembered that crying does no good, but I was powerless to stem the flow.

And Laird, my dear, sensitive, caring son for whom hurting a mouse was unthinkable—what of him? He descended into a darkness as deep as a well, not to emerge for more than a year. Every interaction with him was strained, full of sadness and regret. Trying to tell him he was not to blame produced deep sobs and protestations, sheer agony. I gave up trying to reach him, lost as I was in my own grief.

But Adam, ever faithful, ever true, Adam took over responsibility for bringing our other son back from the depths of despair. They became inseparable, traveling together among the various furnace operations, overseeing every phase of the business, going over the accounts. What they talked about on those long rides around the holdings I didn't ask. Adam had his own grief, but his was bottled up tight, shared only with me in the privacy of our bedroom late at night, where we both gave ourselves over to the staggering grief. Still, Adam managed to reach out to Laird, support him through those dark days, and bring him back to us—damaged but whole.

As for me, I turned to my faithful friend Lindy, no stranger to losing a child, always there with a cup of tea and a hand to hold. When I got myself together to go for a visit, her house was full of grandchildren—one of Phoebe and Lem's, little Tess, that Lindy was raising as her own, and three of Joel and Hattie's, along with a babe in arms from Chad and his wife. It was hard to carry on a conversation with all the youngsters running around, but it was plain that Lindy loved it. Right in the middle of all the fun and nonsense she was almost the old Lindy I'd known in my youth.

"What you need," she'd tell me, "is some of these." Her gaze circled the roomful of children, laughing, whining, crying, fighting, noses running, pants drooping.

It was enough to make me laugh in spite of my grief. "No, Lindy, I can wait for this."

"It'd be good for you, though. Gets you out of yourself. You ought to go down to Cove Forge and get to know that little one."

"You mean Caddie Trethaway's child?"

She gave a laugh. "Sure. Go see if he looks like any of yours. You might be a grandmother already, you know."

I'd visited Cove Forge many times since Caddie lived there, but she was always discreetly busy when I came, and the child never appeared. I wondered about it, but when I questioned Elizabeth David, she brushed me aside and went on to more interesting subjects. Still, since Lindy brought it up, I couldn't get the child off my mind, wondering still if he was, indeed, Robbie's son. In some ways I didn't want to know because it would mean I'd have to encourage Robbie to treat William as his—not neglect and ignore him as his own father had. But polite society forbad the admission of paternity except in legitimate circumstances. Better not to know. Better to get on with one's life and not let youthful indiscretions be a hindrance.

But one winter day, with Edward's death still weighing heavily upon me, I called for the carriage on impulse and bundled up for the trip to Cove Forge. The wind was bitter, and clouds scudded across the sky, portending a change in the weather, not for the good. I arrived at the David's house and was ushered into the parlor, where I found Elizabeth and Wren bent over matching needlepoint chair seats.

"Ellie! How fine to see you. I've been wondering how you are. And your family? Are they well?"

"Well enough, considering our burden," I replied.

Wren looked up, her fingers suspended over her needle work. "How is Laird getting on, Mrs. MacPhail? I haven't seen him in ages."

"He's doing as well as he can. Still lost in his grief, but he sends his best." It wasn't true. Laird hadn't even reacted when I'd announced at breakfast that I was going to Cove Forge. He and Wren had been friends all their lives, and while there seemed no romance between them, Elizabeth and I held out hope that someday there would be.

I turned to Elizabeth. "Can we talk in the kitchen, perhaps?"

There was visible hesitation in her demeanor. She rose and, politely putting aside her needlework, moved toward the door leading into the hallway. "Yes, of course, just let me see if Caddie is busy."

She disappeared into the kitchen and was back in short order, smiling as though she'd shared something amusing.

Caddie's in the middle of fixing lunch right now. I told her we had a guest, and she's adding water to the soup."

I smiled at her little joke and moved toward the kitchen door, but, to my dismay, Elizabeth placed herself squarely in front of it, barring my way.

"Caddie doesn't..."

"It's Caddie I want to see," I said, brushing past her.

The kitchen was full of good smells, meat roasting for dinner, bread just out of the oven, soup on the stove. Caddie Trethaway stood at the table chopping vegetables, a small boy toddling around at her feet. A beautiful child, he reminded me instantly of Robbie at that age: thick, dark hair with a tendency to curl, dark eyes full of the devil, chubby cheeks, and one quirky eyebrow, always raised in a question. I wanted to pick him up and hug him the moment I saw him. I could see Robbie all over him.

Caddie stopped chopping and, looking at me as though I were about to attack, she jerked back, holding her knife as though to parry a blow.

"Caddie! Why he's beautiful. I'm so happy to get to see him."

"You can't have him. Don't you never try to take him away. He's mine."

"No. Nothing like that. I just wanted to see him. He does look like Robbie, though, don't you think?"

"I been trying to keep him from you," the girl said, her eyes darting from me to Elizabeth and back again. "I knew you'd want him soon as you saw him, but no. You can't have him." She even brandished her knife in a forlorn semblance of a threat.

I stepped back. "Caddie, I've no intention of taking your son away. I just wanted to see him. If he is my grandson, I'd like to know him."

"He ain't. You can't claim him, so there. Now git outta my kitchen."

I looked to Elizabeth but saw no help there. It seemed she was siding with Caddie, so I backed off, turned, and left the kitchen by the door I'd entered from. When we returned to the parlor, Wren had left on some errand, and we were free to talk.

"I tried to head you off, but you would go bursting in there. I wanted to spare you. I knew how she felt, unwarranted though it may be. She dotes on the child—never lets him out of her sight."

"What about her family? Does she ever see any of them?"

Elizabeth shook her head. "No, she says she doesn't want anything to do with them, not that I blame her for that."

"Well, I didn't expect this reception. I'd have expected her to try to get money or some kind of handout, but to spurn me when it is so obvious he's Robbie's child, I..."

"That's been her fear all along. She's afraid you'll lay claim to him and take him away because you have the means to give him more than she can."

"Poor child. Abused by her no-good father, cast aside by her lover. No wonder she expects the worst from people. Please try to make her understand that I want nothing more than to know the boy as my grandchild."

Elizabeth reached for a small silver bell on a side table and gave it a gentle shake. The sterling sound brought a young woman properly attired in a maid's cap and apron to the doorway.

"Tea for Mrs. MacPhail and me," my hostess directed. Then turning to me, she said, "What do you hear from your eldest son?"

"Very little. He came home for Edward's funeral but couldn't stay long. Missed Christmas this year. He seems happy down there in Berks County."

"Do you think he'll stay there, then?"

"Perhaps. He's deep into the fur trading business and doesn't seem to miss us very much."

When the tea was served, Elizabeth poured as I sat lost in thought about young William. "Do you think she'll ever relent?" I asked.

"Maybe some day. Give her time. She really is a good cook and a good mother. I should tell you, though, that she has a suitor."

"Suitor?"

"Yes, Brinton English. You know him. Christian English's son."

I furrowed my brow trying to place the young man, but no. "How does he feel about the child?"

"Seems to like him. Willy's such a sweet child, it would be hard not to like him."

"If they marry, would they stay around here? Not move west, I hope."

"Come, now, Ellie, I'm not privy to all that goes on. I'll try to talk to Caddie, get her to change her mind about you, but we'll have to wait and see."

"I did help her when she came to me. Got her this place with you."

"Yes, I'll remind her."

Suddenly it was urgent that I see the child, watch him grow, be part of his life. I knew I was making more of it than needed but, looking back, maybe it was a way to ease the pain of losing Edward. I finished my tea and rose to leave. "Tell Wren to come down to Mt. Etna sometime. The girls would love to see her, and maybe she can help bring Laird out of his grief."

I returned home with a heavy heart, burdened more by Caddie's rejection. It seemed no use to go on. Life was too hard sometimes.

Chapter 62

1850
Adam

The years after Edward's death seemed to run together. Every one of us had our own grief to deal with, but it was hard to tell who suffered more—Laird from the guilt, or Ellie from the loss of her youngest child and being deprived of her only grandchild. Caddie Trethaway remained adamant that she wanted her son to have nothing to do with his grandparents—neither the Trethaways nor the MacPhails. I think Ellie might have had an easier time of it if she'd been distracted by the young William, but his mother had her way.

Our family changed in so many ways after Eddie died. Alyssa married her young Mr. Wilsoncroft and moved to Roaring Spring, where he opened an academy for young boys and they began a family of their own. Having grandchildren in Roaring Spring wasn't as much of a remedy for Ellie as having them close at hand would have been, but she did go visiting two or three times a year and came back with endless tales about the cute and funny antics of young Teddy and baby Melissa.

Bethany announced within months of her brother's death that she wished to go to Philadelphia to study to become a physician. Such a move, unheard of in our day, garnered her mother's immediate approval—but for the distance and loss of another child. Bethany persisted, determined to prove her abilities and be of service. After she struggled to be admitted and get through medical school in the company of all those young men who thought her intellectually inferior, a new women's medical college opened in Philadelphia. I knew she'd be a fine physician, though she'd struggle for respect for the rest of her life. Ellie's daughter, through and through.

Young John, traumatized by the loss of his brother, took to wandering off alone in the woods, fishing, hunting, and gathering roots, bark, herbs, and berries that he shared with Jim Sanders. It was his way of getting over the tragedy, and it eventually seemed to work. Unlike Laird, he seemed barely able to remember that terrible night on Spruce Creek.

As for me, I did the best I could. With so many details to attend to, I was grateful for the distraction running the furnace operation gave me. As I'd always found relief in work, I tried to share that relief with Laird, and it seemed to help—at least for as long as the day lasted. But more than once I passed his door late at night and wondered whether the occupant slept or spent the night awake with his terrors. We all had to get through our grief in our own time and our own way, but it made mine worse knowing he still struggled with his.

One ray of hope abided, though. Miss Wren David began to visit about once a week, and she and Laird would go out walking along the towpath or climb the hills in search of whatever flower or fruit was in season. Wren was ever cheerful, loving, and kind. Her very presence lifted the pall of grief from my shoulders, and I dared hope for Laird.

I entertained the idea of travel as a palliative to Ellie's grief, suggesting trips to Pittsburgh, Philadelphia, even New York. But she declined, making excuses about things that must be done right here in Mt. Etna. I suspected that meant keeping an eye on her grandchild, the elusive William, who I saw every so often when I visited Cove Forge. The resemblance to Robbie was striking and not to be denied. While I didn't share Ellie's need to be part of his life, I sometimes wished Robbie would come home and get to see him, claim him, be a real father.

But Robbie was pre-occupied with his own problems, it seemed. True to his nature, Robert Clifton saw fit to delay changing his relationship with Robbie—or declined to establish it in the first place. Soon after his mother's death a few years ago, Clifton announced to Robbie that he was putting the whole Brighton estate up for sale, as he intended to reside permanently in Philadelphia. Robbie didn't mind, since he still had his grandfather Bratton's place to live.

But the elder Clifton, while promising to take the legal steps necessary to make Robbie his legitimate son and heir, dawdled and stalled until it pleased him to announce that his wife had died, freeing him to marry again. Robbie pressed for action on the legal front, but all was postponed until after the wedding. It was now two years hence, and a child had been born to the new union. A son. Robbie wrote his mother in chagrin over the impending developments, but there was really nothing we could do. So now Robbie stood waiting for some action from his father, but Robert Clifton being Robert Clifton, I doubted that the boy would ever gain the legitimacy he longed for.

My painful relationship with Simon Trethaway continued in spite of my efforts to avoid any contact with him. He'd served three terms in the legislature and even begun making overtures about running for governor. I seriously doubted his ability to gain that office, but he'd surprised me before. In distress over the possibility, I drove to Cove Forge to discuss politics with Noah David.

Noah was getting up in years but was still spry and bright eyed. His young wife and daughter saw to that. When I arrived, Noah was just riding up from downriver, where he'd attended to some business with his tenant farmers.

"Good day, MacPhail. You're just the man I was hoping to see."

"For a good purpose, I hope."

"Good or bad, it's always a pleasure."

We entered the big stone house by the front door and turned right into David's office, where we sat on either side of his broad, walnut desk. As he poured me a draught of brandy, he started the conversation on a controversial note.

"Looks like we might have our first governor from the new county, MacPhail."

"A sorry prospect that is," I replied, swirling the amber-colored brandy in the glass. "I'd never have believed he could even gain the legislature—but surely not the governors office!"

"Well, it isn't all bad—for people other than you, at least. Trethaway remembers where he came from and will make sure the new Blair County gets its due. That's all I care about."

"But the man is a scoundrel. A good-for-nothing churl. His like isn't worthy of the right to vote, less even the right to govern." My anger at Trethaway came hurling out at times like this. Most of the time I held it in check, but, feeling safe with Noah David, I vented my feelings freely.

"I don't disagree with your assessment, but look at the rest of the aspirants. Noble from Lewistown is naught but a boot lick for the railroads, and Fargen from Johnstown is in the pocket of the Cambria Company. At least Trethaway's ears are tuned to our needs."

I had to give him that. The iron industry had a champion in Simon Trethaway—all except me. And even though most of the iron men didn't respect him, they did know on which side their bread was buttered. Politics were politics.

"But I just can't bring myself to support him, Noah. I wish someone else from around here would rise up and challenge him for the nomination."

"Can you think of anybody?"

"It won't be ours to decide, I'm afraid. The power lies in the cities—Pittsburgh and Philadelphia. I don't know how, but I hope they bring someone forward to stop Trethaway."

Noah David took a sip from his glass. "At least being in Harrisburg keeps him from haunting you all the time."

"You've a point there. Maybe I should hope he does get elected."

Hope, indeed. My preferences had nothing to do with it, but Simon Trethaway didn't even gain the nomination. Having given up his seat in the legislature to run for governor, he found himself unemployed after the election, and he returned to his home across the river, with nothing better to do than resume his harassment of me.

I went about my business, doing my best to avoid him, but when our paths chanced to cross, it was the same old Trethaway spewing venom and making cutting remarks. More insulted by it than I was, Elinor took every measure to avoid him or his wife. She would turn around and go the other way if she met either of them on the track, or send young John to the company store rather than meet any Trethaway coming or going.

The clan had shrunk to just the parents and the youngest boy, Jude, who, at thirty, seemed content to do nothing but hang around his parents' cabin and hunt with his coon hounds at night. Caroline Trethaway had stayed at home during her husband's service to the state. Privately, Ellie opined that her appearance was too common even for her husband to overlook. With the two oldest boys gone west and Caddie refusing to have anything to do with them, the couple seemed to cast about for social connections. Simon's loud mouth, full of threats and bragging, hadn't made him many friends, and once his political influence was spent, no one bothered with him much at all, except to buy liquor, which he continued to deal in despite my requests that he not sell to my workers.

Chapter 63

Adam
1851

I managed to have little to do with Simon Trethaway after his return from Harrisburg, and that suited me well enough. Then, one cold autumn day, a gentleman entered the store downstairs, asking for me. He was escorted up to my office by the store manager, who stood by while we talked—as though to make sure the visitor wasn't trouble.

The man approached me wearing workmen's clothes, stocky, blue eyed, and handsome in a common sort of way. He offered his hand. "Good day, Mr. MacPhail. Hugh Evans. I'm a mining engineer from Luzerne County, late from Wales. I come looking for word of my brother, Geordan Evans. I'm told he worked for you some time back."

"Oh, yes. Evans. Have you had word of him?"

"Not for twenty years. I was just a bit of a lad when he left home. Our mother grieved for him ever since. She's gone now, rest her soul. But I promised her if I ever got to Pennsylvania I'd find out his fate."

"I see. Well, Mr. Evans, there isn't much I can tell you. Your brother disappeared without a trace just about twenty years ago."

"Can you take me to his place of work? I could ask around. Maybe somebody who knew something then would be ready to talk now."

I felt a vague discomfort at dredging up that old mystery, but my sympathy for his family made me decide to do what I could. "I could take you down to the Porter Quarry, where he was my manager. There aren't many men still there who would remember him. I don't expect you to find anything, but you're welcome to ask."

The man nodded and stepped aside while I called for a gig for the drive down to Porter. The ride along the river was a bit chilly, and when we arrived, the manager's shanty, with its pot bellied stove, looked inviting.

"I'll introduce you to the only fellow I think might remember anything," I told him. Then to the manager: "See if Mike Morgan is around."

About ten minutes later the door opened and an older, grayer, broader Mike Morgan entered. When I greeted him and introduced Mr. Evans, Mike's face clouded over,

"What? Ye come here to try to dig up something on me? I had naught to do wi' it. Can't say I weren't glad to be rid of him after how he done my dad, but I didn't do it."

"Don't worry, Mike. No one thinks you did. The man just wants to know what happened to his brother. It's too old now for the law to care, and anyway, there's no body ever been found."

"Right. The killer seen to that. Blew him up the next day in a blast."

"You knew this, Mike?" It was the first time anyone had said a word to me about what might have happened to Geordan Evans.

"Aye. I knew it then, but telling you or anybody else would have meant I'd be next."

Mr. Hugh Evans leaned close to Mike Morgan, hanging on every word he said. "Were you and Geordan at odds, then?"

"He were a bastard, yer brother. Sent me dad down where they was blastin'. Knew he couldn't hear the call to cover. I mighta kilt him myself if Trethaway hadn't done it fer me."

"Trethaway?" Suddenly Trethaway's boast about having taken care of Geordan Evans came back to me. "Really, Mike? Are you sure?"

"Who's Trethaway?" asked Hugh Evans.

"Lazy, good-fer-nothin' son-of-a-bitch that Evans rode pretty hard. Lousy worker. Stole anything that weren't nailed down. Evans kept threatening to fire him, so he went away and laid low until Evans went to Water Street one night. Caught him on the way home, bashed his head in with a bar, and carried him back to the far end of the quarry. Covered him up with rocks right where the charge was set to go come morning." He turned to me. "By the time you got here, he'd been blown to Kingdom Come."

I let go a long sigh. "I wish you'd told me then, Mike. He'd have been hanged. As it is, he's still around harassing me."

"No way I'd have told. I was glad to be rid of Evans and scared to death of Trethaway. He went around bragging about taking care of Evans and then left pretty quick. Back up your way, I heard. Good riddance, I say."

I turned to Hugh Evans, shaking my head. "I didn't know. I tried to find out, but the whole crew closed up on me, and there was no body, so I figured he could have just left. Didn't really believe that, but didn't have anything else to hold onto."

Hugh Evans face was contorted in a grimace. He looked like he might cry, but instead let out a sound—half groan, half roar. "Geordan was me brother," he cried. "Me only brother, and good to me and our ma. Where is this Trethaway? I want to see him!"

"No. No, Mr. Evans. You can't go seeking revenge now, after twenty years. Too much time has passed. Let it go."

There was no stopping him, no calming him down. It was as though the murder had occurred only yesterday, so bent he was on finding Simon Trethaway. I wouldn't tell him where Trethaway was, but I knew there were plenty about who would welcome the opportunity.

"Come on, Mr. Evans. You and I need to sit down over a drink and talk this over. We'll go down to Water Street for a draught."

The man wasn't to be easily put off. He turned back to Mike Morgan. "What else can ye tell me? Who else knows anything? Are ye sure you be telling the truth?"

Mike looked from him to me and back again. "It's the God's honest truth. He may have been yer brother, but he needed killin'."

Evans pulled back, fists clenched, staring at Morgan. "Say one more thing about my brother, and I'll give you what they gave him."

Then, without warning, he doubled over, engulfed in deep, heaving sobs, and slumped to the floor. "He were my brother, dammit. My only brother."

Moving to his side, I tried to comfort him, but to no avail. Mike Morgan picked up his work gloves and stalked out the door. Two others, the manager and his clerk, pretended to be occupied with their work. Slowly, I raised Evans to his feet and led him to the gig. I wanted to get him to Water Street, the opposite direction from Mt. Etna, hoped to get him on the next coach back to Luzerne. We arrived at the inn, cold and hungry, at well past the dinner hour.

"I'll get you a room here and you can catch a coach tomorrow," I told him.

He seemed amenable to the suggestion and sat in morose silence as I ordered dinner and two draughts of ale. We ate without further conversation. The man didn't want to talk, and I could only guess what thoughts were racing through his brain. Once dinner was over I apologized for my part in his brother's death, urged him to go back home and forget about the whole thing, and took my leave. For all I knew, he stayed the night at the inn and left for his home the next day.

It was young John, tearing down the path from the company store two days later, who brought me the news I feared. Simon Trethaway was dead. Someone had lured him from his house the night before on the pretense of buying some liquor, and he'd been found that morning on the riverbank, his head bashed in with some kind of iron bar. The irony of the weapon was not lost on me.

I felt an obligation to express my condolences to his widow and son, so I took young John along, crossed the river, and trekked up to the Trethaway cabin on old Tussey as soon as I heard the news. The dead man's body had been gathered up from the riverbank, washed, dressed in his finest legislator's suit of black broadcloth, and laid out on the table in the cabin. Caroline Trethaway made a great to-do of her grief, moaning and crying out like a she-wolf howling on a cold night. She rocked back and forth on her chair, keening and sobbing what a good man her Simon was. Young Jude sat looking at the corpse, not moving, not even blinking. He didn't acknowledge my presence or accept my condolences. He just stared at the body of his father, lying dead on the table.

The news that Simon Trethaway had been murdered by parties unknown brought out the authorities, and it wasn't long before they came to question me about the man who'd come inquiring about his dead brother. I told them the whole story, corroborated by Mike Morgan and the manager and clerk at Porter Quarry, adding that I knew nothing other than that he'd left Water Street the next morning.

Efforts to locate Mr. Evans failed. He was not found to live anywhere in Luzerne County, and it became pretty clear that Mr. Evans had covered his tracks quite well. The conclusion of the sheriff was that Evans had done the deed but had gotten away to who knew where and was at large and not apprehendable. That was the end of it as far as the sheriff and all of us were concerned.

Chapter 64

1851
Ellie

It took several weeks for the excitement of Simon Trethaway's murder to die down, but things were generally back to normal by Christmas. We were excited at the prospect of a Christmas visit from Robbie, and I'd made feverish and frenzied preparations and purchases for all the children and grandchildren with special care.

On Christmas Eve, the family gathered in the parlor where Robbie, Laird, Alyssa and her family, Bethany, and John joined me in singing carols around the pianoforte. Our accompanist was Wren David, whose parents had also joined us. There was food and presents and laugher aplenty as we celebrated fully for the first time since Edward's death. Then Laird stepped forward and, taking Wren's hand, addressed the assembly.

"Mother, Father, brothers and sisters, friends," he began. "It gives me great pride to announce that Wren and I will be married in the coming year. In June, we hope."

He looked at his bride-to-be, his eyes shining with pride, lifted her hand to his lips, and kissed it. Amidst great cheering and congratulating, the young couple danced a slow waltz to the music played by Elizabeth David her approval from the pianoforte.

"Aha, little brother. Looks like you've beaten me to the altar," Robbie called, lifting his glass in salute.

"That's because you're too busy racing horses," his sister Bethany returned. "The only female that interests you has four legs!"

Everyone laughed at that, for Robbie's fascination with horses hadn't abated. He smiled and offered his congratulations to his brother but couldn't resist a little snippet. "At least I know a mare from a filly and a stallion from a colt. More than I can say for some of this company." Laird's apathy toward horses was well known. He'd just as soon walk as ride, and took no joy in driving a team except as a means to get him where he was going.

Later I saw Elizabeth David take Robbie aside and speak with him in quiet tones. I wondered what she would have to say to him, but I resolved to get it from Robbie later. When I inquired, he laughed and said, "She thinks I should visit Caddie Trethaway and her child. She thinks he looks like me. What if he does? Didn't father pay them off?"

"Let's put this conversation off until after the holidays. I'll tell you all about it, but now is the time for celebration."

And so we left it, but, when the holidays were over, Robbie seemed anxious to get back to Berks County, while I was of a mind to argue the case for seeing his son.

"Mother, it isn't that simple," he told me. "Whether or not he is my child is of no consequence to me. He's being taken care of."

"Oh, Robbie, don't be like your own father. Surely, you would feel something for the boy if you saw him. And if you were kind to her and the child, Caddie might decide that it would be all right for us to see more of him."

"That, my dear mother, is your problem. I have more important things on my mind at present. I must get back to Berks County with all haste."

"What more important things?" I was afraid to ask, more afraid to know.

"It seems my 'father' has now a second child and in negotiations with my solicitor has declined to legitimize my claim. His new wife insists that her two sons take precedence over me, and I fear that all hope of gaining any inheritance is lost."

"Oh, Robbie. I'm so sorry. I was afraid he'd do something like this. He has no scruples whatever. I'm lucky not to have married him."

"Yes, mother. There's more. Spurred by the promise of inherited wealth, I've been somewhat indiscreet, acquired some debts. Betting on the horse races. I'm in some trouble, I'm afraid."

"Debts? What sort of debts?"

My son just stood there, hands at his sides, eyes on the floor.

"Robbie! By how much?"

"A lot, Mother. More than I want to tell you."

"Who else would you tell?"

More silence. Robbie stood before me, handsome as ever but chagrinned and looking helpless, still not man enough to take responsibility for his own actions. More to remind me of his father at that age.

"Surely not Adam. Surely you wouldn't expect him to rescue you."

"No. Not Adam. You. You're the only one who can."

"I? How can I rescue you? Robbie! What have you done?"

He lowered his head in shame, turned away as though he couldn't bear to face me. Then he turned and reached for my hand. "Forgive me, Mother. I didn't mean it. I never meant to."

"To what?"

"To lose the Berks County property. Your father's farm. I put it up against my gambling debts, and now I can't pay."

I turned and walked away, up the stairs to my bedchamber, holding my face in my hands. How could he? How could this happen? I never should have trusted him. I knew in my heart he was too weak to resist temptation. I knew it, but I wanted to trust him anyway. How could I have been so foolish?

Now the prospect of having nothing of my own to pass on to my children brought anguish. The farm itself was of little consequence to me; I'd not lived there for more than twenty-five years, and bitter memories of my courtship with Robert Clifton remained. But I'd taken some pride in its monetary value, knew my father would have wanted it to go to his grandchildren. I sat down in a chair by the window looking out on our snow-covered lawn. The wintery scene made me shiver, devoid of any spark of joy now that I could no longer ignore Robbie's shortcomings. There was no making excuses for him this time.

I must have sat there for more than an hour before Adam came looking for me. "Come, now, Mother. Your children have organized a skating party on the canal. They're building a fire on the towpath and calling for you to come join them."

"I'll be down soon," I replied, but the flatness in my voice was enough to give him pause.

"What is it, my dear? I hope you won't let some small thing spoil the children's fun."

"No, no. I'll be down. I just want to . . ."

Adam turned and looked into my face, noticed there a mother's sorrow, and took my hands in his. "What is it, Ellie? Is it Robbie? Is he refusing to see his son?"

"Yes, that, but more. Much more." I poured out my story, haltingly, my voice breaking. "Oh, Adam, why? Why has he turned out so much like his father? He looks like him, walks like him, talks like him, thinks like him. I saw it early, but I didn't want to believe it. Went on thinking he was just a boy, that he'd outgrow his selfishness and pride. Now he's ruined my father's estate, and there are no real consequences for him. If I thought he'd learn from this I'd feel better, but I'm afraid he'll just keep doing the same things, being the same irresponsible churl."

Adam raised me from my chair and took me in his arms. It felt so good to be there. The world was changing too fast. Our children were standing at the ready to replace us in almost every endeavor. But Adam. Adam was still there as always, ready to understand and comfort me.

"We can't mold our children no matter how much we want to. People think they can, but the forces of nature oppose us at every turn. Robbie is who he is—not what you would have wanted him to be. but still worthy of your love. You know the essence of love is acceptance. He's weak, easily tempted, not ready to take responsibility for all he does, but there's good in the boy. After all, look who his mother is."

I lay my head against his chest and closed my eyes. After all the years of resentment and spite, dissatisfaction and rebellion, I was eternally grateful to be here in this place with this man. We'd seen so much, worked so hard, and achieved a success neither of us had ever dreamed of, and I attributed it all to him. To his kindness, patience, willingness to accept what I was willing to give. Suddenly I was again overwhelmed by shame at how I'd treated him, how I'd behaved like a petulant child, punished him for any and every infraction, real or imagined. Now, in the twilight of our lives, I'd finally learned to appreciate him.

"Adam, forgive me."

"Forgive you? For what?"

"For all of it. All the years of pettiness, anger, resentment. You didn't deserve that. I was nothing more than a spoiled child."

He smiled. "Well, you've grown up into quite a lady. No complaints here."

I raised my face to look into his eyes, ever steady, ever deep, and kissed him, long and soft. "I love you."

After twenty-six years, long and harder than they needed to be, I was finally comfortable with those words, words I'd vowed on my wedding day would never pass my lips. Now I nestled my head against his shoulder and let it all go, gave myself over to serenity, composure, peace.

Adam

Young Robert brought us disconcerting news when he came home for Christmas. Disconcerting to his mother, most of all. I care for the boy—nay, the man. He's almost twenty-seven. But I've known since he was a baby that he cared not a bit for others, took his share first, walked away from the consequences of his deeds. Now I must admit that I will be careful in my dealings with him—not give him access to control over money or operations. The rolling mill in Pittsburgh would be a good place for him to learn the business. He's had modest success buying and selling pelts, but he's grown up with iron. Yet I couldn't ask Noah to take him on without first warning him of

Robbie's shortcomings. I want to see Robbie set up in a good job with a bright future, but more, I want to see him stand up and take the consequences of his actions. Ellie is with me on this, but I'm still not sure she's yet ready to stand back and let him fail on his own.

On another front, time really does heal all wounds. Ellie and I have come to our place of contentment as pertains to our marriage. I would even venture to say we are happy. The experiences of the past few years, the loss of our son, her father's death, her deep desire to be allowed access to her grandson, have mellowed her, given her pause, and taught her to appreciate what we've built together here.

Last night she said once more that she loved me. How I have longed for that sentiment, wished for it, hoped for it. I have loved her since the first time I saw her in her father's parlor in Berks County, but for most of our time together I despaired of ever hearing those words. I take responsibility for the lengthy adjustment. I could have been more communicative, should have tried harder to understand, to reach out to her.

But that has passed like a leaf floating in the canal. We have finally reached that common repose, the balance of purpose and sense of commitment all couples wish for. My commitment to this union has always been deep and wide, but knowing that she shares it, too, gives me unanticipated joy.

Chapter 65

1852
Adam

It would seem that all was right with the world as we approached our twenty-seventh summer at Etna Furnace. Furnace and forge worked day and night, turning out Juniata Iron for the world. Our home bore witness to our almost grown family, our financial success, and a bright future. Laird and Wren had decided to be married in the new, red brick Keller church atop a high, round hill at the head of Fox Hollow. The place of worship was resplendent, with two doors leading in on either side of the altar. The brand new pump organ sat on a raised platform on the left, with two aisles leading back between the pews. The altar, behind which sat a horsehair settee in a blue and star-studded alcove, was situated behind a low banister on another raised platform. The lamps on the chandeliers were all lit, the shutters open, the windows polished.

As the father of the groom, I had little to do but greet guests as they arrived on horseback, in buggies, or on foot. The bride arrived in appropriate style, riding in her father's new carriage, purchased expressly for the occasion, dressed in an ivory wedding gown and veil that complimented her soft, creamy complexion. Laird was inside the church, waiting in a little anteroom that served the parish as a library.

I smiled when Jeff Baker drove up in a wagon his children had decorated in bunting reminiscent of the Fourth of July. Jeff helped

Lindy down as Jenny and Lane, the only two children still living at home, jumped down and quickly mingled with the crowd.

"Glad to see this day come, eh?" Jeff asked.

"Glad for Laird. He seems to be getting along well now. Grief took its toll, but the love of a good woman seems to have healed him."

Lindy nodded. "You never get all the way over it, but you do manage to move on."

A gaggle of little ones came tearing across the lawn. "Granny!" they shouted, and threw themselves into Lindy's arms.

I smiled and looked around for Ellie. Here she came, holding the hand of a young boy of about six, smiling down at him with joy in her eyes. "I'm so glad Caddie said he could come," she beamed. "He's grown up with Wren, so it's only right that he should be here." She knelt down to straighten the boy's jacket. "My, what a handsome grandson you are, William."

The child looked at his shoes, too shy to respond but clearly basking in his grandmother's love.

The wedding was lovely from any point of view. Laird, so tall and handsome, and Wren, a classic beauty, stood before the low balustrade, their backs to the congregation, and spoke their vows with deep emotion. Hard not to remember the sad little service that united Ellie and me so long ago. But there was joy here—for the young couple and for us, to have come so far from such an unhappy beginning.

I looked at Ellie beside me, her face set in determination not to shed a tear. I squeezed her hand and whispered, "It's all right. Let it go."—and watched a single tear wend it's way down her still-beautiful cheek.

Following the service, we returned to Mt. Etna and gathered on the lawn at our home, before long, plank tables weighed down under enough food to feed Napoleon's army, much of it prepared by my workers' wives.

Old Mathias Corbin, hobbling around on a cane, still overseeing the roasting of a pig, hailed me as I approached.

"Good pig this time, sir. Raised it myself. Fed it the best slop every day. Grew up nice and fat. Ye'll find it to yer liking."

"No doubt, Mathias. You've never disappointed me yet."

Walking around greeting guests and enjoying the lovely afternoon, I happened to glance across the river and saw Jude Trethaway standing among the trees, watching. He'd taken his father's death hard, withdrawing ever farther from the outside world. His mother had died in the spring, leaving him alone in the cabin with three hundred and sixty acres of land still his. There'd been no word from the two oldest boys, Zach and Luke, since they went west after Lem was killed. Caddie maintained her distance from Jude, spurning association with any of her family. Seeing him standing there alone, I motioned to him to come over and join the party, but he just turned around and walked down along the riverbank, his gun across his shoulders.

Too bad. I'd always thought he might turn out better than the rest. It seemed when he was a boy he might be different, but as a man, it gave me a turn to run into him alone. The look in his eyes, especially since his father's death, was sinister. I always greeted him when we passed on the track, but he never met my gaze, let alone returned my greeting. I'd hoped once the old man was gone Jude would take a different tack, become part of the community, but it didn't look that way now.

I turned back to the celebration, enjoying the praise and good wishes heaped on the young couple. I watched Alyssa's children run around trailing paper streamers, and enjoyed young John's victory over several other young men in a game of horseshoes. Ellie was on the front porch, cutting slices of pie for the guests as fast as Mrs. Gwynn could carry out a fresh one.

Bethany came and stood beside me, laughing at young William's efforts to throw a ball up in the air and catch it. It came down in front of him, behind him, beside him, bonked him on the head, but he persisted. "That's Robbie's son," she laughed, "if there was ever any doubt." Robbie, absent due to his now-estranged relationship with his mother, had a well-earned reputation as a poor athlete—except when it came to horsemanship.

I found myself a place in the shade of one of our huge sycamores and sat down on a wooden lawn chair brought in for the occasion.

The afternoon was warm and sunny; the hay cut the day before lay drying in the fields, filling the air with its soft scent. I wondered how much time we had before we'd be too old to enjoy this life we'd forged. Only in my fifties, I hoped to live maybe another twenty-five years. See a great grandchild or two. Life was good.

Ellie

As the excitement of the day was dying, the newlyweds departed on a canal boat for a wedding trip to Pittsburgh and Lake Erie. They would spend their first married night at the U.S. Hotel in Hollidaysburg before traversing the Alleghenies on the Portage Railroad. Many of the guests from farther away had already climbed into their buggies and driven off. I sat down on the front porch, where I could see most of what was going on. I hadn't seen much of Adam that day. The last I looked, he was sitting on a lawn chair under the big old sycamore. I looked again, and he was still there, so I wandered over to sit with him. Not like him to stay in one place this long. As I approached I could see his head resting on the back of the chair, the breeze playing with his graying hair. I wished I could stop time right there and keep us both as we were; happy, comfortable and in good health. Serenity had been a long time coming, and I wanted it to last.

I was only a few feet away when I heard the shot, reverberating through the hollow, echoing against the hillsides. At first I thought it was part of the celebration, maybe someone who'd had a bit too much wedding cheer. Then I saw the red stain spreading across his white shirt, his head listing to the side. Adam! Adam!

And he was gone.

Ellie

Adam died on our son's wedding day, murdered by persons unknown. Oh, there were suspicions, rumors, stories, blame aplenty, but no proof. Nothing to link his death directly to anyone. Jude Trethaway was the prime suspect, having been seen lurking around the fringes of the celebration with a rifle over his shoulders. But no one had seen anything. No one could prove anything, and I was too overwhelmed with grief to push for his arrest I wasn't ready. Is anyone ever ready for tragedy?

And now it has been decreed that I should go on alone. Tragedy for me. Tragedy for Laird, whose fragile and delicate balance with life hasn't had time to solidify. I grieve for him, thrust so abruptly into full responsibility. I grieve for the other children, deprived of the good and faithful father they loved. I grieve for the world in which good men are few and the need for them is great. Ahh, fate. Who has a right to decree that another's life should end? Where is honor? Where is justice? Where is right?

About the Author

Judith Redline Coopey was born in Altoona, Pennsylvania, and holds degrees from the Pennsylvania State University and Arizona State University.

A passion for history inherited from her father drives her writing. Her first book, *Redfield Farm* is the story of the Underground Railroad in Bedford County, Pennsylvania. The second, *Waterproof*, tells how the 1889 Johnstown Flood nearly destroyed a young woman's life. *Looking For Jane* is a quest for love and family in the 1890s brought to life through the eyes of Nell, a young girl convinced that Calamity Jane is her mother.

As a teacher, writer and student of history, Ms Coopey finds her inspiration in the rich history of her native state and in stories of the lives of those who have gone before.

Preview of Redfield Farm

Ann Redfield is destined to follow her brother Jesse through life—two years behind him—all the way. Jesse is a conductor on the Underground Railroad, and Ann follows him there as well.

Quakers filled with a conviction as hard as Pennsylvania limestone that slavery is an abomination to be resisted with any means available, the Redfield brother and sister lie, sneak, masquerade and defy their way past would-be enforcers of the hated Fugitive Slave Law.

Their activities inevitably lead to complicated relationships with other Quakers, pro-slavery neighbors and the fugitives themselves.

When Jesse returns from a run with a deadly fever, accompanied by a fugitive, Josiah, who is also sick and close to death, Ann nurses both back to health. But precious time is lost, and Josiah, too weak for winter travel, stays on at Redfield Farm where Ann becomes his teacher, friend and confidant. When grave disappointment disrupts her life, Ann turns to Josiah for comfort, and comfort leads to intimacy. The result, both poignant and inspiring, leads to a life-long devotion to one another and their cause.

Author Judith Redline Coopey brings the Underground Railroad alive, giving us characters to remember—both real and compassionate—and conflict to explore when belief in equality for all demands action, even when that action puts another principle, pacifism, to the test.

Preview of Waterproof

On May 31, 1889, an earthen dam broke and sent a thirty-foot wall of raging destruction down on the city of Johnstown, Pennsylvania. Fifty years later, Pamela McRae looks back on the traumatic events with new perspective. How do you—how does anybody—cope with such tragedy?

The flood wiped out Pam's fondest hopes, taking her fiancé and her brother's lives and her mother's sanity, and within a year her father walked away leaving his daughter—now the sole support of her mother—to cope with poverty and loneliness.

Determined not to let the flood define her, Pam makes her own way as a society reporter for the *Johnstown Clarion*, trekking back and forth across town gathering her stories, witness to all manner of human tragedy as people who seem to be on the road to recovery reel and falter under some seemingly minor setback.

But when Davy Hughes, Pam's fiancé before the flood, reappears, instead of being the answer to her prayers, he further complicates her life. Someone is seeking revenge on the owners of the South Fork Fishing and Hunting Club, the millionaires who owned the failed dam, and Davy's bitterness gives rise to suspicion that he might be involved.

In this story the 1889 Johnstown Flood, one of the greatest tragedies of the nineteenth century, takes center stage, and Pamela McRae stands firm in the face of prejudice, vengeance, violence and despair to emerge fifty years later a whole woman, guided by her principles and inspired by love.

Preview of Looking for Jane

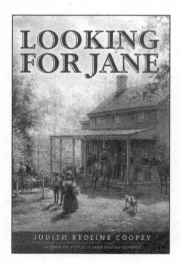

"The nuns use this as their measuring stick: who your people are. Well, what if you don't have no people? Or any you know of? What then? Are you doomed?" This is the nagging question of fifteen-year-old Nell's life.

Born with a cleft palate and left a foundling on the doorstep of a Johnstown, Pennsylvania con-vent, she yearns for a place in the world—yearns to find her mother, whose name, she knows, was Jane.

When the Mother Superior tries to pawn her off to a mean looking farmer and his beaten down wife, Nell opts for the only alternative she can see: running away. She steals a rowboat, adopts a big, black dog and sets out downriver. A chance encounter with a dime novel heralding the exploits of Calamity Jane, heroine of the west, gives Nell the purpose of her life: to find Calamity Jane, her own true mother.

Thus begins Nell's quest, down rivers, up rivers and across the country all the way to Deadwood, South Dakota. Along the way she meets Jeremy Chatterfield, a handsome young Englishman who isn't particular about how he makes his way—as long as he doesn't have to work for it. Together they trek across the country meeting characters as wonderful and bizarre as the adventure they seek, learning about themselves and the world along the way.

This coming of age novel is a story of stubborn determination, self-discovery, adventure beyond measure, acceptance and love—always love—the foundation of everything. You'll take Nell with you to that special place where you keep the best characters. She'll stick with you, beat you down, buoy you up, and teach you a thing or two about life. You'll wonder at her single mindedness, her patience and her courage, but you won't forget her. Not for a long time.

Part Three

1835–1851